MEN OF INKED SOUTHSIDE

COPYRIGHT

Published by Bliss Ink & Chelle Bliss
Published on May 27th 2019
Edited by Silently Correcting Your Grammar
Proofread by Julie Deaton & Rosa Sharon
Cover Photo © Sara Eirew
Cover Design Lori Jackson Designs

MANEUVER

www.chellebliss.com
CHELLE BLISS
USA TODAY BESTSELLING AUTHOR

Xanax,

Thanks for lifting me up and pushing me through the hard times.

The world could've crumbled and I would've watched in fascination because of you.

CHAPTER ONE

DELILAH

"Get the fuck out." My father pulls over at the corner and slams on the brakes.

I gawk at him with my mouth hanging open as he puts the car in park. The look in his eyes is nothing short of ice-cold, devoid of all emotion and completely loveless.

"Dad, just let me drive." I don't move even though I know he won't back down. He never has when he's drunk. I keep my eyes on the flashing red traffic light in front of us, trying to keep my voice even and nonjudgmental. But really, I am judging the hell out of him. How dare he kick us out like trash? "You're drunk, and it's not safe for anyone."

"I'm done with you and your self-righteous bullshit. Survive on your own two feet, Delilah."

I jerk my head backward as my mouth falls open. I'm used to his drunken ramblings and angry fits, but he's never been as cruel as he is tonight. "What about Lulu?"

Lulu is in the back seat, oblivious to everything and somehow sleeping through my father's tirade. My father has kicked me out plenty of times, or at least, that's what he'd say, but I always had my credit cards and bank account to fall back on. He has never cut me off completely.

It has been over a year since his last outburst. Well, before Lulu was born. I thought her birth would change things. I thought he'd stay sober for her, but I should've known better. He never found it in his heart to stay clean for me. The invisible pull of his addiction outweighed any love for his child. Why would his granddaughter be any different?

"Leave her with me," he snaps and leans over me, pushing open my car door. "But you gotta go." His lip curls as he says the last word, showing the wildness the alcohol has soaked into his veins as he settles back into the driver's seat.

My eyes fill with tears, and my vision blurs. I hate this side of him. When my father was sober, he was a nice guy, but when he was drunk, he could give the devil himself a run for his money. Lately, he's spent more and more time drinking, and the old him, the one I loved, barely surfaced.

"I'm not leaving her with you," I tell him and shake my head. I don't care if I have to steal to make ends meet, I would never subject my daughter to my father's alcohol-induced treachery without being there to protect her.

He leans back against the door, holding the steering wheel with one hand while balling the fingers of the other into a tight fist as it rests on his leg. "Both of you are ungrateful little bitches. You have five seconds to get the fuck out and take the little bastard with you."

I move quickly at that point, but I don't dare step out of the car without Lulu. I turn in my seat, avoiding all eye contact with the maniac next to me and pull her from the car seat. Without saying another word, I cradle Lulu in my arms and climb out of the car. Before I can grab my purse, my father speeds away, fishtailing down the wet pavement with the door still open. He swerves around the corner at the end of the desolate street, and the car door slams shut on its own.

"Fuck," I groan, realizing not only did he take my purse, but my phone too.

Here I am with my little girl, no money, no credit cards, no way to call anyone, and it's well after midnight in the middle of nowhere-good downtown Chicago.

I press my lips to the soft skin of her forehead, letting the tears roll down my cheeks as I whisper sweet words to replace his vicious comments. "Mama's got you, baby. I'll always protect you."

Holding Lulu close to my chest, I shield her from anything and everything as I turn around, hoping to find someplace to make a call. I can't stand on the street corner too long. Not in this neighborhood. There is bound to be someone walking by and probably not the type of person I want to ask for help at this hour of the night.

The sound of a bell and laughter down the street draws my attention as a young couple, probably my age, staggers onto the sidewalk, practically hanging off each other. I walk toward them but don't yell out. They look nice enough, but they are clearly in the middle of something and in the middle of a lip-lock.

Walking quickly, I head toward the doorway the couple just walked away from, glancing from side to side because, in all honesty, I am scared as hell. Light from inside streams out of the windows lining the front of the building, falling on the sidewalk near my feet as if signaling to me like a beacon. I step forward, peering through the glass to get a better look before I dare walk through the door.

Gallos' Hook & Hustle South Side.

The place looks nice enough. Not swanky or

anything I'd find on the North Side, but not a complete shithole either. But it's still a bar and the last place I'd want to walk into, especially with my daughter. I step backward and glance both ways, hoping to see the faint glow of a nearby gas station or drug store, but there's nothing but darkness.

I take a deep breath, hold Lulu a little tighter, and reach for the handle. For a moment, no one seems to notice us as we step inside. They're too busy talking and drinking to even look up. These are not the type of people I'd see at my father's country club, sipping martinis and other pretentious drinks while holding their noses high in the air as they try to one-up each other with the size of their bank accounts. Nope. Not even close.

The door closes behind me, and the bell rings overhead, and sure as shit, half the bar turns around. No one yells or shoos us away. They're too busy staring at and judging me for having an infant in a bar at this time of night. It's like I can practically read their minds by the way their eyes are zeroed in on Lulu.

I was thinking so far, so good, but then Lulu lets out a blood-curdling scream like she just saw the boogeyman in her dreams, and I think about bolting for the door. Instead, I softly bounce her tiny body in my arms to quiet her down and smile nervously.

The gentleman sitting the closest to me holds his beer near his lips, looking me up and down in much the same manner my father often did when he was drunk. "It's a little late to have a baby out, don'tcha think?" he asks, tipping his head and completely judging me as a shit mother.

"I just need to make a phone call." I bite my tongue to stop myself from saying something about his late-night middle-of-the-week drinking, clearly doing it often based on the size of his beer belly. Instead, I look at the floor and head toward the other end of the bar.

The woman behind the bar is handing someone a drink and paying no attention to me or the sleazeball hitting on me. "Excuse me," I say, tapping Lulu's bottom as I bounce her to keep her from crying out again, but the bartender doesn't give me the time of day.

"I'm talking to you, beautiful," the same man says, but the word comes out like *beauful* because he's had one too many. He tries to touch me with his dirty, chubby hands, and I step sideways.

"Ma'am," I say, but this time a little louder.

"C'mere," the guy says again and moves faster than I expect, finally touching my arm.

My skin crawls from the contact. "Stop. Please," I beg, trying to inch away from his hold, but he only tightens his grip.

"Harry, get your filthy paws off her, or I'll put your ass on the ground."

I jump and let out a little squeak at the sound of

another man's voice I hadn't been expecting. If Harry wasn't scared, I was enough for both of us.

Harry's lip curls as his eyes finally leave my breasts to somewhere behind me. "Sorry, Lucio. No disrespect, man. Didn't know she was yours."

Didn't know she was yours? For a second, I think about not looking. If someone's claiming me, I'm not sure I'm ready to know who he is. I glance over my shoulder with one eye closed, almost too scared to turn around even though I want to get far away from Handsy Harry.

My eyes land on a huge chest, traveling upward to a wide set of shoulders before finally settling on a handsome face.

"You okay?" he asks.

For a moment, I can't seem to form words. I just stare at him with my mouth hanging open. "I…" I pause, not sure if I am okay and too caught off guard by him to finish the rest of the sentence.

Lucio, at least that's what Handsy Harry called him, raises one eyebrow, looking at me funny when I don't say anything more. When he cracks a smile, I'm a total goner.

"Are you hurt?" he asks as his gaze slowly travels down my body. I shake my head, still rendered mute. "Is the baby hurt?"

I shake my head again. *Earth to Delilah.* I better find my voice quick because I can't imagine a guy like him has much patience for a strange woman walking into a bar at this hour.

"I was wondering if I could use your pecs," I blurt out, and my stomach instantly knots.

He tilts his head to the side and laughs. "Come again?"

Gah. I want to hide or at least go back about ten seconds and get a do-over. I've never been so embarrassed in my entire life. Where the hell did that come from? It doesn't help that he's built like a brick shithouse and the only part of him at eye level are his pecs, extremely large and, based on the looks of them, rock-hard too.

"Your phone. I'd like to use your phone," I correct my earlier statement, but the damage is done.

"You only want my phone?" he teases.

I swear his pecs move up and down, taunting me, but my eyes may be playing tricks on me. I nod, but I don't dare speak. I've already done enough damage and don't trust myself to say another word.

"Daphne," Lucio calls out, pulling his backward baseball cap off his head and running his fingers through his dark brown hair. Everything in the room seems to slow as he drags his long, thick fingers through the wavy strands. "She needs to use the phone."

The woman, Daphne he called her, reaches under the bar, lifts a glass, and sets it on the bar near me.

"It's for paying customers only. What can I get you to drink?"

I close my eyes, wishing I could be anywhere but here. "I don't have any money." The words are bitter on my tongue and harder to say than I ever imagined.

"No drink, no phone," the woman says without an ounce of remorse and ticks her head toward the doorway. "The police station's down the street. You could try there."

God, she's a bitch. Cold as ice and not an ounce of sympathy for a woman without a dollar for a shitty beer, holding a baby.

"We don't treat people like that," Lucio tells her, stepping around me and staring her down. "You know better than that."

"Whatever, Lucio." She rolls her eyes and walks away like her shit doesn't stink.

Lucio takes a step toward me, looking down at Lulu, and I force myself to stay still and keep my mouth shut. "Follow me." He motions for me to go with him as he heads toward a hallway at the side of the bar.

Where the hell does he want to take us?

"What's wrong?" he asks, walking back toward us when I shake my head and stay still.

"Why can't I use the phone here?"

Every nightmare scenario I've ever seen in a horror movie plays through my head. Maybe he's secretly a serial killer, or he could be a human trafficker and my kid and I are the perfect prey for his lucrative business.

"He's taking you upstairs to our mom's apartment," Daphne, the bitch bartender, says as she tosses a white towel over her shoulder. "He's too nice."

"Oh," I mutter and feel like a fool.

"You can stay down here with all these drunk shitheads, or you can make the call upstairs in the comfort and safety of my mom's place. This really is no place for a baby," he says.

He has a point.

I have to wait for the car service to come, and they are never quick. I don't want to wait on the street or in the bar being hit on by drunken strangers either.

"Lead the way," I tell him and finally take a step forward, hoping like hell this isn't some sort of trap.

CHAPTER TWO

LUCIO

The woman doesn't take her eyes off me as we enter my mother's apartment. I can't tell if she's scared of me or completely infatuated. I've seen the look before—wide eyes, parted lips, barely able to speak.

"The phone's in the kitchen," I tell her, pointing toward the old rotary dial telephone my mother refuses to get rid of. They've been out of date for over twenty years and sit in museums, but she hates change.

The woman walks toward the mustard-yellow telephone hanging on the wall across the room. "Wow. I haven't seen one of these in…"

I keep my distance. The last thing I want to do is spook her. I know from having a sister, every man is a potential threat. I've taught them as much, and I try to remember how they'd feel in the same situation.

"Yeah. I know," I say, shaking my head because my mother is a special bird. "My mother is a little stuck in the good ole days." I smile, trying to put her mind at ease.

She holds the baby in one arm, grabs the phone with the other, and stares at me. I don't move a muscle. I'm barely breathing at this point. I imagine her fear is more for her baby than herself. She has no idea if I am some crazy person or the harmless semi-asshole I really am. Her gaze sweeps across my body, focusing on my arms at first and then my feet for a moment.

She's hot as hell for a mom. The woman doesn't look to be more than mid-twenties. Tall, though not as tall as me, but she's wearing heels which make her appear bigger than she really is. Her brown hair is wavy, ending near the middle of her back, but the top is pulled back and away from her pretty face.

The blueness of her eyes is unlike any I've ever seen before. They're almost turquoise, matching Lake Michigan on a sunny day. For her just having had a baby, her body is smoking hot and her tits are freaking spectacular. I almost feel like a total sleazebag for checking her out the way I am, but I'm a guy and I'm turned on because she is totally a MILF.

She takes her eyes off me for a moment to dial each number, but in between each swish, she glances back at me. We stay like this—her holding the baby, waiting for me to pounce, and me barely breathing—as she cradles the receiver on her shoulder. "Hello," she says to whoever is on the other end. "This is Delilah Miles, Roger Miles's daughter. I need a car as soon as possible."

I tip my head to the side, looking at her in a totally different light. She is a rich girl and definitely not from this part of town. I wonder why she is slumming it so late with her kid in tow. Her clothes are fancier than most of the customers in the bar. She looks like one of the wealthy, hipster kids who come down to Hook & Hustle for a dose of culture and reality every once in a while.

Her eyebrows draw together, and for the first time, she turns her back to me, hiding her face. "Excuse me?" she whispers, dropping her voice so I can barely hear her. "I have an account. I don't understand." She tips her face upward and grunts.

My mother walks out from her bedroom, wearing the most hideous pink robe and bunny slippers with her bright red hair in curlers because she has some weird aversion to curling irons. My mom looks at Delilah and then to me, raising an eyebrow. I shake my head and wave my mom off, because I'm not about to explain the little bit I know while Delilah is talking on the phone.

"Please," Delilah begs quietly. "I can pay for your car service myself. You should have my credit card on file." Delilah pauses and glances over her shoulder at me for a second, not seeing my mother standing nearby. "Fine, but I'll have your ass along with your job for refusing service to me." Delilah slams the receiver down and lets out a little grunt as her shoulders hunch forward.

My mother clears her throat and marches into the kitchen, bunny slippers and all. "Would anyone like anything to drink? I'm parched," Ma says, trying to be cordial even though it is after midnight and way past her bedtime.

Delilah nearly jumps a foot off the floor and spins around, clutching the baby for dear life. As soon as she sees my ma, her entire demeanor changes. My mom looks like someone straight out of a comic strip, not a murderer ready to do harm to a fly, let alone a person like Delilah.

"Since we're having a party, I have tea or whiskey. Pick your poison." Ma smiles, standing near the sink with the streetlight cascading through the window, giving her an angelic glow.

"Nothing. Thank you," Delilah replies as her eyes rake across my mother's outfit, and the corner of her mouth twitches. "I'm Delilah."

"I heard," my mother says sarcastically, letting a

little of her devilish side show. "I'm Betty—" Ma motions toward me "—this big lug's mother."

Delilah's gaze moves to me, and there is almost a smile on her face. "It's nice to meet you, Betty. Thanks for letting me use your phone."

"Tea or whiskey?" Mom asks again like it isn't well past her bedtime. She seems oblivious to the fact that Delilah isn't sticking around.

"I can't stay. I have to get Lulu to bed." Delilah turns toward me and peers down at the floor. "Do you think you could give me a ride?"

I scrub a hand down my face. "I only have a bike, and my mom doesn't drive." Times like this, I regret not having a car of my own.

"Those things are deathtraps," Ma says quickly, adding to her crazy factor and reminding me again how much she hates my motorcycle.

"It's fine." Delilah waves her hands in the air. "I'll just catch a taxi."

Ma fills the kettle before placing it on the stove, still ignoring the fact that neither of us is staying. "Why don't you sit down for some tea, and Lucio can go downstairs to find someone's car to borrow?"

I nod, liking that idea because there is something about Delilah that fascinates me. She's like a tragic story. Rich girl, stuck in the hood with no way out. Maybe I can swoop in and be the hero of the story. Who am I kidding? I could at least have a night with the hot chick before she rides off into the sunset with some other guy.

"I'm sorry to be so much trouble. I lost my purse and phone, or else I wouldn't be such a bother."

"Oh dear," my mother gasps, covering her mouth with her hand and being overly dramatic like only Betty Gallo can.

My blood pressure skyrockets as I imagine someone stealing Delilah's shit and almost hurting the tiny, beautiful creature in front of me or her baby. "Did someone hurt you?"

"No, no. It's a long story, but we're fine," Delilah says as my mother points toward the couch for her to sit.

"Will you be okay up here?" I ask as Delilah sits down, resting the baby on her knees as the plastic underneath her crinkles. "I won't be gone long." I give my mother the same look she gives us as a warning. While I love my mother, she can be a tad bit overbearing.

"Just go. We're fine," Ma tells me, answering instead of Delilah.

"I wasn't asking about you, Ma."

Delilah laughs softly and relaxes on the couch, pulling the baby into her lap. "We're safe and warm. We'll be just fine."

I glance over my shoulder before closing the door, and I catch sight of Ma grabbing two teacups from the cupboard. I know they're going to be more than a few minutes because once you get Ma talking, there is no stopping her until she is out of things to say. I hope Delilah is in the mood to listen to the sage wisdom of Betty Gallo because, like it or not, she is about to get some.

"Where's the chick?" Daphne asks as soon as she sees me.

I point toward Ma's apartment and shake my head at the strange turn this night has taken. "Having tea with Ma."

Daphne's eyes widen in horror, being just as dramatic as my mother. "You woke her up?"

"We were quiet, but she heard us anyway." I rub the back of my neck, hating the idea of asking Daphne for a favor. My darling sister will want to be paid back, and her favors are always enormous and costly. "You think I can borrow your car?"

"Dude." Daphne quirks an eyebrow as she folds her arms in front of herself. I can tell by the way she tilts her head that she is about to read me the riot act about her precious baby.

"Please. You know I'd never ask to borrow it, but this is important."

"This about her?" She juts her chin toward the stairwell to our mother's apartment.

"Yeah. She needs a ride. I can't take a baby on my bike."

"Bet you never thought you'd say those words." She points at me with her skinny index finger, totally mocking me for buying a motorcycle. She's always hated the damn thing. She told me I wasn't being practical and that someday I'd need to grow up, but the girl drives a vintage Jeep, so she has no room to talk.

"Just get the damn keys," I tell her and hold out my hand, wiggling my fingers.

"Don't get your panties in a bunch. Watch the front of the house. I'll grab them for you, Big Daddy." She giggles as she hands me the damp towel she's been using to wipe down the bar half the night.

"The girl gone?" Johnny, a regular and one of my father's oldest friends, asks as I take away his empty beer glass to give him a refill.

"She's upstairs with Ma."

Johnny jerks his head backward like I am insane for leaving them alone. "Alone?"

"Uh, yeah, man. She's fine."

"You don't know that girl. She could be a murderer. Think about your mother."

"I don't know too many killers who bring their children with them when they want to off someone." I lean forward and stare him straight in the eyes, sliding his fresh beer across the bar. "Did you ever bring yours?"

His eyes narrow into tiny slits as he grumbles under his breath and grabs the beer, busying himself and not bothering to answer my question.

Johnny isn't only my dad's dearest friend, but he

is a longtime business associate of my father's. I've always stayed out of their business dealings, but I'm not a complete fool. I know Johnny is, or maybe was, my father's number two, and he did some pretty shady shit in his time. I don't doubt for a minute that he's murdered a person or two over the years.

Daphne places the keys next to me but keeps her hand on top of them. "Let me go over a few things with you first."

"It's a Jeep, Daph. I think I can figure it out." I cross my arms and lean against the bar because I have a feeling this isn't going to be a quick conversation.

"No, she's special," she tells me, putting me in my place and reminding me she's just as crazy as our mother.

I roll my eyes, but she is dead serious.

"You want it or not?"

"Fine. Go ahead," I tell her and throw my hands into the air, giving in to her insanity.

"Sometimes the brake pedal sticks. You have to be very careful how hard you handle her. Ease off the brake slowly, but don't take too long, or she'll stall."

"Seriously?"

"Yeah." She nods at me like I am a complete moron. "She's temperamental."

"Shocking," I mutter because the car sounds a lot like my sister. "I'm sure I'll figure it out."

"If the baby pukes on the seats, you're cleaning it

up." She points at me again, twisting her lips. "Got it?"

"Yeah, sis. I got it." I reach for the keys, but she moves them out of the way before I can grab them. "Fill her up too before you bring her back, but none of that low-grade crap either. She needs premium gasoline."

"Anything else?"

She finally moves her hands, leaving the giant keys along with a freakishly large fuzzy heart on the keychain. "Nope."

I'm going to look like an idiot carrying around her set of keys, but at least it's dark, and I don't have to worry about running into any of my friends. I try to jam them into my pocket, but the heart's too big to fit, and the damn thing dangles near my hip for the world to see.

My mother's waiting at the top of the stairs, standing outside the door. "What's wrong?" I ask as soon as I see her.

"She's asleep."

"The baby?"

She shakes her head. "The girl."

Well, fuck. "How? It's only been a few minutes."

She shrugs. "Babies are exhausting, and she's going through something. One minute she was talking, and the next…"

"I'll wake her up."

My mother puts her hands up in front of herself,

stopping me from moving past her. "No. Let her sleep. You can take her home in the morning."

"The baby, Ma."

"We'll set up a little sleeping area for her too. I need you to carry Delilah to the bedroom for me."

Somehow, I'm the only one who sees a problem with this. I want to argue, but this is my mother, and I know there's no way I'll win. This girl who we don't know is going to wake up in the morning and totally lose her shit. I know I would if I were in her shoes, but my mother doesn't feel the same.

"I'll stay too, then. I'll move the girl and then be back after I help Daphne close up for the night."

"Before you get busy working, go down to the corner store and grab formula and a bottle."

"Is there a certain type?" I ask, knowing nothing about what babies eat. I've never had to buy a baby bottle, and I didn't think I'd ever have to either.

"Just get one with a decent nipple."

I stop myself from making a joke because I don't feel like getting smacked upside the head as my mother follows behind me and has the perfect opportunity and angle. Ma gently lifts the baby out of Delilah's arms. I hold my breath, waiting for her to wake up and start swinging, but Delilah just mumbles under her breath for a moment before going still again.

"We can just leave her here, no?"

Ma rocks the baby, sniffing her hair like she often

did when my niece and nephew were little. "I miss that smell," she says with a look of sorrow and happiness all at once. "No, I want her to be comfortable. The poor thing couldn't keep her eyes open. She deserves a good night's sleep. Being a mother isn't easy, Luc."

"I know, Ma. You keep reminding me."

Thankfully, Ma has her hands full, or I'd get a smack upside the head for my smartass reply.

I watched my three-year-old niece and one-year-old nephew for a week after my sister-in-law died after a short battle with cancer. I have never been so exhausted in my entire life. I could barely find time to shower with the two of them around, but it was something I did for my brother and the rest of the family so they could grieve.

Delilah's lighter than I imagine as I lift her into my arms. Her head rests on my chest and tips back, giving me the perfect view of her delicate, soft features. She has a set of freckles on her left cheek, and they almost form a tiny heart. Her skin is flawless and without makeup. She's nothing short of a natural beauty. I'm so used to the girls at Hook & Hustle with their layers of makeup. Sometimes when I wake up the next day, they don't even look anything like the girl I banged the night before.

I walk carefully, taking small, steady steps toward the bedroom so I don't startle her awake and earn myself a black eye.

There are so many ways this could go bad, but I do it anyway. Delilah can lay into me tomorrow. Scream. Yell. Whatever. I can take the anger from a stranger and move on, but there is no way I'm going to go against my mother on this one.

I place her on Daphne's old bed just below her poster of Mandy Moore that's started to curl at the corners. I grab an afghan from the dresser and cover her under my mother's watchful eye.

"Formula and a bottle. Don't forget, babies like big nipples."

"We all do," I mumble as I walk out the door, typing out a message to cancel my date for later.

CHAPTER THREE

DELILAH

For a brief second, I don't have a care in the world. The room is dark, warm, and it's nice to be wrapped in such soft blankets. I blink a few times, stretching my muscles, but then it hits me.

Bar. Strange guy. Woman in bunny slippers. Lulu.

I leap out of bed like a superhero, and all tiredness and comfort leave me in an instant. I race out of the bedroom, peering in every room as I run down the hallway and grip my chest, trying like hell not to lose my mind.

Don't overreact. I inhale slowly, telling myself she's perfectly fine.

If Lulu's gone, I will tear apart the entire city and bring the wrath of God down on these people. I'm flooded with guilt at the fact that I fell asleep, leaving my baby vulnerable and without my protection in the presence of complete strangers.

How could I have been so irresponsible and stupid?

Rounding the corner to the kitchen, I see the guy from last night, holding Lulu and whispering in her ear. I stop dead, watching the two of them from the hallway.

Seeing Lulu being held in a man's arms does something to me I hadn't expected. When her father skipped out, leaving me high and dry six months into my pregnancy, I told myself good riddance. Who needed him anyway? We sure didn't. But somewhere deep in my heart, I knew Lulu would be missing out on something special. Not that Dwight Jones, the spineless, tiny-dicked man who'd knocked me up, was a prize, but still—she needed a male figure in her life.

My father was worthless. No. He was less than that, and I turned out okay, after all. But there have been so many times in my life when I wished I had a real dad…someone who would treat me like a little princess and make me feel like his number one.

Instead, I had a drunken asshole who left me on

the side of the road with his granddaughter and not a penny to my name.

My eyes fill with tears as I watch Lucio and Lulu together. He's so sweet and tender with her, and it's probably the first time I've seen a man be that way with Lulu in her short little life. I slap my hand over my mouth when I feel the sob crawling up the back of my throat.

Lulu's staring up at him, sucking on her bottle and completely captivated by the man. I don't blame her either. He's dreamy in a blue-collar beefcake kind of way.

Last night, he was wearing a tight-fitting long-sleeved white dress shirt, but I barely noticed much about him besides his size. But in the light, with Lulu in his arms, I can see his entire upper body clear as freaking day.

Damn.

His torso and arms are covered with ink. The pictures on his skin almost dance with each movement of the muscles underneath. I've never really been into guys with tattoos, but on him, they are absolutely perfect. I grip the wall, trying to keep myself vertical as my knees start to go weak.

Get yourself together, woman. It's just a guy holding your kid.

"Aren't you a pretty little thing?" he says, bouncing her up and down in one arm as he sets the bottle on the table.

I take a step back, still holding the wall, and I'm careful not to make a sound. I can't stop the stupid smile on my face from spreading as I wipe away my tears.

He places his ankle on top of the opposite leg, creating a little pocket before placing Lulu in between his huge thigh muscles. "So beautiful like your mommy."

Heat creeps up my chest, and I fumble with the collar on my T-shirt. It's been ages since anyone has called me beautiful and even longer since I'd felt that way. I'm too busy in mom-mode with a messy bun, no makeup, and smelling like rotten formula to think I'm even remotely pretty.

I never thought being a mother would be easy, but I didn't think it would be this hard either. There's nothing in the world which could've prepared me for the lack of sleep. And don't even get me started on the stretch marks lining my body like a topographic map. I don't have time to worry about the way my body has gone to shit and how my tits are unrecognizable after Lulu fed off them for the first three months of her life.

Lucio takes a sip of his coffee, still carefully bouncing her, but keeping a close eye on her. I want to rush in and tell him to burp her, but he seems to have things under control. I don't know why I don't step forward and snatch my kid away from his muscular legs which are probably harder than the wood beneath my feet, but I don't.

Lulu makes a little noise, reaching upward and blowing spit bubbles tinted white from the formula at him. He laughs and scoops her in one arm, holding her tiny head in his giant palm, and places her on his shoulder. He does everything so gracefully that I can't stop myself from watching in amazement and a little in awe.

He sets his coffee aside and gently rubs her back, tapping her a few times. I want to tell him to watch out because Lulu is a world-class puker. She doesn't just burp. Nope. Not my kid. She's ruined more outfits than I care to remember, and her baby formula has become my new perfume, which is something I'm not entirely proud of either.

Lulu lets out a burp that's so loud, Lucio starts to laugh, but then it happens. As if everything is moving in slow motion, the burp turns liquid, and a pretty big splash of formula vomit lands on his shoulder before dribbling down his back. I cringe, waiting for the moment when he loses his shit. I mean, here's this hot-as-fuck guy, covered in muscles and tattoos, trying to do me a favor and taking care of a kid who isn't even his, and she pukes on him.

"Well, aren't you a messy little princess?" he says, his laughter getting a bit louder when he brings her face-to-face with him. He's holding her with ease like she doesn't weigh more than a sack of potatoes, and using one finger, he wipes away the formula left near her mouth. "Feel better?"

God, why does he have to be so freaking hot holding her?

The blush that had started moments ago has now turned into a full-blown furnace, radiating from the inside out. I haven't wanted to touch a man since Dwight left town, but Lucio, the hottie with my kid, makes my hands itchy to reach out and touch him. It doesn't matter that he's covered in Lulu's throw-up. I'd happily help him get clean.

Stop being a whore.

The words my father had said to me when he found out I was pregnant echo in my mind as I let my thoughts wander to dirty and dark places about the handsome stranger in front of me.

Betty, the lady with the bunny slippers from last night, walks through the front door, going right to Lulu and Lucio. "Delilah still sleeping?"

"Yeah, Ma," he tells her. "Want me to wake her?"

"You will do no such thing. A mother needs her sleep, and besides—" Betty leans forward and grabs Lulu out of Lucio's arms "—look at this darling face. I could give her a million kisses."

"Ma, she's not yours."

"She could be. I need some more grandkids, honey. I'm not getting any younger, and neither are you." She gives him a funny look, and I cover my mouth to stop myself from laughing. "Why don't you settle down with a girl like Delilah? You'd already have a head start in the grandbaby department, and it would make you my favorite child."

"Ma."

"Lucio."

"Ma, come on. A girl as pretty as her, she probably has a husband, and it doesn't work that way. If I dated her, that doesn't mean this is your grandbaby by default."

"If you were her man, would you let her be out on her own that late at night? And besides, blood isn't required to be a family. You bring her in, and they're both my kin."

I don't know why, but the floodgates open, and tears start streaming down my face like a torrential downpour. No one in my family talks this way about each other, let alone about complete strangers. Even with my father and me sharing the same blood, he treats me, and Lulu too, like trash. My mother is no better after running off with a guy half her age, never to be heard from again.

"She's a rich girl. Why would she want some schmuck from the South Side?"

"You're handsome, and don't even get me started on your heart. Anyway, money doesn't matter when it comes to love."

"You're crazy," he tells her as she gives Lulu a soft kiss on the forehead.

"You keep dating these cheap and easy bimbos

who are more interested in what you can buy for them than they are in you, honey, and you deserve better than that."

He pinches the bridge of his nose and leans forward, resting one elbow on his knee. "What am I supposed to do? Just ask her out?"

"Yes, son. It's that easy."

Oh my God. Oh my God.

Is he really going to ask me out because his mom told him to? Does that mean he wants to, or is he being strong-armed by his bunny-loving red-haired mother?

I don't want a pity date, not even from the hot, shirtless guy holding my baby.

I step backward, heading toward the bathroom, leaving Lulu with them for a moment while I try to pull myself together. When I get in front of the mirror, I look worse than I ever could've imagined. My normally tame locks are a hot mess and tangled, the little bit of mascara I managed to wear last night is smeared down my face, making me look like something straight out of a horror movie. On top of that, all the sleep I got last night did nothing to alleviate the bags under my eyes.

Quickly, I scrub my face, grab some toothpaste and use my finger as the brush, and try to pull myself together, making myself as presentable as possible. I am officially lame. I've done this routine before, but usually after a night of hot sex. Never after falling asleep because I was exhausted.

I grab the handle, ready to walk out in yesterday's clothes and feeling worse than yesterday's trash. As soon as the door opens, I come face-to-face with the half-naked hottie looking like someone straight out of the *Magic Mike* movie. Not only that, but I walk straight into his chest, unable to stop myself.

"Hi," I squeak like a teenage girl with a crush as I gaze up into his eyes.

"Hey." He smirks down at me, holding on to my arm.

I go dumb with the way he is looking at me. I stare at him without being able to form a thought or say a single word. How can I? The guy is more like a Greek god with his rippling muscles, perfect skin, haunting green eyes, and a smile that could make any girl, even a nun, have the dirtiest thoughts, leading to a stint in hell for sinning.

"Sleep okay?" he asks, still holding on to me.

I nod my reply, because words are too complicated with him being half naked. That's the problem when you've been basically celibate for well over a year. Something as small as a shirtless man can make a girl, even me, stupid. If it were another man, maybe one with a dad bod, I probably could stammer out a response, but not with this hot hunk of man meat.

"Hungry?" he asks then, but I'm too busy staring at the ink on his chest to bother with a reply.

That song "Your Body is a Wonderland" had to have been written about a guy like Lucio. My fingers want to play now too. Skate around that fleshy amusement park, touching every inch, until I've explored each curve and splash of art across his body.

I don't think I've been staring long, but when he touches my chin, bringing my eyes to his…I know he caught me. The smirk from a few moments ago is bigger and more devilish.

"Are. You. Hungry?" he asks the words again, but he is speaking each one slowly like I have trouble understanding the English language.

In all fairness, I am having trouble processing even the simplest questions. But in my defense, my girl parts are long overdue for a tune-up or at least a quick adjustment.

My lips fall open a little, just enough to draw his attention, and I'm thankful for a momentary reprieve from his watchful gaze. "Yes," I finally say, trying to pull off a totally sexy, seductive voice, but I sound more like my aunt Maud, which, trust me, will never be hot.

He drops his hand from my face, and somehow, I don't whine. But I want to… Oh, how I want to. "Ma's making breakfast."

"Where's Lulu?" I ask, playing dumb and doing a bang-up job.

"My ma has her in the kitchen. I just wanted to wash up." He turns around, giving me a full view of the mess Lulu left down his back, adding to her long list of victims. "Your little girl has quite the appetite."

"Oh my God. I'm so sorry." Somehow, I manage to get the words out, but nothing about speaking is easy. His back is just as magnificent as his front and on full display. Even with Lulu's mess, the damn thing is a masterpiece.

"It was no trouble. Don't be sorry. She's a kid. They throw up. No big deal."

I stare at the floor as he turns back around. I can't look at him anymore and get more than a few words out. The carpet is a much safer focal point. "It's so sweet that you fed her. You should've woken me up. She's not your responsibility. I feel awful." I finally look up because I realize I'm acting like a weirdo, and I'm more than a little embarrassed.

He shakes his head and holds up a hand, stopping me from the verbal diarrhea I'm in the middle of. "You were tired, and I enjoyed spending time with her. And besides, my ma is over the moon to have a baby in the house."

"Oh." I try to hide the excitement in my voice, but it's impossible. On top of being hot as fuck, the guy says everything a single mother wants to hear. It's like he fell out of the sky, landing straight in between my very available and needy legs.

Don't be ridiculous.

This guy probably has a list of chicks he bangs on the regular. The old-school yellow pages probably have nothing on Lucio. What girl could honestly say no to him? He's not even my type, but I'd drop to my knees and pray for salvation later.

"Why don't we eat something, and then I'll give you a ride?"

My eyes widen, and there's no hiding right where my mind went. The blush creeping up my chest and scattering around my neck doesn't help mask the way his words affect me either.

He smiles again, probably knowing exactly where my dirty-ass mind went. I can tell by the way his eyes sparkle he's getting a kick out of my unease. "A ride home," he adds.

"I'll call a friend to come get us. There's no need to put out." I cough and pound on my chest because, again, I can't seem to speak like a normal person around him. "I mean, I don't want to put you out. I'm sure you're a busy man."

Fuck my life. Seriously. I'm in the presence of a hot guy, who held my daughter and stared at her with such adoration that I've gone all stupid.

"Spending a little time with two beautiful girls…" He steps back, his eyes traveling up my body and rumpled clothes. "I can't think of a better way to spend my morning."

I blink a few times, wondering if I heard him wrong because he seems a little too good to be true. Even his mother, the way she talked about Lulu, is like something right out of a weird, inner-city *Brady Bunch* episode.

I need to eat and get the hell out of here because this hot playboy won't lead anywhere I need to go. Yeah, I wouldn't mind a ride or two, but in the end… all men disappoint, including this one.

CHAPTER FOUR

LUCIO

"This is so good." Delilah moans softly before shoving the last piece of blueberry scone into her mouth. Crumbs fall from her lips and drop onto the plate, but she gathers them on her fingertip. "Your mom is an amazing cook. I've never had something so delicious." She places her finger in her mouth, sucking the tip, and I'm a complete goner.

The semi-hard-on I'm sporting underneath the table suddenly becomes a huge issue. I can't get comfortable, and it's impossible to think about anything other than sex. I shift in my seat, trying to find a position to relieve the ache, but nothing helps. Just when I am about to start picturing something horrific to try to take care of the issue, my ma walks into the room, and all horniness I feel dies instantly.

"I'll pack some up for you to take home," Ma says, bouncing Lulu on her hip like she did with her own grandchildren when they were small.

Delilah's face changes as soon as she hears the word home. Every ounce of pleasure and joy the scones brought her evaporates and dies in that second. Delilah pushes the plate forward, twisting her mouth before chewing on the inside of her lip.

I want to ask her what happened, why she was on the street so late at night, but it isn't my business, and she isn't mine to pry into her personal life or about her family.

I know all about complicated families. Hell, mine has never been a walk in the park or like any sitcom family I've ever watched on television. Maybe the Bundys from *Married with Children*, but our level of dysfunction sometimes far outweighs even their insanity.

Ma sets a bag of scones next to Delilah, and her eyes dip to the bag, noticing the bakery label as she reaches for them.

"My ma is an awful cook. Be thankful they weren't hers." I laugh and earn the evil eye from my mother. I duck just as she tries to smack me in the head.

"Your father has never complained," Ma adds, as

if his opinion matters the most. Just because my father's taste buds are dead, doesn't mean the rest of the world's are too.

"Well, I better get going. I'm so sorry for intruding, but thank you for the great night's sleep and breakfast," Delilah says as she stands from the table and reaches for Lulu who was playing with the pearls around my mother's neck.

My ma whispers something in Lulu's ear before kissing her forehead and closing her eyes.

Delilah practically has to pry Lulu's hands off my mother's pearls. Ma laughs, eating up every moment of baby she can. "I'm so sorry," Delilah keeps saying as if she thinks my mother is upset, even though Ma's clearly enjoying the entire situation.

"Don't apologize, dear. She's precious," my mother tells her and kisses Lulu one last time before Delilah is finally able to wrangle her away from my mother completely.

"She's not usually so attached to people so quickly."

"We're lovable," I tell her for some odd reason. "I mean, at least my mom and I are. The rest of the family… It's debatable."

Ma waves me away, but we both know it's true. "Oh, be nice, Lucio."

"How many siblings do you have?" Delilah asks as she rubs Lulu's back in small, gentle circles.

"Well, three that I know about."

Delilah's beautiful face scrunches, and the smooth space between her perfectly shaped eyebrows wrinkles. "Know about?"

"Well, there could be a few I don't know about. You never know what's hiding in the branches of our family tree."

This time, I'm not so lucky to avoid my mother's smack to the side of the head. "Be respectful to your father."

"Sorry, Ma," I say, but I'm not.

My father was a world-class asshole back in the day. As he grew older, he slowed down, but I know for a fact that he had more than one side piece when I was a kid. I watched as he cheated and snuck around on my mother. I promised myself I'd be nothing like him when I grew up. So far, I've kept my word, but I haven't settled down yet either.

"I like your mom," Delilah says with her lips turned up in a big smile. Why women always like to see a mother put her son in his place, I'll never know. But every single time it happens in mixed company, it always brings some laughs at my expense. But seeing Delilah's face light up again is entirely worth the embarrassment.

"Betty's a bit crazy." I stand, avoiding the second shot that was headed my way for calling her by her first name. "You ready?" I ask Delilah as I reach out to fix the collar on Lulu's dress.

"I can call a cab," she says softly, watching my hands closely.

"I can't allow you to do that. I'll take you home. I won't be able to relax until I know you're safe."

My ma stands behind Delilah and gives me a thumbs-up along with a goofy smile. In her head, she's already planning our wedding day, and while I like Delilah, my ma seems to be getting ahead of herself.

Delilah bites her bottom lip as her cheeks turn a pale shade of pink. "It's very kind of you to put yourself out in that way."

"It's not a bother."

It's not like it's a hassle to spend a little extra time with a beautiful woman. Even if she has a baby, I still like her. There is something that draws me to her. Maybe it's the sadness in her eyes and my always wanting to fix things that make her more alluring.

"I already installed the car seat, so we're ready to roll."

"Oh," she mutters, cocking her head to the side. "You have a car seat?"

"My nephew's. Ma used to babysit, so she had one in the basement. I dug it out while you were sleeping."

To a sophisticated woman who uses a car service to get around, we probably seem like a bunch of middle-class crazy people. Here, she spent the night above a South Side bar in a part of town very few people in her economic class even drive through for fear of losing their lives. My ma's apartment is a decent size, but a complete throwback to the 1980s, complete with her love of plastic coverings on all the furniture. We are not *her* people, but Delilah didn't seem to mind in the slightest.

"If you're ever in the area again, please drop in and say hello," Ma tells Delilah as she gives her a hug.

"I'd love that, Betty." Delilah smiles and wraps one arm around my mother with poor Lulu smashed in the middle.

I'd love that too…and that shocks the hell out of me.

Delilah lives on the North Side in one of the largest high-rise buildings on the lakefront. Swanky doesn't even begin to describe the place or the neighborhood. There isn't a beggar on the corner, hustling to sell water or some other small item to pay for their liquor later, like in my neighborhood. Everyone walking on the sidewalks is in a business suit or some variation.

"Thanks for the ride, Lucio. I really appreciate your help and kindness," she says as she gathers Lulu from the back seat of my sister's Jeep.

"It was my pleasure."

I want to say something else, but I can't. We barely spoke on the way to her place, or at least, not about anything substantial. I didn't learn much about her in the thirty minutes it took to head up Lake Shore to her condo. We kept everything general, and I was okay with that. I didn't want to pry and come off like an asshole. I knew she was already embarrassed about the phone call last night, and I didn't want to make her any more uncomfortable with the entire situation than probably she already is.

Delilah stands outside the Jeep on the passenger side, holding Lulu, and she smiles at me for a moment. I want to ask for her number, but hell, she's a mom with no time for an asshole like me. What mother from the North Side, swimming in cash, wants to date a South Side guy who owns a bar? I'm not hurting for money, but I'm probably not the type she was brought up to marry.

"I'm going to wait here to make sure you get in," I say instead, trying to be a gentleman like my mother raised me to be.

"We'll be fine. The doorman will let us in."

"I'll feel better if I stay and know you're safe," I tell her, memorizing her beautiful lips and deep blue eyes.

She backs away slowly with her eyes locked on mine, maybe trying to remember every inch of my face too. A few seconds later, she turns her back to me, and I shake my head, chastising myself for being such a fool. I always ask women for their phone numbers. Never had an issue with it before, but there's something that stopped me today. Hell, I still don't know if she is married or single, and the lack of a wedding ring means nothing in my book.

She looks over her shoulder and gives me a small wave before pushing through the revolving door, disappearing.

"Way to be a pussy, asshole," I grumble to myself and tap against the steering wheel, trying to stop myself from running after her.

My ma has hated every woman I've ever brought home. And while Delilah isn't a girlfriend and just happened to wander into my bar, Ma took to her immediately. Well, she took to Lulu, and that's all that seems to be needed to win her over.

Not that I need my mother's approval, but it makes shit a hell of a lot easier when Betty likes the girl sitting across from her. My ma may be a tiny thing, but her mouth most certainly is not. I can't live out the rest of her life with her hating the woman I decide to marry. I would rather spend eternity single than listen to Ma go on and on about my poor partner choice.

My phone pings from the center console, and I lean forward to see my mother is sticking her nose in my business…again.

Ma: Get her phone number.

I type out my reply, erasing and retyping it three times before hitting send.

Me: She's already gone.

Ma: How could you mess this up so badly?

Me: She has a kid.

Ma: That means she's stable and a good choice.

Clearly, my ma doesn't know some of the girls from the neighborhood who have children and are more off their rocker than many of the people in the mental ward at County Hospital. Popping a tiny human out of your vagina does not mean you're a good person, normal, or stable. It only means you got laid and nothing more.

As I slide my phone back into the center console, I notice Delilah coming out of the revolving door with Lulu on her hip and tears streaming down her face. I rush out of the Jeep and stalk toward her, calling her name.

When she sees me, she cries harder, practically falling against my chest as I touch her arms. "I got you," I tell her.

Whoever her family is…they are pieces of trash. I grab Lulu from her grip and wrap an arm around Delilah's back, ushering her toward the Jeep and away from this place. "Let's get out of here."

CHAPTER FIVE

DELILAH

Lucio places Lulu back in the car seat without asking me any questions. I stand on the sidewalk, staring up at my father's penthouse and hating him more than I've ever hated another human being. Lulu's father is a piece of shit, but at least he had the decency to leave before she had any memories of him crushing her heart like I do with my father.

I wipe away my tears, trying to collect my thoughts and calm down before I throw myself into a full-blown panic attack. Eli, my doorman since I was in kindergarten, said he was under strict orders not to let me upstairs. I begged him to let me get my things, and although I saw the pain in his eyes, he still turned us away.

My knees start to grow weak as I think about everything that's happened in the last twelve hours. Suddenly, I'm not only a single mother, but homeless and penniless too.

Lucio opens the passenger door and grabs me by the waist, basically placing me in the car with as much care as he did Lulu. "In you go, sweetheart," he says softly, and I move with him.

I don't put up a fight and push his arms away. Besides being completely devastated and in shock, I like him…and the way he treats my daughter. He is a total stranger, but in the few hours I've known him, he's shown me more kindness than my father has in the last ten years.

Sitting in the front seat, I fiddle with the hem of my T-shirt and stare down, waiting for Lucio to climb inside. I don't know what to say or where to tell him to take me. I have nowhere to go and no one else to ask for help. I don't have any identification, and probably by now, not a dollar in the bank account I shared with my father.

"You can just drop me off at the nearest shelter," I tell him because I assume that's what happens in situations like this. I mean, where else does a penniless person go with a baby? I can't live on the streets, and without any family, I have nowhere else to turn.

Lucio leans against the door of the Jeep and turns in his seat. "Absolutely not." He shakes his head as I start to open my mouth to say something. "I'm not taking you and Lulu to a homeless shelter. That's out of the question."

"It's just for a few days. We'll be okay until I figure out what to do," I explain, figuring what I'm saying makes complete sense. But he isn't having any of it.

"Have you ever been in one of those places?" He raises an eyebrow.

I shake my head, twisting my fingers in my lap. "I don't have anywhere else to go," I whisper.

"You have me."

My belly flutters. "We're not your problem."

"Not another word," he tells me. "The place next to mine is empty. You can stay there."

My mouth falls open immediately, and my hands still. "I don't have any money, Lucio. Like, not even a penny to pay for a place."

"Lucky for you, I know the landlord." He smirks and makes everything seem so easy when it isn't. "Do you have a job?"

I shake my head, totally embarrassed. I wanted to stay home with Lulu for as long as I could and live off the trust fund my grandmother left me that I got when I turned twenty-one.

"You can help out at the bar if you'd like to earn some cash. You know, to get back on your feet."

I widen my eyes for a moment before they fill with

tears again. I don't know what to say to this beautiful man sitting next to me, offering us a roof over our heads and a place to work. He doesn't owe me anything. He definitely doesn't have to be nice. Lord knows, my own father couldn't find it in his heart to be kind to me or his granddaughter.

"I don't know what to say," I mumble between my sobs. I'm somehow happy, thankful, and crushed all at the same time. I don't know what else to do but cry and fling myself into his arms. "Thank you." I plant a big kiss on his cheek, finding comfort in the warmth of his skin and the hardness of his body. "I don't know how I'll ever repay you."

Lucio rubs my back, soothing me in the same manner I often do Lulu when she is upset. "It'll be nice to have the little squirt around. Life's been way too quiet anyway."

Even through my tears, I smile. This beautiful mountain of a man is lying through his teeth, but I'm not going to call bullshit even though I know it is. For now, I'll take Lucio up on his offer and try to stay out of his hair as much as possible so we don't ruin his life. "I promise you won't even know we're there."

"Sweetheart, you're doing me a favor, not the other way around."

I back away, untangle my arms from his body, and stare up into his deep green eyes, completely confused as I wipe away my tears. "How's that?"

"The place has been empty for far too long. I need

someone to live there to keep everything working until I can find a new tenant."

"Oh." I nod, pretending like I understand, when I don't have a clue what he is talking about. "So, you want me to fix things?"

He rests his thumb against my cheek and brushes away a few tears I missed. "Absolutely not, but if a place is empty too long, things start to go bad. I just want you to make yourself comfortable for a while and not worry about anything."

I gaze up at him, not moving away from his touch because it's nice to have someone be there for me in a way no one else ever has been. "We'll be gone as soon as I can save enough money to give you your place back."

"Or you can just stay there and rent the joint from me. Don't have one foot out the door the entire time." When he smiles, it's like the entire world shifts and the dark cloud that's been following me around moves away.

"Thanks, Lucio. You're almost too good to be true." I grimace, knowing that's a shitty thing to say. I don't mean the words in a bad way, but where the hell did this guy come from?

Out of all the places on the South Side of Chicago I could've walked into, I went into his bar…a guy who's more like a knight in shining armor than a super-muscled, womanizing hottie.

"I mean..." I stammer, trying to think of a good recovery, but fail.

"Listen, Delilah. I have no doubts about how people look at me and what their first impressions are because of my good looks and hot body—" he waves his hands in front of himself and flexes at the same time "—but I'm not some asshole who bangs everything with two legs and kisses his own reflection in the mirror every day."

"You sure about that?" I laugh because this man does love himself. He can deny it all he wants, but there is no getting around his ego. "I mean, not many guys say they're good-looking and have a hot body."

He lifts his chin at me as one corner of his mouth turns upward. "They just don't say it out loud, but they're all thinking it."

I roll my eyes and swat his arm. "Well, at least I know."

"Know what?" He quirks an eyebrow and somehow looks even more handsome.

"That you're not just a pretty face." I shrug and try to maintain a straight face, but I can't with the way he looks at me. Lucio is nothing short of drop-dead gorgeous, but the problem is...he knows it too.

"I'm totally yanking your chain, Delilah. All men are dicks. I'm no different, but I was brought up to respect women and do a little good in the world while I'm here."

"So, you don't think you're good-looking and have

a hot body?" I resist the urge to let my eyes drop to his very well-formed muscles peeking out from the sleeves of his T-shirt. Even worse, I want to feel them with my fingertips.

"Do you think I'm good-looking and have a hot body?" he asks, turning the tables.

"You're all right," I tease, because Lucio is, in fact, all of that and more. But at his core, he's a good guy who is willing to help me out when no one else will.

"So are you," he says with a wink before he picks up his phone and sends a text message. He starts the engine without another word and takes off for wherever I am going to call home.

Lucio has a way about him. At one of the lowest points in my entire life, he is able to make me forget the shitshow and laugh. No matter what, I'll forever be grateful to him for giving me a moment's peace and a little security, as well as a place to sleep.

"Where's the apartment?" I ask as we pass the bar I wandered into last night.

The neighborhood looks different in the daylight. Way less scary than I let myself imagine on the moonless light with nothing illuminating the two- and three-story buildings except the nearby streetlights.

"It's a block away from the bar, and it's a house, not an apartment."

I turn my head toward him and try not to ask too many questions because I don't want to seem ungrateful. "So, we're going to share a house?"

"I live downstairs, but the upstairs unit is empty. Don't worry. There's a door with a lock at the top of the stairs for your privacy."

I wasn't really worried. I mean, how could I be? He didn't ask anything of me. He hasn't even come on to me and has barely flirted. Who really wants a homeless chick without a penny to her name? He could probably have any woman he wanted flat on her back in under five minutes, me included, so why would he bother with me? Nothing in my life is easy, and he seems like the type of guy who likes everything easy…including his women.

"That's good to know."

"You'll have everything you need to get started. The place is even completely furnished, and my ma is bringing over some hand-me-downs, so there's no need to worry."

I almost let out a sigh of relief, but although the physical things are being taken care of, I have no way to feed either of us. I can't even afford a container of formula for Lulu. I couldn't care less about myself. I could go a few days without eating and survive, but not my baby girl. Nothing in the world is more important than her.

When we pull up to what I assume is his place, there are two cars and no less than four people unloading groceries, boxes, and a crib. "What the…" My voice drifts off because I can't believe my eyes.

Who does this? What kind of people help out

strangers? My family never did. Definitely not my father. Sure, he gave to charity, but they were always nameless, and the entire thing was only to get a tax write-off at the end of the year.

"We got your back," Lucio says as he puts the Jeep in park and tips his head forward. "This is how my family is. When someone's in need, we rally."

"But…"

Lucio places his finger against my lips and stops me from speaking. "Don't say another word. Grab Lulu, and we'll head up to your new place."

I can't wipe the smile off my face. Less than an hour ago, I thought my entire world had ended and Lulu and I would spend the night in a shelter huddled together for safety. Now, we have an apartment, food, and an entire group helping us out when I'm not sure what we did to truly deserve it.

CHAPTER SIX

LUCIO

Delilah hasn't moved from the landing at the top of the stairs. She's just gawking at the upstairs apartment with her mouth open as my two brothers, sister, and mother walk around her, dropping items on every available surface before they head downstairs to grab more.

"I just can't believe this," she whispers before she takes an uneasy step forward, as if she moved too fast, everything would disappear.

"This is the last box," Vinnie says as he pushes past me, knocking into my shoulder just like he did the last three times he made the trip up the steps. The once punk-ass teenager is now a college kid with more muscles than brains. "Where would you like this, ma'am?"

Delilah's eyes sparkle as she stares at the box in my kid brother's hands marked *Little Kid Shit*. "Anywhere you'd like." She looks almost as happy as she did this morning when she ate the blueberry scone.

Vinnie grunts, lifting the box higher because he always likes to show off his strength, even if the woman is way out of his league. As the star quarter-back in high school and now the sophomore starter for one of the biggest football colleges in the area, he thinks he's God's gift to all humanity, especially women. Delilah might have thought I was full of myself, but she doesn't know Vinnie and how his ego barely fits in the room with the rest of us at Sunday dinner.

My ma grips Delilah's shoulders, and Lulu instantly grabs at Ma's pearls again, but my mother doesn't seem to mind. "Dinner's at one tomorrow. You know where I live, honey."

"What?" Delilah's face scrunches up again, the tiny wrinkles returning toward the tip of her nose. She turns to me, looking for help, but I only shrug.

I'm not about to say anything. Family dinners have always been a special time and a requirement if you were born into this ragtag group of people I call my family. Although my mother seems warm and fuzzy, she doesn't often invite people we just met to sit down at our table. But Ma being Ma, she is doing her best to make Delilah feel included, and I'm sure she's pushing us together in some way. As if living under the same roof and working at the same place isn't enough, Ma wants to make sure we don't spend a moment apart.

"Family dinner is always on Sunday at one."

"But I'm not…"

"Don't say it," Ma tells her, beating me to the words, and gives Delilah her very stern, motherly, don't-mess-with-me look. "The more, the merrier. Family is more than blood, baby."

Delilah seems to eat it up, smiling bigger and brighter than she has before. "Thank you so much, Betty. It's very kind of you to offer, but I think it's going to take me days to unpack everything and get settled."

"Hush now." My ma waves her hand in my direction. "Lucio will help, and besides, you need to eat. One o'clock. Don't be late."

Delilah only nods.

"We'll be there, Ma," I say, saving Delilah because she looks overwhelmed.

Ma walks over to me, throwing her arms around my shoulders and putting her mouth right next to my ear. "Don't fuck this up," she whispers as I stare at Delilah and she stares at me. "You help this girl and keep them safe."

"I know, Ma," I whisper, but neither of us is speaking softly enough for Delilah not to hear us.

Ma doesn't say anything I don't already know or think. In the short amount of time Delilah and Lulu have been around, they've grown on me, and I feel responsible for their safety.

As quickly as my family gathered to save the day and fill the upstairs apartment with so much baby stuff the place looks like we robbed the going-out-of-business sale at Toys "R" Us, they disappear, leaving us alone.

"So, your family is…" Delilah looks around the room and pauses with wide eyes. "I don't know how to describe how I feel."

I rub the back of my neck and start to laugh. "They're crazy at times, but—"

"They're amazing, Lucio. You're so lucky to have them."

She moves into the small, well-stocked kitchen which I had outfitted with new appliances after the last tenant moved out. I follow, keeping my distance because I don't know what type of traumatic shit she's been through, and we don't know each other well enough for me to start looming over her.

"This place is beautiful. Are you sure you don't want to give it to someone else?"

"And what, put you guys on the street?"

She turns then, facing me with little Lulu staring at me too. "You could've." Her eyes dip to the floor, but I stay quiet because I wasn't trying to be a hero in this situation. I did what most people would do when someone is in need. Especially when they have a baby in tow. "I mean, my father didn't have a problem doing that to us."

"Listen." I move forward, closing the space between us now because I want her to understand I want them here. "I don't know what bad shit you had happen or what type of people you're used to having in your life, but you needed help, and I had a place. I couldn't sleep at night if I dropped you and Lulu off at a shelter when I had the means to help."

Lulu holds her hand out, reaching for me, and I take her from Delilah's arms without thinking. Even Delilah doesn't put up a fight and just hands her over like we've known each other for years.

"I'll repay you for everything."

"Stop right there," I say sternly. "I'm not looking for money." I laugh as Lulu touches my lips, plucking at them with her tiny fingers and blows her own raspberry.

"Everyone's looking for money."

"I have a house, a bar, a great bike, and a nice family. I got everything I need. You're helping me out by keeping the place in working order and lending a hand at the bar."

I feel like a broken record, repeating the shit I've already told her, but she doesn't seem to get it.

In her world, the one flooded with so much

money they practically drown themselves in decadence, she probably doesn't understand how someone could open their home to a perfect stranger. But as Lulu plays with my face like I'm a Mr. Potato Head toy, Delilah finally seems to relax and let everything sink in.

"We're done talking about it," I say to her, but not like an asshole. I don't want her to continually thank me or think she owes me something for helping her out. "There's two bedrooms over there." As I try to tip my head, Lulu's grip intensifies, and those tiny little nails dig into my skin.

"Oh Jesus. I'm sorry," Delilah says, moving toward me to take Lulu back. "I should probably feed her and put her down for a nap before she gets cranky."

"I don't think this kid ever gets cranky."

"Trust me, she does, and it's like the nine circles of hell when she has her moments." Delilah laughs softly before kissing Lulu's head.

"I have the bottle and formula from earlier. Just relax on the couch, and I'll get it ready. Once she's asleep, we'll start unpacking."

Delilah tilts her head and stares at me like I am part of some freak show act at the cheesy carnival that rolls into town from time to time.

"I can't let you do this all alone," I tell her because I know what she's thinking.

"Cause your ma told you to?" she asks.

"Because I want to, and to be honest—" I rub my hands together, knowing I am going to drop something on her she may not care to hear "—I like you and the kid."

Her eyes widen like my words are a shocking revelation.

I want to ask her if she has a boyfriend or anything, but I assume she doesn't. If she does, he is a piece of shit for not helping out her and the baby instead of me. If she were mine, she wouldn't be dealing with any kind of stress and certainly not living with her asshole father.

"Go sit," I tell her, angling my chin toward the couch behind her. "I got this."

She stares at me with her mouth hanging open, not moving as I walk toward the kitchen and start to prep Lulu's bottle. A few moments later, Delilah walks through the living room and peeks into the two bedrooms. "The crib's already set up."

"We work fast," I say as I measure the formula and heat the water. It has been years since I prepped a bottle, and my mother did it this morning, but it isn't any more complicated than making a drink at the bar.

The leather of the couch squeaks as she sits down. I finally turn around, catching sight of her holding Lulu across her lap and looking comfortable for the first time since she walked into my life. Her eyes are moving fast, checking out the place and all the boxes of God knows what my family decided to drop off.

What kind of idiot would fuck this up?

Hot chick. Cool baby.

Not too much is complicated about the situation. I could never abandon my kid and baby mama, but that's just how I was brought up. Then there's the fact that my mother would have my balls in a vise for doing that shit to my own blood.

I shake the bottle, mixing the chalky formula with the water as I walk into the living room, watching them. "I'll start unpacking while you feed her."

She looks up at me with her big, beautiful blue eyes and long eyelashes, blinking for a second like she is trying to process what I said. "I'm sure you have things to do."

"I don't." I kind of lie. I didn't have anything solid planned, but I was supposed to play a game of football with the guys.

I hand her the bottle and make myself busy, giving her some space and time to think while she feeds Lulu.

I've done some fucked-up shit in my life, but never once did my family turn their backs on me. I can't imagine what is going through her head after her father basically disowned her, leaving her without any money or a place to live.

I don't even make it through the first box when she starts to speak. "I just want you to know no guy is going to show up on your doorstep, demanding to see me or Lulu."

"I'm not worried," I tell her and keep my back to her, slowly pulling out the baby items and placing them on the counter. "You're allowed to have anyone over you'd like."

"Lulu's dad took off before she was born. I haven't heard from him since and have washed my hands of him entirely. I haven't been in a relationship with anyone since, so…"

"It's not my business, Delilah." My heart hurts for Lulu, and Delilah too. Not only do I want to beat her father's ass, I want to strangle the prick who knocked her up and then abandoned them both.

"But I want you to know because—" she pauses as I finally turn around to face her "—I like you too." She speaks so quietly I almost don't hear her, but those words change things forever.

CHAPTER SEVEN

DELILAH

Saying those words wasn't easy either. I didn't want Lucio to think I only said I like him because he's helping me out. Of course, that is part of the reason, but not the only thing I like about him.

Why wouldn't I love the guy who swooped in and rescued us from the clusterfuck that's become my life?

But it's more than that.

Here's this drop-dead gorgeous guy, muscles for days, owns his own house and bar, and he's willing to help some woman he just met, along with her baby. Lulu's father couldn't even be bothered, and I dated him for over a year before he knocked me up. Lucio has the qualities every woman's looking for but rarely ever finds.

Clearly, it isn't just his physical appearance that draws me to him, but damn, it is impressive nonetheless. Even standing in the kitchen, holding a teddy bear in one arm and a little girl dress in the other, he is hot as fuck. His tanned skin, bulging arms, and tattoos scream sexy stripper guy. I probably would've made that judgment about him if we'd crossed paths on the street. But he isn't any of that. He is the only person in the city who didn't turn his back on me.

"Give her here," he says, motioning for Lulu. She's fast asleep in my arms with the bottle still in her mouth. "I'll put her down."

I hand Lulu over without saying a word. I stare at him, and he meets my gaze but doesn't acknowledge what I just admitted. Maybe he doesn't like me in *that* way, and I'm totally off base. He could've meant he liked me as a sister or a good friend. Not that he wanted to jump my bones in quite the same way I want to hop on him.

"What the fuck? Way to go, Delilah," I whisper to myself as he disappears into Lulu's bedroom down the hallway.

Pushing off the couch, I scrub my hands down my face and try to overcome the embarrassment as I kneel on the floor. I open a box of baby clothes sitting next to the couch as Lucio walks back into the room. I don't dare look up because I don't want to throw myself at him again and make an even bigger fool of myself.

We work in comfortable silence, stealing glances at one another as we unbox all the items his family brought over. I rarely get flustered around people, but Lucio has me all kinds of off-kilter.

"Are you hungry?" he asks as he stops in front of me.

"A little," I lie, because I am starving.

"Stay here. I'll go grab something."

"Okay," I say as he runs down the stairs, leaving me alone.

Without him here, I walk around and check out my new, but temporary, place. Opening cabinets and drawers, I find the place filled with everything we need. The clean, modern kitchen has stainless-steel appliances, white lacquered cabinets, and black granite countertops. It's stuffed with pots and pans, dishes, and anything else I'll need to whip up a feast.

The decent-sized bathroom has a bathtub with a shower, pedestal sink, and everything else I'd expect to find, including towels, soap, and even bubble bath. The bedroom where Lulu sleeps has a crib and a dresser, but not much else. My room has a comfortable queen-sized bed, nightstand, dresser, and even a small walk-in closet.

What more could a woman ask for? This isn't my father's penthouse, but it is absolutely perfect for Lulu and me. But I don't want to make myself too comfortable. I know this is only temporary. Lucio is a good man, but I don't want to overstay our welcome.

I lie on the bed, staring up at the ceiling and listening to the sirens screeching down the street below. They will take a little getting used to, but Lulu can sleep through a hurricane…thank God. I close my eyes, moving my fingers across the soft comforter and humming to myself when it becomes too quiet.

"Comfy?"

I jump off the bed and grab my chest as soon as I hear his voice. "You scared the shit out of me," I say as my heart pounds underneath my hand. "Jesus."

"I'm sorry. I was quiet so I wouldn't wake Lulu." He leans in the doorway to the bedroom, arms folded in front of his wide chest, watching me with a devastatingly beautiful smile. "I got pizza. Is that okay?"

My stomach growls and flutters at the same time. I've never felt anything like that before. "You look like a meat kind of guy, yeah? Lemme guess. You got sausage," I say as I follow him into the living room and hope he's not the pineapple type. Because pineapple on pizza is a total deal-breaker.

"Pepperoni. It was the only one they had ready, and I didn't want to make you wait." He opens the lid of the box, and the smell smacks me right in the face.

"It's absolutely perfect," I tell him as my mouth starts to water just looking at the gooey masterpiece. The cheese is perfectly melted, a little brown near the crust, and covered in loads of pepperoni, without a slice of pineapple in sight. Thank God.

"You okay with sitting on the floor?" He looks to the coffee table across the room. It's the only surface in the apartment that isn't covered with boxes or items that need to be put away.

"Of course." I nod and can't hold back my smile.

How could I have a freaking problem with the floor? I don't have a literal pot to piss in without him. I'd eat on the roof if he wanted. I grab two plates from the cabinet along with napkins before kneeling down next to Lucio. He grabs a slice and motions for me to take one too.

"So, tell me about you," I say as I hold the slice near my mouth, moving slowly, trying not to shove the entire piece of pizza in my mouth out of sheer starvation.

He takes a bite, swallowing down the first mouthful with a shrug. "Not much to tell. Grew up in this neighborhood, and I own the bar with my brothers and sister. It used to be my parents', but we bought them out a few years ago after my father ran into some legal issues."

I cover my mouth, feeling like a complete asshole. "I'm sorry," I mutter with a mouthful of food.

"Don't be," he laughs and waves the pizza slice in the air. "Santino knew his house of cards would come crashing down someday. He was into some pretty shady shit, but I'm happy we were able to save the bar before the government had a chance to seize it."

My heart flutters at the way he stares at me. It has been ages since anyone has looked at me like that. Having Lulu in my arms is always a surefire way for no man to see me as anything but a mom. But Lucio is different; he gazes at me like I'm a woman and not a breeding machine.

I set my pizza down and place my hand on his arm. "You didn't have to tell me that. I really am sorry."

He shrugs it off, but I can tell the entire thing bothers him. "He did the crime and has to do the time. I'm not proud of him, but he's still mine. He was always a good dad, just did some questionable stuff we all knew would catch up with him someday."

"He's still a better man than my father," I tell him, going back to my pizza to stop myself from touching him again. I already let my hand linger a little too long.

"Do you mind telling me what happened?"

Typically, my personal home life is private, but Lucio deserves to hear the entire gruesome story. He opened his home to us and needs to know what happened and why. I spend the next ten minutes spilling my guts about my alcoholic father, my missing-in-action mother, and the downward slide of my father's career and how it changed him into an unforgiving and sometimes reckless asshole.

"That's some pretty fucked-up shit, Delilah." This time, Lucio reaches out and touches my arm, sweeping his thumb across my skin. "I'm so sorry you had to go through all that with him."

Goose bumps cover my flesh, and my heart, which is already in overdrive, speeds up a little more. "I'm just sorry I stayed as long as I did. I should've moved out a long time ago. I wouldn't be in this situation if I had."

His fingers still, and he tightens his grip on my arm. "But then you wouldn't be here," he says without even blinking.

All the air I have in my body evaporates as I stare into his dark green eyes. The small apartment suddenly feels even smaller as he stares at me, touching my skin. I swallow down the lump that has settled deep in my throat and try to regain my composure. Something I've failed at multiple times with him. "You'd probably be out having fun on a Saturday instead of saddled with me and my kid."

I regret the words as soon as they come out of my mouth. I sound like I'm fishing for a compliment, and I hate people who do that. I really meant what I said and wasn't looking for him to say anything about how spending Saturday with me is far better than hanging out with his buddies. We both know that isn't true.

Lucio moves closer, and I hold my breath, leaning forward. Part of me is hoping he's going to kiss me. Our bodies are still connected. He's still holding on tightly to my arm. I close my eyes as he moves his face near mine and wait for the moment.

"Delilah," he says softly. I barely hear him whisper my name over the whooshing of my pulse in my ears and the rapid beating of my own heart.

"Yes?" My voice sounds needy, and I am. My body is on fire, the nearness of him and his scent overpowering my common sense. The fact that I haven't been touched by a man in so long amplifies everything.

"Lulu's awake."

My eyes fly open, and I realize he wasn't moving in for a kiss. He was trying to get up because Lulu is crying in the other room. I'd been so wrapped up in him, I hadn't even heard her.

I cover my face with my hands, letting out a little groan as Lucio disappears into Lulu's room. My face is red and heated. All I want to do is crawl under a blanket and hide. I'm sure Lucio knows I expected a kiss. How could he not? I had my mouth open, leaning forward, eyes closed like a dumb-ass teenager waiting for her first kiss.

"You're an idiot," I whisper to myself.

"Delilah," he says as he walks back into the room with Lulu in his arms. "I'm going to kiss you, but not until the moment's right, and definitely not over a box of pizza."

I don't know if I want to spin around the room, celebrating the fact that Lucio does, in fact, want to kiss me, or if I still want that blanket to hide my embarrassment over sitting on the floor with my eyes closed and my lips puckered. "Right," I say, going back to my pizza and keeping my eyes off Lucio as he sits down with Lulu in one arm.

"Hey." He touches my face, forcing me to look at him. "You're hot, li'l mama," he says as his thumb brushes near the bottom of my lip. "I don't want to rush things. You've been through a lot. When the time is right, if it is, I'll kiss you. I don't want to ruin you just yet."

"Ruin me?" I ask, almost choking on my pizza.

"Once I kiss you, you'll never want another man again."

I wish I could say something witty about how he is full of himself, but something tells me Lucio isn't lying.

CHAPTER EIGHT

LUCIO

"MAYBE I SHOULD JUST GO BACK HOME," SHE SAYS AS we walk through the front door of Hook & Hustle.

"No, no. My mother wants you here." I wrap an arm around her back and curl my hand over her hip, stopping her from leaving as she tries to take a step backward. "I want you here," I admit, shocking her as much as myself.

"Oh." Delilah blushes and smiles, tucking a strand of brown hair behind her ear.

"Besides, if you leave now, Betty will track you down."

"She will?" she whispers as her eyes grow wider.

"She's been known to do crazier shit."

She lets out a nervous laugh before glancing around the empty bar. "Where is everyone?"

"We're closed on Sunday afternoons. It's Gallo time until eight when we reopen again."

"It looks so different in the daylight."

"Not as scary?" I try to make light of the situation. I know the other night she was practically shaking in her shoes when she walked through the front door of Hook & Hustle.

"Definitely not as scary." She rests her head on my chest like she's done it a million times before. I have to remind myself she isn't mine—well, not yet, at least.

Last night, we flirted. I knew she wanted to kiss me more than once, but I was trying to play it cool with her. And that had never been my thing. I'd forced myself to give her space, but it was almost like torture.

I had the worst night's sleep in my entire life. Every time I heard Delilah walking across the floor or Lulu crying, I wanted to run upstairs to see if they were okay. Somehow, I stopped myself from doing just that because the last thing I wanted to do was scare her away.

Especially after the things she told me about her family. It was awful. They are awful. There hasn't been one person in her life she could depend on. I didn't want to be added to the ever-growing list of assholes who'd fucked up her life.

"Lucio," she says as she turns her face upward, piercing my heart with her baby blue eyes. "I…"

I know shit is about to get heavy, and whatever she is going to say is something I'm not sure I am ready to hear. "We better get upstairs. We're already late."

She nods and drops whatever she was about to say. I reluctantly release her from my grip, letting her walk ahead of me up the stairs. I can't help but stare at her perfectly round ass and the way her hips sway as she slowly walks in front of me.

Delilah's foot doesn't even land on the top step when the door flies open. My ma looks down at us with the biggest smile. "Finally," Ma says, holding out her arms and motioning for the baby. "Let me see that angel."

Without hesitation, Delilah hands Lulu over to my mother. "Jesus," Delilah whispers when she gets her first full look at everyone busy setting the table and preparing the food. "This is a small army."

Sometimes, I forget not everyone has a big family like mine. "You saw almost everyone yesterday, but I never formally introduced you."

"It was kind of hectic," she snorts and somehow makes the noise sound adorable.

"That's Vinnie. He's the baby." I tick my head toward my little brother who is standing in the kitchen and the only one not helping with dinner.

"Yo," he calls out, barely looking up from his cell phone.

"Hey." Delilah gives him a small wave, but Vinnie is too busy to even notice or wave back.

"He's an asshole and thinks he's God's gift to women," I tell her because there's no better way to describe my little brother.

"Must be genetic," she mumbles and starts to giggle, getting in her small little dig about me.

"I'm God's gift to everyone," Vinnie corrects without making eye contact.

Daphne rounds the kitchen counter, walking toward us. I know Delilah was most nervous about seeing her because, let's face it, my sister can be a complete bitch. "Hey. I'm so sorry about the other night."

"It's not a problem," Delilah says and shakes her head.

Daphne grabs Delilah, pulling her into a giant hug. "You got to understand. We get a bunch of assholes who wander into the bar all the time asking for shit. You'll see. It was nothing against you." Delilah doesn't hug her back immediately, but Daphne isn't letting her go. My sister is relentless in everything, including her hugs. "I was in a shit mood, and I wasn't feeling overly friendly. Please forgive me."

"It's okay, Daphne. I do understand," Delilah says, finally putting her arm around Daphne. Maybe Delilah knows she isn't getting out of my sister's grasp without accepting the apology and hugging her back.

"I swear I'll make it up to you. We'll have a girls' night."

Delilah glances back at me, looking for a rescue, but I have nothing to give. My sister is a pit bull, and I'm not about to get into an argument over a girls' night out. "We'll see. I don't go out anymore. Lulu takes all my time."

Daphne waves her hand in my direction as she finally releases Delilah. "Lucio can babysit," she offers without even asking me first.

"I couldn't ask him to do that."

"We're not asking," Daphne laughs. "He'd be happy to do it."

"I'll watch the tiny squirt any time. Everyone needs to blow off a little steam every now and then," I tell Delilah without even thinking about it because I like seeing her happy.

Plus, she could use a friend, especially someone like my sister. I haven't heard Delilah mention one girlfriend she could count on, and there is no one quite like Daphne. She'd happily kick any guy in the balls without a second thought. My brothers and I probably did too good of a job preparing her for the onslaught of men we knew would go after her as she grew up.

Delilah turns to face me, holding her chest. "You'd do that?" she stammers.

"Of course." I'd rather stay in and entertain her, but I keep that shit to myself.

Delilah lunges forward, wrapping her arms around my neck. "Thank you, Lucio," she whispers, standing on her tiptoes with her mouth so close I could've kissed her.

I hug her back, enjoying the way she feels in my arms. Even with her mouth almost touching mine, I don't kiss her. Daphne is too busy staring at the two of us, and I don't want our first kiss to be in front of my entire family, especially Daphne.

"Come on." Daphne grabs Delilah's hand, pulling her toward the kitchen. "Let me introduce you to everyone."

"Go," I tell her when Delilah hesitates, looking to me for permission.

"You're whipped already, huh?" Angelo, my oldest brother, says as soon as the girls are across the room and out of earshot.

"I think so," I mutter, rubbing the back of my neck, unable to take my eyes off Delilah. "I know I don't want anyone else touching her."

"Then claim her," he tells me, like it is the most natural thing in the world.

"Dude, she's not a prize."

"The way you're looking at her, I'd say she is."

His words render me speechless. I've never really looked at someone the way I look at Delilah. That much is true, but I've never really had a girlfriend either. I am more a play-the-field type of guy. Not because I am a playboy or an asshole, but I saw my father struggle to stay faithful for so long, I was scared I had some of him in me.

"She's got a kid, man."

"What's your point? I'm sure you've slept with other mothers."

I don't want to tell him I don't even really know because I've never bothered to get to know them well enough to find out. "Yeah, probably."

Angelo places his hand on my shoulder, doing the big brother crap. "Well, I think your whoring days are numbered, little brother."

I blow out a long breath, knowing what he said is probably true. "Fuck, this could be bad."

Angelo laughs, squeezing my shoulder rougher this time. "Might be the best damn thing ever to happen to you."

"Says the unattached guy," I mumble.

"I think Pop fucked you up in a way. We're all scared of commitment because of the way he was when we were kids, but he's not that man anymore, and neither are we."

"It's hard to be a cheater from behind bars," I remind Angelo.

"He stopped a long time ago. I think he was scared Ma was going to kill him in his sleep if he kept up with his bullshit."

"He finally wised up, and I have no doubt Betty could've offed him."

"Johnny probably would've done it for her," Angelo says.

"The man has never gotten over her picking Dad instead of him," I agree as I glance at my mother, who is still holding Lulu.

Angelo steps in front of me, blocking my view to make sure he has my undivided attention. "If you like this chick, make her yours."

"You make it sound so easy."

Is it really that simple? Life is already going to be complicated. With Delilah living above me, working at my bar, nothing is going to be easy. Our lives are about to become so intertwined I'm not sure if a relationship is the smartest route, but then again, I've never been known for making the best decisions.

The one thing I know for sure is I want Delilah. In the short amount of time she's been in my life, I haven't thought about anyone or anything else. Nothing seems to matter except for her and Lulu.

I want them safe.

I want them happy.

I want them with me.

"I see the war going on inside that head of yours." Angelo nudges me as I space out. "Stop thinking and just do it already. If you don't, I will."

"You're a bastard," I hiss, knowing he's pushing my buttons and it's working.

He laughs and slaps my back. "I'm a motivator."

"A fucker, maybe."

"Careful or I'll be a mother fucker."

I hate him.

CHAPTER NINE

DELILAH

The Gallos are nothing like my family.

Growing up, dinner was always a silent affair with only the adults allowed to speak to one another. When I finished the food on my plate, I had to remain seated, waiting for my parents to finish eating before being excused.

Lucio's family is the exact opposite. They don't stop talking. Not only that, more than one person talks at a time, making it almost impossible for me to follow any single conversation. I spend most of the time trying to memorize everyone's names and details because trying to talk is useless.

I asked Lucio to tell me about his siblings before we came to his mother's house. When they dropped everything off yesterday, I was too in shock to process anything. Plus, they came and left so quickly, I barely got to say hello.

Angelo, the oldest brother, is just as tall as Lucio, not as freakishly large, but not small by any means. His eyes are a beautiful shade of ice blue, popping against his olive skin and dark hair. He seems to be more serious than everyone else, but maybe because of everything he's been through, especially losing his wife and being a single parent.

Vinnie, the youngest Gallo brother, is super cocky and probably a lady-killer. He is the golden boy and star quarterback, winning the state championship three years in a row in high school. Although he is a part owner of the bar, he is gone most of the year but sometimes comes home on weekends. He's just as handsome as his brothers, but he still has a boyish quality which makes him appear to be innocent when he is the furthest thing from it.

Daphne is two years older than Vinnie. She is pretty straightforward, speaks her mind, and doesn't take shit from very many people. She either likes you or she doesn't, and she makes her feelings very clear.

"What do you think, Dee?" Daphne asks, but I am so lost, I have no idea what she wants my opinion about. She's staring at me, and I shift in my seat, feeling the weight of her gaze.

"Sure," I say because I don't want to seem like I'm not paying attention. Hell, I am paying as much attention as I possibly can to every conversation around the table and failing miserably.

"Yeah?" She looks shocked, and I know I'm in trouble.

When Lucio turns to me with his eyebrows almost to his hairline and asks, "You really want to do that?" I pretty much know I'm fucked.

I look at her and then back to him. "What am I missing?"

"A whole lotta skin," Daphne replies with a wicked smile, pretending to spank the air with her palm. "And muscles for days, girl. Dat ass, though."

"I think she has to work," Lucio says, rescuing me even though I didn't ask him for help from something that doesn't sound like all that much fun.

Strippers used to be fun before I had Lulu. But now the very thought of a bunch of gyrating, naked men doesn't seem as interesting or exciting as a nap, due to my current state of exhaustion.

"Yeah. I heard the boss is a real prick too," I add, giving Lucio a sideways glance as I bounce Lulu on my lap and try to be funny.

I should've been pissed he answered on my behalf, but I'm not. Sitting around, getting drunk, and watching half-naked men doesn't sound like as much fun as a quiet evening at home alone with Lucio. But I know I am being delusional. The dancers and Lucio have one thing in common…they aren't the type to settle down with a single mother.

"He totally is," Daphne laughs. "But the other boss, the more beautiful one"—she points to herself—"says you can have the night off."

Somewhere along the way, Daphne and I became total BFFs. The woman behind the bar is nothing like the one sitting across the table from me now. Maybe there's a work version of her which is tough as nails and takes no bullshit. Daphne Gallo at her mother's dinner table is sweet as pie. Either that, or she's trying to get me into a world of trouble.

"She has a baby to take care of," Lucio tells Daphne like I'm not even in the room, let alone sitting next to him.

"I'm sure Ma will watch Lulu," Daphne shoots back before staring at her mother, waiting.

I think all hope is lost for a second, but then Betty speaks.

"Although I love Lulu already, I'm busy next Saturday."

Everybody in the room goes silent, turning toward her with their mouths hanging open. It's the first time since I walked through the door there's not a single sound.

Vinnie shakes his head like he can't believe the words that just came out of her mouth. "What the hell are you doing Saturday, Ma? You never go out on the weekend," he asks, finally laying down his phone next to his dinner plate.

Betty stabs at the chicken on her plate, pretending she doesn't hear the question, but she doesn't look at anyone either.

"Ma." Angelo taps on the table in front of her. "Where are you going on Saturday?"

"I have plans," she says between bites.

"Plans?" Daphne cocks one perfectly plucked eyebrow and leans back in her chair, staring in her mother's direction. "You never have *plans.*"

"I have a life too, honey." The features on Betty's face tighten suddenly. "Drop it. End of discussion. I can't watch the baby. Delilah will just have to stay home."

Why do I get the sneaking suspicion Betty doesn't have a damn thing to do next weekend? I remember the words she said to Lucio. She seems to want to push us together, and so far, it's worked.

"Fine," Daphne sighs and tosses her napkin on her plate.

"Thanks for asking me to go. It means a lot to me." I try not to seem overly happy I can't go, even though I am relieved.

"You're welcome." Daphne smiles, sitting up a little straighter and pushing her long brown hair behind her shoulder. "We'll do it another weekend."

The momentary silence evaporates, and everyone

starts talking again, but no one presses Betty any further.

"So, Delilah, do you have any waitressing experience?" Angelo asks from the other end of the table.

I glance down at Lulu's smiling face and think about lying for a second, but I know he'd be able to tell as soon as I started on the job. "I don't. Is that okay?"

"It's fine." He waves me off and almost cracks a smile. "I'd be more than happy to show you the ropes."

I peer up at Lucio as he sits next to me, but he is staring at his brother, paying no attention to me at all. "I'll be training Delilah," Lucio states quickly.

"If you think you can handle it," Angelo says with a small smirk and returns his brother's stare. "I know how much you hate training new employees."

Lucio's eyes narrow, and he still doesn't look at me. "We haven't had a new employee in four years."

"Dudes," Vinnie interrupts and points at himself with his thumbs. "I'll train the new chick." He winks in my direction and is immediately smacked in the chest with the back of Angelo's hand.

Part of me wants to laugh because Vinnie is adorable, but Jesus, the way Angelo and Lucio are glaring at each other, I am ready to duck for cover.

"I don't want to be any trouble," I say softly as an uneasy feeling settles deep in my stomach.

Without looking down at me, Lucio places his

hand on top of mine. "It won't be any trouble. I want to train you."

"I'm sure you want more than that," Vinnie whispers under his breath and is again met with the back of Angelo's hand, but this time a little harder.

"Delilah." Betty breaks the awkward silence and changes the subject pretty quickly. "Want to take Lulu for a walk with me?"

Just as quickly as Lucio placed his hand on top of mine, it's gone.

"Sure," I say and try to hide the sadness from my voice.

"The kids can clean up." She smiles as the *kids* grumble. "I usually take Angelo's kids for a walk after dinner, but they're with their other grandparents."

"That's so sweet." Neither of my parents has ever taken Lulu for a walk. My father barely held Lulu, and my mother still hasn't bothered to see her once. "They must love that."

I am envious of the people around this table. I would've given up growing up with money if it meant I'd have half the support system they do. All the money in the world means nothing without love. I know that firsthand after my parents pawned me off on nannies and boarding school as I grew older. Even when they were physically present in my life, they weren't truly there.

"Lucio, can you get the stroller for us?" his mother asks him.

Lucio stands with me, finally making eye contact. "Want me to come?" he asks.

"No. You stay here and relax," I tell him. He looked so hopeful before those words left my mouth, but I am being selfish. I want a little time alone with his mother, someone I would've loved having as my own.

"I promise to be on my best behavior," his mother says.

Lucio doesn't look convinced. "I think I should go too. Make sure you two are safe." He takes a step forward, but his mother places her small hand on the middle of his giant chest and stops him.

"You'll stay here. Give the girl a little room to breathe, son. Let your momma handle this," she says as if I'm not even in the room, listening to the entire conversation.

It seems to be a theme in this family. I don't know if it's because I'm the new girl or maybe they just like bossing each other around, but it's starting to drive me a little crazy.

"Delilah, why don't I show you where we store it in case you want to use it again?" Lucio motions for me to follow, and I glance at his mother.

"That's a splendid idea. I'll just run and get my hat." She smiles and shoos me toward the stairwell where Lucio is waiting. "Gimme that sweet girl," she says, taking Lulu from my arms before I can take a step.

We don't speak as I follow him through the bar, down a hallway, and to the storage closet where I think they keep the stroller.

Before I have one foot in the doorway, Lucio has his arms around me, pulling me in closer until there's no space left between us.

"I'm sorry," he says as he leans forward, staring into my eyes so intensely my knees start to go weak.

"For what?" I ask as he moves his mouth closer to mine. My voice is so soft I'm not sure he heard me because he doesn't answer right away.

"For this." He presses his soft, full lips to mine and holds me tighter, stealing my breath. He sweeps his tongue across my bottom lip, and I tip my head back, opening to him. In this moment, as our tongues tangle together, I know one thing for sure. He was right.

I *am* ruined.

CHAPTER TEN

LUCIO

"I CAN'T QUITE PLACE THE LOOK ON YOUR FACE," Daphne says as I stand behind the bar, looking out across the room filled with customers.

I know where she's going with the statement. I've been walking around in a haze ever since I kissed Delilah, but I didn't think it was noticeable. I should've known Daphne would be all over me, sticking her nose exactly where it didn't belong.

I fill a pint at the tap, trying to busy myself. "Shut up, Daph."

I walk to the other end to get away from my

sister's prying eyes, but she follows me. "You really like this chick, don't you?"

I set the beer down in front of Johnny before I turn to face her. I know she isn't going to back down. That's never been my sister's style, especially when it comes to her brothers and our love lives. "I do," I admit, turning to face her and crossing my arms in front of my chest.

"Huh," she mumbles and shakes her head slowly. "Never knew you had it in you."

My muscles tighten, and I'm instantly defensive. "Had what?"

"The love gene." She punches my shoulder playfully and laughs. "I'm pretty sure it's the end of the world."

"I'm not in love, Daphne. I just met the girl." I may not have been there yet, but I could easily fall in love with Delilah. My ma was right about one thing; Delilah is more stable than most of the women I've dated. She doesn't ask for much, and even though she grew up with a silver spoon in her mouth, the smallest things seem to make her happy.

"You doth protest too much."

I roll my eyes, stalking away from her, done with the conversation. But Daphne's not ready to move on. She follows me, almost face-planting in my back when I stop too quickly. "What are you doing?" I ask, trying not to lose my cool as I glare at her over my shoulder.

Daphne comes around in front of me, blocking

the path to the back room and wags her finger in my face. "You had sex with her already, didn't you?"

"Not that it's any of your business, but I haven't." I don't know why I tell her. She doesn't need to know everything that happens in my life. Working together has added a new level of brother and sister closeness I never expected when I agreed to buy the bar with them.

Daphne staggers backward, holding her chest like she's heard the most shocking news. "You haven't? Oh. My. God. It *is* the end of the world."

"Stop being overdramatic." I push her aside and stalk toward the office.

"You sleep with everyone, Lucio. She's been under your roof for more than twenty-four hours, and you haven't nailed her. That can only mean one thing."

"Don't say it," I tell her as Michelle, my sister's best friend and our best waitress, walks into the office just behind us.

"What the hell are you two doing?" She places her hands on her hips, staring back and forth between the two of us before tipping her head toward the door. "We have a bar full of customers waiting."

Daphne waves her hand at me. "Lucio hasn't slept with Delilah yet," she says, not answering Michelle's question and totally selling me out to Michelle.

My sister says I sleep with everyone, but I don't. Hell, I haven't slept with Michelle even though she's smoking hot and totally my type. She's way too connected with my sister for me to even think about sleeping with her. Something about the very thought has always grossed me out.

Michelle's eyebrows shoot up, and she steps inside the office, forgetting about all the waiting customers she came in here to tell us about. "Oh, do tell me more."

"Both of you get out," I tell them, shooing them toward the door.

They step backward in unison, giving each other a look before laughing. "Someone's got it bad," Daphne teases and nudges Michelle's arm with her bony elbow.

"Get. Out," I repeat as I push them into the hallway, needing some time alone to get my head on straight.

I HEAD HOME EARLY, leaving Daphne and Michelle to clean up because they wouldn't get off my case. I tiptoe through the front door finding Delilah sitting on the steps to her apartment, leaning against the wall, and sound asleep. She doesn't even flinch when the front door clicks and I engage the lock. She looks so peaceful, so beautiful as she sleeps, but in no way does she look comfortable.

Delilah mumbles something as I lift her into my arms, and her face falls against my chest, making it impossible to understand her words. I'm tempted to carry her to my bed, but I know we may not hear Lulu crying, so I take her upstairs instead.

My life went from carefree to complicated the moment Delilah walked into the bar. I've never been one to turn my back on a friend in need, but strangers are a different story. Not that I'm a heartless bastard, but I have too much other shit to deal with on the daily to put a whole lot of thought into helping someone I don't know.

If she had been alone, I might have reacted differently, but I couldn't turn my back on her and Lulu both. Lulu is an innocent in the entire situation, and as far as I can tell, so is Delilah. In all probability, I wouldn't have turned my back on Delilah either because I'm a sucker for a pretty lady, especially one in crisis.

My ma has said more than once that I attract the crazy chicks, but there's a reason for that. They're safe. I never worry about falling in love when the girl is one step away from a padded room.

Delilah isn't safe. Not for my heart, at least, and it's a scary place for me to be in, as well as totally uncharted territory.

"Lucio," Delilah whispers as I place her on the bed.

"Shh," I say softly as she stretches. "Go back to sleep, sweetheart."

I expect her hands to fall away from my neck, but

she tightens her hold. "Lie down with me," she begs, and in that moment, I can't say no.

I crawl under the covers, placing my front against her side. She curls into me, smashing her face back against my chest again. I'm not sure where to put my hands, not knowing her well enough to touch the parts I really want to. Instead, I set one hand against the small of her back and use the other to prop my head in my palm.

"How was work?" she asks, pulling her face away from my body and staring up at me with sleepy eyes.

"It was good. You okay?"

She looks sadder than usual, but she nods. "I'm fine. Just had a long night. Lulu wouldn't stop crying."

"Is she sick?"

"No. She was just fussy. Thank God she's sleeping." Delilah groans and brings her hands between us, wrapping her fingers around my T-shirt and holding on to me tightly. Her breasts press against me as she shifts, and no matter what I do, I know my body's going to respond to the feel of her.

I move my face and bury my nose in her hair, recognizing the lavender scent of the baby shampoo my mother gave to her after the family dinner. "Is there anything I can do to make things easier?"

She peers up, tightening her hold on my shirt. "Kiss me," she whispers.

I don't know what I thought her answer would be, but I like where she takes my offer. I'm not sure kissing her again will make things easier, but I know it sounds like way more fun than anything else.

I don't hesitate in moving my lips to hers, our eyes locked on each other as our breathing grows harsher and more labored.

I struggle to keep my composure as my mouth crashes down on hers for only the second time since I met her. The feel of her lips is no less spectacular or mind-blowing than it was the first time I kissed her.

She slides her arms around my shoulders, pulling me on top of her as I tug on her lip with my teeth, teasing her and myself in the process. She lets out a small moan, making it damn near impossible for me to take things slow.

I slide a hand under the hem of her T-shirt, finding the soft skin near her waist. It takes everything in me to keep my fingers there because I want to slip the thin fabric from her body and mine, removing every obstacle between us. The only noise in the room is our lips smacking against each other, and it sounds like pure heaven.

"I want you," I murmur against her lips. God, I want her more than anyone I've ever wanted before. But restraint is key with a girl like her. A single mother needs to be treated with kid gloves. Having her as a roommate makes everything more complicated. I know once we go down this road, there's no turning back.

She laces her fingers through my hair, holding my

face and lips to hers. I wasn't going anywhere, though. Nothing could stop me from taking what she had to give.

I slide my tongue across her bottom lip, feeling her softness and tasting her sweetness. Her tongue meets mine, sending shock waves through my system, and the haze I've been walking in for most of the day seems to vanish.

I don't know what I was thinking when I kissed her in the bar, but in all reality, I wasn't thinking at all. I let my body lead the way, and I'm doing it again. I know I shouldn't be touching her, but I can't stop myself.

"I want you too," she admits, and when she wraps her legs around my back, the small sliver of resistance and common sense I had slips away.

I kiss her harder, loving the way she responds with soft moans and by tightening her legs around my body, pushing my cock into her.

She wants me. I want her.

This should be simple, but I know nothing about what's about to happen is.

Just when I'm about to make my move, Lulu starts to wail from the other room. For a moment, we don't stop. It's like some invisible force is holding us together, but as Lulu's cries become louder, we both pull apart. I roll to my side, staring up at the ceiling with my cock hard as a rock and throbbing with need.

"I'm so sorry," Delilah says as she crawls off the bed.

"Don't be," I tell her before she walks out of the room to grab Lulu.

Lulu may have saved me from a big mistake. I don't want to sleep with Delilah because I'm horny and she's barely awake. I want the moment to be right, the feelings to be there. Once it happens, there's no turning back.

I already know I can't imagine them walking out the door, never seeing them again, but can I get over the worry I've carried around my entire life about being too much like my father? I owe it to Delilah and Lulu not to go any further unless I know I can be the man they both need.

CHAPTER ELEVEN

DELILAH

It's official.

I'm going to be the world's worst waitress.

"Again," Lucio says as he sits in the back corner of the bar, pretending to be a random customer.

Lucio's been patient with me, setting up the afternoon for us to train, and he hasn't complained once. But I know I'm bad. Bad isn't even a good enough word to describe the level of awful I am at taking orders and serving drinks. Carrying a tray is easy when it's empty, but add a few drinks, and I'm a hot mess with absolutely no balance.

Thankfully, the bar is almost empty. There're a few regulars hanging around, but they're too busy arguing about politics to watch how epically I'm failing.

I turn around, trying to regain my composure before facing him with a kind smile. I've already spilled three drinks and dropped the tray half a dozen times. "Good evening. Can I get you a drink?" I say, changing up the script we've gone over a hundred times.

"Good evening?" He raises an eyebrow.

I drop the straight face I've been able to maintain. "What? It sounded good." I shrug. "No?"

"Delilah, look around the bar." He waves his hand across the table toward the few guys sitting on the stools near the bar. "What do you see?"

I peer over my shoulder. "Some guys."

"What kind of guys?"

"Regulars, I assume."

"Yeah, but do they look like the type to say good evening?"

I peer down at the floor and kick the hardwood with the toe of my shoe. "Well, no."

"This isn't the country club, and the men who come in here don't wear a suit and tie. Keep it casual."

I shrug and blow out a breath. My feet hurt, and I'm irritated with myself. "Whatcha wanna drink?"

Lucio covers his mouth, but I know he's laughing.

The words are so foreign coming out of my mouth I can't even stop myself from laughing too.

"That's closer than good evening. Just be yourself."

I go right back into my role, taking his advice to be casual and act more like myself. "So, whatcha want? I don't have all day, mister."

"I'll take a gin and tonic."

I have my tray tucked under my arm, scribbling his drink order on a pad of paper. "How about a double for three bucks more?"

"Nice touch and upsell. Make it a double. I'll also take a Sex on the Beach and a Blow Job."

I blink a few times with my pen hovering over the pad of paper, but I can't seem to write out the words or make enough saliva to swallow without sounding like an idiot. My face heats, and I can't deny both sound pretty damn good about now. I imagine the sun bouncing off his tanned skin as the waves splash over our bodies.

I'm so lost thinking about screwing Lucio, the tray falls from under my arm and bounces off the floor, bringing me right back to reality. "You want a what, again?"

"They're drinks, Delilah. Sex on the Beach and a Blow Job."

Last night, we were so close to having sex until Lulu used her magical kid powers and put an end to mommy time. It was probably for the best, but I can't stop thinking about what could've happened and what the repercussions would've been today.

"Oh." I'm sure he hears the disappointment in my voice because Lord knows I do nothing to hide it. "Coming right up." I snatch the tray off the floor and march toward Angelo, fanning myself with the tiny pad of paper.

Angelo's leaning against the bar, watching me as I approach. "Lucio being too hard on you?" he asks, giving me a kind smile as he stops whatever he's been doing to give me his full attention.

I shake my head and blow the hair out of my eyes that had fallen when I bent down to pick up the tray. "No. He's great. I just suck at this."

"You don't suck. Give yourself some time to adjust. Why don't you lose the tray and leave the paper in your pocket? Only use it when you have a large order you're worried you won't remember."

"I can do that." I somehow muster a smile through my embarrassment. "I hope I don't mess things up tonight."

"You won't. Strangers are easier to serve than someone you know."

"Lucio makes me nervous," I blurt out and instantly regret letting that little nugget of truth slip.

Angelo's ice-blue eyes sparkle as his smile widens. "I think the feeling's mutual, Dee."

His statement makes me feel better. Lucio always seems to have his shit together, while I'm a mess of emotion. "I don't know about that. He's a pretty smooth talker."

Angelo leans forward, closing the space between us. "I'll let you in on a little secret," he says as I lean in closer too, dying to know what he's about to say. "My brother is a smooth talker, but you fluster the hell out of him. I've never seen him so unlike himself around a woman until you walked through the door."

"Waitress," Lucio calls out from across the room. "How's my drink coming?"

"See," Angelo says as he backs away. "He doesn't even like me talking or getting that close to you."

I peer over my shoulder at Lucio, who's watching us carefully and doesn't look one bit happy. "Coming, sir." I smile in his direction, but he doesn't return it.

"What did he order?"

"Double gin & tonic, Sex on the Beach, and a Blow Job."

Angelo rolls his eyes and grabs three glasses before filling them with water. "Carry them without the tray and try not to spill more than a few drops this time."

I carry the shot glass in one hand and the other two drinks in the opposite, walking as smoothly as possible toward Lucio.

His eyes never leave me as I get closer. "Here're your drinks, sir," I say, sliding them onto the table without being covered in water.

"Thank you." He grabs the tallest glass and

guzzles down the water like he's been walking in the desert for days.

"Did I do better this time?"

"You did." He wipes his mouth with the back of his hand, green eyes still on me, blazing.

I resist the urge to grab a glass of water and down the damn thing too. The way he's looking at me makes me want to crawl into his lap and beg for his kiss again.

"Grab the credit card reader from Angelo and make it quick this time."

Is Lucio jealous of his brother? I never would have pegged him for the insecure or jealous type, especially not when it comes to his family.

Angelo has the credit card reader on the bar top by the time I make my way across the room. He dips his head but doesn't say a word. I give him a small smile, not lingering too long because I know Lucio's patience is already wearing thin.

I'm halfway to the table when the door to the bar opens with the familiar little bell chiming overhead. "Can I help you, sir?" Angelo asks the person, and I continue walking, ignoring everyone in the room except Lucio.

"I'm here to see my daughter."

I can't stop the credit card reader from slipping from my grip and crashing to the floor near my feet. All the blood drains from my face, and all the playfulness I was feeling is gone when I hear his voice.

"Your daughter?" Angelo asks as I turn around with wide eyes, seeing my father standing near the doorway.

"Delilah," my father says, rushing in my direction with his hands outstretched. "Thank God you're okay."

I back up, moving closer to Lucio and farther away from my dad. He's the last person I want to see. My eyes are already filling with tears, my vision blurring, and I can't seem to walk away fast enough.

When my father grabs my arm, I pull away and glare at him. "Get the hell out," I snap, not caring who hears or what kind of scene I'm making. I figure the few guys sipping beers only a few feet away have heard worse. "You're not welcome here."

"Baby, don't say that," he says, trying to touch me again, but I jump backward, slamming into a wall of muscle.

"You heard the lady. Get out." Lucio's voice is loud and deep. He wraps an arm around my waist and moves himself in front of me. "You're not welcome here, Mr. Miles."

"I'm her father. I have every right to speak with my daughter. She's none of your concern, boy. This is family business."

My father looks normal, dressed in one of his best suits with bright eyes and no slur to his words. He's sober and doesn't look as disheveled as the night he kicked me out of the car. So any hatred he spews is coming from a clear head and not the alcohol.

I grip the back of Lucio's shirt, hiding my face as I wipe away the tears with my free hand. I don't want my father to see me crying. He's hurt Lulu and me enough to last a lifetime, and I'm not about to let him have another round at bruising my heart.

"Family business?"

I can't see Lucio's face, but every muscle in his back is tight, and there's a low rumble, almost a growl, deep in his chest.

Angelo rounds the bar and starts to walk in our direction, when Lucio holds out his hand, stopping his brother from entering the fray.

"You have five seconds to get out before I toss you out on your ass," Lucio tells my father.

God, I love this man for the way he defends me when no one else in my life ever has. My father should've always been my protector, but he's been nothing but a nightmare. I'm done being his whipping post.

"Wait." I yank on Lucio's T-shirt and peer up at him.

Lucio looks over his shoulder, and I can see the anger in his eyes, but it's not toward me. "You want to talk to him?"

"I need to say my piece," I tell him. I know that I need to have closure and leave my father in the past. "Let me have this."

It's the only way I can move on and start over again. Pushing him out the door will only make him come back, and next time, he'll probably be shit-faced.

Lucio nods, stepping aside without another word or an argument.

"Outside," I say, not moving until my father starts toward the door first.

"Hey." Lucio grabs my hand as I take a step forward. "I won't be far."

"Thanks." I muster a smile, but inside, I'm shaking like a leaf. "I need to do this."

He releases my hand, and I walk toward the doorway, where my father's waiting. There's pain in his eyes, but it's always there after he has a drunken episode like the other night. Next, he'll beg for forgiveness and promise to attend meetings, but this time, I won't believe a word that comes from his lying mouth.

My father paces on the sidewalk in front of the bar, dragging his hands through his hair as I lean against the wall near the entrance. "You wanted to talk, so talk," I tell him and pick at my nails because I can't bring myself to even look at him.

I've had a lifetime of dealing with his drunkenness, so you'd think I'd be better at handling the aftermath by now. I've always forgiven him in the past. I never forgot, but I found a way to move on, especially after I found out I was pregnant. He made so many promises, and stupid me thought he'd clean up his life for his granddaughter, but I should've known better.

He comes to a stop and faces me, but he doesn't bring his eyes to mine. "I'm sorry, Delilah," he says and runs his fingers through his perfectly combed hair. "I was having a bad night."

"You have a lot of those." My voice is even, which is surprising because my insides are burning with rage.

The hurt in his eyes would've probably affected me a week ago, but standing here now, I feel nothing.

"I want you to come home," he pleads.

"No," I say firmly.

He looks up at the building and makes a face of disgust. I know what he's thinking. He's always looked down at people who didn't fit his perfect, wealthy mold. "You don't belong in a place like this." He waves his hand toward the bar.

I push off the wall, walking toward him quickly, and I stick my finger right in the middle of his chest. "The thing I didn't deserve was being tossed out on the street with my daughter, your granddaughter, without a penny to my name. What I didn't deserve was a narcissistic father who was more worried about getting his next drink than his own family." I poke him a little harder this time because it feels good, and my anger's rolling harder and deeper than it ever has before. "What I didn't deserve was putting up with an asshole like you for the last ten years. I never walked out on you, Dad."

"I know."

"Mom left because she couldn't deal with your drinking, but I stayed." My voice grows louder because my anger is at a boiling point, and I'm close to blowing.

"She left you, too," he says, reminding me of the fact that my mother couldn't even be bothered with me, choosing the hot pool boy over both of us.

"Shut up!" I push him backward using my finger, and he doesn't fight back. "I will not go back home with you because it has never been anything more than a shelter. There's no love between us. You don't give a single shit about Lulu or me. You made that perfectly clear when you left us here."

"I need you," he says, but I don't believe a word of what he's telling me.

"Hire a housekeeper. I'm sure someone will put up with your drunken tirades for enough money. I'm done with you. I've spent enough of my life dealing with your verbal abuse, and I will not subject my daughter to it too." He steps backward, trying to get away from my finger, but I follow. "If you really feel bad, put my money back in my account. It's not yours to take. It's mine and Lulu's. If you really care, you'll make sure at least her future's secure."

He stares at me, and there's a flash of emotion on his face, but I'm not sure if it's sadness or something else. My father's never been one to share his feelings unless he's filled with a bottle of vodka.

"It's my account too," he says like he's justifying his theft of well over a million dollars that was left to me.

I pull my finger away from his chest and take a step backward, glaring at him. "Because I was under eighteen when Grandma died. It's not yours."

"Come home, and I'll return the money. Or stay here, and see what it's really like to survive on your own."

"I would rather live on the streets than live under the same roof as you again. Unlike you, my daughter is my first priority."

"Don't be a fool, Delilah. These aren't your people," he scoffs, and his facial features tighten. "I brought you up better than this." He waves his hand through the air again, motioning toward the bar.

"*These* people have been kinder to me in a few days than you have been in the last ten years. I'd rather Lulu be around people who shower her with love than throw money at her in hopes of winning her affection."

"Already sleep with one of them?" He throws the familiar words in my face, but this time, he's wrong.

"Just go, Dad. Don't look for me. Forget I even exist."

"You'll always be a whore just like your mother. Your bastard child will always be a reminder. I was sorry for what happened, but I can see you have no forgiveness in your heart. You're no better than her."

His words are meant to hurt me, but they don't mean anything anymore. I'm nothing like my mother, or my father either. I will always put Lulu first. I will never let her feel like less than the amazing little girl she is, and I will never allow her around anyone who's willing to hurt her.

Whether they're blood or not, no one will have that power over her or me again.

I glance to the side and see Lucio peeking around the corner of the building. I shake my head, waving him off. I know he wants to rush to my side and physically remove my father, stopping the last words I hope I'll ever speak to him. I want this moment. I want the goodbye to be final and leave no room for him to come back.

"Goodbye, Dad," I say and turn my back to him. "Don't come back. We're no longer your problem or your family."

He curses at me as I walk back through the door to the bar. The few people inside scramble back to their seats, clearly having been listening to the exchange and sticking their nose in my business.

My face turns red, and I'm completely embarrassed, ready to sprint toward the bathroom to hide. But then the guys in the bar start clapping.

"You did good, kid," one of the men says, punching me lightly in the shoulder as I walk by.

"You have some balls, little girl," another one adds and dips his head. "Lemme buy you a drink."

"No, no." I half smile and laugh because they're so happy and sweet, although a little strange. "Thanks."

The sadness I would've felt in the past isn't there anymore. I'm not sorry for the things I said to my father or the fact that I cut him out of my life once and for all. I was done being his carpet to step on when he felt his life wasn't going the way he wanted. He has shit to deal with, and I'm not going to be there to watch him crash and burn.

CHAPTER TWELVE

LUCIO

"I'M TAKING HER HOME FOR A WHILE," I TELL ANGELO as Delilah runs into the bathroom, probably crying her eyes out.

"Take all the time you need. Delilah needs you." He nods, tipping his head toward the mostly empty bar. "We won't be busy tonight, and Michelle's coming in soon."

"Tell Ma we'll be back for Lulu later."

"Don't rush," Ma says as she comes down the stairway, holding Lulu in one arm. "I heard every bit of that nasty man. You take that girl home, and don't let her out of the house until she's ready. Words like that don't leave a child's mind, no matter how old they are."

"I know, Ma."

My father may not have been the best partner, but he was a great dad. He was always kind and patient, even when we probably didn't deserve it. Raising four kids couldn't have been easy for either of my parents, but they never made it seem like a hardship or a duty.

Never once, no matter how many times we fucked up, did they talk to us the way Delilah's father just talked to her.

"Go make her whole again, baby." Ma kisses my cheek as I run the back of my finger down Lulu's soft, pudgy cheek, hating the idea of her ever hearing such hateful words. "Lulu and I are fine together. We're about to go for a walk. Now, get moving. There's a woman who needs you back there."

Delilah's sitting on the floor, leaning against the wall of the bathroom as I walk inside to make sure she's okay.

"He's such an asshole," she says as soon as she sees me, but there're no tears on her face. "I'm sorry you had to see that."

I sit down next to her, touching her shoulder with mine. "Don't ever be sorry."

"I'm so mad right now, I want to punch something."

I push against her shoulder and point at my chest. "You can hit me if it'll make you feel better."

She glances up at me with a small laugh. "You're the last person I want to punch, Lucio."

"You won't hurt me," I promise her and pound on my chest to prove how solid I am.

"I can't," she tells me.

"You'll feel better, though." I'm pretty sure her punch would barely make me flinch. Delilah's so tiny, and her hands are so dainty, I'm not even sure she could hit much harder than a little girl.

"Don't be ridiculous."

"Let's get out of here, then." I stand and hold my hand out to her, hoping she'll take me up on my offer to help her relax a little.

She slides her hand into mine without hesitation, and I pull her to her feet. "But what about work?"

I shake my head and pull her tightly into my arms. "I know the boss. We're good."

She laughs a little and rests her head against my chest. "I can't say thank you enough."

"Hush now," I tell her as I press my lips to the top of her head. "Don't thank me. I haven't done anything heroic."

"You treat me better than my own parents."

"Well, I want in your pants," I joke, but my words aren't entirely false.

I want more than that from Delilah. I can see much more than a great fuck. I see a future. I see a woman who's fierce, kind, and willing to take a risk instead of bowing to someone else's will for a boatload of cash.

She slaps at my chest playfully. "Don't be a dick."

"It's so difficult, though. Sometimes you make it so easy to let that side of myself shine."

She peers up at me with a soft face and kind eyes. "You're really a good guy, Lucio."

"Don't tell anyone. I don't want to ruin my reputation around here."

She rolls her eyes and stands on her tiptoes, trying to bring her face closer to mine. I cup her cheeks in my hands and press my lips against hers. There's nothing hungry in this kiss. I don't rush through the action because this is about emotion, not lust.

"I'll be by your side, Delilah. No matter what happens, I'll never turn my back on you," I promise her.

"Why are you so nice to me?" Delilah's blue eyes never leave me as I carry the dishes to the sink.

"Why wouldn't I be nice?"

Delilah shrugs and plays with the napkin in front of her. "Your family may be the only genuinely nice people I've ever met who weren't looking for something in return."

Leaning against the countertop, I stare at the

woman who's been beaten down but refuses to be broken. "Maybe it's all a ruse, and I'm secretly going to sell you into sex slavery when you let down your guard."

"Stop being silly. I mean it, Lucio. People aren't nice."

"Maybe where you come from. But down here, people tend to be kind and look out for each other. That's why I never moved out of the neighborhood."

She sighs. "I wonder what it would've been like to grow up like you. Loving parents, siblings, and nice people. I bet it was the best ever."

"Don't get me wrong. There're some real assholes around here too, but I don't ever regret where I come from. I'm proud to be a South Sider."

She stands and rounds the island, coming to a stop in front of me. "Do you like me, Lucio?" she asks point-blank.

"I do," I answer honestly as she steps between my legs. "I thought I made it pretty clear."

"Do you like me as a friend or…"

I place my finger under her chin, forcing her eyes back to mine when she glances down. "I want to be more than your friend, Delilah. I don't make a habit of kissing my friends."

"Thank you for this," she says, pressing her body to mine and pushing against my cock.

Sliding my palm along her cheek, I run my thumb across the bottom edge of her lip. "For what?"

"This," she states and leans forward, taking a play right out of my book.

The air's knocked out of me, just like the first time I planted my lips on hers. I said I'd ruin her, but in reality, she devastated me. Changed me forever. There was no turning back. No other kiss in the history of kisses could compare to kissing Delilah Miles.

Grabbing her by the waist, I lift her into the air and place her on the countertop before pushing her legs apart. "I want you," I murmur against her lips, not wanting to miss a moment of her sweet taste.

Her fingers find their way under my T-shirt, and her nails scrape the tender flesh of my ribs. "I need you," she moans as I gently pull at her bottom lip with my teeth.

My eyes search hers, looking for any signs of hesitation, but her blue eyes burn for me. My thumbs slip under the hem of her T-shirt, sliding across the soft skin near the waistband of her jeans, and she shudders. I deepen the kiss, needing something to focus on before I tear her shirt over her head and move too fast. I want to savor every inch of her body and enjoy every dip and curve, reveling in the taste of her flesh and the softness of her skin.

But when she moves her hands down the front of my stomach, slipping them into the waistband of my shorts, I just about lose control. Her fingers are met by the tip of my cock, begging for more than a little attention.

"Oh my God," she whispers and pulls away, glancing down. "Is that…"

"Pierced, baby."

"I've never…"

"I'm about to blow your mind."

"I gotta see," she says and slides off the counter, yanking on my shorts on the way. Her head's against the cabinets, and she's staring at my package, which is currently waving at her, hoping she's going to do more than look. "Can I touch it?"

I'm like a proud peacock, showing off my goods and hoping like hell she digs the fuck out of the piercing. "As much as you want," I say with a smile, stroking her hair and stopping myself from pulling her lips toward my mouth.

Using the tip of her finger, she traces the metal piercing, scraping my super-sensitive skin with her fingernail. I suck in a breath and close my eyes, rocking forward toward her touch.

"It's amazing," she whispers, and her warm breath glides across the tip of my cock, turning the throb into a full-on ache. "Can you feel it?"

"My cock?" I ask, tangling my fingers in her hair and praying for a little mouth action.

"No, the piercing. Does it feel different?"

"It'll pull a little when I'm in you, but you'll feel more than I will because of it."

She glances up, lips parted. "I'll feel it?"

"Wanna find out?" I waggle my eyebrows, hoping the show-and-tell portion of the evening is over.

She licks her lips, and my knees go weak. She grabs on to my ass with one hand, digging her fingernails in, and steadies me like she knew I was about to go down. "It's so…" She moves closer, and I can feel the heat of her skin. "So shiny."

I don't care if she thinks it's blazing like the Statue of Liberty on the Fourth of July, as long as it makes her happy and doesn't scare her away. Between the size of my cock and the piercing, I've had more than one woman walk out the door practically in tears.

"Touch it again," I tell her. "Explore all you want." I'm being an asshole, but God, I'm so horny I'm on the verge of pulling her off the floor, tearing off her jeans, and ramming my dick into her warm, wet pussy.

She leans forward, and I hold my breath and squeeze my eyes shut. I can't watch. I can't move. I'm too turned on to do anything but stand here, waiting for the moment her…

Fuck. Her tongue tugs at the piercing, and shock waves radiate through my system. Every muscle in my body tightens, and for a second, I can't breathe. When her lips close around the head, colors explode behind my eyelids, making me think I found heaven on earth. I'm so turned on, I know I won't last long, and I don't want this to end before we have a chance to really get going.

I grab her shoulders, hauling her up from the floor, and instantly, I miss the warmth of her mouth as her lips slide off the tip. "I need to taste you," I tell her and lift her shirt upward.

She raises her arms as the material easily slides over her head, exposing a white lace bra and a perfect set of tits. My mouth waters. My hands itch to feel their weight in my palms, but I want to explore her with my mouth and have her begging for my cock.

I slide her bra straps down her arms as she stares at me, barely breathing. She moves her hands in front of her stomach and grimaces.

"What's wrong?" I ask, seeing nothing but perfection.

"I have stretch marks." She closes her eyes, and I cradle her face, wanting her to know how I feel.

"Baby, look at me," I say, waiting for her to open her eyes. "I see nothing but a playground built for me. Don't hide what I'm dying to explore."

I fall to my knees and push her hands out of the way, exposing the tiny lines across her belly. The very lines that once held Lulu deep inside her. They're not scars, but a badge of honor…a reminder she gave someone life. "They're beautiful," I say as I lean forward and kiss the edge of the largest line.

She tangles her fingers in the top of my hair and sighs. "You don't hate them?"

My lips glide across her stomach, following the lines as I moan my appreciation for the softness of her skin. She's perfection no matter what's on her skin. "They're like my tattoos," I tell her, my head level with her stomach, but looking up into her blue eyes. "They're a reminder of a life experience. They mean something. They're not scars. They're life."

She doesn't move to cover them again as I run my tongue across her skin this time, tasting the saltiness of her skin and smelling her need. Unable to wait any longer, I unbutton her pants, and she lifts up as I pull them downward along with her panties before tossing them both across the room.

She's nervous. I can see it in her eyes. "Say you want me," I tell her, needing to hear the words from her lips once more.

"I want you, Lucio," she says, clear as day.

I pull her forward, sitting her ass on the edge of the counter and giving me the perfect view of her beautiful, glistening pussy. She leans back, resting her palms on the countertop, readying herself.

Reaching up, I palm her breast, wishing I had more time, but I know what she needs and how to make her feel good. My thumb brushes against her nipple, and she pushes her chest into my touch.

My mouth waters, and I lick my lips. There's nothing more beautiful than a naked and needy Delilah. I lean forward, placing my head between her legs, close enough that she can feel my warm breath moving across her skin.

She rocks forward, silently pleading for my mouth.

I give her what she wants, dragging my tongue through her lips, capturing her wetness on the tip. "So fucking sweet," I say, causing her to moan.

My fingers tug on her nipple as I bury my face between her legs, sucking her clit into my mouth. The salty sweetness of her explodes across my tongue and makes my cock even harder than it was before. The way she moans my name as the tip of my tongue flicks against her spurs me on.

I devour her skin, lavishing her most needy part with every bit of my mouth until her fingers curl around the edge of the counter and she grinds her cunt against my face. She's moaning, screaming, as her body quakes in pleasure.

"Fuck!" she shouts and throws her head backward, jutting her tits out more.

I don't let up. Don't stop sucking until she's limp and gasping for air.

"Jesus." She licks her lips with her eyes still closed.

I give her pussy another kiss before making my way up her body, positioning my cock between her legs.

"Condom," she says as her eyes fly open.

"Of course," I tell her, fishing one out of the drawer next to us. She looks at me funny but doesn't ask me why on God's green earth I keep condoms in the kitchen.

I rip open the package with my teeth before cautiously pushing it over the tip of my cock, careful not to catch the latex on my piercing. She grabs my face, crashing her lips to mine, ending all conversation. When she spreads her legs and presses her ankles into my ass, I know I have permission to bury myself deep inside of her.

Her legs tighten as I slip the tip of my cock along with the piercing inside her. She moans into my mouth, and I swear my eyes almost roll backward. I take it slow, moving a little deeper with each thrust until she's pushing me forward and grinding into me.

Then I'm buried deep inside her, and I know I'll never be the same again.

CHAPTER THIRTEEN

DELILAH

"Are you feeling better today, my dear?" Betty asks as she takes Lulu from my arms before I'm even three steps into the kitchen of her apartment.

"I am. Thank you."

Better doesn't even begin to describe how I feel. Waking up next to Lucio, tangled in a pile of sheets and limbs makes me feel more than better… I feel like a new woman.

"I was worried about you after your father stopped by." She motions for me to sit, and I do without hesitation because I'm not crazy enough to argue with her. "Even though you handled him like a pro, I wanted to make sure you're okay."

"I've had a lifetime of practice."

I thought I'd wake up this morning feeling awful about everything that happened, but I don't. For the first time in a long time, I'm hopeful. There's a new sense of freedom I've never felt before. I'm no longer walking on eggshells, waiting for the next drunk tirade from my father.

She sits across from me, rocking Lulu back and forth. "If you don't mind my asking, why did you stay so long?"

I lean back in my chair, trying to figure out why I did stay as long as I did. "I've asked myself that very question a million times."

"We all do what we feel is right at the time, sweetheart. Don't be too hard on yourself."

"I didn't want to abandon him like my mother did to both of us. At first, I was too young to leave. And then I stayed with him through college because I was barely ever home anyway, so it didn't matter. He still got drunk, but I couldn't be his whipping girl if I wasn't around."

She nods her head but stays silent, listening to me spill my guts. The look on her face isn't judgmental, and I'm comfortable talking to her. She's been nothing but gracious and kind, treating me better than anyone in my family ever has. So, I keep going, figuring I could use a little motherly advice on where I go now and if I'm headed in the right direction.

"When I found out I was pregnant with Lulu, my father promised he'd change if I'd only stay with him to raise his granddaughter. He remained sober through my entire pregnancy, going to every doctor's appointment with me after Lulu's father took off."

Betty gasps. "He just left?"

I nod. "I haven't seen him since, and he's never even tried to contact me. Dwight is no better than my father, but at least he gave me a beautiful daughter out of the situation and has left me in peace."

"She's a dream," Betty says as she leans forward to kiss Lulu's head. "This baby girl deserves all the love and kisses."

I smile and keep talking so I don't start crying over all the love Lulu's missed out on already. "For a few months after she was born, my dad kept up his sobriety. But slowly, one drink turned into two, and then he'd down an entire bottle. Somehow, his temper didn't return with the drinking like it had before. Not at first, but over the last week before he kicked me out, he became more aggressive and rarely had a sober moment."

"Did something change?" she asks.

"Yeah." I pause and chew on my bottom lip, remembering the job offer in California for the first time in days.

"How about some tea?" she asks before I can answer.

"I'd love some," I tell her and stop myself from asking for whiskey instead.

I could use a drink, but I've never let myself use alcohol as a crutch or to relieve stress. I didn't want to end up like my father, and I knew enough about alcoholism to know, typically, it is passed on through genetics.

She carries Lulu on one hip like she's been doing it a lifetime, grabbing the teapot and filling it with one hand. "We don't have to talk about it anymore," she says as she turns the stove on, and the flame licks the bottom of the pot.

"I'm fine. I want to talk about it."

"I never want to make you uncomfortable."

"You have never done anything but make me feel welcome and comfortable, Betty."

She leans against the countertop, and Lulu grabs at her pearls. "We love having you here."

"I took Lulu out of town for a few days for a job interview on the West Coast."

"Oh." Her eyebrows shoot up, and I know the information is something I haven't shared before. Betty seems to have grand plans for Lucio and me. While I like the idea, and could probably be happy here forever, I'm not sure we'll work out in the long run.

"Anyway, after we left, he started drinking more

and more. He'd call at all hours of the night, yelling and cursing me for leaving him." I blow out a breath, still hearing the scathing words my father strung together over the phone echoing in my ears. "The day before we were scheduled to come back, he went to a meeting and promised he'd get his life back together."

"People make grand promises when their backs are against the wall, but they never seem to remember to follow through during the small moments. Those matter the most," she tells me.

"They do." I nod. "When he picked us up from the airport after a long flight, I didn't think he was drunk, or I never would've gotten in the car with him. But after a few blocks of him swerving, I knew he was too drunk to drive. He couldn't even keep his promise for twenty-four hours and pick us up sober."

"I'm sorry, dear."

I wish my father could be half the person Betty Gallo is. Even on his best day, he couldn't hold a candle to her love and charm.

"He didn't just put our lives in danger that night, he cleaned out my bank accounts and cut me off completely."

She lifts the teapot, removing it from the hot burner and placing it on a cool one as soon as it whistles. "Earl Grey?" she asks, and I nod. Using one hand, she carries two teacups with little pink flowers around the rim and sets them down on the table before grabbing the pot along with two tea bags. "Would you like cream and sugar?"

"If you're having it, yes." I've never been a tea drinker and I'm not sure what proper etiquette is when sipping tea, but I'll follow Betty's lead.

"So, what about the job on the West Coast?" she asks as she pours the hot water in the cups, watching me as she does.

"I was offered a position at an entertainment company. It's entry-level, but perfect for someone like me. I can't take it, though."

"Why not?" She plops two cubes of sugar in my cup along with a splash of milk before doing the same to hers, but her eyes are on me and I feel the weight of her stare.

I tug on the tea bag, waiting for her to sit before I continue. Lulu's too busy playing with Betty's necklace to care that I'm in the same room. It's nice to have someone else she's comfortable with because, any other time, she doesn't want to leave my arms. "Without the money I had in the bank, I can't afford to make the move and earn the small salary they were going to give me to start."

She tilts her head to the side. "Is that the only reason?"

I frown and peer down at my tea. "I don't know, Betty."

"What about my son?" she asks.

"He's kind of great," I say and can't stop the

goofy smile from spreading across my face.

She places her hand over mine. "He really likes you, Delilah. I know Lucio's heart, and it's the biggest of all my children. Sometimes he's hard to read, but when he loves, he loves deep."

"I've never had someone treat me the way he does," I admit.

Before I left California, I wanted to take the job, but something had stopped me. I asked for a little time to think over their offer, and they agreed, giving me one week to make my final decision. The only reason I applied was to get as far away from my father as possible, and now that he's out of the picture, I can't imagine uprooting my life and moving clear across the country.

"Lucio has never fallen in love. He's been so scared he'd be like his father that he wouldn't open his heart, but he's different around you."

"You're not the first person to say that to me."

"Angelo?" she guesses.

"Yeah."

"He's the only one of my kids to have already fallen in love, but when his wife died, I think it scared everyone. My relationship with Santino already had them skeptical. But after Angelo found someone who made him happy and she passed away, no one wanted to put themselves out there."

"Do you regret being with Santino?" I ask even though it's none of my business.

She sighs as she sets down her teacup. "No. Even though our love wasn't always easy, there has never been a time when I regretted being with him. How could I?" She cradles Lulu in her arms, rocking her gently. "He gave me four wonderful children."

"Were there moments when you wanted to leave?"

"Sure. I think there's a point in every relationship when people could walk away. Sometimes it's easier than fixing what's wrong and building a stronger foundation."

"But he's in prison, right?" I grimace as soon as the words leave my mouth. "It's none of my business."

"Santino is in prison for a little while longer, but I never thought about leaving him for that or the long, drawn-out trial that was splashed across every newscast and paper in the city."

Suddenly, I put two and two together, realizing why the name Gallo sounded so familiar. The trial of Santino Gallo was one of the biggest news stories a few years ago. Many people in Chicago claimed organized crime was dead and there was no such thing as the mafia, but after Santino's arrest, they could no longer make the same statement.

"I remember now," I tell her, and my face heats. "I'm sorry."

"Santino did the crime, and now he has to do the time. He knew what could happen, leading the life he did. I turned a blind eye to his business dealings, but I never let him slide when it came to his extracurricular activities."

"Lucio mentioned that."

"There's so much my children don't know. They think I was complacent with his behavior when I wasn't. For a long time, I believed Santino was faithful. No one wants to think otherwise. But I wasn't a fool either. I'd smell the cheap perfume on his clothes when he came home at night. I got sick of it and took matters into my own hands." She laughs, and there's nothing sweet about it.

"Yeah?"

She nods with a smirk. "He knew if he wanted to keep his vital organs, he'd leave the broads in the past and learn to be a faithful partner. I wouldn't leave him, but I wasn't above torturing him. He knows my temper better than anyone, and he came to his senses after a little convincing."

"Convincing?" I swallow, almost choking on the word. I'm not sure I want to know the lengths Betty would go to in order to rein her man in.

She pats my hand, still laughing. "It's best if some things stay a secret, dear."

"I think you're right," I whisper. "You're an amazing person, Betty."

"Delilah, if you want to go to California, we'll understand," she tells me, but while I feel she's being sincere, I don't hear the conviction in her voice.

"You would?"

"I wouldn't be happy, but I'd let you go. I'd love to see you with my son and sitting around my dinner table with this bundle of joy every week. But you need to do what's best for you and your little one."

"Betty," I tell her, covering her hand with mine and squeezing. "To be honest, I've never felt more complete and content than I do here with Lucio, you, and the entire family."

My words bring the smile back to her face. "Does he know?"

I shake my head, because I didn't really know until I just said the words. "I don't think so."

"If you want to love my son, love him fiercely, but don't wait too long to tell him."

"Don't you think it's a little soon for me to love a man I barely know?"

She laughs softly and shakes her head. "I knew Santino much of my life, but we were never more than acquaintances, growing up on the same block. He was older and I always knew he was a player, but after one kiss, he asked me to marry him."

"Really?"

"I told him he was crazy, but every night, he'd come to my house, crawl onto the roof of my parents' front porch, and knock on my window to ask me again."

"And you said yes?"

"After thirty nights and not a single date, I said I'd move in with him."

"Move in with him?" My mouth falls open. "Why didn't you marry him?"

"I knew marriage wasn't for me. I don't know." She shrugs.

"But you have the last name Gallo."

"I went to court and had my last name changed. I wanted the same name as my children."

"Why not just marry him?"

"His business was complicated. We knew he'd eventually get caught—everyone always does—and this was the best way for me to protect what's mine."

"Will you ever marry him?"

"Maybe. As we get older, I do regret not being his legal wife."

"Well, it's not too late," I tell her, trying to picture her in a wedding dress. "He sounds like he's romantic. He swept you off your feet."

"I was young and stupid back then. But every day, I'd wait for the sun to set so Santino would come to my window. Nothing else mattered. I couldn't even look at another man because I was so smitten."

"So, you kissed him, and that was enough?"

"He was relentless in his pursuit of me. No one else went to the lengths he did. It didn't matter how many times I said no, he wasn't going to give up. He was foolish and so was I, but sometimes our heart wants what it wants. There's no rhyme or reason to any of it. You can't overthink love, baby. You just got to jump."

CHAPTER FOURTEEN

LUCIO

"Please, Lucio." Daphne begs me for permission like it's mine to give.

"Why are you asking me?"

Although I hate the idea of Delilah going out to a bar with God knows who hitting on her, I have no right to say no. She could use a break from me and everything that's happened.

"Someone has to watch the baby," Daphne says, batting her eyelashes at me because she knows I'm a sucker.

I point to myself, drawing my eyebrows down. "You want me to babysit?"

"Well, duh." Daphne rolls her eyes. "Do it for Delilah," she tells me, knowing I can't say no when she puts it that way.

"I don't like this," I tell her and rub the base of my hands into my eyes.

"No strippers." She uncrosses her fingers and shows them to me like the childish gesture means a damn thing. "I promise."

"I'm trusting you, Daphne."

"Come on now. I know you love this girl. I won't do anything to mess that up."

"Fine, fine. I'll watch the baby. Just don't have too much fun."

Daphne throws her arms around me, peppering my face with sloppy kisses. She knows I hate when she does that, but she doesn't stop. "You won't regret this," she tells me, but I already do.

"YOU'RE SURE ABOUT THIS?" Delilah asks for the fifth time as she slips on the high heels Daphne let her borrow. She's leaning over the couch with her cleavage on full display, but only because of her current position. Her outfit is tasteful, which is surprising because Daphne gave her the dress. I never would've thought my sister had something that didn't reveal too much skin, but somehow, Delilah found the only such dress in my sister's closet.

"We'll be fine," I tell her, not really answering the question. I'm not sure about the entire thing. Spending the night with Lulu should be easy, but imagining what's happening at the bar is a different story. "Go and have some fun."

At least she's going with Daphne. My sister knows how I feel about Delilah and hopefully will have my back, not letting anything get out of control.

Delilah gives me a quick kiss as she reaches for her purse, but I don't let her get away so easily. I wrap my arm around her back, hauling her body against mine and crash my lips down against hers. I want her to feel my kiss all night, remembering who's waiting at home for her.

Maybe it's a dick move, but in that moment, I don't care. I've slept with dozens of women and never cared what they did afterward, but Delilah's different. The thought of another man touching her makes my skin crawl and sends my temper into overdrive.

When I pull away, her eyes are still closed, and her lips parted. "I'll wait for you," I say.

She blinks slowly and licks her lips, making me want another taste. "I won't be late."

Daphne walks into my place without so much as a knock. Much like she did when we were kids. She never cared much for boundaries or privacy, unless it was her own being stepped on. "Ready?" she asks in the most annoying and cheery voice. "Don't want to keep the others waiting."

"Others?" I ask as my stomach knots.

"Michelle's coming and a few other girls from the neighborhood."

"Like who?"

"Colleen and Carmen," Daphne says, glancing around the room because she knows I'm not going to be happy.

Fuck. More than half the women going out together I've slept with. This could be a complete shit-show and the end to Delilah and me. I wasn't a saint. I never claimed to be, but no woman wants to come face-to-face with someone their partner has shared a bed with.

"Maybe you should stay in." I pull Delilah backward before she gets too close to the doorway.

"Don't be an asshole. She's coming. She already knows about Colleen and Carmen."

"You do?" I squeeze my eyes shut for a moment and groan.

"There's nothing to be sorry about, Lucio. We all have a past," Delilah says with an easy smile. "I don't care what you did before I got here. I'm sure it'll be fun."

Fun isn't the word I'd use to describe the conversation that will no doubt be taking place tonight. I'll be the main topic and won't be there to defend myself. Although Colleen and Carmen are nice and hella good in bed, I didn't give either of them the relationship they both begged for in the end.

"Have fun, but not too much," I tell her.

"I've never been drunk, remember?" She places her hand on my chest, peering up at me with her baby blue eyes. "Don't worry so much."

I give her a soft kiss, and my sister grunts, practically gagging behind us. "Let's go," Daphne says, tapping her foot against the marble tile in the entryway. "We're wasting precious time."

"Bye," Delilah whispers, holding my hand as long as possible as Daphne starts to pull her out the door.

When they're gone, I look around the house, rubbing the back of my neck and wondering what I'm going to do with my night off. A few weeks ago, I would've called any number in my contacts, finding some hottie to spend a few hours with to pass the time, but with Delilah around, that's a no go.

I collapse onto the couch, keeping the volume low enough so I can hear Lulu in case she starts crying. I never thought this would be my life, at least not without doing the marriage thing first.

I flip through the channels, surf the internet on my phone, and grow so freaking bored I text a few of the guys and invite them over for beer and pizza. They quickly remind me that they're out for the night, busy living the life I'd been taking part in up until a week ago.

My life before Delilah wasn't better. I have already

grown used to hearing her pad around the upstairs apartment and the tiny cries and giggles of Lulu I hear even from my bedroom. I never realized how empty my life was until she came into it.

But I wouldn't change a damn thing. That's the funniest part. I loved my life before Delilah walked into the bar. There wasn't a part I didn't enjoy the fuck out of either. But now, all I want to do is spend the night eating pizza on the floor with Delilah and Lulu. Nothing sounds as perfect or as sweet as something that simple.

Just when I start feeling the weight of the silence in the house, Lulu begins to cry in the other room. I rush in and pluck her tiny body from the crib.

"Hey, doll," I whisper, rocking her in my arms as I hold her tightly against my chest. "Don't cry, baby girl. I got you."

I spend the next twenty minutes heating a bottle and watching Lulu as she sucks down every drop like she's never eaten before. I don't know where she puts it, but I'm quickly reminded when she spits up all over the back of my shirt.

"I still haven't learned."

Based on the smile on her face, she's happy with the way the evening is turning out. There's not much I can do with an infant, so I do the only thing I can think of, throw on some cartoons and stare at the clock.

"Yo," Angelo says, walking through the front door

just like Daphne. "I was heading home from the bar and saw your light on. Thought I'd stop in and check on you."

"I don't know how you did this alone, man." I shake my head. I've been with Lulu for only a short time, and I can't imagine handling two kids, nonstop, day after day, with no end in sight. My brother makes everything seem easy, and even through his grief, he's never once complained.

"There's nothing easy about it, and without Marissa, everything is harder." He plops down on my couch, in no hurry to leave. "But I thank God for the month in the summer when her parents take the kids. I need the time to recharge and feel human again."

"Have you thought about dating again?" I ask, still standing because I'm covered in Lulu's sour milk. We've had the conversation more than once, and he's always quick to change the subject.

He rubs his forehead, clearly hating this conversation. "I don't think it's fair to the kids."

"Angelo, don't be ridiculous. You can't hide behind those kids forever."

He juts out his chin, and I know he's about to say something shitty. "And what are you hiding behind?"

Bingo. He's always turning the tables, trying to draw the attention away from himself, but I won't let him this time. "They deserve two parents."

"Lucio, I know you think you know best, but you don't quite understand what it means to be a parent."

"Enlighten me, then."

He stands and takes Lulu from my arms. "Go shower. You smell like shit. And then we'll talk."

I don't argue. With Delilah gone and Lulu not on a regular schedule, I don't know another time I'll be able to shower without someone else to watch the little squirt. "I'll be out in five."

"Take your time," he calls out before I disappear into my bathroom and think about the question my brother asked me.

What was I hiding behind?

"Figure it out, Einstein?" Angelo asks as soon as I walk back into the room. "What are you hiding behind?"

For a moment, I feel like I can conquer the world again with all remnants of baby vomit removed from my body. But it's short-lived as soon as Angelo starts playing twenty questions.

"I always thought you were a pussy," he says with a cocky smirk on his face because he knows just what to say to get me going.

"I'm not a pussy," I tell him as I plop down on the couch next to him and pull Lulu from his arms. "You know Dad was an asshole when we were kids, and I don't want to be like him." I pause for a minute and look down at Lulu as she wraps her tiny hand around my finger. "Look at this kid. Am I really a father figure?"

"Did you think I would be?" he replies quickly, raising a single eyebrow.

"You know you're a great dad." Angelo's like Super Dad. If there were a medal given out for that type of shit, he'd get first place. There isn't a thing he wouldn't do for his kids, and somehow, he's managed to keep them alive and thriving even after losing Marissa. I'm not so sure I could've done the same in his shoes.

"Maybe I should be with Delilah. We both have kids. We can make our own Brady Bunch-type family. It'll be perfect."

I stand quickly, pointing toward the door with Lulu in my other arm. "Get the hell out!"

Angelo laughs and shakes his head as he stands. "You got it bad, brother. Make her yours. Stop thinking, and just act for once. Let your heart do the talking." He pats me on the chest before he steps away. "But don't wait too long. I'm sure I won't be the only guy to try to take her off your hands."

"Fuck off, Angelo," I mumble as he walks out the front door. I can still hear his laughter as he jogs down the front steps and onto the sidewalk.

"No one's taking you," I tell Lulu, and she smiles, pulling at my cheeks. "Your momma and you were meant to be with me."

CHAPTER FIFTEEN

DELILAH

It's after three a.m. by the time I stumble to the front of the house. I'm drunk. So drunk I'm almost seeing double and can barely feel my legs as I make my way up the stairs.

I turn and wave at Daphne, Michelle, Carmen, and Colleen as they wait on the sidewalk, making sure I can actually make it inside on my own. They were taking bets on how many times I'd fall in my high heels because they had to hold me upright for the last two blocks.

I want to hate them for laughing at me, but I like

them, even if they didn't warn me that a Long Island Iced Tea didn't really have any tea in it at all.

"Bye!" I yell, waving and leaning against the front door for a little support.

"Bye, girl. Don't do anything we wouldn't do!" Michelle yells back, and all the girls giggle.

"Or haven't done." Carmen reminds me of the fact that she's slept with Lucio. I can't even hate her for it. She explained it was years ago, just after high school, and he wasn't all that good, but she was sure he'd argue that point.

"Jesus," I mutter as I try to focus on the handle and take a deep breath. I can pull this off. I can pretend to be sober, right?

I nearly trip over the threshold but catch myself on the doorframe, nearly slamming the door into the back wall. "Shh," I tell it and hiccup through the laughter.

I lean over, holding the door handle to stay as steady as possible, and pull off my high heels. The lights are off, but there's enough of a glow from the television for me to make my way through the living room without knocking over any furniture.

Peeking over the back of the couch, I see Lucio asleep with Lulu sprawled out across his massive chest. Her tiny cheek is resting in between his pecs, drool running down the side of her face and pooling against his skin.

Holding on to the arm of the couch, I make my

way to the wooden coffee table and sit. I blink a few times and wait for the room to stop spinning as I rest my chin in my palm and my elbow on my knee.

The way he's holding her with his hand against her back, making sure she doesn't slip or move, brings a smile to my face and tears to my eyes. I find it hard to believe Lucio doesn't think he'd be a good father. He's been more than amazing with Lulu, and tonight is proof.

Her little leg twitches, and I hold my breath, trying hard not to wake either of them. I wish I had a camera to capture this moment forever, but I still haven't replaced my cell phone. Lulu stills for a moment before her hands flatten and her tiny fingernails bite into his skin.

He doesn't open his eyes as he removes her claws from his chest with one hand and rubs her back in small, soft circles with the other. I can't stop staring at the way he loves my daughter. I want that type of love for her. I want her to have something I never did, a man who will always put her first.

Lucio could be that guy. He may not believe in himself, but I do. Daphne made it quite clear tonight that her brother has feelings for me, but she didn't tell me anything I didn't already know. She told me, no matter what I hear, to remember he's the most loyal guy she knows. No one would fight harder or defend me stronger than her brother. Part of the night, I felt she was pitching me on all the reasons I should love her brother, but I didn't need her input to know how I already felt.

"You're home," he says softly as I wipe away my tears. "What's wrong?" He reaches out and touches my knee, leaving Lulu balancing on his chest.

I shake my head and bite my lip, wishing the tears would stop streaming down my face. I'm acting like a fool, and the alcohol isn't helping. "Nothing," I whisper and place my hand over his. "I'm just so…"

"So, help me God," he says, placing his other hand under Lulu's bottom as he sits up.

"No. Nothing happened. I'm just so happy," I tell him, waving my hands around because I know I must seem foolish. "Coming home and finding the two of you snuggled on the couch, I realize all the things we've missed."

"Baby." He touches my cheek, wiping away a few tears with his thumb. "I like seeing you happy."

I turn my face, capturing the pad of his thumb between my teeth, suddenly overcome with need. "I want you," I murmur against his skin. "I need you."

His lips part and his eyes close as I pull his finger into my mouth and suck hard, twirling my tongue around it like I've done with his cock. He sways back and forth as his breathing grows more ragged and labored with each passing second. "The kid," he says like I forgot he's holding Lulu.

"Upstairs," I say around his thumb and waggle

my eyebrows because I'm more than ready to put my daughter down and get busy taking Lucio to bed.

He groans as he pulls his finger from my lips, and I suck harder, teasing him as much as possible. He's on his feet, almost gliding up the stairs as he takes them two at a time. I'm not as fast, the alcohol still working through my system. I hold on to the railing, swaying just like Lucio had on every step, but somehow, I don't fall backward.

He's waiting for me, having already put Lulu down, watching with a mix of laughter and horror as I make my way to the landing. Before I get my feet flat on the floor, he scoops me into his arms and stalks toward the bedroom.

"Eager little beaver, aren't you?" I snort because I'm a drunken idiot.

"You got the eager beaver, baby." He laughs. "Greedy thing too."

"It's that damn piercing," I say and try to reach down and grab his dick.

He shakes his head, probably wondering what the hell got into me, but I'm sure it's pretty obvious. Any type of shyness or worry I had about sleeping with Lucio again has vanished. Thanks to the Long Islands, I don't care about anything other than feeling his cock buried so deep inside me I can't even breathe.

"You like it that deep?" he asks as he sets me down on the bed and slips the spaghetti straps of the dress down my arms.

"Did I say that out loud?" I'm momentarily horrified, but I forget everything as soon as his lips close around my nipple.

He pushes me backward and hovers over me, holding himself up with his thick, muscular arms. I tangle my fingers in his hair and hold him against my skin. God, his tongue is like magic, sliding across my breast and bringing me one step closer to heaven.

I hum my approval, hoping this feeling never ends. When he starts to move down my body, I pull him back up by his hair and look him straight in the eye. It's like I'm possessed by a sassy version of myself. "Don't," I tell him, and his eyebrows draw downward. "I don't want your mouth. I want your cock."

He gives me a smug smile and climbs back up my body. "You like the piercing, don't you?"

"I like your dick, Lucio. Pierced or not, it's all I want." I don't know where the words are coming from, but he seems to enjoy this side of me because his smile grows.

He pushes himself up and stands at the foot of the bed. All I can do is watch as he shoves down his shorts, revealing that perfectly straight cock with the shiny tip. If I hadn't drunk so damn much, I'd crawl down there and use my tongue to tease him, but I'm not sure I could pull it off without falling off the bed.

"Fuck me," I say instead, hoping it's enough.

"You don't gotta ask me twice." He leans over and

grabs his wallet as his cock bobs like it's doing a dance of pure joy.

"How deep you want it, baby?" he asks as he tears open the condom and slides it down his shaft.

"Deep." I barely get the words out because the throbbing between my legs is so intense I'm not sure I won't orgasm as soon as his body slides against mine.

He crawls between my legs, placing the tip of his glorious cock against my pussy, and hovers above me again. He slips his hand between my legs and touches my clit, causing my ass to rise off the bed and shock waves to shoot across my body.

"So wet," he says, telling me something I already know.

"Fuck me, Lucio. Fuck me hard."

I don't have to ask again. He thrusts deep in one push, stealing every ounce of breath in my lungs. He grinds his hips, hitting every inch of my insides before pulling out. "Like that?" he asks, toying with me.

"Harder," I tell him, wanting more. Needing more.

He leans forward and closes his lips around my nipple as he slams into me, pushing me up the bed a little. I scream out with nothing but joy and pleasure coursing through my veins.

His deep green eyes bore into me. "You're mine, Delilah."

"Yes!" I cry out. His words wash over me, sending tiny sparks throughout my body.

"Only mine," he tells me, driving the point home as he pumps into me.

No one's ever kissed me like him. No one's ever fucked me like him. And Lord help me, I never want another man again.

CHAPTER SIXTEEN

LUCIO

WHEN EVERYONE'S LEFT THE ROOM, ANGELO FINALLY decides to speak to me. "Did you lock it in?"

I look at Angelo funny. "What?"

"Delilah, dumbass. Did you lock her down?"

"You can put your dick back in your pants. She's mine, bro," I tell him, pointing my finger right at his face.

"Good," he says with a big smile. "Maybe you're not as foolish as I thought you were."

I lean back, throwing my arm on top of the chair-back next to me. “I’m never foolish when it comes to women.”

“Wait.” He pauses and narrows his eyes. “Did you have an actual conversation with her about your relationship, or did you just fuck her?”

“I told her.”

“Smooth.” He shakes his head and glances up at the ceiling.

“Well, we’re not in high school anymore. What was I supposed to say to her? ‘Delilah, would you wear my class ring?’” I wave him and his silliness off. “Get out of here with that bullshit.”

“Make sure there’s no doubt in her mind.”

“Did I miss the memo that we’re back in the fifties?”

“Listen.” He leans forward, resting his hands flat on the table and looking at me with one of the most serious faces I’ve ever seen on him. “I’m telling you this because I love you. I know what it’s like to love a woman—and to lose one too.”

It’s hard for me not to listen after he makes a statement like that. I loved his wife from the day I met her. She was the best woman I’d ever known and the perfect match for my brother. We were all devasted by her death, but no one more than him. I watched my brother’s easy, carefree attitude turn serious and sometimes sour. It’s hard to stay happy when the one person who brought you the most joy disappears.

“I’m listening,” I tell him, being respectful because

he's been through more in the last few years than I have in my entire lifetime.

"You can't just tell a woman she's yours. I'm sure that's the dumb-ass shit you did. You need her to know you're hers too. She needs to understand there won't be another Carmen or Colleen."

"You heard about that?"

"Daphne has some balls on her." He scrubs his hand down his face and shakes his head. "I've already had the talk with her."

"How'd that go?"

He laughs and shrugs. "How do you think?"

"Well, I don't see any claw marks."

"What are we talking about?" Vinnie asks, walking in the room before plopping down in the chair next to Angelo.

"Women," I say.

He suddenly perks up and sets his phone down. "About Delilah?"

"Yeah." I nod.

"Did you lock it down?" Vinnie asks, sounding just like Angelo.

"What is this? Now you two are talking the same."

Vinnie looks at Angelo, and they both shrug.

"You lock it down with any of those girls you're always messaging?" I ask, putting some of the pressure on him instead of focusing only on me.

"I have them all on lockdown, Luc."

My eyes widen, and so do Angelo's. "All of them?"

he asks, turning toward our youngest brother, staring at him like he has three heads.

"I don't want them with any other guys."

"Dude—" Angelo smacks him in the chest "—that isn't cool."

"Hey, don't hate the player."

We both roll our eyes at the little egotistical asshole who takes pride in stringing girls along. "How does that work?" I rub my forehead, trying to figure out the logistics of the entire situation he's put himself in. "I mean, you have to get caught eventually. Then what?"

Vinnie smiles proudly. "I never say I'm committing to them. I just let them know they're mine and no one else's."

Angelo points at Vinnie, but he's looking at me. "This is what I'm talking about."

"I get it. I get it," I tell him and realize the error I've made. "I'll lock her down."

"Speaking of lockdown," my mother says, startling the shit out of all of us as she walks in, "your father called yesterday." She sits down at the head of the table but doesn't say anything else.

"And?" Angelo rolls his hand in the air.

"He's been granted early release. He'll be home in a few months."

"That's amazing, Ma," Vinnie says, but Angelo and I aren't as overjoyed as my little brother.

"I've missed him," she says, looking back and

forth between Angelo and me. "I know you two have issues with your father, but I want you to bury that in the past."

I've never had issues with the man as a father, but as a partner, he treated my mother like garbage for too long for me to turn a blind eye to it. Angelo feels the same way, but Vinnie is too young to remember our father's shenanigans.

"We'll make it work," Angelo says quickly, knowing it'll make my mother happy, and always trying to keep the peace.

"There's another thing." She plays with the clean spoon still left on the table in front of her but doesn't look at any of us.

"We're listening," Vinnie says, a little too enthusiastically.

Angelo and I are staring at each other, knowing whatever she's about to say none of us is going to like. I ball my hand into a tight fist, hoping it'll be enough for me to keep my mouth shut. The last person in the world I want to piss off is my mother.

"As part of his parole, he'll need a job."

Angelo kicks me under the table, opting for using me as a punching bag instead of his own hand like I'd planned to do. I flinch and bite down on my tongue to stop myself from swearing after his size-twelve shoe smacks against my shin.

Ma looks at me, waiting for me to say anything, but I don't dare open my mouth. "I'd like you to hire him on at the bar to keep him in compliance. He received special permission from the parole board to live above and work in the bar."

"No problem, Ma," Vinnie tells her like he's the only one making the decision. He owns twenty-five percent of the business, and he's barely there, so his vote doesn't even count in anyone's book but his own.

"We'll talk to Daphne about it," Angelo tells her because he knows my answer will be no. "We can't say yes until we're able to talk it through."

"Talk with everyone, but I don't ask for much and I'm asking for this favor," she states, letting us know that we better say yes, or there'll be hell to pay.

Either way, we're totally screwed.

I TAKE Delilah by the hand after she puts Lulu in her crib. "Sit down, baby."

She moves slowly, touching the couch with one hand as she lowers herself onto the cushion. Her eyes never leave mine, and I can see the fear in them plain as day.

"It's nothing bad. I swear. We just gotta talk," I tell her as I touch her face to calm her nerves.

She smiles nervously, watching me with those beautiful blue eyes as I sit on the coffee table in front of her. "Is everything okay?" She fiddles with her long brown hair, wrapping the strands around the tip of her finger. "You're making my stomach hurt, Lucio."

"There was a lot going on last night, and you were drunk."

She covers her mouth and gasps. "Oh God. What did I do? Did I say something stupid?" She pulls at her bottom lip, and her eyes roam around the room. "I remember we had sex, but not much else."

I mentally slap myself because I realize my brother is right. I hadn't even thought about the fact that she was totally shit-faced when I told her she was mine. I thought by the time I told her, she'd sobered up enough she'd remember, but that was my mistake.

"Yeah, baby. We had a lot of sex. It was hot too." I smile.

She blushes. "Well, that's good to know, at least. If you're going to tell me you don't ever want to do it again."

I place my finger over her lips, stopping her from finishing that sentence. "I love you," I blurt out, laying my cards on the table.

"Say that again," she says against my finger before chewing on her bottom lip.

"I love you, Delilah Miles. I want to be yours and for you to be mine."

Her eyes fill with tears again. "Yeah?"

I reach out, cradling her face in my palms, and stare into her eyes so there's no question where my loyalty and love lies. "Yes. There's no one else for me. I only want you. I want Lulu. I want us."

"You're sure?" she asks, tears streaming down her face and her lip trembling.

"I know it's quick and crazy, but I've never been happier in my entire life. I want you here, by my side, in my bed, with me—forever." I scoot forward, leaving very little space between us until I can feel her warm breath skid across my face. "I want that little girl as my own. I want to shower her with love and be the father she needs. I don't want to be alone anymore, and I don't want you to ever be afraid of anything for the rest of your life."

Delilah throws herself into my arms, grabbing my face with her small hands and kisses me so hard I'm sure I'll have a bruise. "God, I love you," she murmurs against my lips. "So, so much." The words come out garbled because she's too busy kissing me to let me speak.

I pull her closer, wrapping my arms around her back, and tangle my hand in her hair. "You love the piercing," I tell her when she finally lets me up for a little air.

"It's a bonus." She says those words with a straight face. "But that's not the only reason. Kiss me again. Mark me," she says, and that's all I need to hear.

I grab her by the waist, flipping her over the edge of the couch and lifting her skirt to expose her beautiful ass. "I'm going to bury my cock so deep, you'll never forget I've been here," I say as I cup her bare pussy in my hands.

She peers over her shoulder with a wicked grin. "Who do I belong to?" she asks quietly.

"You're mine, sweetheart. Now and forever. I own this pretty little pussy as much as you own my cock."

"Forever," she repeats my words, and nothing has ever felt so right.

CHAPTER SEVENTEEN

DELILAH

"Hey lady," a woman says from table three, snapping her fingers in the air and looking me up and down like I'm a piece of trash.

I walk up to the table and smile, somehow keeping my composure even though I want to dump a glass of water over her head. "Can I get you something?" My voice is so sugary sweet and about an octave higher than normal.

She's chewing gum and popping it between her teeth in the least classy way I've ever witnessed. "We'd like another round." She runs her fingers through her black hair, catching her fingers a few inches away from her head in the tons of hairspray keeping the nest in place. She recovers well, pretending she meant to do it when she fluffs the bottom of the strands with her palms. "Can you handle that?" she asks when I don't reply right away.

"I can handle it," I tell her before repeating their earlier drink order back to them to make sure I remember. "Sound about right?"

"It's right," another woman at the table answers before the Aqua Net queen practically shoos me away.

I grumble under my breath, knowing these bimbos are going to leave me a shit tip. If Angelo or Lucio were serving them, I'm sure they'd get more than a few bucks, but I can tell these women are going to be cheap because I don't flip their switch.

"What's wrong?" Lucio asks as I walk up to the bar, mumbling under my breath.

"Nothing." I give him a fake smile, pretending that my night is going amazingly well.

For the most part, it is. I've only spilled one drink. Thankfully, I was still at the bar when it happened and managed to keep the orders straight. I'd call it a victorious night in my book, except for some of the customers.

The men who have walked through the front door

have been nice. Some were overly flirtatious, but I was able to shut them down pretty quickly. No one got handsy either, but the night is still young and the customers haven't consumed enough alcohol to get too aggressive. Besides the table of bitchy girls with their teased hair and long, fake nails, I've enjoyed mingling with the crowd at Hook & Hustle.

"I know that look," he says, studying my face closely. "You're upset about something."

"No. I'm fine. Everything's fine," I tell him.

"What's their order?" he asks, pointing his head toward the table of women currently gawking at him.

"Two Whiskey Sours, a Long Island Iced Tea, and a Screwdriver."

He grabs the empty glasses and starts to make their drinks, but he keeps looking at me, waiting for me to spill my guts. "They giving you shit?"

"Nope. I swear. I'm fabulous." I'm not telling him anything. I refuse to complain about a couple bitchy women. I'm sure they won't be the last group of classless hussies who walk through the door of Hook & Hustle.

He pushes their drinks forward, and I snatch them up, walking off like I've been doing this a lifetime. Carrying four drinks isn't hard, but resisting the urge to dump them over their heads is the bigger struggle.

"Who's the tall drink of water?" the gum-popper asks as soon as I set the drinks down on the table.

"The owner," I tell them before walking off, done talking to them. There's no point in being nice and overly friendly when they already hate me. The fact that they're staring at my man just adds to my level of agitation.

"Doll," a man says, wrapping his arm around my legs as I try to walk by. "Why don't you bring me something cold?"

I glare at him, my eyes going from his arm to his face and back again. "You better remove your hand if you want to keep it."

"Oh, I like'm feisty." He laughs. "I'll throw in an extra twenty if you bend over and show me your panties."

I smack his arm away and move out of arm's reach. I have my hand in the air, ready to slap him, when Lucio touches my arm.

"Out you go," he says, hauling the guy up by the collar of his shirt. "There's no touching the ladies."

The guy tries to twist out of Lucio's grip and swings at him, but Lucio's too fast and his arms are too long for the guy to connect.

"You ever come back in here again, you won't walk out on your own two feet." Lucio pushes the guy out the front door, kicking him in the ass at the very last second.

The room erupts into cheers, and Lucio bows to the right and then the left. Within seconds, the bar goes back to normal with loud voices talking about everything and anything as they drink.

I stalk toward him, a little upset because I don't want him to step in any time someone gets a little too touchy-feely with me. "I could've handled him," I tell Lucio with my hands on my hips.

I shouldn't be so upset. He saved me a lot of trouble, and it was nice to have someone come to my rescue. But I wasn't sure Daphne or Michelle were given the same treatment. No way did I want to be treated any differently from the other girls at the bar.

"He was bigger than you."

"And?" I tap my foot, crossing my arms over my chest.

"What were you going to do with that hand? Slap him?" He raises an eyebrow.

"Of course."

"And then what would've happened if he hit you back?"

I blink a few times, thinking about what he just said. I never thought about someone actually coming back at me. I was defending myself, after all. "Well, I…"

"If he would've hit you, I would've murdered him right here in the middle of the bar. For your safety and my sanity, I took out the trash before this place became a crime scene."

"Thanks," I say slowly, changing my tune because I hadn't thought about how Lucio felt about the entire situation, or the fact that the guy could've cracked me back.

"If any man touches any of the ladies in this bar in an inappropriate way, they'll get the same treatment. Don't ever try to handle it yourself."

I nod, feeling a bit like a fool. I had become used to taking care of myself. Lord knows my dad was never there to rescue me from uncomfortable situations. Then there was Dwight, but besides being a bad lay, he was one of the biggest pussies I knew.

"Are you okay?" Lucio asks, following me behind the bar when I go to pour myself a little water.

"I'm fine, Lucio," I tell him. "I've handled assholes before. He didn't hurt me."

"But he could've," he reminds me again, driving the point home.

"I got it." I keep my back to him and guzzle down an entire glass of cold water before I face him again. "I'm sorry," I say after I've cooled down a bit. "I just want to make sure I'm treated no differently from anyone else."

He brushes my hair over my shoulder. "I can't help it if I treat you a little different, Delilah. I love you, and no one gets to touch you or be mean. I'll always step in to protect you."

"Give me a chance to handle things on my own first, okay?"

"I'll try."

"If I can't, I'll call you in as backup. Deal?"

He holds on to my arm for a few seconds, his green eyes searching mine. "Deal," he says before releasing me.

"I have to get back to my tables," I tell him with a sigh before heading back to work.

Aqua Net knocks into me as I make my way across the room. She doesn't say excuse me or even seem to notice that she almost makes me lose my balance. I turn, watching her as she stalks toward Lucio like a woman possessed.

A new couple sits down at my table near the window, and I try to give them my full attention. "Good evening. Welcome to Hook & Hustle. Do you know what you want, or would you like a few minutes?"

Somehow, I get the sentences out even though I can't stop looking toward the bar as Aqua Net primps her hair and applies another layer of lip gloss. She's a few feet away from Lucio, staring at him like he's her next victim.

"I'll take a pint of Guinness," the man says to me as I finally make eye contact. "She'll have a glass of Moscato."

"Anything else?" I ask, glancing over at the bar again.

"Peanuts or chips, if you've got them."

"Coming right up." I give them both a quick smile before marching toward the bar. But this time, I go to Daphne for the drinks.

"I need a Guinness and a Moscato," I tell her when she stops in front of me.

Aqua Net's talking to Lucio, tossing her petrified strands behind her shoulder, shamelessly flirting with him. He's not smiling or laughing, but she seems to be enjoying herself.

Daphne follows my eyes and snaps her fingers in my face when she realizes who I'm staring at. "Ignore them," she tells me.

"She looks like she's about to jump his bones." My lip snarls out of reflex.

"Lucio isn't enjoying himself." She tips her head in their direction. "Look at him."

"That tramp hasn't been nice from the moment I waited on her, and now she's all over my man." I narrow my gaze, and I imagine myself grabbing her by the back of the hair and hauling her ass to the door like Lucio did to the scumbag.

Daphne places the two drinks on the bar and smiles at me. "I like this side of you."

"What side?" I glance at her for only a second, because if Aqua Net touches him...all bets are off.

"The bitchy, territorial side. If I didn't know better, I'd think you were born here." She laughs and smacks my arm. "I like it."

Lucio catches my gaze from across the room and smiles, giving me a little wink. Aqua Net turns to see who he's looking at, and her nostrils flare.

He says something to her and she turns around,

but he isn't there for more than a few more seconds before he walks away. Aqua Net watches me as she walks back to her table and says something to her girls before picking up her purse.

I walk quickly, sliding their bill down on the table before they can walk out. They look every bit the type to leave without paying their tab.

"The guy said it's on the house," Aqua Net tells me with a straight face.

"He did not."

"Yeah. He did."

"Listen, lady. You owe the bar money and you're gonna pay up, or I'm calling the cops."

She looks me up and down, her lip curling at me in disgust. "I don't know who you think you are, talking to me like that, but I don't owe you anything."

"Just pay the bill, Jinny," her friend tells her, yanking on the side of her black leather coat.

Jinny swats the woman's hand away. "Fine, but the bitch isn't getting a tip."

I'm not even the least bit shocked. So instead of being upset, I give her my best smile and say, "It's okay, Jinny. I'm taking the owner home, and that's reward enough for a hard night of putting up with your bullshit."

Jinny's mouth falls open, and her head snaps backward. "I'm sure you're a lousy lay. He'll come to his senses eventually, and I'll be around to make sure he gets what he needs."

"He's not into bimbos, Aqua Net. Sorry to burst your bubble, but you'll never get that man. He's mine. Always will be. So you can move on to your next victim and spread your infection elsewhere."

She throws a twenty on the table and bares her teeth. "You're nothing more than a high-class cunt," she says, trying to wound me.

"He loves my cunt too," I tell her with an even bigger smile.

She stalks away, giving me the evil eye as she slams her hand against the door and walks outside. Her girlfriends follow, whispering to each other and looking at me over their shoulders.

"Wow." Daphne slaps my back. "Definitely a South Sider now. Those country-club folks would've had a stroke if they'd heard that shit coming out of your mouth."

"Fuck them," I say, but I'm not just talking about Jinny, I'm talking about all the people in my past. No longer am I anyone's doormat, and I never will be again.

"My girl," Daphne says and throws her arm around my shoulder. "It's worth coming out of my own pocket to pay the rest of their tab for that kind of entertainment."

"What happened?" Lucio asks, coming toward us with a concerned look.

"Delilah's got a mouth on her," Daphne tells him, laughing as she talks.

"I know." He winks, and I about die of embarrassment.

God, I love every person in this family, even his crazy-ass sister. I finally feel like I'm part of something bigger. Something more. Something lasting.

CHAPTER EIGHTEEN

LUCIO

I've been standing against the back wall, arms folded, watching the ticket counter move at an excruciatingly slow pace.

We'd already spent a few hours applying for a new Social Security card and getting a copy of her birth certificate, so she could get a new license. The DMV is my least favorite place, but it's unavoidable in Delilah's current situation.

She waited a few days, hoping her father would at least send her things so she wouldn't have to replace everything. But the bastard hadn't returned her purse or her money.

I'm fuming over the entire situation, but Delilah begged me to let her handle things. Me being me, I work in the background, trying to figure out how to get her money back along with all her stuff out of her father's penthouse.

My phone buzzes from the lawyer I contacted, a regular at Hook & Hustle, asking him to figure out a way to make her whole again, while avoiding court.

"The letter will be delivered today," Sal says without even so much as a hello.

"Thanks, Sal." I tick my chin at Delilah as she bounces Lulu in her lap, watching me. "I hope he comes to his senses."

"I'm fairly certain he'll want to remain out of the public eye and avoid court."

"If he has any brains, he'll do as you asked."

"He has no legal standing and will lose if we end up in court. But," he says, drawing the word out and lowering his voice, "you can probably convince him somehow if he drags his feet."

"Sal, I can't." I know where he's going with this. There's no way in hell I'm asking Johnny or any of my father's people to step in and strong-arm Delilah's father.

Not that he deserves better treatment, but I already promised Delilah I'd let her handle things.

And shit would blow up in my face if Johnny used his special methods.

"The guy isn't going to want to go to court. He has a reputation to uphold, Sal. Just handle that shit."

"You got it. I'll contact you as soon as I hear from him or his lawyer."

"Thanks, Sal," I say, disconnecting the call because I know Sal isn't one to say goodbye. Drives me crazy too.

"What's wrong?" Delilah asks as she walks toward me with Lulu in her arms.

"Nothing, baby," I tell her as I pull her into my arms and have her lean against me. "Why don't we go shopping after this? I know you and Lulu could both use some of your own clothes."

"Lucio." She peers up at me and shakes her head. "I made forty-three dollars in tips last night. Forty-three. I'm not buying much with that amount of money."

"I have money."

She pulls away, sliding Lulu to her hip and staring at me. "I'm not letting you buy me clothes."

"I know you're not letting me, but I'm doing it anyway."

She narrows her eyes, and I ready myself for an argument, which I have no doubt I'll win. "I can't let you."

I tap her nose with my finger and smile. "You're cute, doll."

"I'm serious, Lucio," she says sternly, as if her mom voice has any effect on me.

"While you look hot in my sister's clothes, I don't think cutoff shorts, heavy metal T-shirts, and dresses cut so low you can almost breastfeed without actually moving the fabric aside is quite your style."

She glances down at the worn-out Metallica T-shirt and twists her lips. She knows I'm right. I can see by the look on her face she hates what she's wearing. "Only if I can pay you back."

I grab her waist and pull her forward again. "We'll add it to your tab."

"Number 156," a woman calls out.

"That's me," Delilah says, handing off Lulu to me before she sprints toward the counter, weaving through the sea of people.

"Does Lulu want some pretty dresses?" I ask the kid like she has the ability to talk back. "I know Mommy does." Lulu smiles as she reaches up, playing with my lips again.

Delilah pulls out a wad of ones and sets it on the counter next to her paperwork, pushing it toward the woman on the other side. The lady rolls her eyes, throwing all kinds of shade at Delilah, not knowing everything she's been through in the last few days.

Delilah looks over her shoulder and smiles, but I know the entire situation has to sting. She's not used to any of this, but she takes it all in stride and doesn't complain.

A lesser woman would've caved and run back to daddy to cash in on her trust fund, but not Delilah. Maybe it's her attitude which drew me to her the most. She was a damsel in distress but didn't let any of it beat her down. She seemed to pick herself up, brush herself off, and move on without a bit of trouble.

When the woman hands her the driver's license, Delilah has the biggest smile, thanking the woman like she'd done something grand for her rather than just her job.

"Lookie what I got," she says, swaying her hips as she approaches. By the way she's acting, you'd think she won the lottery, not had her identification replaced.

"Let's go try that bad boy out," I tell her and slide my arm around her shoulders as we make our way to the door.

"Try it out?" I can see the confusion in her eyes, and I know she wants clarification, but I'm not going to give any.

"We've got a big day ahead of us," I say, leaving it at that. Delilah doesn't press me for more as she takes Lulu back into her arms and we walk outside. "First stop, the biggest department store in Chicago."

"Lucio," she says. I can hear the warning in her voice. "I don't need new clothes. These are fine."

"If you're a teenage girl from the nineties maybe, but not a grown-ass woman and a mom."

She narrows her eyes while she glances up at me as I open the door for her. "Do not put me in mom clothes. So help me God, I'll…"

"You'll what, sweetheart?" I tease.

The last thing I want on her body is a bunch of frumpy clothes, but she deserves to have nice things.

"We won't go crazy, but I'd like to see you in some grownup clothes, showing off that banging body, but in a classy way."

She leans over, placing Lulu in the Jeep while I check out her tight little ass. "I thought you liked the dress I wore the other night."

"I did, but not so much with you wearing the flimsy thing without me around."

"Jealous?" She smiles as she turns around.

"Greedy." I shut the door before pressing her against the side of my sister's Jeep. I grab her waist, digging my fingers into her skin. "I don't share, sweetheart."

She places her hand on my chest, curling her fingers into my shirt, and smirks. "I don't either, baby."

"What about this one?" she asks when she walks out of the dressing room and twirls in a circle as the skirt lifts, showing off her lace panties.

"Not for work," I tell her quickly, and Lulu claps

her hands, mesmerized by the way the fabric moves, "but it has a lot of other possibilities."

My ass is numb from sitting in the tiny chair inside the dressing room area for the last hour, but the smile on Delilah's face is entirely worth the pain.

"I love the fabric." She runs her hand over her bottom, smoothing the material. "Wanna feel?" She grins.

"You're torturing me today." If I feel the fabric, I'll touch her ass. If I touch her ass, it won't lead anywhere good but probably a trip down to the police precinct because I won't be able to stop myself. "I'm good. Just take that fine ass back into the dressing room and put something else on."

She sways her hips as she walks, laughing at the way I adjust myself in the seat. "You sure you don't want to touch it?" She shakes her ass before turning around to face me. "Just a little?" she teases, raising an eyebrow along with the front of the skirt.

I cover Lulu's eyes, and her hands immediately go to my fingers, trying to pry them free. "The kid, Delilah."

Delilah practically cackles as my gaze heats, and I know I'm going to make her pay for this. I hate shopping, but with her, it's a mix of pleasure and pain.

"You have five more minutes, and we're out of here," I tell her, done with the fashion show and ready to get her home.

"Patience is a virtue." She smiles, slowly closing

the door and staring at me with a sexy smirk on her face through the crack.

"So is generosity, baby." I watch under the door as the skirt drops to the floor. "And you're about to understand how generous I can be."

"I said I don't want you to buy me clothes." She slides on her shorts, and the dressing room door opens again. "I never asked for this." She grabs a hefty stack of hangers with all the items I liked, and I can see this bothers her.

"I'm not talking about clothes."

"You want me to pay you back in sexual favors?" She fakes disgust, but I know she's going to love every inch of what I'm going to give her.

I grab her chin between my fingers and move my lips within an inch of hers. "No, sweetheart, I'm going to be the one doing the pleasing."

Her blue eyes sparkle as she tips her head up, staring at me with so much need I can feel the heat coming off her in waves. "I like your style, Mr. Gallo."

"Baby, you haven't seen nothing yet." I pull on her bottom lip with my teeth.

Lulu smacks my arm and lets out a little grunt, reminding us both she's there.

"Let's go home," I tell her. "The kid needs a nap, and I need some Delilah."

"Fuck," she groans as she pulls away. "Between work, Lulu, and you, I get nothing done."

"Baby, we're all you need doing." I swat her ass as we exit the dressing room, already pulling out my wallet because I can't waste another minute. All I want to do is to be on top of her, touching her, consuming her.

CHAPTER NINETEEN

DELILAH

LUCIO CRAWLS OUT OF THE BED, AND I ROLL OVER, too comfortable and exhausted to bother getting out of bed with him. There's someone pounding at the door, but I don't care if it's God himself, I'm not leaving the warmth.

The birds chirp outside the window. They're a little too cheery for me. I open one eye and stare at the clock, groaning when I realize Lulu will be up any minute.

Suddenly, I can hear the loud rumble of Lucio's voice, and I jump to my feet, padding across the floor to the window. I pull back the curtain, trying to hide my face because I don't want him to think I don't trust him.

My heart stops as soon as I see his face. Dwight's on the walkway to the front door, waving his hands at Lucio and yelling back. Lucio takes a step forward, and Dwight backs up, knowing he's no match for Lucio's size and power.

I grab a pair of jeans off the floor and slide them on before I find a clean T-shirt, pulling it over my head as I walk to the living room. I'm practically stomping my feet with every step, marching toward the door and the man who abandoned us.

I'm so pissed my hands are shaking, and I'm breathing so fast I'm on the verge of hyperventilating. It's been nine months since Dwight vanished into thin air. I'd say he has a huge set of balls for showing up now, but I know that's not even remotely true.

I can hear Dwight's voice clear as day from the living room as he yells at Lucio. "I want to see my kid!"

"Daughter or son?" Lucio asks. I can't see his face, but his arms are crossed in front of him and he looks like the Hulk compared to Dwight.

Dwight stares at him but doesn't say anything back. The fucker doesn't even know because he left before I found out we were having a daughter, and he's never so much as called or texted to see if either of us survived.

My hand's on the doorknob, but something stops me from going outside. I hate him so much, but I'm thankful he left when he did. Lulu never had a chance to get attached to him and will never know the hurt of being abandoned.

"I want to see my son!" Dwight screams, putting the nail in his coffin.

"You have a daughter, asshole."

"Fuck you. She's my kid, and Delilah's my girl."

"You lost that right long ago. They're mine now."

A thrill runs through me when I hear Lucio say those words. I don't think I will ever get sick of hearing him call me his. The fact that he claims Lulu too makes my heart swell with pride, love, and hope.

"Where's Delilah?"

I turn the knob and step onto the front step, feeling stronger than I ever have. I'm no longer the timid girl, always trying to be proper and kind. "What do you want, Dwight?"

His eyes travel up my body, looking at me like I'm a prize he's already won. "I came back for you, baby."

I tip my head back and laugh as I hold my stomach. "What makes you think I want you?"

"We made a life." He takes a step toward me, but Lucio holds out his arm and presses his palm into Dwight's chest. "We are in love."

"We are?" My mouth drops open, and I widen my eyes, totally fucking with this worthless human. "Was that before or after you ditched me?"

Dwight's eyes narrow and he tries to push Lucio away, but he's not strong enough to even make him sway. "Don't be that way. You know I had to go."

I step forward, descending the cement stairs as slowly as possible with my eyes locked on him. "Did you get arrested?"

"No."

"Did you get called away on some secret mission?" I ask as I stand a few feet away from them, letting Lucio stay between us.

"Don't be ridiculous."

I tap my chin and glance at the sky. "That's right. You couldn't handle having a baby. You were a coward and decided you needed to live a little, like somehow I was trying to trap you."

Dwight drags his hand through his dirty-blond hair and stares at the ground. "I…" He starts to speak, but I don't give him a chance to come up with another lame excuse.

"I'm not your woman." I point toward Lulu's bedroom window. "She's not your daughter. You're nothing to us, just like we were nothing to you."

When he tries to move toward me again, Lucio grabs him by the arm and holds up a finger. "Take one more step, and I'm knocking your ass out."

"How the hell did you find me anyway?"

"Your dad told me where you were," he says as he reaches out his hand. "We can make us work again.

You can't want this." His eyes go to Lucio and back to me. "You're better than this, Delilah."

I touch Lucio's shoulder, knowing he's about to knock Dwight's lights out with one punch to the jaw. I should let him, but I've never been one to use my hands when my mouth will do the trick.

"Sweetheart, can you give us a minute?" Lucio turns to me with worry all over his face. "I'll be fine," I tell him, trying to make him comfortable. "I need to do this."

Lucio shakes his head and keeps his hand wrapped around Dwight's arm. "I don't think it's a good idea."

I touch his face, and his eyes close. "Please," I beg. "She's probably awake and hungry by now." I don't dare say her name. Dwight doesn't deserve to walk away from here knowing anything about Lulu.

Lucio nods before turning around and leveling Dwight with his gaze. "I see you try to touch her, and you're not leaving this front yard without a broken bone."

Dwight swallows, turning pale as a ghost, but he nods slowly. Lucio releases him but not before lunging forward, causing Dwight to flinch. There's a smirk on Lucio's lips when he turns to face me.

"Dwight won't hurt me." I slide my hand across Lucio's cheek. "He's never been that kind of man. He's a coward, for sure, but not a hitter."

"You have five minutes, and then I'm coming back out."

I lean forward, popping up on my bare tiptoes to give him a hard kiss. "Understood," I murmur against his mouth. "But I won't need that long."

Lucio touches my waist, holding on to me as he walks away. His hand slips away as he makes his way up the stairs, and I watch him, waiting for him to go inside before I lay into Dwight about his disappearing act.

I turn, narrowing my eyes, and stick my pointy finger square in his chest. "How dare you show your ugly face, you bastard."

His eyes widen as he backs up, clearly not expecting me to be pissed off and ready to vocalize every bit of that anger.

"You take off, leaving me with my father and a baby on the way. I know you were scared, but be a man, for fuck's sake. I was scared too, but I couldn't just walk away from the situation like you did." He tries to touch my hand, but I swat his arm away and keep going, pressing harder into his chest. "You need to forget we exist. You did a good enough job with that since the day you left, so it shouldn't be that hard to do it again."

"But she has a right to know her father."

"You were a sperm donor, Dwight. Let's not fool ourselves. Your name may be on her birth certificate, but—" I turn for a second, seeing Lucio watching from Lulu's bedroom window "—this man has been more of a father to her than you could ever be."

"Delilah, please."

"I don't know what you were thinking showing up here, but you're not getting a happy ending. I'm going to a lawyer and getting papers drawn up for you to relinquish your parental rights. Sign them. If you don't, so help me God, I'll go to everyone at the country club and tell them you knocked me up and took off."

His mouth hangs open, and I know I'm hitting him right where it hurts. "What will your daddy think when he finds out you ran away from your responsibilities?"

"I'll tell him." He steps forward and tries to touch me again, but I back away. "I'll make him understand. Don't cut me out of her life. Out of yours."

My hand slams into his chest, knocking him backward and causing him to stumble, almost losing his footing. "Sign the papers, Dwight, or…"

"Or what?" He challenges me, finding a pair of balls I never knew he had.

"Or I won't be able to stop what happens to you."

"What's that mean?" His lips twist.

I have no idea what it means, but I'll find a way to make him pay. The only thing I need right now is for him to believe I know of ways to hurt him that stretch beyond the law.

"I know people," I say simply, wondering if I

could get Johnny to strong-arm Dwight. I'm sure he'd do anything for me; he seems to have taken to me like the rest of the family.

"You know people?" He looks confused.

"Never mind," I tell him, knowing the only thing Dwight cares about is money. "You know what?" I stalk forward. "I don't have any money anymore, but I sure could use some child support. What are you making now? Ten thousand a month?" I smile as his face pales. "I'm sure I can make a case to get a hefty payment from you each and every month."

The last thing I want is his money, but it's the only motivator I have for his dumb ass.

He jerks his head back. "You're broke?"

"Not a dime." I draw out the word, following him as he's already heading toward the sidewalk. "My father stole it, but I'm sure you can help us out, right? We could use all that back child support to get a new place."

"Back child support?" He almost chokes on the words, and I know he's doing a calculation in his head.

"Yeah. I figure you owe us about—" I tap my chin and stop near the sidewalk, but he keeps moving "—about thirty grand by now."

"What? That's insane!"

I'm lying through my teeth. I have no idea how much I'd be awarded by a judge for child support, but Dwight is too stupid to know any better.

"Sign. The. Fucking. Papers."

"Fine," he says, throwing his hands up in the air. "You're nothing but a broke-ass hood rat anyway."

I roll my eyes, not feeling the sting from his country-club, cardigan-wearing, dumb-ass words.

"Fuck off, Dwight. Thanks for the lousy lay and the great kid," I hurl at him as he walks around the corner and out of my life again.

This time, he's not coming back.

Lucio's out the door before I have a chance to turn around. "He gone?"

"He's gone," I say, turning toward him and burying my face in his chest as soon as he gets close enough. "He's an asshole."

He wraps his arms around me and holds me tightly. "I'm proud of you."

His words warm my insides, making me feel better than anything else in the world. Lucio does that to me. He makes me feel better about myself, more confident, and tougher than I've ever been in my entire life.

CHAPTER TWENTY

LUCIO

"I GOT THE SHOTS," DAPHNE SAYS AS SHE ROUNDS THE bar and heads toward the middle of the room.

We're cleaning up, readying the bar for tomorrow's service. The bar was busy tonight. More crowded than we've been in a long time.

"I'm exhausted," Delilah says, wiping off the last table.

"It's Saturday night. We can't go yet." Daphne sets down the bottle of vodka, along with a plate of cut-up lemons and sugar. "I'm putting my foot down and requiring us to do a team-building activity."

Angelo raises an eyebrow and glances in my direction. "It's my last weekend without the kids," he says like he's justifying something.

"That's exactly why you deserve to get shit-faced," Daphne tells him and motions toward the table. "We have a new employee, and this will be great for team building and morale." When I groan, Daphne stalks across the room and grabs me by the hand. "We could all use a little downtime before the shitshow starts."

She's referring to my father. As soon as word got out that he was going to be released from prison soon, people started showing up in droves to get a glimpse of the local mafioso.

Delilah walks toward us, sitting down first and slipping off her shoes to rub her heels. "My feet are killing me," she says and makes a noise so close to the one she makes when I slip my cock inside her, I almost go rock hard. "We have time for a drink, Lucio, don't we?"

"One hour," I say and take the seat next to her.

"Come on, everyone." Daphne claps her hands. "And I mean everyone."

"What's your team-building activity?" Angelo asks, knowing it's useless to argue with her.

"Two Truths and a Lie." She smiles and stares down at us. "It's the best way to get to know each other."

I don't know how this will help anything. Most of

us grew up together, and there isn't much we don't know about each other.

"This might be your dumbest idea yet," Angelo grumbles.

Daphne sits down, ignoring our brother's grumpy mood and starts to pour the shots. "We have a new employee. Wouldn't it be nice to get to know her a little better?"

"I'm all about a drink to unwind, Daph, but shots are a little much," Michelle says as she takes the seat next to Daphne and pulls the glass in front of her.

"You're not a lightweight. Stop complaining."

Everyone's finally seated except for Vinnie. He's not here. Not like he ever is, but it's his final weekend home before he returns to school to finish out the spring semester.

Delilah places her hand on my leg and rests her face in her other palm. "I've never played this," she admits.

"Oh, girl. It's easy. You come up with two truths and a lie about yourself. You tell the table, and we have to guess which one is the lie."

"Where's the drink come in?" Delilah asks, staring at a shot glass filled with vodka.

"If you guess wrong, you gotta drink."

"I'm a human lie detector." Delilah smiles. "Prepare to get slaughtered."

"You got a lot of shit talk for a little girl," Angelo teases. "I can see why you two work so well." His gaze bounces between the two of us. "I'll go first." The table gives him their full attention. "I lost my virginity at fourteen, I was once with a woman twenty years older than myself, and I haven't been touched by a woman in two years."

I raise an eyebrow. I know his first two are true, which means the last one is his lie. He's been with someone, which is surprising because he hasn't bothered to mention it to anyone.

Delilah tips her head to the side, studying my brother's face. "That's easy. The last one's your lie," she answers like she's known him his entire life.

"Why d'you think that?" Angelo asks, leaning back in his chair.

"There's no way you've been celibate for two years. You're not grouchy enough. I mean, you're intense and everything, but not near enough for that to be true."

The entire table bursts out laughing. Daphne suddenly stops and slams her palms down on the table. "Wait." She turns and gawks at him. "Who have you been seeing behind our backs?"

"None of your business," he says before downing the shot and grimacing. "You don't need to know everything about my life." I catch the subtle glance he gives Michelle from across the table, but I don't say a word because it's none of my business who my brother is sleeping with.

"Delilah, it's your turn," Daphne says, but her voice isn't as cheery as it was only a minute ago.

Daphne hates not being in the loop. She's used to having her nose so far up in our business that the revelation has to sting.

"So, wait. You slept with a woman twenty years older than you?" Delilah looks shocked. "Who was that?"

"Mrs. Kinsey," I answer for him because all the guys had a turn with her as we grew up.

"Who?" The tiny lines between Daphne's eyebrows deepen. "Who the hell is that?"

"It's a dude thing, little sister." Angelo pats her on the shoulder, and she stiffens.

"The old lady from down the street?"

"She wasn't so old back then," Angelo says.

Mrs. Kinsey was a widow in her forties, but damn if she didn't look a day older than thirty back then. The boys in the neighborhood knew about her and her wild sexual appetite.

"You banged her, man?" I ask Angelo because I couldn't do it. I tried, God how I tried, but she didn't do it for me.

"I let her blow me." He smirks.

"Today her ass would end up in jail." Daphne turns toward Delilah, already a little hot under the collar. "Go." She waves her hand.

"I speak three languages, I met Brad Pitt, and I was once arrested."

"Shut the fuck up, you met Brad Pitt?" Daphne says quickly with wide eyes. "Tell me everything."

Delilah laughs and pushes Daphne's drink in front of her. "Drink up."

"Fuck. Seriously?" Daphne's lip snarls as she takes the shot glass. "What the hell were you arrested for?"

I'm just as shocked as everyone to hear the news. I never pegged Delilah for someone with an arrest record. I'd been booked into County more than once, but I was a minor and had a bad temper.

"Public nudity." Delilah smiles.

There's not a sound in the room, and everyone's staring at the prim and proper Delilah Miles.

"You can't just say that and not explain," I tell Delilah, and I am fascinated once again by my girl.

The entire table is just as interested as I am. We all have our opinions on Delilah, and so far, every single thing we assumed about her has been wrong.

"It's no big deal. It was freshman year in college, pledge week." Delilah sits up straight and twists the shot glass between her fingertips. "The sisters in the sorority thought I was a stuck-up prude."

"Shocking." Michelle giggles.

"Shut it," Delilah tells her like she's been here for years. As far as I can tell, the girls bonded the night they went out, but thankfully, Carmen and Colleen haven't decided to come around. "Anyway, as part of my initiation, I had to run across the football field naked during warmups."

"Impressive." Daphne waggles her eyebrows. "Never knew you had it in you."

"I hadn't planned on the security guards practically tackling me on the fifty-yard line and being hauled out of the stadium in handcuffs."

Daphne downs the shot and clears her throat, not bothering with the lemon or sugar. "Okay." She pauses, and I can almost see the wheels spinning in her head. "I once puked on a guy in the middle of having sex, I've never seen *The Notebook*, and I hate when guys call me baby."

I rub my hand down my face, hating everything about playing this game with my sister. The last thing I want to know about is her sex life. I like to pretend she's celibate, preferring to live like a nun than the wild child she's always been.

"Easy," Michelle says as she starts to laugh. "You've never seen *The Notebook*."

"You're not allowed to play when it's my turn," Daphne tells her, pointing her skinny little finger in Michelle's face. "You know all my secrets."

"Wait, you puked on someone while you were doing it?" Delilah's mouth is hanging open.

"Move on. I'll go," I say because I've learned way too much already, and I don't want the gory details.

"I once danced for money, I've never done drugs, and I have never lied to Ma."

"What about me?" Ma says as she walks down the staircase, scaring the shit out of all of us.

"Lucio says he's never lied to you," Angelo tells her, throwing his hand in my direction.

"That's some bullshit," Ma says, ending my round of Two Truths and a Lie.

"You dance?" Delilah's eyes light up as she looks at me. "Like a stripper?"

"Don't lie, man. You did that shit more than once." Angelo's so quick to throw me under the bus.

"I was young."

Delilah squeezes my leg and winks. "I want to see your act later."

"Baby." I lean over and touch her cheek. "I'll show you what I got anytime."

"I'm gagging," Daphne says and pretends to hurl on the floor next to her.

"I'm done. I want to get Lulu home and my girls to bed." I stand and hold my hand out for Delilah.

"Damn, I wanted to play," Ma tells me, giving me puppy-dog eyes like they're going to work on me.

"I'm already scared enough after tonight. My heart can't take much more." Delilah's laughing as she takes my hand, and I help her up. "You guys play. I'm sure it'll be enlightening."

"Nope. I gotta go. I have a date," Daphne says suddenly.

"Me too," Angelo stands, and so does Michelle, leaving Ma sitting there alone.

"One o'clock tomorrow. Don't be late," Ma calls out as we head in opposite directions.

"I'll grab Lulu. Wait down here for me," I tell Delilah before kissing her on the lips.

I'm halfway up the stairs when I hear my mom tell Delilah, "Once when I was younger and much more flexible, Santino would…"

I cover my ears, taking the steps faster because no way in hell do I want to hear the rest of that sentence. There's such a thing as too much information, and tonight, I've already hit my limit.

CHAPTER TWENTY-ONE

DELILAH

I'M TOWEL-DRYING MY HAIR, SITTING ON THE EDGE OF the bed when the music starts. I'm barely awake, not having had nearly enough coffee to be coherent or energetic for a Monday morning.

Lucio comes sliding into the room, wearing a pair of black athletic pants, a white tank top, and a baseball cap. My mouth waters the moment I see him, and suddenly my hair isn't so important.

I'd know the song anywhere. It's the theme song from *Magic Mike,* and based on the way he's moving his hips, he knows the routine by heart.

I'm mesmerized as he turns his baseball cap around, exposing his beautiful face and deep green eyes. His gaze meets mine, and my stomach flutters. All I can do is sit here, watching him as he dances around the room, thrusting his dreamy cock in my direction.

I reach out, trying to grab a hold of his waistband, but he pushes my hands away and waves his fingers in my face, telling me no.

He turns his back to me, teasing me as he slowly lifts his shirt over his head. The muscles of his back ripple, moving to the beat of the music. I'm impressed by his ability to control his body the way he does. Sometimes I can barely walk in a straight line, but he has such control, I'm envious and totally turned on.

"Take it all off," I say, careful not to scream too loud because Lulu's still asleep. "Show me whatcha got."

He spins with his feet together, running his hand down his abdomen as the muscles of his arm flex and become more defined. When he grabs his crotch, I almost slide off the bed, so turned on I want to throw myself at his feet and beg for his cock.

But then he jumps on the bed, placing his feet on both sides of me and grinds his dick in my face. I bite through the thin material, teasing him as much as he's teasing me.

I can imagine him doing this in a room full of women, the money flying in his direction because he's that damn good and so freaking sexy. I grab his ass and try to pull his pants down, but he's off the bed, dancing again before I have a chance.

But I'm not in the mood to play fair. I pull my robe open, exposing my breasts, and palm one in my hand. His eyes are locked on my movement, watching as I swipe my thumb across my nipple. His dancing slows a bit when I open my legs and slide my other hand down, running my fingers through my wetness.

He moves toward me and pushes me backward, dancing his way between my legs. I watch down the length of my naked body as he twists down to his knees, bringing his beautiful, lush licks right to where I ache the most.

I close my eyes as his tongue runs over my clit, sending waves of pleasure through my entire body. My fingers close around the comforter, balling the material in my palms as he lifts my thighs over his shoulders and closes his lips around my clit.

I cry out, loving every second of the way he loves me with his mouth. He's an expert and has learned my body so quickly, but I'm not surprised since I'm not a quiet lover.

When he moans, matching my own, the vibration joins his tongue in delivering a one-two punch. The orgasm comes quickly, way faster than either of us expects, especially me. The air in my body vanishes, and my toes curl along with my legs, burying his face in my pussy. I grind against him, smothering him, but he doesn't seem to mind as he sucks harder. The waves crash over me like a thunderstorm rolling through a mountain valley, overshadowing everything in sight.

"Fucckkkkk," I moan, sucking in a breath as my head spins. "That was so…"

"Amazing and the best you've ever had," he says with a smirk, before running his tongue across his lips, taking in every last drop I gave him.

He tries to help me up, but I push him down and mount him. "That was quite the performance," I tell him as I rub my pussy against him with only his pants separating us.

He smirks, showing off his stunning white teeth against his tanned skin. "Which parts?"

He's cocky, but damn if he hasn't earned the right to be. "All. Of. It." Leaning forward, I lick his lips, tasting myself.

"But the tongue…"

"That's my favorite, but…" I pause and slide down his body. "I think I like this part best." Putting my hand over his cock, I stroke his hard length through the material.

He moans, lifting his ass off the bed just like I do when he licks my pussy. As soon as I pull down the waistband of his pants, his cock springs free, moving through the air as if it's greeting me.

"It's still so fucking pretty. No cock should be this hot," I say, grabbing it with my hand and staring at it.

"None are," he tells me. "Show me how much you like it."

My tongue flicks the piercing, and I'm just about to close my lips around the tip when Lulu starts crying. Lucio's entire body tenses, and I freeze, praying she'll fall back asleep. But we both know it's not going to happen.

"I'll go," he says, pulling me up his body and tossing me onto the bed next to where he just lay. "But you're finishing this later."

"Naptime can't come soon enough," I say through my laughter.

I almost feel bad for him as he pulls his pants up, trying to jam his hard cock underneath the thin fabric. The material does nothing to contain his erection as he stalks out of the room like he has a third arm.

I roll off the bed, closing my robe as I climb to my feet, and I remember there's no time for me to finish what I just started because I have an appointment with an attorney this afternoon.

As promised, Dwight was given paperwork to sign, revoking his parental rights and any future ties to Lulu. After today, there's no reason for me ever to see him again.

Someday, when Lulu's older and has questions, I'll tell her what I can without making her feel bad. I know this is what's best not only for her, but me too.

"Baby."

Lucio lifts Lulu into his arms like he's been doing it since the day she was born. The way he holds her makes my heart skip a beat. He's so tender and gentle even though he's large and covered in muscle.

"Don't forget I have to go to the lawyer's today."

"I'm coming," he says as he rubs Lulu's back, trying to quiet her tears.

"You don't have to. I'm sure you have things to do."

"Delilah." He gives me that look. The one that says I'm being crazy. "There's nowhere I'd rather be than with my girls."

He always includes Lulu. It's not just about me anymore, and Lucio somehow respects and embraces both of us.

"Okay," I tell him, wrapping my arm around his back and leaning forward to kiss Lulu. "I want you to come with me more than anything."

"Hey." He pauses, waiting for me to look at him. "You'll never have to go through anything else alone. I'm here and not going anywhere."

I'd say thank you, but the words don't seem adequate enough for how I feel. I've never truly had someone I could depend on who didn't let me down. Lucio's only been in my life a short time, but I can't imagine ever being alone again.

CHAPTER TWENTY-TWO

LUCIO

"Sal," I say, shaking his hand as we walk into his office.

"Looking good, man." Sal takes a step back and stares at me. "It must be because of this beautiful lady."

Delilah blushes and smiles, but when Sal reaches out and sweeps his finger down Lulu's pudgy cheek, she laughs.

"Of course, I'm talking about you, Ms. Miles, but I know Lucio's fondness for little Lulu too." He motions toward the small table near the window. "Sit, please."

"Thank you for taking this case so quickly." Delilah walks at my side, holding my hand. I pull out the chair for her, being a gentleman, and wait for her to sit before I take the seat next to her.

"Anything Lucio ever needs, I'm always there for him."

Delilah looks at me and places her hand over mine. "I don't know what I did to deserve him."

"I think you have it backward, sweetheart. I'm the lucky one here."

Sal's watching me with a funny look. We go way back, and he knows my past better than anyone. Neither of us is innocent. We did some pretty dumb shit as kids, but somehow, he went to law school and passed the bar even though I never would've guessed he was smart enough. I guess he hid his intelligence and learned to fit in, because on the South Side, in our neighborhood, muscles beat out smarts every day of the week.

"Did you have any trouble with Mr. Jones?" Delilah asks as she turns to face Sal.

"None." Sal shakes his head. "I called him, and he came into the office the same day to sign the paperwork."

"Not surprising. The bastard." Delilah whispers the last part and covers her mouth, trying to hide her disgust.

"He understood that he'd lose if the case was brought in front of a judge. He abandoned you and your daughter." Sal slides a manila folder in front of Delilah, and she takes it. "He may have been able to get supervised visitation, but he'd have to start paying child support immediately."

"He's too cheap to part with his money. Even for his daughter." Her hand's lying on top of the folder with her and Lulu's names written in black ink on the front. "So, it's done?" she asks.

"You just need to sign the paperwork too, and I'll file it with the court."

She peels back the cover and studies the first page before flipping to the end where Dwight has already signed.

Sal sets a pen down in front of her. "Do you need a moment alone?" he asks.

"No," she says, waving her hand before snatching the pen off the table. "There's no sadness in my heart. No regret about doing this. He doesn't deserve to be her father even if it's only on paper." Delilah scribbles her name next to Dwight's, almost stabbing the dot over the "i" in her last name. She drops the pen and pushes the entire folder back toward Sal. "How long until it's final?"

"The courts are slow and backlogged, but it should only take a few weeks."

"Perfect."

I turn to Delilah and grab her hand. "I want to

ask you something," I say, and her eyes widen. "Not that."

I wasn't too smooth with that sentence. If I were going to ask her to marry me, it sure as hell wouldn't be in Sal's office.

"I love you."

"I love you too," she says quickly.

"I love Lulu."

"She adores you."

"What do you think if I…" God, I'm about to say words I thought would never come out of my mouth, and my stomach is knotting and my pulse quickens. "What do you think if I adopt Lulu?"

Delilah only blinks as her lips part, and she stares at me. I'm not sure she quite heard me right because she doesn't say anything right away. Her lips move, but no words come out.

"She needs a daddy, sweetheart. I want to be that for her. I love her like she's my own and never want her to think she wasn't wanted."

"Wait." Delilah turns a little more in her chair, and I can already see the tears forming in her eyes. "You want to adopt her?" she repeats like she really didn't believe the words I just said.

"Yes." I nod, squeezing her fingers between mine. "More than anything in the world."

"You want to be her father?" A tear runs down Delilah's cheek as she blinks. "Like, forever?"

"It usually works that way."

I know this is a huge step and she might tell me I'm completely insane and refuse to let me adopt Lulu, but I have to try.

"I had a long talk with my ma. She agrees with me on this. We all want Lulu to be part of our family forever."

"I don't know what to say," she whispers, and more tears start to fall.

I brush away the tears with the back of my hand before resting my palm against her cheek, cradling her face. "I've never loved anyone like I love you, Delilah. But Lulu, she has me wrapped around her little finger. I want her to be mine. If you say no, I'll understand, but I…"

I don't get the next words out before Delilah's mouth is on me. Her hands come to my face, and she peppers me with kisses. The tears haven't stopped. She's crying harder than before, but she's happy.

"Yes!" she exclaims, causing Lulu to jump in my arms and scream for a moment.

"You sure?" I ask between kisses.

"You're already an amazing father to her, Lucio. Better than my own ever was to me, and more of a man than Dwight will ever be. Lulu would be lucky to have such a wonderful man as her daddy."

"Sal," I say, peering over at him without turning. Delilah's still attached to my face, kissing me a dozen times. "Draw up the papers."

Sal nods and claps his hands loudly, and Lulu cries this time, startled by all the excitement in the room.

Delilah takes her from my arms and hugs her tightly. "You have a daddy now," she tells her, and I almost choke up.

"As soon as this form is accepted by the court, I'll start official adoption proceedings." He nods and is all smiles. "One more thing," Sal says and pulls another folder off his desk. "Lucio told me about your father, and as a personal favor, I sent him a letter to restore the money he removed from your account."

"You did?" Delilah gazes at me, and I give her a nervous smile.

I may have overstepped my bounds with that favor, but fuck her father, he did not deserve to keep the money which rightfully belonged to her.

"Yes, and I received a letter of response yesterday along with proof that your bank account has been made whole again."

Delilah's eyes widen as Sal slides the folder in front of her, peeling back the front to show her the deposit slip.

At least the prick had enough sense to give her every dollar back. I wasn't going to let a sleeping dog lie. He was going to pay her back one way or another, but I'm glad it only took a strongly worded letter to scare him into action.

She runs her fingers over the paper, staring at the

number. "I can't believe it. I don't know how to thank you both for everything."

"No thanks needed," Sal says, taking the words right out of my mouth. "It's always nice to help someone who deserves it."

Delilah's eyes are filled with tears, and she's so choked up she can't say another word.

"I'm going to take my girls to lunch to celebrate," I say as I stand and hold out my hand to shake, thanking Sal for his help.

He comes around the table, capturing me in a giant bear hug. "I never thought I'd see the day you'd go all soft on me, buddy. It suits you."

I don't even grumble. There's nothing in the world that can bring me down from the high of knowing I'll be gaining a daughter and, hopefully soon, a wife too.

Lulu's asleep in the stroller next to the table. She's worn out from the excitement of earlier. The sun's shining overhead as we sit on the patio at the Park Grill overlooking Grant Park.

My finger's in my pocket, and I'm fiddling with the diamond ring I picked out yesterday with a little help from Angelo. I went overboard, but I couldn't help myself. I didn't want Delilah walking around with a shitty ring. No matter how many times someone says size doesn't matter, I know it's a crock of bullshit.

"Champagne," the waitress says, holding out the bottle to us for approval.

"It's perfect," I tell her before she pours two glasses.

"I can't believe we're celebrating," Delilah says, and she still hasn't come down from the high of earlier.

"I was worried for a second," I admit.

The entire thing could've blown up in my face. Delilah could've shot me down, going on with our relationship just as it had been. Other people would think we're crazy. We've only known each other a few weeks, but I can't imagine letting her or Lulu walk out of my life at this point.

"I'm sorry I scared you." She touches the base of the champagne flute and gazes at me from under her lashes. "I was just so in shock."

I know what I'm about to do is going to be another shock to her system, and I pray to God she says yes. We're both in too good of a mood to have something destroy the happiness we both deserve.

I'm almost certain she'll say yes. I've never seen her smile as easily as she does with me. When she first showed up at the bar, she was an entirely different person. It took a little time for her to relax and open up, but once she did, there was no turning back.

A noise across the way draws Delilah's attention,

and I know it's my one shot to surprise her. I slide to my knee and pull the ring from my pocket before she turns back around.

When she looks across the table and I'm not there, she almost panics. But when she sees me… God, when she sees me on one knee, holding a giant ring that's sparkling in the sun like a beacon, her eyes widen and she gasps.

"Ms. Delilah Miles, would you do me the honor of being my wife?" I say quickly because I know she's about to cry again, and hell, I might too.

My heart's pounding, and all the voices around us seem to quiet. Everyone's watching, waiting with bated breath as I kneel before her, praying she'll say yes.

"Fuck. Are you kidding me?" she says.

"No jokes, sweetheart. I've never loved another person more than I love you. All I think about every day is you and Lulu. The only place I want to be is by your side. I want you to be mine forever. I want to marry you in front of my family and God. I can't imagine another day on this planet without you."

"Yes! Yes! Oh my God. Yes!" she yells, and the tears start falling as I slide the ring onto her finger.

She doesn't even look at it or notice the size. I agonized for hours over the perfect one. Learning everything I could about cut, clarity, and all the other bullshit that comes along with diamonds.

She leans forward and wraps her hands around

my neck. "I love you, Lucio. I want nothing more than to be yours forever."

The people sitting around us clap and smile, feeling the excitement in the moment. Engagements always make people happy, even if they're miserable in their own lives.

I pull her into my arms and know this is meant to be.

CHAPTER TWENTY-THREE

DELILAH

"Lemme see," Daphne says as soon as we walk through the front door of the bar.

I hold out my hand and wiggle my finger, showing her the extravagant ring Lucio bought for me. I would've been happy with a small rock. Size never really mattered to me. How could it when I have a guy like Lucio by my side?

"It's so beautiful." She stares at the ring, bringing my hand closer to her face. "He did damn good. I'm impressed."

"Where is she?"

I turn as Betty comes down the stairs with the biggest smile on her face. She's wearing the most magnificent black-and-white polka-dot dress with her hair styled like a 1950's pinup. She's absolutely stunning and smiling bigger than I've ever seen before.

"There's my girl," she says, holding out her arms. For a second, I think she's going for Lulu, but when she wraps her arms around me, I can't help but smile. "You've made me so happy." She pulls back and grabs my cheeks. "So, so happy."

Lucio clears his throat, getting his mother's attention. "I wouldn't let you down, Ma."

She pats his chest, always proud of her son. "I never had any doubt, baby. Now let me see my granddaughter."

"Ma, it's not official yet."

She rolls her eyes as she takes Lulu from my arms. "I don't need a court to tell me she's one of my own." Lulu laughs, grabbing for those pearls again, just as attached to Betty as she was the very first time she held her.

"When's the wedding?" Daphne asks, almost chomping at the bit to know more.

"I don't know." I look to Lucio because we haven't even talked about when we'll actually say I do.

"As soon as possible," he answers easily.

"We must book the church immediately. No child of mine is getting married at city hall. Father Michael must be the one to marry you."

"I'll let you ladies plan everything," Lucio says and shakes Angelo's hand as soon as he walks over.

"Finally growing up," Angelo teases him. "Locked it down like I told you."

"Locked it down?" I ask.

Lucio leans over and kisses my cheek. "Made sure I never let you go, sweetheart."

"Oh." I laugh. It's a bit cavemanish, but I kind of like it.

Angelo grabs Lucio by the shoulder and announces to everyone, "My brother's getting married. Beer's on the house."

The few regulars, people I've come to truly like, erupt into cheers, congratulating us on our upcoming wedding; although they are probably more excited about the free drinks.

"There's so much to do." Daphne grabs me by the arm and ushers me to a nearby table. "Dresses, reception, invitations."

"We can keep it small. I don't really have anyone to invite." The words sting a little, but besides my father and mother, there's no one left in my family who hasn't been driven away.

"Girl, our family is huge."

"How big?" I ask.

"Between the cousins, we're talking well over a hundred people."

My mouth falls open, and all I can do is blink. "For real?"

"Italians always show up at weddings."

"Always?"

"Always. I can bet my mother is going to invite everyone from the neighborhood, then we have the customers, and the family too. It's going to be enormous."

I'm suddenly nervous, thinking about all the strangers staring at me as I walk down the aisle. "Maybe we should just keep it small. Do it right here in the bar." I like my idea. It sounds simple and more intimate.

"Don't be crazy. We have a wedding shower to plan and so much to do. You're going to look like a princess on your big day," Daphne tells me, and my mind's reeling from all the information she's hurling at me.

I was so excited about the engagement, I didn't even think about all the things that would come with it.

"I'm planning the bachelorette party," Michelle says, coming to sit with us finally.

"I'll let you, but you better make it good."

I smile because I don't know what else to do.

I'm so overwhelmed by their love and excitement I can't even talk anymore. I just look around the bar, watching their happy faces and know I've found my forever home.

Michelle places her hand over mine as I watch Daphne walk away. "You okay?"

"Yeah. Just overwhelmed."

"The Gallos don't do anything small, but I promise we'll be there to help. Don't get scared. You're about to be part of something amazing."

"I know," I tell her, and my smile comes easily. "I've never been so happy in my whole life."

"Daphne and I have been planning our weddings since we were kids. We're excited about this and hope we can help you."

"Of course. I want your help in everything."

I don't even know where to start. After watching my parents' marriage end in spectacular fashion, I never thought I'd be willing to take the plunge. I didn't have the best role models, and the thought of making the same mistakes scares the shit out of me.

"Do you want to postpone the wedding?" Lucio's standing in the doorway to my bedroom, watching me.

"No. Why would you ask that?"

He walks across the room and sits next to me on the bed. "We can elope, then."

"We can't do that."

He grabs my hand and kisses my fingers. "You seem overwhelmed."

I stare at him and smile. "I am, but I've also never been more certain about anything in my life either."

"What can I do to make this easier for you?"

God, how is he always so great? So patient. So understanding. "My parents were a terrible example, and"—I lean over and put my head on his shoulder—"what if we mess the entire marriage thing up?"

He turns on the bed and grabs my face between his giant hands. "Listen, sweetheart. My parents were basically a shitshow most of my life. I know how my mom talks, you'd think they had the type of love you only see in movies, but it's not true. I never want to be like my father. Never."

"His actions don't define who you are," I tell him as I place my hands on his thighs.

"And neither do your parents."

He has a point.

He slides his hands to my shoulders, and he strokes my neck with his thumbs. "I promise to love you and only you. I've always been so scared to commit to someone because I thought I'd be like my father, but I know now, I'm nothing like him."

"I'm nothing like mine," I say.

"Even though my father wasn't the best partner, he was a great dad."

"Neither of my parents was spectacular in any area of their life."

"But you're an amazing mother," he tells me, and I smile, happy someone has noticed.

"Thank you, Lucio."

He turns his eyebrows inward. "For what?"

"For everything."

"Sweetheart." He pulls me into his lap and wraps his arms around me. "Don't thank me. I should be thanking you. Until you showed up, my life was empty."

"Looked pretty full to me," I say and giggle.

He peers down at me and shakes his head. "I'm being serious." His finger finds the engagement ring and moves it. "I never let myself get close to anyone. Never had any real connection. But then this scared girl turned up, and nothing else mattered but keeping her and her baby safe."

"So, we were basically a pity case?" I'm totally joking. Well. Sort of.

"I wouldn't ask you to be my wife out of pity. I've never loved another person as much as I love you."

I sit up straighter and slide my arms around his shoulders. "I love you too, and I don't want to postpone the wedding. I want to be married to you more than anything in the world."

He tightens his hold and presses his lips against my forehead. "As soon as the adoption paperwork is ready, we'll get married. I'll talk to Sal and find out when everything should happen, and we'll plan around it. I don't want to waste another day without you being mine."

I peer up into his beautiful green eyes. "I am yours, silly."

"Forever," he tells me before he moves his face closer and steals my breath in a devastating kiss.

All doubt. All worry. Everything disappears as his mouth covers mine. I know where I'm meant to be. Whom I'm meant to be with. Nothing else matters. The past is the past, but our future is just beginning.

EPILOGUE

LUCIO

Three Months Later…

My palms are sweaty, and my heart's pounding so hard I'm sure the entire church can hear the crazy rhythm over the piano music. When the church doors open and Delilah steps out on Angelo's arm, my heart practically stops for a second before beating faster than before.

She looks stunning in the all-white gown with her hair pulled up off her shoulders and the lace veil down over her face. I can't take my eyes off her as she makes her way up the aisle, almost floating over the hardwood.

When she steps up to the altar and I pull back the veil, revealing her tearful but happy face, a sense of bliss comes over me. It's like the entire room disappears, and only Delilah and I exist.

Her hands are in mine as we stand in front of the altar, listening to the priest. The entire church is filled with our family and friends, dabbing at the tears in their eyes as we say our vows.

I haven't taken my eyes off Delilah since the moment she walked into the church. How could I? She's everything I ever wanted but never knew I needed. I can't imagine a day without her or Lulu in my life. My heart's filled with so much joy, I'm not even sure how I can stand as still as I am.

I turn to Angelo on cue and take the ring from his finger. He smiles, but his eyes are teary too, maybe remembering the day he married Marissa. I touch his hand before I turn back around, and he nods, giving me the sign to move on.

The platinum band seems too small as I hold it between my two fingers to face Delilah, one step closer to her finally being my wife.

The priest clears his throat, reminding me of what we rehearsed last night. I slide the ring onto Delilah's finger, staring into her eyes as I see my future come to life. "Repeat after me," he says quietly.

"Delilah, receive this ring as a sign of my love and

fidelity. In the name of the Father, and of the Son, and of the Holy Spirit."

I don't speak right away. My fingers are holding the ring and Delilah's hand as I stare into her sparkling blue eyes. "Delilah, receive this ring as a sign of my love and fidelity. In the name of the Father, and of the Son, and of the Holy Spirit."

She bites her lip, holding back the tears I know are about to fall again, only harder this time. Even I can feel my nose tingle, but I take a deep breath, pushing any tears away.

Delilah turns toward Daphne and takes the ring from my sister. She's smiling when she faces me again, looking more confident and beautiful than I've ever seen before. I glance to my mother, who's holding Lulu in her arms. My daughter.

"Repeat after me. Lucio, receive this ring as a sign of my love and fidelity. In the name of the Father, and of the Son, and of the Holy Spirit," the priest says again as Delilah touches my hand.

She keeps her eyes on me as she starts to slide the ring on my finger. "Lucio, receive this ring as a sign of my love and fidelity. In the name of the Father, and of the Son, and of the Holy Spirit."

I squeeze her hands, wondering if that feeling of peace washes over her like it does me in that moment. We've said our vows before the eyes of God and my entire family. Even though the priest hasn't said the words, we're officially husband and wife.

We kneel, waiting for the silent blessing, and our hands are connected. I can't stop turning the ring on my finger, still a little shocked that I'm married. I'm not scared for the future. Not worried I'll mess up like my father anymore.

I sneak a glance at Delilah, and she has her head bowed, but she's watching me too. The mass seems to take forever when all I want to do is take my wife out of this place so I can show her exactly how much I love her.

"Please stand," the priest says, closing the bible in his hands as soon as he's done with the prayer. He nods at us when it's time to face the crowd.

I smile at Delilah, happier than I've ever been as we turn toward our family and friends while they rise to their feet too.

"I present to you Mr. and Mrs. Lucio Giovanni Gallo. You may now kiss the bride."

I know my mother's praying I keep it tasteful. And while I want to abide by her wishes in theory, the ceremony has been entirely too long, and I'm dying to give my wife a real kiss. One that she'll remember forever. One that's bigger and better than any I've given her before.

As Delilah turns toward me, I place my hand against her neck, sweeping my thumb across her cheek as I wrap my arm around her back. She stares at me, tears hovering in her eyes as I lean in. She holds her breath, and I hold mine as I pull her close and fuse our mouths together.

The cheers of the crowd die away, and my mind and body buzz with excitement as she places her hand over my heart and kisses me back. The moment's one I burn into my brain, never wanting to forget how I feel in this moment when we've become each other's.

When I pull back, I gasp for air and my head spins, knowing the ceremony's over and the good hasn't even begun.

As I walk down the aisle with my family looking on, I know the best is yet to come.

"Why are Carmen and Colleen here?" I ask, leaning over and whispering in Daphne's ear as we stand in the receiving line, greeting the last few guests.

"Delilah invited them." Daphne shrugs. "Honestly, if we couldn't invite any woman you've been with, there wouldn't be many people here you aren't related to."

Only my wife would give the okay to invite everyone from the neighborhood. I heard her say something about making it clear to every female in a five-mile radius that I was officially off the market. I didn't expect her to invite them all to the wedding. I just had to shake my head and know I probably would've done the same.

"What's wrong?" Delilah asks as the last wedding guest steps down the stairs to the dining area.

"Nothing, sweetheart." I touch her face and resist the urge to haul her into the storage room to officially consummate the marriage.

"I'll announce you to the guests after the wedding party, as you make your way down the stairs, and then we'll go right into your first dance as husband and wife," the DJ tells us so fast I can barely understand his words. Thankfully, I've been to enough weddings to know the spiel without being told.

"Sure," I say, still holding on to Delilah.

He heads toward the dance floor, and Delilah and I finally look out over the crowd, which has more than doubled since church.

"Holy hell, who are all these people?" she asks with wide eyes.

"Your family," I answer simply.

"I never thought I'd have a family quite this big." She squeezes my hand, and I can see the tears coming again.

"Don't cry, Mrs. Gallo." I like how her title sounds coming out of my mouth. I'm not sure I won't say it on the daily because it's still too damn unbelievable.

The wedding party, which consists of Angelo, Daphne, Vinnie, and Michelle, marches down the stairway, forming a line for us to walk through as the DJ plays the theme music to *Rocky*, even though I told him not to.

But I can't be mad. It's my wedding day, and I married the girl of my dreams. "Ready?" I ask her, bringing her hand to my mouth and pressing my lips to her soft skin.

"Yes." She smiles, and it's like my whole world is complete. "I've never been more ready for anything in my life."

I raise my hand, along with hers, in celebration as we make our way down the stairs, going slowly so she doesn't fall over the ridiculously long dress and her crazy high heels. Everyone in the room is standing, clapping loudly, probably still not believing I actually tied the knot. Hell, I have a hard time believing it myself sometimes.

How the hell did I get this damn lucky? Of all the places her father could've left her, it was in front of my bar. Anywhere else and we probably never would've crossed paths. I'd still be alone, and she'd be… I put the thought out of my mind, trying not to think of what could've happened when that bastard abandoned them.

Angelo slaps my shoulder as we walk by, and for the first time in a long time, he looks happy. Ma's waiting at the end of the line, just before the dance floor, with Lulu in her arms.

Lulu's smiling as she looks at us and holds out her arms. I take her and hold her tightly, bringing my mouth close to her ear. "My baby girl. I love you so much. I'll always love you. Always protect you. You're mine now too. Forever and always."

She makes a little noise, blowing out a raspberry before grabbing on to my ear and giggling. Over the last few months, she's grown so much, and every day's like a new beginning. Watching her grow up, seeing her personality come alive, has been something I never could have explained to another human being without experiencing it.

"I think she needs a little brother," I tell Delilah as she touches my arm to lean in to kiss Lulu.

"Getting ahead of yourself, aren't you?" she says.

"Oh no. I want a house full of little ones running around." She pales a little, and I laugh, giving Lulu a kiss on the cheek before handing her back to my mother.

"Nothing would make me happier," Ma says, looking more than excited about the possibility of more grandchildren.

"Think of all the fun it'll be," I say as I usher Delilah toward the dance floor.

"What? A house full of kids?"

"Making all the babies," I correct her as I pull her into my arms, and the music starts.

She laughs, swinging her arm around my shoulder and taking my hand. When Luther starts to sing, her smile almost touches her eyes. She let me pick the song, and there's no one more romantic than Luther Vandross singing about love.

I hold her closely and sing the words to "Here and Now" to her. Every damn word of this song is exactly how I feel about Delilah.

She doesn't take her eyes away from mine as we dance around the floor. Everyone else in the room doesn't seem to exist. Just the two of us, moving as one to the words of Luther.

My heart's pounding as the realization comes crashing down on me. Delilah's mine forever. As I sing about loving her faithfully and promises for the future, I know when I look into her eyes, I'm the luckiest son of a bitch in the world.

With Delilah and Lulu by my side, anything's possible. I thought I had it all before they walked into my life, but I realize I had nothing. I was a shell of a man with no real purpose or future.

But now, with them, I have everything I ever could've wanted and more.

Delilah places her chin on my shoulder and brings her mouth close to my ear. "I love you," she whispers.

"I love you too, sweetheart," I tell her before singing the words to the song in her ear. I want her to hear the promises, the love, the way I plan to love her forever.

Her thumb strokes the back of my neck, brushing the skin just under my hair. As the song comes to an end, I start to back away, but she pulls me back. "We're not done," she says in my ear.

Luther melts into Celine, and Delilah takes

another page out of my book, singing "Because You Loved Me" in my ear. I listen to every word, holding my wife tight, and close my eyes, reveling in the moment.

She thinks I gave her strength, but I didn't. It was always there, waiting to break free. She gave me a daughter, love, and more than I could ever give her. But damn it, I'll spend the rest of my life trying to show her what she means to me and how grateful I am for her to become mine.

As she sings the last word and our bodies stop swaying to the beat, I grab her face and cover her mouth with mine. The moment's sweet, slow, and everything it should be.

We turn to take a bow, and I see him. Standing in the back of the room, clapping slowly and leaning against the wall with a smile, is my father.

"Fuck," I mutter, and I know shit's about to get crazy.

FLOW

www.chellebliss.com
CHELLE BLISS
USA TODAY BESTSELLING AUTHOR

Flow

Men of Inked: Southside

by

Chelle Bliss

COPYRIGHT

Published by Bliss Ink & Chelle Bliss
Published on October 2nd 2018
Edited by Silently Correcting Your Grammar
Proofread by Julie Deaton & Rosa Sharon
Cover Photo © Wander Aguilar
Cover Design © Lori Jackson Design

Grandma,
I've been blessed to have you in my life. I won the lottery the day I was born into this fun, crazy, and sometimes loud Italian family.

Thank you for making me always feel loved and being the best grandma in the world.

Chelle

CHAPTER ONE

DAPHNE

I didn't think I'd feel this way. Laying eyes on my father after years of him being in prison is kind of like seeing someone rise from their grave.

He's aged a bit since the last time I visited him. Two years into his sentence, he denied any further visitors, including my mom, which didn't sit well with anyone in the family, but most of all her.

I suppose spending years behind bars can age a person prematurely, even someone as strong and stubborn as my father. From everything I know about prison life, nothing is easy, and the evidence is written all over my father's face. The lines around his eyes, which used to be faint and barely visible, are deep and stark against his olive skin. His black hair has larger swaths of white, mostly framing his handsome face.

Ma's the first one to make her way to him, throwing her arms around his shoulders as soon as she's close enough. My father holds her tight, tucking his face into the crook of her neck as he lifts her off the floor and spins her in the air.

They've been through this before. My dad has spent most of my life in and out of prison, never learning his lesson.

There's a brief moment of hope as I watch them embrace, hoping he's *reformed* after this last stint. But then again, he's Santino Gallo, and he's never seemed to learn.

They say you can't teach an old dog new tricks, but I disagree. My father learned; he just ignored the hell out of the lessons, preferring to live life on his own terms, always bucking the system.

Lucky us.

At first, no one seems to notice my father's presence besides my mother and me. But then, just like something out of a movie, the music stops playing, and the entire room goes silent. All eyes are on my parents, watching as they embrace.

I lift the whiskey to my lips, taking another sip as I try to collect my thoughts. The moment should be a happy occasion, but part of me is pissed. This is Lucio and Delilah's day, not my dad's, but he always finds a way to make everything about him.

"Well." Angelo comes up behind me and places his hands on the bar. "This should be interesting."

"One word for you." I set down my empty glass and turn to face him. "Clusterfuck."

"Maybe he won't be so bad this time," he tells me, and we both start laughing.

We know the thought is utter nonsense.

We know Santino.

We know his tricks.

His lies.

At my father's core is a good man. A loving father and mostly, at least the last time he was out, a faithful and caring partner.

"Pop's back," Vinnie tells us like the entire wedding reception isn't seeing him with our very own eyes.

"Way to go, Captain Obvious," Angelo teases.

Vinnie has had the least amount of time with my father. Being the youngest, most of his life my dad was in prison. Even with that, Vinnie still idolized my father and always thought the best of him. We knew better. Years of disappointment will do that to people.

If it weren't for Angelo and Lucio, I don't know where Vinnie would be. They made him the man he is today, giving him guidance and advice as he navigated his teen years.

"He has the oddest timing. Why can't he ever be

normal?" I ask as I shake my head. "The man has no limits or shame."

"Shit's about to get sideways," Lucio says as he comes to stand near the three of us, with Delilah at his side.

"Aren't you guys happy?" Delilah glances between us. She doesn't know the complexity of my father and the years of his bullshit either.

"Of course we are. He's our dad, but he doesn't make life easy for anyone." Lucio pulls her tighter to his side and kisses her head. "You'll learn soon enough."

"He can't be any worse than my father," Delilah says, putting things into perspective for all of us.

Delilah knows all about messed-up fathers. I'd rather deal with my dad's revolving door at the local prison than her father's alcoholic tantrums.

Even after months apart, her father hasn't bothered to contact her. He really just washed his hands of her, preferring to pretend she never existed than to clean up his act and beg for her forgiveness. At least my dad never did anything to hurt me. He may have been a selfish prick at times, but he never did us any long-lasting harm.

"My *bambini*," my father says as he walks toward us with his arms outstretched like a proud papa and not an ex-con.

He's wearing a new suit, no doubt having planned to make his grand entrance during the wedding without clueing the rest of us in on his release date.

My mother's behind him, glaring at us. We aren't running into our father's waiting arms like she did, and she's not too happy. I love my mother. There's no other person on the planet I adore more than her, but man, she doesn't seem to have a grip or any willpower when it comes to my dad.

I turn around, glancing over at Lucio and pretending my mother isn't giving us the evil eye. "Is he serious?"

Lucio doesn't answer back. Just shakes his head, at a loss for words.

Papa clearly didn't get the memo about our not being overly thrilled about his return. The fact that our mother is asking for us to hire him on at Hook & Hustle—which means telling us, because there's no saying no to Betty—just adds another layer of complication. It sure as hell doesn't help in the feelings department either.

Vinnie's the first one to grab my dad, almost lifting him off the floor in a giant bear hug. "We missed you," he tells him, like he's speaking for all of us.

Which he's not.

I remember a time when I felt like Vinnie. But after the third, or maybe it was the fourth, time we went through the prison release celebration bullshit, I became jaded.

Who wouldn't be?

Saying goodbye to my father over and over again because he can't follow the law gets tiring after a while. When all my friends' dads were attending Father-Daughter dances at school, I had one of my big brothers at my side because my dad was doing hard time for some stupid shit he easily could've avoided. But he always chose crime over his family.

"Jesus," Papa says to Vinnie as soon as his feet touch the floor again. He gazes up at his youngest son and grabs him by the shoulder, squeezing his muscles. "You've grown." My father practically beams with pride.

There's a smart comment on the tip of my tongue about missing Vinnie's last growth spurt. Angelo elbows me, knowing I am about to open my big mouth and probably say something I'll later regret.

Vinnie was in high school when my father last got popped and sentenced to seven years hard time. Papa missed so many milestones. He wasn't there when Vinnie won the state championship or became Illinois Quarterback of the Year during his senior year. Both of which were things we celebrated as a family, minus my dad.

While my dad was away, Vinnie had a big growth spurt, adding a good six inches to his then-already six-foot frame. He's a monster. Wide. Muscular. And everything a star football player should be.

"He's a big boy," Ma says. "Wait until you see him

play."

My papa's staring at Vinnie with wide eyes. Maybe surprised at his size or sad at everything he's missed. The reality of the time he'll never get back has to hit him square in the face when seeing a full-grown man standing in front of him, instead of the teenage boy he left behind.

"I'll be at every game," my father promises.

It's hard for me not to roll my eyes. This happens every time he gets out of the joint. He's full of promises. He means well and probably thinks he'll follow through, but he's always pulled back into the criminal world and away from us.

Lucio leans forward and whispers, "Are we doing an over-under this time?"

The last two times he came out of prison a changed man, we bet on how long it would be before he ended up behind bars again. This time won't be any different. So far, Angelo's two for two, always nailing the exact amount of time before my father is arrested again.

"Years or months?" Angelo asks in a hushed tone.

"Years may be too optimistic," I tell them. "I give him six months."

"I say a year," Lucio replies.

"Nine months, tops," Angelo adds.

I'm not the only jaded Gallo kid. We know my father all too well and aren't fooled by his false promises anymore. Vinnie, though, he's still too innocent and hopeful to let our sourness seep into his system.

My father closes the space between us, arms outstretched like we're having a grand homecoming and couldn't wait to see him again.

I used to be a daddy's girl a long time ago. There was a time when I'd leap into his arms and squeal with delight. She's gone now, but the reality hasn't quite caught up with my father.

"Look at my kids. So grown. So beautiful," he says.

"Dad." There's no warmth in Angelo's voice.

"Pop." Lucio nods.

"Hey, Papa," I say because I've never called him anything else to his face. "You look well."

"Daphne, you've turned into a magnificent creature."

"It wasn't overnight," I blurt out, getting in a small dig about how long he's been gone.

He shakes his head, knowing he's fucked up. "It won't happen again. I'll never go back there. I swear."

My ma's practically hanging on him, happier than all of us to have her man back at her side. She's always been a sucker for my dad. I don't know of another woman on the planet who would put up with his bullshit, but she does somehow.

"This is your new daughter-in-law, Delilah." Ma dips her head toward Dee.

"You're more beautiful than the photos," my

father says.

"It's nice to finally meet you," Delilah replies and runs her hand down the front of her gown, smoothing out the material.

She looks absolutely stunning today. Don't get me wrong, Delilah is always beautiful. But there's something about a bride on her wedding day that'll always knock everyone's socks off.

Lucio and Angelo have their arms crossed, looking like bouncers at a swanky club in their polished suits and big muscles, with absolutely no smiles.

"Don't be that way," my father says and waves his hand in the air. He steps forward and throws his arms around my older brothers at the same time, hugging them. "I'm home now. Don't worry about anything. I have everything covered."

Those are the words we most fear. My dad's idea of having everything covered always involves shady shit and a trip to the police precinct.

"Let's get this party started," my father says, pointing toward the DJ. My father takes my mother under his arm and wraps the other arm around Lucio. "Let's celebrate. This is a big day."

Lucio doesn't even grumble. Maybe the happiness of the day is too big to let my father's presence cast a shadow over everything. The wedding guests start to chatter again as the shock of my father's presence starts to wear off.

"I'm changing my bet to three months," Angelo tells me as we watch them saunter up to the bar. "He hasn't changed a bit."

I know Angelo's right.

Santino Gallo's the same proud, charismatic, law-skirting man he was five years ago when he was arrested. How he convinced the parole board to let him out nearly two years early, I'll never understand. I'm sure he charmed them with his promises of being a changed man. Hopefully this time, he doesn't land on every television news station in the city for whatever crap he pulls because he can't seem to fit into society and be normal.

I crave normal.

I want simple.

But somehow, I never seem to take the easy road…a trait I clearly inherited from my parents.

No one says anything as my father hands out glasses of champagne. We're all staring at each other, trying to pretend we're happy to have him back. We know our mother expects us to act like we're excited, but it's not so easy to pull off. Deep down, we are happy to have him home and safe. How could we not feel that way? He's our father, after all. But that doesn't mean there isn't hurt and anger there too.

"To Lucio, Delilah, and new beginnings." Papa lifts his glass, waiting for each of us to do the same.

"Cincin," my brothers say in unison, finally caving when my mother's eyes narrow.

I chug the champagne, wishing I were buzzed already. Alcohol always seems to make awkward situations like this a little easier to swallow. Right now, I could use a little liquid courage, or as I like to call it, liquid amnesia.

"Santino." Uncle Sal's voice is unmistakable as he comes up behind me.

I turn toward my uncle with the champagne flute still against my lips and lift my eyebrows. I know this is about to get good.

Salvatore Gallo has very little patience for his brother…my father. They are complete opposites except for their faces. If I didn't know better, I'd think they were twins with their salt-and-pepper hair and devilish good looks. But everything else about them is totally different. Uncle Sal is a dedicated family man, where my father cares more about his *business*.

There was bad blood for years. They didn't speak after a falling-out. Tempers have cooled over time, maybe because they're getting older.

Just before my father went back to prison, they had made amends and put the past behind them. But then things changed, and the Gallo name was dragged through the mud, chilling the relationship again. But my uncle Sal didn't let that affect how he treated the rest of us. He knew we were nothing like our father.

"Sal." My father's smiling from ear to ear. "I've missed you, brother."

Somehow, I avoid spitting my mouthful of champagne all over everyone at my father's bald-faced lie.

"You've always had great timing," Uncle Sal says, and his voice is oozing attitude. Standing behind Sal are his children—Joseph, Michael, Anthony, Thomas, and Izzy—waiting for fireworks just like I am.

My father has always called his brother Sal "elitist." He thinks Sal not only snubbed his nose at his roots, but the entire family, when he moved away to Tampa. He did, but not because he was too good for us. My dad was the biggest problem, and the pressure pushing down on Uncle Sal by association was tremendous.

I don't blame him for leaving. I probably would've too if I could have. For years, I thought about changing my name, but I knew it wouldn't help. In my neighborhood, everyone knew my father and our illustrious past, so there was no reason to go through the hassle.

I like my uncle Sal and my cousins too. I only wished they'd stuck around a little longer and been part of my life instead of setting off for the warm sand of Florida when I was young.

My father's attention doesn't linger too long on his brother before turning to Aunt Maria, Sal's wife. "Mar, you're looking better than ever." Papa winks at her in a playful way. No doubt trying to piss off his brother.

"Tino," Aunt Maria says at her husband's side,

but she's not amused or feeling the same playfulness as my dad.

The funny thing is, Aunt Mar is so much like my mother, it's not even funny. They look entirely different, but goddamn, they're both bossy and nosy as hell.

My father's sister looks him up and down. "Hello, Santino." Aunt Fran crosses her arms in front of her chest. "You're looking…" Her voice trails off and her top lip curls.

Her husband, Bear, wraps his arm around her waist like he's trying to hold her back and whispers something in her ear.

In the short amount of time I've spent with Bear, I've found him oddly fascinating. Looking at him, you'd think he'd be all badass, but he's just a giant teddy bear—and a complete pervert too. He has my aunt Fran all tied up in knots, which is something I thought I'd never see again.

After a bad breakup with her first husband, I never thought she'd fall in love again. She was way too fond of track suits and tennis shoes to get much more than a sideways glance from another man. But now, she's like a different person, showing more skin than I'd ever seen her do before.

"Fran, you're a sight for sore eyes." Papa doesn't dare try to touch her.

No other woman, besides my mother, scares the crap out of him quite like his sister. She's a tiny thing, but man, the mouth on her gives me life goals.

"I need a drink," Fran says, glancing over her shoulder at her silver fox husband. "Something stiff."

Bear smirks, brushing his lips against her cheek. "Baby, I got…"

"Don't say it," Fran warns as her top lip flattens.

"What's your poison, Aunt Fran?" I ask.

I want nothing more than to drown the insanity that is my family in the bottom of a few shots of whatever she thinks is stiff.

"Whiskey, baby." She smiles.

"I like it when you drink tequila," Bear whines.

I bite back my laughter. If she's anything like me, I lose all common sense and control when I've had even a moderate amount of tequila. It's not pretty, and I am never proud of the way I behave after I've spent the night with Mr. Cuervo.

"That's why I want whiskey," she tells him and cocks an eyebrow, but he doesn't argue.

"I'll grab a few bottles." I place my empty glass on the bar, ready to go back to the harder stuff.

"My kinda girl," Bear says with a wink.

Izzy, my cousin and Uncle Sal's only daughter, catches up with me as I walk to the other end of the bar, needing a break from my family.

"You okay?" She touches my arm as I lean over the bar and realize my tits are almost spilling out of my dress.

"I'm great. Just fucking peachy." I adjust my strapless bra which is digging into my skin and silently curse Delilah for her ugly-ass choices in dresses.

"I'm here if you want to talk," Izzy says.

My cousin is nothing short of perfect. Her skin is flawless, her hair is spot-on, and her outfit is to die for. But all my cousins are perfect, especially Sal's kids.

Meanwhile, I'm in a hideous strapless chiffon nightmare with so many ruffles on the front, I might as well not have tits because no one can see through the layers anyway.

"Thanks, Izzy. I'd rather not talk about him. Let's talk about you instead. I've heard some pretty interesting rumors."

"Rumors?" She raises her perfectly shaped brown eyebrow and smirks. "Like, what kind of rumors?"

"I hear you have quite the man on your hands. I don't know how you do it. I mean, if some guy bossed me around, I'd probably knee him square in his junk."

I keep my response tame so as not to hurt her feelings. I don't know how much she wants to share, and honestly, what she does in the bedroom is none of my damn business.

Izzy laughs, covering her lipstick-stained mouth with her hand. "It's not what you think."

"He doesn't boss you around and tell you what to do?"

She waves me off. "Only in the bedroom. But everywhere else, I'm the boss."

The bartender walks over and glances at us,

perking up a little even though he's got one foot in the grave. "What can I get you, ladies?"

"Three bottles of whiskey. Top-shelf."

"Three?" He leans forward like he didn't quite hear me right. "You sure?"

I nod and hold up three fingers. "Three."

"It'll be a moment," he says before disappearing.

"A man better give me a whole lot of pleasure for him to tell me what to do in the sack."

"He does." She's beaming, and part of me hates her just a little bit more. "And it's not as bad as you think."

It's my turn to raise my eyebrows and stare. "I can't wrap my head around it."

"You haven't known pleasure until you completely surrender. You should try it sometime."

I want to tell her to fuck off, but I can't. She looks entirely too happy, and her husband is a fine specimen of a man. He could probably make me drop to my knees and beg for an ass-whoopin' too. He's that good-looking. They make a perfect couple with all their perfectness.

It's irritating.

"Here you go," the bartender says, saving me from saying something I'm almost sure I'll totally regret.

"Ready?" I ask her, grabbing the bottles, and dip my head toward the two stacks of glasses the bartender slides across the bar.

She scoops the glasses into her arms and follows me toward the tables where my cousins have already made themselves comfortable.

Our parents aren't there. They're on the dance floor, putting Fred and Ginger to shame.

"We're not waiting for them," Morgan, Fran's son, says as he grabs a bottle as soon as I set the whiskey down on the table.

"Never thought I'd see the day when they'd all be in the same room again." Joe, my cousin, ticks his chin toward the dance floor as he kicks back and takes the glass of whiskey Morgan hands to him. Suzy, Joe's wife, is at his side, curling into her husband but not drinking.

"It's crazy." Michael, Joe's brother, leans back and shakes his head.

I stare at my cousins, wondering what life must have been like for them. Here, there's only us, but there in Florida, they have each other. We used to have Morgan, but that was before my cousins lured him away from us with promises of warm winters and an amazing job.

I hate them all just a little. I shouldn't, though, because they're family. But it's hard not to feel that way. They're all happy and tanned, not looking as pale or miserable as my brothers and me.

"It's weird, right?" Morgan holds a glass in front of his lips and pauses. "But the night's early. There's plenty of time for bloodshed."

CHAPTER TWO

DAPHNE

My legs wobble as I stagger away from the dessert table after consuming more cake than should be allowed for one human being. Walking gracefully is damn near impossible after the amount of whiskey I've already consumed and the ridiculously high heels Delilah made me wear.

I'm making my way through the sea of wedding guests, concentrating a little too hard on each step, when my heel catches. I start to tumble forward and let out a loud screech, knowing I'm about to face-plant onto the dance floor in front of everybody.

My arms flail around, and I'm cursing whiskey for making this all possible as I fall forward. Just as I brace myself for impact, trying to avoid smashing my face, strong arms wrap around my waist and haul me backward.

I blink a few times, staring at the dark green carpet a few feet in front of me where I was no doubt going to land with my dress flipped over my head, letting everyone know I didn't bother with underwear.

My heart's pounding as my back collides with a warm body, and I gasp. "Easy there." The man holds me tightly, saving me from what would've been one of the most embarrassing moments of my life. His voice is so deep, my skin prickles the moment he whispers in my ear.

"Shit." I grab my chest, trying to calm myself after my near-death experience. Okay. Maybe I'm being overdramatic, but at the very least, falling on the ballroom floor in front of the three hundred guests is something I never would've lived down.

"I got you," he says, and this time, the deep honey sound of his voice sends goose bumps streaming down my skin as if a line of dominoes has been tipped over.

His arm is around me, hand gripping my hip on one side, holding me so damn tight I can barely breathe. I turn, glancing over my shoulder at my savior, wondering who the mystery man is, and praying like hell he isn't a cousin.

That would be awkward.

But instead, I'm met by a pair of honey-brown eyes the color of sin and everything unholy. We're face-to-face, his front to my back and his arm still holding me close.

My mouth moves, but nothing comes out. I'm too lost in the way his eyes seem to pierce my soul.

"Are you okay?" the dreamboat asks.

I gawk at him and do nothing to put space between us. All I can do is nod. I don't trust myself to speak without sounding like a prepubescent schoolgirl, and I sure as hell can't seem to walk without totally embarrassing myself either.

His cheeks rise, almost touching the bottom of his eyes, as he stares at me…laughing. Every ounce of mortification I may have felt vanishes instantly, and the dreamboat doesn't seem as hot anymore.

"You can get your hands off me now," I tell him as I narrow my eyes.

How dare he laugh at me. You can't save someone and then laugh in her face at the hilarity of the entire situation.

"Don't be that way," he tells me, as if I'm being completely unreasonable, which I'm not.

"I'm not being any way. Thanks for the save, but you can let go of me now." My teeth grind together, and my body goes rigid.

He tightens his hold and puts his mouth near my ear. "*Bella*," he whispers. "Maybe I like the way you feel against me."

My body betrays me as I practically shudder in his arms because, damn it, I like the way I feel in his arms too.

The deep musk of his cologne permeates the air around us, filling my senses with everything dreamboat. His thumb strokes just below my rib, slowly moving up and down, doing nothing to make pulling away from him any easier.

"Want to get out of here and find someplace quiet to talk?" he asks.

I turn my face toward him again, bringing our lips so close we're almost kissing. I want to ask him if that line works for him, but I don't. There's no doubt in my mind his words sure as hell do work for him.

The whiskey doesn't help me make a rational decision. I should say no. I know that. I should tell him to kick rocks and leave me alone because we're celebrating my brother's wedding and I'm the maid of honor. But tonight, with the way he's looking at me and the heat his body is throwing, I quickly say, "Yes."

Plus, there's the whiskey.

Dreamboat smiles.

I pull away, getting a better look at his face. It's sheer and utter perfection. His honey-brown eyes are only the beginning of what I'd call insanely hot with a dash of let-me-ride-that-face sexy. His square jawline is dotted with just the right amount of stubble to tickle my inner thighs, and his full lips are made for kissing.

This was the first wedding where I didn't expect to

hook up with anyone. Every person in the wedding party was related to me in some way, which left the guests. With hundreds of relatives and people from the neighborhood, I didn't see any orgasms on the horizon when the evening began. But now there's Dreamboat, filling the void of what very well could've ended up being a lonely and miserably drunk night in my hotel room.

Dreamboat licks his lips. I can't stop myself from watching the slow, torturous path of his tongue across his mouth. I should ask his name, but in this moment, I don't really care. He could be named Clyde, and I'd still roll around in the sack with him for a night.

That's the thing about one-night stands…details don't matter—actions do. And based on the way he's holding me and his eyes are blazing, I'm fairly certain he'd be nothing short of spec-fucking-tacular in the sack.

No one notices as we slip into the hallway. Dreamboat's hand is on my back, guiding me through the lobby. I steal a glance his way, risking falling on my face again.

He's staring straight ahead with his chin up, oozing confidence and a whole lotta swagger.

The tailored suit hugs his body in all the right places and is loaded with muscles.

"Wait, I can't just leave like this." I turn to him when we're within feet of the hotel bar, rethinking my stupid decision after coming to my senses. "It's my brother's wedding, and I'm the maid of honor. I can't just ditch everyone."

Dreamboat doesn't even flinch. "You go back. I'll wait," he tells me.

My stomach flutters with the way he's looking at me and the promise of the pleasure he'll no doubt deliver. "Don't do that. It could be hours. If we're meant to be, we'll see each other again," I tell him, drinking in his rugged handsomeness as I step backward and somehow don't end up on my ass.

I'm clearly intoxicated because who says that kind of ridiculous crap.

The answer would be me when I'm plastered.

I leave him standing in the lobby and march away on shaky legs, fanning myself as I head straight back to the ballroom without so much as a backward glance.

The wedding's still in full swing when I step through the double doors. Aunt Fran is dancing on top of the table near the doorway, and a small crowd has assembled to watch her impressive moves. Bear's laughing and trying to get her to come down before the wobbly table collapses, but she bats him away and twists her hips wildly, not giving two shits.

"Happens every damn time," Morgan says as he comes to stand next to me. "She can't hold her liquor."

We stare at his mother, but I can't stop smiling. "I like your mom. Cut her some slack. Someday we'll be old too, and I hope we have enough energy to do that." I motion toward her as she squats down, shaking her ass like she's in a rap video and totally dropping it like it's hot.

"So fucking embarrassing." Morgan covers his eyes with his hand and groans before wandering away.

"Will the bride and groom please come to the dance floor? You know what time it is," the DJ announces, turning the attention away from Fran.

I hate this part of the wedding. There's something so archaic about the throwing of the garter and the bouquet. All the single people at the wedding line up like cattle, exposing our lack of love and our desperation to get hitched someday, with everything hinging on catching an object we'll throw in the trash the next day.

The guests cheer as Lucio and Delilah make their way to the dance floor, holding each other's hand as they walk. They're so happy and so in love, I'm almost a little jealous. I always thought I'd be married by now. I never for one moment figured Lucio would get hitched before me. The man swore off relationships from the day he discovered pussy, but here we are… at his wedding.

Michelle spots me from across the room and makes a beeline in my direction. The ruffled mess Delilah calls a dress looks so much better on Michelle. Her tiny waist and big tits are no match for the layers. And her blond hair, pulled back in a tight bun, shows off her long neck line, her soft facial features just adding to the perfection. "Where the hell did you go?" she asks and points toward the hallway.

"I stepped out for a minute."

The fewer details I give her, the better. I already feel like shit for leaving my brother's wedding, even if it was only for a few minutes.

Michelle's head jerks back like I slapped her. "Stepped out?"

I nod and make a face. I thought my words were pretty self-explanatory. I wasn't about to say I was trying to get my brains banged right out of my head by an absolute stranger before I finally came to my senses.

She puts her hands on her hips, and I know she's about to grill me. "With who? Where?"

"I went to the lobby for some fresh air." I'm lying, but the words slide off my tongue so easily, I even believe my own bullshit for a hot second.

She cocks her head to the side and narrows her eyes. "Who's the guy?" she asks without missing a beat, knowing me better than I know myself sometimes.

That's how it is between us. We've been best friends since we still had training wheels on our Huffys. We were, and always have been, inseparable. In a family filled with men, she's the closest thing I have to a sister and the person who knows all my secrets.

"There's no guy."

I'm sticking to my story. There's no way I'm coming clean.

She ticks her chin in my direction, eyeing something behind me. "Then, who's he?" She crosses her arms and tilts her head, letting me know I'm very much caught.

Shit.

I don't want to turn around. That would be totally obvious. By the way Michelle's looking at whoever is behind me, they know we're talking about them already. No need to fan the flames of embarrassment.

"What do they look like?"

"Tall, dark, handsome, and wearing a suit."

I roll my eyes. "Jesus, Michelle. You just described every man in this room. Be a little more specific."

"Just look," she tells me.

Like it's that easy.

"What color eyes does he have?"

"Seriously?" She shakes her head, and I know she's judging me. "Did you leave with more than one guy or something?"

"No, no. It's not like that."

"Well, prepare yourself. He's walking toward us and…"

"Daphne." The shivers from earlier skate across my skin, and I know Dreamboat's behind me.

I turn my head and smile. "Hey," I say casually because I don't want him to know what he does to me or for Michelle to think something more happened than the tragic truth of my sad, lonely vagina missing out on what I'd assume would be numerous orgasms.

"Can we talk?" he asks, without even looking at Michelle.

"Give me a minute," I tell Michelle and place my hand on her arm, hoping she doesn't make a scene.

She stares at me for a second before glancing at Dreamboat over my shoulder. "He looks familiar."

"He's one of Lucio's buddies," I tell her.

In all honesty, I have no clue who he is, and a few minutes ago, I didn't really care.

"Be careful." She places her hand over mine. "With your father back, people are going to come out of the woodwork."

"But it's a wedding."

"There's no safe time or place when Santino's around," she reminds me.

That's the cold, hard reality of my father's line of work. There's always a willing someone out there, thinking about putting a bullet in our heads as payback for some fucked-up thing our father did.

"I won't leave with him. I promise."

She stares at Dreamboat for a moment before walking toward the dance floor where Lucio currently has his head up Delilah's dress, making a spectacle of retrieving the garter and taking his sweet-ass time too.

I turn to face the man I very well could've been naked with if it weren't for my regaining my sanity. "Who are you?"

Dreamboat doesn't seem frazzled by my question. He has one hand in his pants pocket and the other at his side, standing tall and just as confident as ever. "I'm Leo," he answers, like his name should clue me the fuck in on something.

I don't touch him, but I want to. I like being near him. I like the way my body reacts when he touches me, and I hate myself for it. "One of Lucio's friends?"

Leo shakes his head.

"Delilah's?"

He shakes his head again.

"Well," I say, wasting time because I'm confused, and the whiskey doesn't make anything easier.

If he's not friends with Lucio or Delilah, then why the hell is he here? Then it hits me. Maybe he's a relative.

Jesus, please don't make him family.

"Cousin?" I grimace, hoping like hell he'll shake his head again.

Leo shakes his head again, ending the possibility that I almost banged my own blood.

Thank fuck.

"I know your father," he says casually, like it's not a big freaking deal.

This can't be happening.

I want to slap myself in the face…repeatedly. Out

of all the men at the wedding, I had to almost hook up with someone who associates with my father. A mobster and an ex-con.

Yippee.

I should seriously get the gold star for this one.

By the looks of Leo, he totally fits the mold of the smooth, handsome, and irresistible bad-boy gangster Hollywood has always portrayed.

"My father invited you?"

I didn't even know my father was out of prison until he showed his face tonight. But clearly, other people knew, including Leo.

"Not exactly," Leo replies, being cagey.

I cross my arms over my chest, unable to stop myself from staring at this hot-as-fuck guy. And when I say hot-as-fuck, I mean off-the-charts, panty-melting, ride-him-until-I-die kind of sexiness.

"You're friends with my father, and you tried to sleep with me. That's fucked up."

Leo smirks. "I never said I was his friend."

At this point, I'm confused and too drunk to form any type of rational thoughts. I don't have time to ask any more questions because Johnny, my father's friend and business associate, is heading straight for us.

He doesn't look happy, but then again, Johnny's rarely sporting a smile.

"Look out," I say, because if Leo isn't my father's friend, Johnny isn't coming to say hello.

Leo turns around, and his cocky smirk vanishes as soon as he lays eyes on Johnny. "I better go."

But before he can move, Johnny is so close to Leo, they're practically standing nose-to-nose. "I'm going to be nice about this because we're at a wedding," Johnny says, staring Leo straight in the eye and almost foaming at the mouth.

Oh shit. This isn't good.

Leo doesn't seem fazed by the way Johnny's gritting his teeth like a dog ready to attack. "I was just leaving," Leo tells him.

"You have some balls showing up here, kid." Johnny pushes his fingers through his gray hair, smoothing back the sides.

Leo squares his shoulders, not backing down. "I wanted to see with my own eyes." He's not afraid of Johnny. That much is clear.

"Don't come near Tino's family." Johnny's eyes slice to me, and I know he doesn't like me talking to Leo.

I'm eventually going to get an earful, but it has always been hard to keep up with who's who in the Chicago mob world.

"Especially his daughter. She's off-limits."

His words don't sit well with me. My father's business has nothing to do with me or my life. He stopped calling the shots somewhere around the time he went to the joint for my entire middle school years. But that doesn't stop Johnny from trying to run my life.

"Johnny, I'm grown. I can make that choice," I tell him with one hand on my hip, throwing him tons of shade.

Johnny's eyes darken immediately. I can see he doesn't agree. "Do you have a death wish, Daphne?"

"Who's going to off me?" My eyes slice to Leo the dreamboat. "Leo?" I laugh nervously.

Leo has been a complete gentleman. Well, if you don't count trying to get me up to his room to fuck my brains out not that long ago.

"You know who Mario Conti is, right?"

It's hard not to know Mario. He and my father were friends back in the day until Mario decided to split from the family and form his own. Since that day, my father and Mario have been mortal enemies.

"Uh, yeah, Johnny. I know the name well."

Johnny pitches his head toward Leo. "This is his kid."

I gawk at Leo, wondering if he was, in fact, going to off me as soon as we were alone. The thought doesn't seem as wild and stupid as it did a few seconds ago. Was there a hit on me? Jesus, the thought sends chills down my spine.

"Were you going to…" My voice drifts off. I can't seem to bring myself to say the words. They're horrifying.

Leo shakes his head. "I only had one thing on my mind."

"Get the fuck out," Johnny says and points toward

the door. "You have thirty seconds to get your feet moving, or I'll toss you out on your ass. Wedding or no wedding, I will make an example of you."

"Johnny." I draw his attention back to me as I touch his arm. I want to talk to Leo alone without my father's henchman nearby. "Give us a minute, and then he'll leave. Don't make a scene at my brother's wedding. Please."

Johnny stares at me but doesn't move or speak for a moment. I think he's going to fight me on this, but he doesn't. "Thirty seconds," he says before he steps backward, keeping his eyes on Leo until he's a few feet away.

"I can't believe you."

Anger, rage, and hurt well up inside me.

How could I have been so stupid?

"Daphne, listen." Leo's dark eyes bore into me, and that sexy, sinful look from earlier seems more sinister with the knowledge of who he is. "I wasn't going to hurt you."

"Mm-hmm." I'm not convinced.

Leo reaches between us and takes my hand in his. The warmth of his palm sends tiny bolts of lightning throughout my system, and I instantly wish everything could be different. The way he looks at me is unlike how any man has ever looked at me before. Maybe it's not sexual like I'd imagined, but filled with rage and hatred instead.

He sweeps his thumb across the top of my hand in

slow, steady strokes. "I like you. I like you a lot, and that's dangerous for both of us."

Well, that's the understatement of the year.

"Right now, you're the only one in danger." I pull my hand away even though I like the way he touches me. Then there's his face. Damn, Leo's all kinds of sexy, and it kills me to say my next words. "Just go, Leo. Go before you ruin my brother's wedding."

"See me again," he begs.

Everything in me wants to say yes, but then I see Johnny giving me the stink eye, looking like he's about to go all Tony Montana on Leo. "It's better if you keep your distance. I don't date mobsters anyway."

"I'm a businessman."

"Sure, you are. And I'm Mother Teresa."

"We're not done. I'll find you," he promises.

I don't know if I should be excited about that statement or scared to death.

CHAPTER THREE

DAPHNE

My head throbs as I pull the sheet over my face, trying to block out the sunlight streaming through the annoying little slit in the curtains. My tongue sticks to the roof of my mouth as I try to swallow, getting the first taste, which I'm not sure any amount of brushing will ever wipe away.

Last night, I had way too much to drink. I totally blame Morgan for continuing to ply me with alcohol long after Leo left. Aunt Fran was partially to blame because she got the ball rolling with the bottles of whiskey, sabotaging my plans to stay sober.

"You're awake," a deep, gravelly voice says beside me.

I freeze as my eyes widen.

Who the fuck is next to me?

I knew I was trashed, but I didn't think I'd had so many shots I wouldn't remember inviting someone back to my hotel room, but clearly, I did.

Lying here, thinking about last night, I remember being at the reception, laughing with my cousins. But for the life of me, I don't remember walking through the lobby, the ride up in the elevator, or the last few steps to my room.

Shit.

This could be bad.

Like, really bad.

I squeeze my eyes shut and say a silent prayer, hoping like hell I didn't sleep with one of my brother's friends. Either way…this has to be my dumbest moment of my entire life.

Well, at least the second dumbest because that time under the football stadium bleachers with Tommy Pasquale probably takes the cake. But I've blocked that memory out for so long, I refuse to breathe a whisper of it to another human being for the rest of my life.

Maybe the guy and I passed out, and neither of us will remember a thing about last night. That would be the best scenario at this point. I can at least hope that will be the case. Maybe he was so drunk he couldn't even get it up, or I'll find him completely dressed and on top of the sheets because he was a complete gentleman.

A hand slides across my bare thigh and puts all doubt and hope I have to rest. "Please, God," I whisper.

Rarely has the Almighty come to my aid, but there's never been a time I needed him more than right now.

The bed dips as the stranger rolls closer. When his bare skin touches mine, I know my prayers have most certainly not been answered. By the way his morning wood is digging into my thigh, I can probably assume we fucked too.

"Morning, *bella*," he says.

Oh shit. For real? I close my eyes again, and flashes of leaving the hotel come flooding back like giant slaps in the face in that perfect spot that makes you feel like your skull's going to explode.

My entire body goes rigid. Leo's naked. I'm naked. His cock is touching me, and I can't remember a damn thing.

Just great.

"Did we…?" I suddenly feel ill.

I don't give him time to answer. I don't even care I'm naked as I roll off the bed and run toward the bathroom, knowing I'm about to hurl every single thing that could possibly be left in my stomach into the toilet.

Leaning over the porcelain goddess, I gag, waiting to vomit, but nothing comes. My chest heaves, and tears sting my eyes with the realization I've fucked up by sleeping with him.

Not just a little, but so damn big.

After growing up surrounded by men who easily could've walked straight out of *The Sopranos*, I told myself I'd never get involved with anyone in the family *business*.

My father ruined the sexiness Hollywood had portrayed. I knew the lifestyle wasn't as glamorous as many people believed. Besides that, mobsters were dangerous as fuck. But out of all the guys in Chicago, why the hell did I have to sleep with one who's the son of my father's enemy?

The tears fall fast and hard as the stupidity of the entire situation hits me.

"You okay in there?" Leo asks from the other side of the door.

I can't help myself. I start to laugh as the tears plop onto the seat of the toilet, popping like my shame.

The doorknob jiggles. "I'm coming in."

"No!" I yell and bite down on my lip, trying to stop the giggles that have suddenly taken over. "I'm fine. Go away."

"No, *bella*. Not until I know you're okay."

"I'm fine. Just fucking great." I start to laugh louder than before and slip, falling backward and hitting my back against the bathtub. I howl like an injured wild animal as the edge digs into my skin.

Leo doesn't bother asking if I'm okay again before he barges through the bathroom door in all his naked glory.

Well, damn.

My laughter dies. I gawk at his body. My face is covered with tears, both from pain and embarrassment, and I'm as naked as the day I was born.

I'm a mess and in pain, but damn it…the man is fine.

Thick, muscular thighs. Abs that resemble an old-fashioned washboard, complete with the most perfect happy trail, which leads to a long and perfectly thick cock. His pecs are even off-the-charts hot. The man is built. Then there's his face. His dark eyes, full lips, stubble, and somehow, he pulls off bed head.

Goddammit, why does he have to be nothing short of perfection?

"Jesus." Leo scoops me into his arms, not waiting for me to ask for help.

I'm about to slap his hands away, but my back aches and then there's the fact that I'm so hungover, I'm not sure I could make it back to the bed while staying upright.

"Are you hurt?"

I don't answer.

His hot skin against mine is doing crazy shit to my insides and totally scrambling my brain. I've never been that girl. The one rendered speechless by a guy. Somehow, I've turned into her, and Leo Conti's to blame.

He places my bottom on the bed and then starts to inspect my body for any damage. Leo's hand skates across my skin while I'm face-to-face with his cock. I don't mean it's nearby. I mean, if I stick my tongue out, I'll get a taste.

I can't make myself look away either.

He may be my father's enemy, but that doesn't mean I can't appreciate the man and his off-the-charts hotness along with the sheer perfection of his dick. This is by far the biggest clusterfuck of my life.

"I'm fine, Leo," I lie and cover my face with my hands, totally embarrassed and wishing I could get a do-over. "You should go," I tell him and try to keep my eyes on his face instead of his beautiful cock.

If anyone in my family catches Leo in my room, it'll be game over for both of us.

He backs up, his cock waving around like it's taunting me, and places his hands on his hips. "This is my place. Where do you want me to go?"

Fuck my life.

"Why me?" I groan and drag my fingers down my face.

Leo kneels in front of me and pushes my hands away. "You don't remember, do you?"

"I remember," I say quickly, completely defensive.

I don't want to be *that* girl.

You know…the type I clearly am.

The corner of his mouth turns upward. "Tell me what position we did it in?"

I laugh and wince all at once because the tiny monster inside my head is jackhammering away like a boss, probably etching the word "Whiskey" onto my skull as a reminder. "Come on. That's so easy," I scoff.

He raises an eyebrow. "Then tell me."

I mentally flip through every possibility as quick as I can. Since I was drunk off my ass, there's a high likelihood I wasn't on top because…hello, I could barely walk.

Leo doesn't look like the missionary type of guy either, so that's right out the window immediately.

Two down and only a few hundred to go.

"Doggy," I blurt out. I'm almost positive this guy is an ass man. If ass men had a look, they'd be Leo.

The smirk on his face turns into a full-on smile as he shakes his head.

"Against the wall," I say, trying again. When Leo shakes his head again, I know there's no way I can go on pretending that I can remember any goddamn second of last night. "Fine. I don't remember." I feel all kinds of whorish, like I need to run to the nearest church and beg for forgiveness in the confessional.

"You're cute." He slides his massive hand against my cheek and cups my face. "I didn't think you were that drunk, or else…"

I glance away, trying to avoid his dark, penetrating

gaze. "Now, he has morals," I say before he can finish the statement.

"Hey," he says, drawing my eyes back to his. "I always have morals, especially when it comes to women."

Suddenly, I realize how very naked I am. I was so taken by his bare skin, I completely forgot I wasn't wearing a stitch of clothing and had done nothing to shield myself.

"Fuck." I push his hand away and scramble to my feet, taking the top sheet off the bed with me. Wrapping the material around my body, I glance around the room, trying to find the monstrosity I wore last night. "Where's my dress?"

He pitches his head toward the door. "In the living room."

Living room?

"You have a suite?"

He shakes his head, and that cocky, drop-dead-sexy smirk is back. "We're at my place."

"I've got to go." I rush toward the door, not giving two fucks about anything except getting the hell out of here.

Leo wraps his hand around my arm and hauls me backward. "Don't you want a few memories to take with you?" There's a smug grin on his face.

I glance down to where his hand is against my skin and grind my teeth. "You want to keep your cock?" I raise an eyebrow as I gaze up into his eyes.

"You're feisty. I like it," he teases before he releases his grip on my arm. "Tiger through and through." I know he's loving every moment of my misery.

I don't even have time to ask what the fuck that means. I'm all kinds of sideways. "Pretend I don't exist." I run out of his bedroom, scrambling to find my dress to get the fuck out of his place.

Leo leans against the wall in the living room as I scoop my dress off the floor.

I drop the sheet, giving him a full view because he's seen it all anyway. "Get your last look." I yank the dress over my head.

Leo's standing there, arms crossed, looking all kinds of sexy, with his cock waving in appreciation.

"It's the last time you'll see me," I tell him.

"*Bella.*" He closes the space between us in three quick strides before taking my chin between two of his fingers. "You made promises last night."

I gawk at him, blinking uncontrollably and totally lost. "What?" I ask him, not exactly knowing what the fuck he even means by that statement. "I was drunk. You can't hold me accountable for anything I said or did."

He slides his finger against my jaw as his thumb comes to a rest behind my ear. "It means we aren't done. Not by a long shot," he tells me, like he's making all the sense in the world, and somehow, I'm just supposed to agree.

My eyes are locked on his. I can't bring myself to look away, no matter how hard I try. "We can't do this again, Leo."

"We won't. Next time, you'll be sober and begging for my touch."

Butterflies start to buzz around my stomach at his words. Or maybe it's the liquor still sloshing around, waiting for its perfect moment to remind me of all the ways I fucked up. I swallow down every bit of lust this man fuels in me and lift my chin, ever defiant.

He leans forward like he's about to kiss me. I hold my breath, wanting him to both do it and not at all at the same time.

I pull away, moving quickly toward the door, and I glance over my shoulder. "Forget I exist."

"We're not done, *bella*," he tells me as the door closes.

CHAPTER FOUR

DAPHNE

Michelle calls as I'm trying to pull myself together and somehow make myself presentable for the family luncheon at the bar.

"Whore, where did you disappear to last night?" she asks, because Michelle's nosy as fuck.

"I didn't feel well, so I went to bed early."

"I knocked on your hotel room this morning, but you didn't answer."

She's fishing, but I'm not biting.

"I passed out and didn't hear you."

"Let me walk down there now."

"No!" My voice comes out much louder than I intend. I know I have to cover my tracks and quick. "I already left. I wanted to shower at home before heading to the bar."

There's a pause, and I know she's about to call bullshit. "Hmm," Michelle grunts. "I could've sworn I saw you leave with that guy from last night."

I drop my head forward, wishing she would've just come out and said something to begin with. "You're an asshole."

She laughs on the other end of the phone. "I wanted to see what cockamamie story you'd come up with."

"I was so freaking drunk. Why did you let me leave with him?"

"I tried to stop you. I called your name, but you seemed oblivious to everything and everyone except for him."

"What a fucking disaster."

"Well, we've all been there. It's done now. Move on."

"Michelle, that's the thing." I stare into the mirror, giving myself the look my mother used to give me when she was disappointed in my behavior. "You know who he is, right?"

"The hot guy?" She pauses for a second. "Nope."

"Leo Conti."

She gasps. "Shut the fuck up."

"Yep."

"Stop fucking lying to me."

"It's true. God, I wish I were lying," I groan.

"You seriously fucked Mario Conti's kid?"

"Yeah," I whisper and toss my eyeliner pencil back in the drawer. "But that kid is all man." There's no way I can focus enough to avoid looking like someone out of those *How Not to Apply Makeup* videos on the internet.

"You know that's messed up, right?"

"I don't get involved in my father's world. I drank too much. That's my only defense."

"Daphne." I can picture her shaking her head at my sheer stupidity. "Stay away from that man. His father and your father…"

"I know. I know. I don't have plans to ever see him again."

"Was he good, at least?"

"I don't know. I don't remember." I wince as I say the words.

"That's a shame." Michelle laughs. "There's going to be blowback eventually, and it would be nice at least to have a fond memory or two to look back on."

"Shut up. He said he's a businessman. I don't really know anything about him except I made an epic mistake."

"Did he at least have a bangin' body underneath that suit?"

"The best I've ever seen," I say honestly.

"Better than Tommy Pasquale?"

He follows me everywhere.

"Girl, better than any male on the planet."

"Big dick?"

"Perfect. Long and thick."

"Fuck. All the good ones are either taken, unavailable, or off-limits. I swear, it's tough out here."

"From your lips to God's ears." I pull on my sandals, wishing my mother would've canceled Sunday dinner, but that's not her style. "I got to run. I'll see you at work tonight, yeah?"

"I'm going to do some digging before I come in."

"No. Absolutely not. Do not ask around about him, Michelle. I don't want our names linked even in casual conversation."

But I know, no matter what I say, Michelle's going to stick her nose right where it doesn't belong. That's what we do for each other, and it's why she's my best friend. She always has my back. Always. Doesn't matter if I'm in the wrong, she's willing to go down with the ship.

"I'll be discreet," she promises before hanging up.

I'm not sure she even understands what that word means.

An hour later, I'm at the bar, and my father is standing in the middle of the room, clinking his fork against his wineglass to get everyone's attention.

This isn't a normal Sunday dinner. My mother decided to invite the out of town guests to the bar for one last hurrah to close out the wedding weekend.

Thankfully, she didn't cook and was smart enough to have the event catered from Dino's down the street.

"First, I want to thank everyone for coming to celebrate with us. We're overjoyed to have Delilah as part of our family." My father pauses and glances down at my mother, who's beaming from ear to ear. "Second, as the years pass by, Betty and I understand how important family is, and we wanted you to be the first to know we have officially decided to tie the knot."

"You've got to be kidding me," I mutter under my breath, which earns me a kick under the table from Angelo.

"Seriously, Angelo." I stare at him, arms crossed, totally annoyed. "Why now? You can't be happy about this."

My parents have been together over thirty years, but they have never once seriously talked about getting married until this moment. It makes no sense. The time to do it was decades ago when they decided to start a family, not after we're all already grown.

"It makes total sense. They're getting older, Daph."

Angelo's words don't sit well with me. I know the years are ticking by, but I still can't think of my parents as old. Even though they both drive me crazy at times, I can't imagine a world without them in it.

"I need some air."

I quietly excuse myself from the table and slip into

the back alleyway without anyone noticing. I'm leaning against the wall, scrolling through my social media and catching up on all the funny cat videos I've missed, when my father steps outside too.

We stare at each other for a minute and don't speak.

The last words I uttered to my father before they took him away in handcuffs were not the most heart-warming.

In my defense, I was angry.

What girl wouldn't be when her father's about to be locked up for years because of a choice he made, fully knowing the consequences?

My father runs his fingers through his salt-and-pepper hair and stares at the ground as he kicks some gravel. "Hey, baby girl. How are you doing?"

"I'm fine." I tuck my phone into my back pocket and try to be cordial. "Why aren't you inside with your guests?"

He finally brings his eyes to mine. "I wanted to check on you." He ticks his head toward the door. "I saw you run out of there."

"I just needed some air."

"Want me to go?"

"No," I say quickly.

"Still mad after all these years?" he asks.

"I don't know what I am, Papa," I answer honestly.

Part of me is happy that he's okay and back under

the same roof as my mother. But then there's the other part that knows he's just going to be up to his old tricks soon enough, possibly landing back in prison. Each time, he seems to stay out a little longer than before, which has never been easy for anyone, especially my mother.

"You guys have done really well with the bar," he tells me, changing the subject.

"We've worked a lot of hours."

He comes to stand in front of me. It's my first real chance to get a good look at my father with the sun shining overhead.

My brothers get their good looks from my father. The rich olive skin, the piercing eyes, and strong Gallo features. My father's DNA is definitely more dominant than my mother's. I could've very easily had red hair and ivory skin instead of looking every bit the Italian princess.

"Don't forget to enjoy life a little. It passes in the blink of an eye. One day you're young, thinking you can rule the world, and the next thing you know… Bam!" He smacks his hands together, making me jump. "You're praying you make it just one more day."

This is a side of my father I haven't seen before. He's always taken life by the balls without a single care about the consequences. He's never really discussed getting older, but maybe five years with nothing but time to think will do that to a person.

"What about you, Papa? Do you have another five years in you to spend behind bars?"

My father reaches out and places his hands on my shoulders, much like he did when I was a little girl. "Time is too precious, Daphne. I don't want to spend another moment away from my family."

"But?" I can feel there's more to what he's saying. There usually is when it comes to my father. He talks around things, always avoiding what he really wants to say.

"There's no buts."

There's always a but with Santino Gallo.

"You're giving up the life? Going straight?"

The small dimple on his right cheek deepens. "Something like that, kid."

"You either are, or you aren't." I'm point-blank, unwilling to dance around my father's statement.

"I learned a thing or two in the joint."

That's exactly what I was afraid he'd say. Spending five years surrounded by nothing but criminals has to allow someone an opportunity to hone their skills a little bit more. I'm sure he picked up some tricks of the trade, but he needs to remember, every guy in there wasn't smart enough to avoid being arrested.

"I promised your mom I wouldn't go back." When he speaks, he doesn't look me in the eye. "I'm going to stay clean. Be on the up-and-up."

"I really hope so." I mean those words.

There's nothing I want more than to have my father around. If for no other reason than to be there for my mother.

I worry about her being alone.

The last five years have been hard on her. She found hobbies to take up her time, but there's only so many things a person can make before they hit their breaking point.

I wait for him to release me, but he doesn't. He stares at me, pulling me into a tight embrace. "I missed my baby girl," he whispers in my ear.

I feel like a little girl again. I'm hopeful for a minute. Thinking maybe my father has finally grown up, but then I remember he's rarely truthful and getting out of the life is hard, especially for an old-timer like him.

"I missed you too," I tell him because I did miss having him around. Even though he adds a special brand of insanity, the bar and Sunday dinners haven't been the same without him.

"Come celebrate with us," he says, still holding me tightly.

"When's the big day?" I ask out of morbid curiosity.

"We're not rushing into anything."

Of course they aren't because that would be totally absurd. Only my father would think getting married sooner rather than later would be rushing into something. I swear they've had the longest courtship on the planet.

"It's only been thirty years, Papa." I shake my head as I start to laugh.

"What's on your neck?" He leans forward and brushes my hair off my shoulder.

"I don't know. What is it?" I turn my head, giving him a better look.

"It looks like a hickey." He moves closer, inspecting my skin like he used to after I had a date. "It *is* a hickey."

Son of a…

My eyes widen. I know exactly who left me with a sucker bite like we were in high school. "Jesus," I mutter and instantly want to track Leo down and punch him square in his junk.

"I didn't know you were seeing someone."

I look at the ground, avoiding my father's eyes and any chance I'll tell him the truth. "I'm not." I cover the mark with my palm and take a step backward. "Someone was just being an asshole."

"What's his name?" he asks, trying to be fatherly for the first time in over five years.

"We better get inside. I'm sure everyone's looking for us," I say, trying to avoid the conversation entirely.

All I need is for my father to hear the name Leo Conti.

His head would probably explode.

CHAPTER FIVE

DAPHNE

I'M STARTLED AWAKE BY RUSTLING ON THE FIRE ESCAPE outside my bedroom window. Last night, I slept with my window open and the curtains pulled closed, foolishly thinking I'd be safe. I should've known better. But the night's cool air was too hard to resist in my second-floor loft.

Reaching under the pillow, I wrap my fingers around the cold steel handle of a gun. I always keep it there just in case.

I roll onto the floor, thinking I look like someone in an action movie, but I realize I'm missing the sexy swagger. My knees dig into the hardwood, and I grit my teeth, trying to stop myself from crying. As I crawl toward the window, I'm barely breathing, trying not to make a sound.

I crouch down, aiming the gun toward the curtains and resting my finger on the trigger just in case the visitor decides to come inside. Maybe I'm totally overreacting, but I'm not willing to take any chances, especially with my father now walking the streets.

A black leather shoe peeks through the curtains, and I stiffen immediately. "Hold it right there. I have a gun," I yell, but my voice quivers. I'm holding the gun out in front of me, ready to shoot whoever this dumbass is if he moves another inch.

The person freezes. "Don't shoot," he says quickly, and the sound of his voice sends goose bumps scattering across my skin.

I lift my finger off the trigger and let out a heavy sigh. I could've killed him. Not figuratively, but actually killed Leo Conti because he had to crawl through my window like a stalker and a freaking idiot. "What the hell are you doing here?"

"Can I move now?" Leo asks, still frozen with only a foot inside my place and the rest of his body hidden behind the curtains.

"Yes. I won't shoot you… Well, not yet, at least."

The curtains part, and Leo's head comes through the window, followed by his other half. He's dressed in a pristine suit, looking every bit as fuckable as he did on Saturday night.

"Why are you here?" I ask, still pointing the gun at him. Both turned on by his presence and wanting to shoot him too for scaring the shit out of me.

His eyes slowly rake over my body, drinking in every inch of my bare flesh. "That answers that."

"Answers what?"

He rubs the pad of his thumb down the corner of his mouth, looking all hot and shit. "If you sleep naked all the time." He smirks.

I glance down, my heart still pounding, and I'm so filled with adrenaline, I totally forgot I was buck-ass naked.

I place my free hand on my hip and look him up and down, much the same way he's looking at me. "Are you trying to make me shoot you?" I cock an eyebrow.

He takes a step toward me. "God, you're sexy as fuck."

I back up. "Don't change the subject." I want him way too much, and I need to do everything in my power to avoid his touch. "What the hell are you doing here?"

"I wanted to talk." He doesn't stop moving toward me.

The backs of my knees hit the mattress, and I have nowhere else to go. "How about knocking like a normal person?"

He covers the gun with his hand, pulling the cool metal from my grip. "It's too dangerous."

"Crawling through my window isn't exactly safe." I motion to my gun which is now safely in his hand and ignore the fact that our bodies are almost touching. "I could've killed you."

Honest to God, I was two seconds from pulling the trigger. The mess his death could've created would've been astronomical. How would I have explained why Leo Conti was crawling through my window?

"That'd be pretty hard since the safety's on."

I grunt and purse my lips. "I still could've shot you. It's not that difficult to take the safety off."

His eyes twinkle. "I'll take my chances with you over them." He pitches his head toward the window.

"Them?"

Leo leans forward, and I hold my breath, thinking he's going to kiss me. Even though I know it's a horrible idea, my belly flips and my body tingles, wanting his lips on mine way too much.

Instead, he places the gun on the bed behind me. "There are too many eyes on both of us." As he rights himself, the back of his hand brushes against my thigh, whisper-soft.

I shudder and am suddenly breathless, both from the tidbit of information he just dropped in my lap and his touch. "There's no one watching me," I argue.

He tilts his head and says nothing more, but the look he gives me says everything I need to know.

"Seriously?" My mouth falls open. "I've never seen anyone."

"There's always people watching us, Daphne. Our fathers are too important for us to go unguarded or unnoticed."

I always knew my father had protection, but I never really thought about someone watching over me or my brothers.

"Then I better put some clothes on." I start to move, but Leo reaches out and grabs my hand.

"Let's not panic," he tells me as his fingertips scorch my flesh.

He's the enemy.

I repeat that statement over and over again as Leo stares at me with those dreamy, sinful eyes.

I glance down, staring at the spot where our skin touches, and I know I need to take drastic measures. "Move it or lose it."

"What are you going to do, little girl?" he taunts as he swipes his thumb across the underside of my wrist.

I don't know what kind of women he's used to being around, but the one thing I'm not is weak. Growing up with three brothers and a father who didn't live on the up-and-up made it almost impossible for me to be a damsel in distress or anyone's victim. I could punch like a guy and take down a man twice my size without breaking a sweat. It didn't matter that I was naked; I could still put his ass on the floor.

"I'd hate to wrinkle your fancy suit," I tell him, giving him a once-over before staring him straight in the eyes. The corner of Leo's mouth twitches before he finally releases me. "I'll ask again, why are you here, Leo?"

"I wanted to see you again."

"Well, you saw me. All of me…again." I point toward the door. "So, you can go now."

Leo's eyes narrow as he closes any remaining space between us. I hold my breath as he reaches out and brushes a few strands of hair behind my back with his fingers. Even though my breasts are inches from his face, his eyes are locked on mine and nowhere else.

"We're not done," he tells me again.

I can't help but stare back at him.

"There's no we, Leo. There never will be. There never can be. Whatever happened, happened. We'll leave it at that. Two drunk people fucked. End of story. No big deal."

Leo's eyes darken, and he grips my wrist again, tethering himself to me. I know I should pull away, but there's something about the way he's looking at me that makes moving impossible. "First of all, I wasn't drunk."

"So, you took advantage of me? A drunk chick.

Nice." I know it's a complete lie. He didn't take advantage of me. I can guarantee I was more than willing. But I'm sticking to that as the reason why I slept with the son of my father's mortal enemy.

"*Bella*." He sweeps his hand under my hair and rests his palm against my neck. "Nothing happened."

I'm not even listening to him. I'm too upset, mostly at myself, to even hear what he's saying. "Hell, only a sleazebag would fuck a drunk girl."

His tongue pokes out, dragging slowly across his bottom lip. I watch the smooth movement with my lips parted, making it impossible for me to deny the attraction much longer.

His fingers dig into the back of my neck, just below my hair, sending shock waves down my spine. "Daphne, I'm going to repeat this, and you're going to be quiet and listen."

I blink, taken aback by his bossiness and a little turned on.

"We went back to my place to talk. We made out a little bit, but you were so tired, you undressed in my living room and walked—well, mostly staggered—to my bed and collapsed. Nothing happened. I didn't take advantage of you."

"Oh." I stare into his eyes and then realize he's been lying to me. "Wait. What?"

"I'm not a sleazebag."

"Okay." I nod. I don't know what else to do or say.

I feel like an asshole, but come on, anyone in my shoes would've thought the same damn thing.

"I feel like shit that you left thinking we had sex. I needed to talk to you, and I want to take you on a real date."

With the way he's holding me and how he's looking at me, thinking isn't easy. "You what?"

Leo's hot.

Like *GQ* hot with a dash of *Godfather*. Dark hair, dark eyes, lush mouth, and built for riding. He's totally my dream man, minus the fact that we could never be together and his cocky attitude leaves something to be desired…most of the time.

"I want one date, and then I'll leave you alone."

"That's all?"

Going on a date with Leo Conti wouldn't be the worst thing in the world. I'd done crazier shit for men who were not at the same freakishly hot level as Leo. I take that back. They were all hot, but some weren't too bright. Those were the ones I had put up with long enough to go one round, or sometimes two, in the sack before pushing them away, which was pretty easy and comical.

"If you never want to see me again after that, I promise to go away forever."

"One date," I whisper as my belly flutters. "But how? If we're being watched, that would be damn near impossible."

"You let me worry about that, sweetheart."

I have a few triggers, and men calling me by pet names when they don't even know me is one. Most women would think it's charming, but not me.

"Let's get one thing straight. I'm not your sweetheart, your baby, your doll, or your anything. Got it?"

Leo smirks. "I got it, *bella*."

I'm about to reply and tell him off, but before I can, Leo leans forward. My breath hitches as his lips come near mine. I'm staring into his eyes, unable to breathe, waiting for the moment his soft lips touch mine. Wanting it more than anything.

"I'll text you the details," he says and releases me.

My mouth hangs open, and I can't even form words. My skin is still tingling, waiting for him to kiss me, but he's already heading toward the door.

I'm never the girl at a loss for words.

Never.

But I'm standing in my bedroom, unable to move like a moron. I hate the way Leo Conti plays with my emotions and how my body betrays me every time he's around.

Tomorrow night, I will not be a pawn.

"Why do you keep looking at your phone?" Angelo asks.

I look up, not even realizing how often I've come

back to the counter just to see if Leo texted me about our date.

"No reason," I say and smile, hoping he'll drop the subject.

"You never look at your phone at work," he tells me, pointing out the obvious and never letting anyone's bullshit slide. "And that smile—" he points at me and drops his chin "—is bullshit."

"Fine. If you must know, I'm waiting for a call."

"Must be pretty important."

"It's not, Betty," I tease him.

He's being nosy as fuck, just like our mom. Angelo's usually the one to mind his own business, but tonight he's a little too interested for my liking.

He pushes five beers in front of me. "Take these to table five." When I don't move right away, he says, "Please."

"Only because you asked nicely." I quickly glance down at the blank phone screen before grabbing the beers and hustling toward table five.

"Sweetheart, settle a bet," one of the men says as I set the beers down at their table. I let the little nickname slide because one, he's a paying customer, and two, I've been called worse.

I tilt my head and place my hands on my hips. They're so intoxicated, I'm sure their pressing question is going to be a doozy. "Shoot," I tell him with a quick nod.

"Can we be crass?" the guy closest to me asks, and I'm honestly impressed he uses such a big word.

"Sure."

"Okay, so… You've been dating a guy for a month, and it's finally the big day you two are going to do it." The guys around the table are all giggling like schoolgirls except one, the guy I assume they're all making fun of with this little question. "You're about to get busy, he drops his drawers, and his penis is so small it's almost an innie… What do you do?"

I honestly feel bad for the guy. I don't know what's worse—having the world's tiniest penis, or his friends knowing about it.

"He better be damn good with his tongue," I say.

The looks on their faces are priceless.

"So, you wouldn't end the relationship?" another guy asks.

I shake my head. "Let's face it, boys. Someday, all your dicks won't work and will be useless anyway, but a tongue is forever." I smirk as their mouths hang open.

I turn my back and head toward the bar, but I stop dead when I see Angelo staring at my glowing phone.

Oh no. Shit.

I walk faster, and any sense of victory from moments ago is gone. I quickly snatch my phone off the bar as soon as I can.

"So, who's *The Best You'll Ever Have*?"

I stare at my phone, seeing the funny little name he must've put in my contacts when I was sleeping or you know…passed out.

"We're just friends." I slide my finger across the screen, opening the entire message, thankful Angelo could only see the nickname.

I'm typing out a reply when Michelle walks up to us and looks over my shoulder. "Who are you texting?" she asks, being just as nosy as my brother.

"The best she'll ever have," Angelo tells her.

I glare at him. "Don't start," I warn.

"Daphne, you can't be serious," Michelle says because she knows exactly who we're talking about.

"You know him?" Angelo raises an eyebrow, getting all intense.

I turn to her and narrow my eyes. "Shut your mouth, Michelle," I whisper.

"No." Michelle smiles at Angelo and shakes her head. "I don't know him, know him."

I'm ready to reach out and wrap my fingers around her neck, strangling the life out of her and the ability to rat me out. She's my best friend and is always supposed to have my back, even when I'm fucking everything up.

"He's just some guy we met," Michelle says, covering for me and therefore saving her own life.

Angelo isn't buying what she's selling, but he doesn't have time to argue because a customer on the other end of the bar is waving him down. One of his female regulars who only wants him.

Michelle snatches the phone from my hand. "You can't be serious with this shit. You know how dangerous he is?"

I grab the phone back before stuffing it into my back pocket to avoid anything else being seen. "He said one date and he'd leave me alone," I tell her.

"A man like Leo doesn't do just one date, Daphne."

"How would you know?"

"I heard about him." She raises an eyebrow as her lips flatten.

"Heard what?"

"I'm just warning you now he's not someone you could be involved with." She pauses and rubs the back of her neck, glancing around to make sure no one's listening. "There's your father. Plus, I heard Leo doesn't like to give up control and can be a complete dick."

"It's only one date. What could go wrong?"

Michelle rolls her eyes and glances up toward the ceiling. "Everything."

CHAPTER SIX

DAPHNE

Leo's text was cryptic. He simply said to be ready at six and wear a dress with heels. He didn't drop a clue as to where he's taking me even though I asked many times. He only sent back a quick reply that stated, "You'll see," and left it at that.

When I make my way downstairs and open the door to my building, I expect to see Leo, but he's not here. Instead, there's a man dressed in a black suit with dark sunglasses, and a fancy car parked at the curb.

"Good evening, ma'am," he says, dipping his head slightly.

I peer to the left and then to the right, waiting for Leo to pop out of somewhere and yell surprise.

"Mr. Conti is waiting for you at your destination."

"Where are we going?" I ask with a shaky voice as I pull the door closed behind me and wonder if I'm walking to my death.

I'm headed off to God knows where. Maybe it's a trap. Anything's possible with my father now out of prison. Leo could very well be kidnapping me to hand me over to his father in some crazy-ass Chicago mafia coup d'état.

"I'm under strict orders not to reveal a single detail." The driver walks ahead of me, and I follow like a lamb stupidly heading to slaughter.

"Wait." I stop and grab my phone out of my purse. I shoot Leo a text, asking what the fuck he's thinking sending a strange man to my door when I'm already apprehensive about going out on this date to begin with.

The man folds his hands in front of his chest, watching me, not the least bit amused.

Leo: Just get in the car, Daphne.

Easy for him to say.

He's the one in the know, while I'm clueless and supposed to trust a man I barely know.

Sure, he's hot as hell, but beyond that, I only know our fathers hate each other.

I punch in a quick reply, trying to take deep breaths before I hyperventilate.

Me: You could be kidnapping me.

There's a brief pause before he starts typing something back.

Leo: I could've done that when you were passed out. Just get in the car. It's a surprise.

Me: I hate surprises. They don't mesh well in my world.

The driver's phone rings, and he turns his back to me before answering the call. "Yes, sir," he says quietly. "I understand."

I tap my foot, waiting for someone to give me a straight answer or I'm turning around and calling off the big date. "Well?" I say as soon as he faces me again.

"Mr. Conti has instructed me to tell you we're going to the airport. But beyond that, he'd like to keep it a surprise."

"The airport?" I nearly choke.

"Ma'am, Mr. Conti has chartered a private plane for the evening. Now, if you'll please." He motions toward the car. "I don't like to keep him waiting."

"I'm sure you don't." I walk past the super stiff driver and head toward the car.

He rushes in front of me, grabbing the handle before I can and opening the back door. "Ma'am." He pauses and straightens, somehow looking even stiffer than before.

I slide into the back seat and look around the

sleek, black-leather interior, kind of impressed with the lengths Leo's going to for our date.

The driver gets in and doesn't say a word as he pulls away from the curb. I stare out the tinted windows, wondering if I'll ever make it back home again and know I have to tell someone where I'm going just in case.

Me: Leo's taking me on a plane ride. Private jet. If I don't come back, he did it!

Michelle's going to have something to say about the unplanned trip. She was already pissed I was going out with Leo, but now that I'm taking a plane ride to God knows where, she'll be livid.

So instead of reading her text messages chastising me for being an idiot, I tuck my phone back into my purse and enjoy the view from the seclusion of the back seat of the luxury sedan.

My hands are practically shaking as we pull into the airport on the outskirts of town. The sun's setting behind the trees, splashing the sky with vibrant yellows and stunning oranges like something out of a painting. Leo's standing at the base of the stairway, looking just as handsome as ever in another expensive suit. There's no smile on his face until the driver opens the door and I step outside.

"You made it." He walks toward me. "Decided I wasn't going to ransom you off or kill you?"

I laugh nervously, knowing I had been ridiculous.

"I'm trusting you, Leo." I peer up into his deep, rich eyes. "Don't break that trust. I don't give it easily."

Leo places his hands on my upper arms, and the spark I felt before zaps me again. "I promise to have you back before the sun rises and in perfect condition."

I wouldn't mind a little imperfection if it included a round in the sack with Leo as a parting gift, of course. But then I remember having sex with him will only complicate matters even more than they already are, and I decide I will not sleep with Leo Conti.

I place my palm flat against his chest, feeling his heart beating out of control just like mine. "Something has been bothering me." I keep my eyes locked with his. "I need to know one thing before I get on the plane with you."

"Ask me anything. I have nothing to hide." He doesn't blink.

I glance toward the waiting jet and clear my throat. "My brother's wedding."

Leo nods, bringing my attention back to him.

"Why were you there? I know you weren't invited."

He slides his palms up and down my arms, stirring the lust seated deep in my belly. "It's a long story. Why don't we get on board, and I'll tell you everything? We have an hour before we land."

"Not good enough," I tell him, but I don't back

away. My mind is telling me to run, but my body's not listening.

Leo's palm slides down my arm before covering my hand resting on his chest. "I was in the hotel and just stopped in. I never meant to talk to anyone or be seen. I promise to tell you whatever you want to know once we're on the plane, but we're going to be late."

"Late?"

"For our dinner reservations."

"Which are where?"

I know I'm being difficult and I'm fishing, but damn it, surprises have never been my thing. I've had too many in life, especially when it comes to my father. I like to know what I'm walking into before I'm smacked in the face with reality.

"Nashville," he says finally. "Figure there's no chance of the old guidos seeing us there."

"We could've just gone to the Little Village for some margaritas."

Leo shakes his head and sighs. "Their reach is everywhere in Chicago, even with the Mexican cartel."

I open my mouth to say something, but nothing comes out. Leo's been dropping information left and right when I'm with him, and it's all news to me. I figured my father's business was far-reaching, but I never really thought about how vast his network could possibly be.

Leo holds my chin between his fingers. "I promise you won't regret tonight."

I stare into his eyes, looking for any reason not to go. "Okay," I say when I don't find any.

Leo leans forward, still holding my chin, our eyes locked. "I promise you'll have a good time," he says softly with his lips practically touching mine.

My breathing slows, and time almost seems to stop as he hovers just out of reach. His brown eyes darken, and the way he stares at me leaves me nothing short of needy.

"Not here," he whispers before backing away.

My hand falls from his chest, and I'm left gasping for air, trying to recover from the nearness of him.

I've never felt this way with anyone.

No one except Leo Conti.

I think back to the moment I met him up until now. I haven't stopped craving his touch, his kiss, his everything.

His hand is on the small of my back as we walk on to the plane. He greets the pilot, introducing me, but leaving my last name out of the entire brief conversation.

There's just the three of us for the short flight. A bottle of chilled champagne is waiting near the leather sofa that runs down one side of the plane.

Leo motions for me to sit before he pours two glasses. "Buckle up," he says with a smirk as the plane starts to taxi down the runway. "It may be a bumpy ride."

No truer words have ever been spoken. There's nothing smooth about the storm that's brewing inside me and the hurricane barreling our way if I don't put an end to whatever this is before we touch down again in Chicago.

The takeoff isn't as smooth as I'd hoped or am used to in a commercial airplane. I've never been fond of flying, and being in a small private plane doesn't alleviate the anxiety that has settled deep in my core.

After I quickly polish off the first glass of champagne, I pour myself another and pray it will be enough to calm me down.

Leo places his hand on my knee, which hasn't stopped shaking since the moment the plane lifted off the ground. "Are you okay?"

I smile nervously and wave the champagne flute between us, almost spilling the contents in his lap. "I'm great. Fine. Never been better," I blurt out, making it quite obvious I'm a hot mess.

He squeezes my knee. I take a deep breath, trying to focus on my breathing along with his deep, penetrating gaze instead of the fact that we're high in the air.

He turns on the couch next to me, bringing his knee against mine, connecting our bodies once again. "You asked why I was at the wedding." He pauses as he sets his champagne flute on the table at his side.

"For weeks, I'd heard rumors your father was being released from prison. When I saw the last name for the wedding party in the grand ballroom, I thought I'd stop in and see if he was there."

My entire body rocks backward. "You were stalking us?"

"No, no. It's not like that."

I raise an eyebrow and cross my arms, carefully holding the champagne flute in front of me. "It sounds exactly like that."

"I'm like you, Daphne. I have nothing to do with my father's business, but somehow, his world bleeds into mine. Especially when one of his enemies is after him. We both know the bloody histories of our fathers' business endeavors."

I nod, but I'm not quite sure I have a firm grasp on it like Leo does.

"I needed to see with my own eyes if Santino Gallo was really out, walking the streets again."

"You think my father would order a hit on yours?"

"I have no doubt my father would order one on your father if he deemed it necessary. Why would your father be any different? Hell, they'd probably kill us and not even blink."

I open my mouth to speak and close it again. I'm in complete and utter shock. None of us is involved in my father's hustle. Not in any way are we even remotely tied to his business dealings besides the simple fact that we were born.

"That's ridiculous," I tell him.

Leo moves even closer. "I needed to know if your father was released and if I had to increase the security around my sisters and myself. We're not part of their world, but it's very easy for us to become casualties."

I think back to the wedding, the moment I tripped, and how Leo caught me. "You swear you didn't know who I was when I left the ballroom with you?"

He holds his hands up. "I didn't know at first. I never went to the wedding with the intention of sleeping with Santino's daughter. After you fell into my arms, I wanted to talk to you."

"When you asked me to go somewhere quiet, you were going to fuck me, weren't you?" I'm straightforward with my questioning.

His hand is back on my knee, stroking the spot that makes my belly tighten. "There was a spark between us from the moment I touched you, Daphne. I've never felt that with another person. Maybe it's your fiery mouth or your beautiful lips, but I can't stop myself from wanting you. Couldn't keep myself from taking you home that night and thinking about you nonstop since the moment you walked out of my place, leaving your scent in my bed and turning my world upside down."

I swallow roughly, knowing exactly what he's talking about. From the moment I first heard his voice, my body has responded to him in every way. Even his touch sends goose bumps across my skin. I should hate him. I should stay away, but Leo makes that impossible, and my body's reaction isn't helping.

"Our fathers are enemies. You said it yourself, neither would think twice about offing one of us. Normal people don't hop on private planes to fly to a different state to stay under the radar for a date. There's so much wrong with this, Leo. So much is fucked up about the entire situation."

Leo's grip tightens on my leg. "And yet, somehow, there's so much that's right. Tell me you don't feel it."

God, I want to tell him he's wrong and to go to hell, but I can't seem to get the words out of my mouth. I'm having trouble even thinking. Leo's too close, his skin on mine, and the plane's vibrating, reminding me we're high in the air.

Leo Conti could very well be my undoing.

CHAPTER SEVEN

LEO

Up until the plane ride, I hadn't given Daphne one good reason to think I was an honorable man or trustworthy in any way.

Hell, I didn't even bother to correct her when she thought we'd had sex. It was a sleazeball move, but I liked her thinking we'd done more than actually sleep together.

Tonight, I'd reserved the chef's table at the fanciest and most exclusive steakhouse in Nashville. Dining in the kitchen gave us more privacy, and I didn't want her looking over her shoulder most of the night instead of keeping her eyes on me.

Daphne fidgets, touching the silverware on both sides of her plate as soon as we sit down. "This is impressive."

"Nothing but the best," I tell her, pouring the champagne I selected earlier for this special occasion.

"You really shouldn't have gone to all this trouble," she says as she takes the champagne flute from my hand. "It's beautiful, but I'm really a simple girl."

"There's nothing simple about you, Daphne."

She blushes and looks away before lifting the champagne to her lips.

"Leo, my dear friend," Martin, the chef and owner, says as he approaches our table.

"Martin, thank you for having us this evening on such short notice."

"Ah. Anything for you. Your lady is quite beautiful." He smiles at Daphne, no doubt just as struck by her beauty as I am. Daphne's blush only deepens as Martin continues to talk. "But you've always been a lucky bastard."

"I've never been as lucky as I am tonight." I wink at Daphne, wanting her to know exactly how I feel.

"I have to get back to work, but your first course will be ready shortly."

"Thank you," Daphne says to Martin with the sweetest smile.

"It is entirely my pleasure, madam." He tips his

head, drinking her in in much the same way most men do when they cross her path.

"He seems really nice," Daphne says, watching over my shoulder as Martin is no doubt putting on a show. "Have you known him long?"

"For a few years. We used to work together before he decided to open this restaurant. I helped him get it off the ground, becoming part owner until he was able to buy me out."

"Well, that was nice of you."

"It was purely a business decision," I tell her, but I would've done anything for Martin. He helped me launch my hotel in Nashville, ensuring it was a success in an already flooded market.

"I find that hard to believe," she says, smiling at me over the rim of her champagne flute.

"I'm a good guy, Daphne." I feel like I'm pleading my case, trying to get her to think of me as someone other than Mario's son.

"I realize that now."

"Can I ask you something?" I stare across the table at the most beautiful woman I've ever seen. "What makes you tick?"

She leans forward, holding the champagne flute in one hand and looking way more delicious than anything Martin could ever serve. "My family and my business."

My answer would be the same. But someday, I'd like to have my own family. As the years roll by, I realize I'm not getting any younger, and the need to settle down becomes stronger and more urgent.

I lean across the table and brush a few strands of hair away from her eyes, but my touch lingers. "What brings you pleasure?"

The candlelight flickers across her face as her eyes darken, and she moves into my touch. "Right now, you do," she admits. "And you?"

"Being with you."

"We shouldn't do this," she whispers.

"Do what? We're only talking." I feel absolutely no guilt for how I feel or what we're doing.

I don't care about our families, our friends, or any repercussions that could come out of our evening together.

"We're doing more than talking, Leo," she says softly, blinking slowly and seducing me even more.

Martin clears his throat, interrupting the moment we were just having. "Can I just say you two make a gorgeous couple? Never have I seen two people more perfect for each other."

Daphne and I exchange a look over the table before I reply. "Thank you, Martin. We don't want to get ahead of ourselves. This is our first date."

Martin sets down the plates he's been holding. "I'm so sorry. I misspoke. I never would've guessed this is your first date."

"It's fine." Daphne smiles easily. "It doesn't feel like our first date either."

"Well, enjoy the Oysters Rockefeller. They're the house specialty and an aphrodisiac." He winks before leaving us alone again.

She relaxes back into her seat and stares at me across the table. "You're not what I expected. Not at all."

I raise an eyebrow. "Is that good or bad?"

"Well, I figured you were an asshole."

"Oh." I laugh. "I am."

"Not really."

"No. I really am, but maybe you're too blinded by your feelings for me to see it."

Daphne smirks. "Hardly," she whispers.

We're halfway back to Chicago, and I know my time is running out to get her to agree to another date. Even though I asked her for only one, I sure as hell want more.

"I like you, Daphne. I don't care what your last name is. I don't care who your father is or who my father is. I don't care that it's dangerous to be around you. I don't care that if your father finds out, he'll probably end my life before I can blink. All I care about is you. The way your skin feels against mine. The way your breathing changes when I touch you. I want all of it. I'm not ready to walk away without finding out what this is between us."

"It's a lot for me to process," she says, totally not going where I wanted after professing what's happening in my head.

Daphne's been staring at me all night. Practically undressing me with her eyes like she did the night I met her. Her lips may have said one thing, but her body has always portrayed the opposite.

The straight line across Daphne's top lip dips. "Leo," she whispers and shakes her head as she sits next to me on the plane. "Tonight was nice, but we could never work."

"Why? Give me one good reason." I'm being pushy, but nothing is ever gained without being relentless.

"Um." She laughs softly. "The possibility of one of us dying is a pretty damn good reason, you know?" She shrugs with a crooked smile.

"We're all going to die someday, Daphne, but it's how we choose to live that's most important."

She stares at me for a minute, blinking with her lips parted. I can't tell if my statement was a home run or the proverbial nail in my coffin of anything possibly happening between us.

"Did we at least kiss that night?" she asks.

I cover my mouth to hide my smile. This woman has me all kinds of crazy, and I can't seem to stop myself from wanting more. "You don't remember anything?"

Daphne shakes her head. "Not really."

"Nothing?" I ask again in complete shock.

"Not a minute after the reception," she tells me. "I think I would've remembered things if they were that earth-shattering or life-altering, but I have nothing. There's not even a hint of a memory."

I slide closer, wanting to be near her. "We didn't even kiss. But I want to kiss you," I tell her, needing to touch her lips more than anything in the world. "I'm going to kiss you."

Her eyes widen, but she doesn't pull away or protest. I place my fingers under her chin, holding her eyes to mine.

"If there's no spark, no connection, and you feel nothing, we'll call this quits. You can walk off this plane, and you'll never hear from me again. But," I say and pause, leaning forward a little more and bringing my face closer to hers. "If you feel what I do, we see what happens. We owe ourselves that much."

She doesn't say anything as she stares deep into my eyes. Daphne's barely breathing, and the air around us is thick and crackling with lust.

Her gaze drops to my lips as I move forward. I'm hungry for her. This girl has my body, mind, and soul all tied up in knots. She's like some great cosmic joke, making me fall for the one girl in the entire city of Chicago I shouldn't be falling for.

I slide my hand up her cheek, cupping her face in my palm as I press my lips to her soft, inviting mouth. The same electric shocks I felt before vibrate throughout my system as our bodies connect and our breathing becomes synchronized. She moves into my touch, her body craving the kiss as much as my own.

I want her. I want her more than I've ever wanted anything or anyone in my entire life. I'm used to getting what I want, but Daphne Gallo isn't going to be an easy conquest. She's going to fight me tooth and nail, and I'll use any weapons necessary to win.

My fingers press into the nape of her neck, tipping her head back and allowing me to kiss her deeper and harder than before. She moans softly, sending the electric sparks scattering across my nerves, shocking my heart out of rhythm.

Sliding my other arm around her back, I pull her closer, wanting to feel her body against mine. As if on cue, she crawls into my lap, settling her warm, lush pussy against my agonizingly stiff cock. She digs her fingers in my hair, kissing me back with more fervor and passion than she did the night we met.

She feels. She can't deny what this is. The lust. The passion. The want. The need. It's there. It's undeniable. It's not love. It's not caring. It's sexual and inescapable for both of us.

She tips her head back, giving me full access to her neck. I slide my lips down her jaw, following a path to her pulse. Her heart's pounding feverishly, matching my own. I tangle my fingers in her hair, holding her in this position so I can feast on her flesh.

The plane drops, and Daphne gasps, stilling in my

arms. "We're safe, *bella*," I whisper against her skin before distracting her with my touch. "I got you."

When I bite down gently on the soft spot near her shoulder, she relaxes in my arms and lets out a soft moan. She grinds against me, rocking her core across my cock. I'm a goner. Any resistance I have is quickly slipping, making it impossible for me to go slow.

"I want you. I need you," I admit, knowing full well the explosive pleasure our bodies produce together. I'm not the type of man to admit such things. Especially not so early and with an unknown outcome. But Daphne Gallo does that to me. She makes me different from my usual self. She makes me…better.

Her fingers fall from my hair and are at the buckle of my belt, working quickly to release the metal prong, and I'm silently thanking the man above for letting her feel the spark too.

I release her hair, sliding my hands down her sides until I find the hem of her dress. Her skin's soft and warm, calling me to touch every inch and lose myself in her completely as our mouths fuse together again.

She pulls at my zipper, yanking the metal down easily and exposing the head of my cock. Her fingernail brushes against the tip, and I'm momentarily breathless. When she reaches inside, wrapping her silky fingers around my hard shaft, I almost lose it.

I need to be inside her. I need to feel her around me more than I need the air I breathe. I shove her dress upward, exposing her bare pussy, and dig my fingers into the tender flesh of her ass. She scoots forward, placing her wetness against my hardness.

She lifts her bottom, one hand on my shoulder, and stares at me. With my cock in her hand, she says, "I feel it too, and I'm about to fuck it out of my system."

I don't argue.

I'm up for the challenge.

I'm about to fuck her so good, she'll be begging for my cock again. This isn't our goodbye. I refuse to let her throw me away, making me nothing more than a warm body and a hard cock with an expiration date.

Daphne drops down on my dick, impaling herself on my entire length as she digs her fingernails into the skin underneath my dress shirt.

The pain and pleasure mix has my head spinning and my ability to breathe almost nonexistent. I don't want this fast. I want her slow. I want to feel every inch inside her and for her to feel me buried deep within her for days.

I grip her hips, slowing the pace as I swivel my hips, making sure to hit every pleasurable spot inside her. Her head tips back as she moans, giving up control to me. Rocking into her, I thrust my hips upward as I pull her downward, slamming our bodies together in unison.

She cries out, her hand still on my shoulder, nails

digging into me, and I'm fucking loving every moment of this. Daphne's brown hair cascades down her back, sweeping against my pants as she tethers me to her with her grip.

"You feel that?" I ask as I pummel her slick pussy with my entire cock.

She moans, not giving me the answer I want verbally, but her body convulses as I speak.

"Do you feel the way I want you? The way I need you?" My voice is rough and my breathing even more ragged than before. "Look at me," I order her, wanting the connection deeper than just the flesh.

Her dark brown eyes connect with mine, and something snaps. I pull her face to mine, crashing my lips against hers as I pick up the pace, thrusting my cock deeper and harder than before. I'm chasing the high only Daphne Gallo gives me.

Her insides constrict around me, sucking me deeper, stealing my breath. Her body's pulling out the orgasm I'm not ready to give. I want more of this. I want more of her.

She bucks against me and pushes my hands away, bucking and bouncing on my dick as her tongue dances with mine.

I'm lost.

I'm a goner.

I'm completely addicted to Daphne Gallo, and I've never been so completely fucked in my entire life.

CHAPTER EIGHT

DAPHNE

"What's that?" Michelle moves my collar aside and gasps. "Did Leo do that again?"

I slap her hand away and cover the spot I thought I had concealed. "I fell," I blurt out, but we both know it's bullshit.

That bastard. He left a bruise on my neck where he bit me on the plane as I rode him through multiple orgasms. I no longer regret the claw marks I no doubt left on his shoulder either. I now realize he's quite fond of leaving a mark somewhere on my body, and not in a discreet place, which I'm sure is part of his master plan.

Michelle grabs the side of her head and grunts. "Are you fucking stupid, or do you have a death wish?"

At this point, I'm thinking a little bit of both. Why else would I be drawn back to Leo…repeatedly?

Angelo walks behind the bar and narrows his eyes, zeroing in on the hickey on my neck.

"Lower your voice." I motion toward my brother with my chin, not wanting him to hear a word of our conversation.

She glances at Angelo and smiles like she's covering our tracks and totally failing. "Answer the question." She doesn't even move her lips when she speaks.

"I ended things," I tell her.

At least, that's what I told him when I kissed him goodbye as we stood outside his plane on the runway. Even though we fucked like rabbits and he quite possibly may have given me the best orgasms of my life, I wasn't sure I could see him again.

There is no future for us.

How could there be?

Our families are enemies, and by extension, so are we.

Michelle crosses her arms over her chest, cocking her head to the side and giving me a look. "Are you sure?"

"Of course," I scoff and wave my hand in the air. "Totally."

She narrows her gaze. "He may be on the up-and-up, but we both know his father isn't."

"Neither is mine," I remind her, but she knows my father just as well as I do.

Michelle grew up in the life too. Her father worked for mine until he passed away five years ago in a tragic car accident. She wondered for a long time if it was a hit, but so far, we haven't found any evidence. My father swears there was no war going on and everything that happened to Eddie, Michelle's dad, was accidental.

She glances up at the ceiling. "Is it really over between you two, or are you bullshitting me?"

"Yes. It's really over," I say, but I don't even convince myself, and I know Michelle doesn't buy it either.

"So, it was that good, wasn't it?"

"What was?" I play stupid.

"The sex." She shakes her head, annoyed with me. "You said he had a perfect penis and the best body you'd ever seen."

"Girl." I let out a loud sigh. "He was the best ever."

"Toe-curling?" The corner of her mouth ticks up.

We've always been honest with each other and never hid anything before… Why start now?

"Everything curling. I'm in trouble here, Michelle. Real trouble."

"Daphne, your phone is vibrating across the bar," Johnny says as he lifts my cell phone up and stares at the screen. "Who's The Best You'll Ever Have?"

"Oh fuck," I mutter and leave Michelle behind, marching straight to Johnny and plucking my phone from his grip.

Angelo looks at me, and I can see the questions already swirling around in his head. "Who you seein', Daphne?" Angelo finally asks as I jam my phone into my purse underneath the bar. "It's not the first time he's called."

I don't turn around, keeping my back to him because it's easier to lie when I don't have to face him. "No one."

The words are almost truthful. I'm not seeing Leo. Well, not anymore, at least. We aren't a thing. We fucked. Okay, we fucked a few times, but that doesn't make us a *thing*.

"You were MIA last night, and now you show up with a hickey on your neck again," he says.

"Fuck," I whisper and close my eyes, pretending to dig in my purse for something that's not there. "I fell down. That's what the bruise is from. It's not a hickey, jagoff."

"So, you fell and hit your neck?" His voice rises on the last word.

I lift my face to find Michelle staring at me,

twisting her lips as she tries to hide her laughter. I give her a look that's nothing short of deadly. "Something like that." I stand, finally turning toward my brother and somehow keeping a straight face. "Anyway, I'm fine."

"And the phone call?" He raises an eyebrow.

"Just some random dude."

Angelo looks to Michelle and she nods, but there's no smile on her face. She's the lamest liar on the planet. Although she'd be the first person at my side to fuck shit up, she'd also be the first one singing to the cops and confessing all our crimes, especially if Angelo were the detective. She's always had a thing for him, even though she tries to hide it. I'm not stupid or blind.

"Yeah. He's no one, really," Michelle says with the fakest laugh I've ever heard.

Angelo doesn't say anything more, but his eyes are still on me. There's no way in hell I'm telling him anything more than he needs to know. And right now, he doesn't need to know about Leo.

I start to walk away, satisfied that the conversation's over, when Angelo says, "Billy saw you at the little airport outside of town last night."

I freeze mid-stride with one leg in the air, waiting for the proverbial other shoe to drop. My eyes are wide and locked on Michelle, and she looks just as horrified as me.

That fucker has been leading me on, knowing full

well I was with someone, but playing stupid, trying to get me to crack. But I'm a pro. Growing up Gallo has taught me a thing or two…evasion being one of those skills.

"He said you were with some guy getting on a private jet last night. Billy said the guy looked familiar, but he couldn't place his face. Well, not yet, at least. Did you take a little trip, sis? Maybe with the Best You'll Ever Have."

I spin around on one heel like I'm a freaking ballerina and stare down my brother. "I don't have to tell you anything. Mind your own business." He dips his head, and the corner of his mouth tips upward, making me angrier. "I don't ask you who you're screwing, and you don't get to ask me, big brother."

I give Michelle a smile, feeling mighty impressed with myself and my ability to hold it together even under Angelo's penetrating gaze. Well, to be fair, my back was to him most of the time, but still.

"I don't care who you're with, Daphne. Just be careful and be smart."

Careful—I had been careful. Leo was careful because he knew there were eyes on us. Smart. That was something entirely different. If I were smart, I wouldn't have agreed to the one date, and I most definitely wouldn't have banged him, officially becoming a member of the mile-high club.

I stalk back to the bar, grabbing my purse and

phone from under the countertop. "I'm always smart, Angelo. Always," I lie.

I march out of the room, making my exit, and head to the alley. I'm already listening to Leo's voice mail when the door slams behind me.

Daphne. I can't stop thinking about you. You said goodbye, but I know you didn't mean it. I'll be at your place tonight. Don't shoot me.

I can't wipe the smile off my face, but then I remember the possibility of one of us winding up dead.

Me: It's too dangerous. Someone saw us at the airport.

I tap my foot, waiting for him to text me back, but when nothing comes, I take a step back inside. I'm not even three feet down the hallway when my phone finally rings.

"What do you mean someone saw us?" I can hear the worry in Leo's voice.

"One of my brother's friends works at the airport. He ratted on me."

"Fuck," he hisses.

"I don't think we should see each other again, Leo. It's too dangerous. You were careful, and someone still saw us."

"Do they know who I am?"

"Since the guy works at the airport, I'm sure he can figure it out."

"The plane's registered in the company name."

"And which company would that be?"

He still hasn't told me much about his work besides the fact that he's in no way involved with his father's business. I wasn't going to push the subject, but since he brought the topic up, I think, what the hell. Why not?

"Excellence Hotels."

"Like *the* Excellence Hotels?"

My brother's wedding was at the Excellence. Now, the reason for Leo to be at the hotel made perfect sense and how he knew which couple was celebrating in the grand ballroom that evening too.

He wasn't stalking my family, after all.

"Yes," he replies.

"Are you, like, the CEO or something?"

"I own the hotel chain, Daphne."

My mouth hangs open. I knew Leo was wealthy, I knew Leo had class, but never did I think he was the owner of one of the biggest and most elite hotel chains in the country.

"Well, okay," I say, still in shock from the truth bomb he just dropped on me. "We still shouldn't see each other again. When I said goodbye, I meant it."

"We'll talk about it tonight," he says and hangs up.

I gawk at my phone in disbelief.

He hung up on me.

Fucking Leo Conti just hit end on our conversation without letting me get another word out, and I had plenty to say.

"Are you working, or are you going to chitchat all day?" Angelo asks, scaring the living hell out of me.

"Jesus," I mutter, grabbing my chest. "I'm coming."

Angelo stares at me. He knows something's up. I just hope he doesn't find out who I've been seeing because I know he'd have something to say about it. He hates my father's business as much as I do.

I jam my phone into my back pocket and walk toward the bar, brushing against his shoulder as I pass by.

I'm busy pulling down the new bottles for tonight's service when my mom pushes through the front door, carrying an old bicycle frame in her arms with the biggest smile on her face.

"Look at this beauty." She lifts the rusty heap higher when she approaches us.

"It's… It's…" I don't know what to say to her. I know she wants to hear how wonderful the hunk of junk is, but I just can't seem to find the right words. It's a rusty mess, but to her, it's a work of art.

"It's great, Ma," Angelo says quickly, saving me before I utter something I know I'll regret.

Her smile grows larger as she rests the frame on the floor. "I know exactly what I'm going to make, too."

My mother has become interested in reclamation art or, as I call it, junk. When my father was sent away to prison, Ma needed to find a hobby to pass the time, and why she didn't pick up crocheting or knitting, I'll never understand.

Instead, she takes what other people throw out and repurposes it to create a "work of art"—her words, not mine—that no one ever wants to buy.

I feign interest because well…she's my mom, and I can't be disrespectful. "What?" I ask, but I don't really care to know the answer.

She holds the frame with one hand and takes a step back, staring at the rusting disaster. "Picture this." She waves her hand between the frame and herself. "I'm going to use this as the base for a coffee table. Maybe I'll use glass for the tabletop. Wouldn't that be fabulous?"

"Sounds great, Ma," Angelo says, always the one to kiss my mother's ass.

"Ass-kisser," I mouth, rolling my eyes so only he can see.

"Daphne wants it for her living room," he tells her with a shitty smirk. "She's been talking about getting a new coffee table for a long time."

My mom starts to clap, excited at the thought of me finally displaying a piece of her work in my place. "It's serendipity," she chirps.

With my back still to my mother, I glare at Angelo and flip him off. "I'll get you back," I mutter quietly before turning to face my mother. "I'd love to have it, Ma, but I hate glass. Can you at least make the top metal or wood?"

Part of me is hoping I'll kill her vision and she'll decide to keep the table for herself, but I should've known that wasn't my mother's way.

"Sure, honey. Anything you want." She's so happy I almost feel guilty that I want a solid top to hide the fact that there will be a piece of junk holding the entire thing up. "I'm going to go out back and start working on it." She grabs the bike frame, and before either of us can say another word, she scurries toward the hallway to her "art studio" in an abandoned garage behind the bar.

"That's going to look amazing in your place, Daph." Angelo laughs.

"You're an asshole!" I yell as he walks toward the other end of the bar, avoiding the dagger I'm pretending to throw his way.

CHAPTER NINE

LEO

I'M WALKING THROUGH THE LOBBY ON MY WAY TO SEE Daphne when I spot my father sitting at the hotel bar, sipping on a glass of brandy. He never comes here. Not unless he wants something.

We've always had an agreement. He keeps his business out of my hotels, and I try to ignore the fact that he's a criminal.

"Hey, Pop," I say, motioning to the bartender to pour me a drink because I have a feeling I'm going to need it. "What brings you here tonight?"

"I heard you were in the old neighborhood the

other night." He swishes the brandy around the inside of the glass, beating around the bush instead of coming right out and asking me what he really wants to know.

That's my father's way.

He'd always pry but pretend he wasn't actually fishing for information.

Tonight, my father looks tired. The lines near the corners of his eyes seem deeper than the last time I saw him. There're more gray streaks running through his perfectly placed black hair. Time is catching up with a man who has seemed invincible my entire life.

"I was," I tell him, sliding the whiskey in front of me as soon as the bartender sets the glass down.

"It's not safe for you there." My father glances across his shoulder at me. "I thought you were smarter than that, Leo."

"I have nothing to do with your business, Pop."

His brown eyes narrow. "You're my son. Whether you like it or not, you're a target because you're my blood."

I take a sip of whiskey, listening to him go on and on about the danger I put myself in by going into enemy territory. I let him say his piece without argument because there's no reasoning with the man.

"I forbid you to go there again," he tells me like I'm a little kid and, somehow, he's still in charge of my life.

I lean back and stare at my father, wondering if

he's high on a power trip or growing senile. "I'm a grown man. You no longer get to tell me where I can and can't go in the city."

"The Gallos are dangerous, my son. Santino is out of prison now, and I'm sure there will be a power play for him to regain some of the territory he lost in his absence."

"Maybe he's done with the hustle and is a changed man after prison."

My father laughs cynically. "There's no such thing. Prison only makes someone harder." He pauses for a moment as he takes a sip of brandy before continuing. "And a better criminal."

My father should know. He's spent his fair share of time behind bars. Mostly when I was younger because he was a hothead, craving the spotlight and trying to live out his *Scarface* fantasies.

"If something happens to me, the blood will be on your hands. I'm not part of your business and won't let your world dictate my life."

His stare turns colder. "If someone touches you, a war will break out. You are my child no matter how old you are, Leo. I will always try to protect you."

"Maybe it's time to retire, Pop. Ever think of that? Live a normal life away from the violence and without having to look over your shoulder constantly."

He cracks a smile. "There's no other life for me. Since your mother died," he pauses and does the sign of the cross, "God rest her soul, there's no reason for me to quit."

My chest tightens. "Then we'll have to agree to disagree."

He places his hand on my arm, which is as close to affection as my father can seem to muster with me. "Nothing good can come of you going there."

He's wrong about that. If he knew I was meeting with Daphne Gallo, he'd literally shit a brick before stroking out on the barstool next to me. But that's his problem, not mine.

I polish off my drink before rising to my feet. "I have to run, Pop. Anything else?"

He stares straight ahead, looking at the mirror behind the bar. "I don't like getting reports on your whereabouts, Leo."

"Then stop having me watched. Call your bulldogs off and remind them I'm not part of your business. I'm off-limits."

"Naïve," he mutters before I walk away.

I leave him sitting at the bar, nursing his drink and probably stewing over the fact that I don't seem to follow his advice.

My sisters are so much better than I am at listening to my father. They always have been. They're all pampered princesses, willing to take the dirty money to maintain the cushy and over-the-top lifestyles they grew accustomed to.

But I am nothing like them and never will be.

DAPHNE DOESN'T LOOK EXCITED to see me parked next to her Jeep behind the bar a little after midnight. "What are you doing here?"

"Get in."

She stares at me, blinking a few times, but she doesn't move. "You hang up on me, and now you're telling me to get in your car?"

"Yeah." I smirk.

No matter what she's saying, I know she's going to get in. She can act offended all she wants, but I know it's a front. The way she kissed me said everything I needed to know when it comes to Daphne Gallo.

"It's not safe for me to be here. So, get in the car so we can find someplace more private to talk."

Daphne glances around, looking into the darkness. I planted the seed, and that's all I needed to do before she marches around the back of my car and slides into the passenger seat.

"I'm here," she announces as she slams the door and then clears her throat. She folds her hands in her lap and stares out the front window, practically ignoring my presence.

I pull onto the street, heading toward my place where I know there's no one watching. "We've got to talk."

"I thought I said everything I needed to at the airport."

God, she's such a hard-ass. The woman doesn't give in about anything, especially when it comes to her feelings.

We're sitting at a stoplight, and she still hasn't glanced in my direction. "You didn't mean it." Those words make her turn, and I could give two shits if it's out of anger. I have her attention now. "We both know that."

"I promised you a date. I gave you what you asked for, and I kept my word. We both know we'd never work. So, why force it?"

I don't answer her question as I pull away and maneuver through the streets of Chicago. I spend a few minutes planning my next move, my next words, and how I'm going to proceed with Daphne to get her to admit what she's feeling.

I don't need a profession of love, but knowing we're both on the same page physically would be nice. Everything else can be figured out later.

Since neither of us is involved in our father's businesses, there's nothing stopping us from seeing where this goes.

Once I pull into the secure underground parking below my building, I stop looking in the rearview mirror to see if we've been followed and finally relax. "Are you seeing someone else?" I ask as I park the car in my reserved spot and cut the engine.

"That would infer I'm seeing you, which I'm not. I'm seeing no one."

I shake my head and smile. I don't know if I've ever met someone as maddening or stubborn as her. Why I enjoy her sharp tongue is beyond me. There're plenty of women who would enjoy being with me, and hell, they wouldn't put up this much of a fight.

Maybe that's why I like Daphne so much.

She isn't easy.

She doesn't give a rat's ass who I am or what I have, unlike some of the women I've had in my life.

"Come up for a bit, and then I'll take you home," I tell her as I open my car door, trying to at least get her into my place. Once I have her, I know she won't be so fast to leave.

She stares at me for a moment, not saying anything. I figure she's about ready to tell me to fuck off and take her ass home. Everything that's coming from her mouth is hinting in that direction, but she surprises me. "No kissing. Only talking. Got it?"

"Of course. I'll be a complete gentleman," I promise her.

She's out of the car before I am, stalking toward the bank of elevators just a few feet away. Her hips sway with each step, shaking her ass at me in a silent tease. She knows exactly what she's doing. She knows she drives me wild.

"Don't you miss the old neighborhood?" Her back is to me as she looks up, watching the floor numbers ticking by as the elevator descends.

"Sometimes."

Daphne and I grew up only a few blocks from each other. Back then, our fathers weren't enemies and life was less complicated. I remember her brown hair, pulled tight in pigtails, blowing in the wind as she'd ride her bike down the street, terrorizing the other kids. She was a pistol then and hasn't mellowed with age.

She gives me the side-eye as she glances over her shoulder. "Why are you looking at me like that?"

"Just remembering you as a little girl." My smile widens. "You haven't changed all that much."

"That's funny," she says, turning back around as the elevator dings. She steps inside, walking all the way to the back before facing me again. "I can't seem to remember you."

"I remember plenty about you." I don't take my eyes off her. "I remember the pink bike you rode around the neighborhood, bullying half the kids to get your way."

"I loved that bike." Her eyebrows draw downward. "Why don't I remember you?"

"I'm older, and I didn't go to St. Catherine's."

"Ah. Wait. So you did know who I was at the wedding, then. I mean, we grew up with each other. How could you not know?"

"The last time I saw you, you were seven. You've changed a bit."

When shit went south between my father and hers, we moved out of the neighborhood and away from everyone and everything I ever loved. It wasn't until years later that I really understood why we'd had to move.

She grabs her breasts, lifting them higher and giving me a show in her V-neck T-shirt. "I know I didn't have these," she teases, knowing full well she's driving me mad and loving every second of the sweet torture she's inflicting.

I close my eyes, wishing the elevator moved a little faster or I lived on a lower floor. "Your mouth hasn't changed at all."

CHAPTER TEN

DAPHNE

Leo's penthouse is nothing short of amazing. With the floor-to-ceiling windows, sleek hardwood floors, and modern furniture, everything about the place screams single male and excess wealth.

"Make yourself comfortable," he says as he tosses his keys on a table near the door.

I walk toward the windows, soaking in the decadence. The city lights twinkle in the distance like a cloudless sky, sparkling against an endless backdrop. "The city's beautiful from up here."

Leo stands behind me, his body heat licking at my

back. "I've spent many nights staring out across the city."

I smile over my shoulder, but I don't let my gaze linger too long. His cocky smile and luscious mouth are like my kryptonite, making it almost impossible for me to hold true to my promise to be done with him. "I can see why. It's so beautiful," I say, keeping my focus on the skyline in front of me.

"Want to sit outside?"

"Yes," I say quickly. I know staying inside means we'd sit on the couch, and the likelihood I'd end up in Leo's lap or in his bed is extremely high. I need to maintain a safe distance because my willpower around him is damn near nonexistent.

Leo grabs a bottle of red and two wineglasses before I follow him onto the patio. I'm not planning on staying long enough to polish off a bottle, but Leo doesn't seem to care. I settle into the chair near the railing, on the opposite side of the table, and swallow down my fear of heights.

The best course of action is to get right to the point and not to veer off topic. "What did you want to talk about?"

Leo stares at me for a moment as he pours two glasses. I drink him in, noticing the silver cuff links sparkling like the stars above our head. They're expensive, just like his penthouse.

"I need to know who saw us at the airport."

"You're not going to…" I pause and look out

across the city, wondering if I should tell Leo the man's name. While the physical attraction to Leo is undeniable, I don't know enough about him to know if he's dangerous or not. I bring my gaze to his and soak in his piercing eyes. "You know…"

"I'm not going to hurt anyone, Daphne. I'm not my father," he says.

"Fine. All I know is his name is Billy. I don't know a last name or what he does, but he knows my brother and was all too quick to call him and report on my whereabouts."

"I'll take care of him." He hands me a wineglass like he didn't just say he was going to off someone, and my eyes widen in horror. "I'll talk to him," Leo corrects and shakes his head slowly. "Again, I'm as much like my father as you are yours. Stop thinking the worst of me."

I glance down, running my fingers along the base of the wineglass. I feel so out of place and like a fool. "What are we doing here, Leo?"

"Talking," he says like it's that simple.

"I know that, but why?" My gaze flickers to his for a brief second, but the lust is too strong, and I have to look away. "I told you we were through. I sound like a broken record at this point."

"If my father wasn't my father and your father wasn't yours, would you still be telling me there's no future for us?"

I don't answer right away. I ponder the question

along with the complexity and simplicity of the entire situation. I want to lie to him. It would be easier for both of us if this were nothing more than a passing attraction. I really wish I'd fucked him out of my system, but that only seemed to make matters worse.

"I don't know," I say honestly. "You're busy. I'm busy. There's not much time to plan a future when we're both dedicated to our work."

He studies my face, and I can feel the heat of his gaze. "What's more important to you, work or family?"

"Family, of course."

That's a no-brainer. Family always trumps business. It's the main reason we shut down the bar for half the day every Sunday. We decided that we didn't want any interruptions during our family dinner, and there always seemed to be a crisis at the bar that needed our attention.

Leo leans back and undoes the top button on his dress shirt, exposing just enough skin to draw my attention back to him. "Do you want a family of your own someday?"

"Someday," I say in a deeper tone, unable to hide what the sight of him does to me. "But not yet."

His fingers work at more buttons on his shirt. "So, if we were just Leo and Daphne, not Conti and Gallo, we'd have a shot?"

He knows what he's doing to me. The smirk on his

face tells me as much. It's only fair since I toyed with him near the elevators first.

"Maybe," I sigh and look away. "Who knows. I don't spend much time thinking about what could be when reality seems to smack me in the face every day, constantly reminding me I'm a Gallo."

"My father questioned me today," he confesses.

"About us?" I swallow the lump that's now lodged in my throat.

"No, but he heard I was in the old neighborhood." Leo rubs his hand across his face, trying to cover the frown I know is there. "He warned me to stay away. He said your father was a dangerous man."

I laugh at the stupidity of the entire situation. "See? We would never work."

"Maybe," he admits as his gaze drops to his wineglass. "But I've never been one to let my father dictate my life."

"Me either." But that doesn't mean I don't heed my father's warning every once in a while.

Leo leans forward and pushes his glass to the side. "I'm not ready to give up on whatever this is, Daphne." He slides his hand across the tabletop and places his palm on my arm, reminding me of the sparks I feel every time we touch. "Life's too short to deprive ourselves of finding out."

I stare across the table, wanting to say yes, but something stops me. I could easily fall in love with Leo

—hell, I was in full-blown lust already. "I need time to think," I say, hoping it's enough to satisfy him.

"Stay the night."

"I can't." My heart wants to stay, but I know nothing good will come from another night with Leo. I'll fall a little harder and a little deeper, making my ability to resist him even weaker.

"Another time, then."

I shake my head, because there won't be another time. There can't be. "You're persistent."

His stare intensifies. "Only when I know what I want."

I pretend to ignore his statement even though my stomach flutters and my heart practically skips a beat. "I think I should go." I need to get away from him before we fall into bed and I never want to go back to reality.

"I'll take you back to the bar."

"No," I say quickly. "I'll grab a cab."

"It's late, and the bar is far, Daphne. Don't be silly."

My phone rings in my purse, and I scramble to answer it, without looking at the caller ID. It's well after midnight, and there's never good news at this hour. "Hello," I say, watching Leo across the table.

"Where the fuck are you?" Michelle asks. "Your Jeep is here, but you're not. Angelo is going to stroke out when he notices."

"Tell him I'll be back in thirty minutes. I had to help a friend or something."

"Are you with him?"

"Michelle…"

"Daphne, so help me God—" she starts to say, ready to give me a lecture, but I cut her off.

"Don't breathe a word to my brother. Cover for me."

"I'm not a good liar," she tells me like I don't already know this. "I'll buy you some time, but you better get your ass back here because I can only entertain him for so long."

"Find a way," I say. "Flirt with him or something."

There's a pause from the other end. "I'll do my best."

I jam my phone back into my purse as I stand. "I have to leave now. Things are getting too complicated, and someone's bound to find out."

Leo follows me to the door. "This is it, then?" he asks, and the look in his eyes tugs at my heart.

"We're both in danger. This has to be the end." My voice wavers on the last few words.

Leo moves closer. "I want things to be different."

I resist the urge to say the same thing. It won't make this easier or change anything. We can wish all we want, but that won't do a damn thing. I'll still be a Gallo, and he'll be a Conti, making any type of relationship between us impossible.

He snakes his arm around my back and pulls my

body flush against his. He's staring into my eyes, intense as always, and he leans forward. I love being in his arms, surrounded by his scent and caught in his intense gaze. I slide my hands up his arms, gripping his delicious biceps and tethering myself to him.

"Goodbye, Daphne," he says softly with his lips only a few centimeters away from mine.

My gaze dips to his mouth, hoping he'll kiss me. "Goodbye, Leo," I whisper before locking eyes with him again.

His eyes search mine, and all the air inside his penthouse evaporates. My breathing's shallow as I wait for the moment his lips touch mine, praying he'll kiss me one last time. The wait isn't long before he leans forward, bringing me closer, and crashes his mouth down on top of mine.

Any breath I have left is instantly stolen. His kiss is demanding, rough, and makes my toes curl. There's no goodbye in the way his tongue slides against mine. Only a promise of something more, something better.

I pull away, breaking the kiss before I become too consumed and lose the willpower to walk out the door. My grip on his arms increases as I hold him at a distance and gasp for air.

He stares at me, breathing just as heavily as I am, but he doesn't say a word. I can't bring myself to say goodbye again, but I know I have to leave. Without speaking, I back up, waiting until the last moment to pull my hands away from his body and open the door.

Leo stands in the hall, watching as I walk backward into the hallway, eyes locked on his for only a few seconds before turning my back and heading toward the elevator.

Why is it so damn hard to say goodbye to him? I don't love the man, but the lust is there and totally undeniable.

A week ago, I barely knew the name Leo Conti, but now… Now, I can't seem to get him out of my system.

CHAPTER ELEVEN

DAPHNE

One month later

"Daphne!" Vinnie yells from the other room as he slams the front door, making me jump. "I'm home."

It's been four weeks since Vinnie went back to college and I said goodbye to Leo. They've also been the longest thirty days of my entire life. Every few days, Leo has two dozen red roses delivered to my place with nothing but the letter L on the card.

They're constant reminders of what could've been if I'd only said yes, but I know I made the right decision, even if my heart doesn't agree.

I drop the pillow I've been holding and run into the living room. "Vinnie!" Flinging my arms around him, I pepper his face with kisses, happy he's here and hoping he'll get my mind off Leo for a few days.

"Hey!" Vinnie wraps his massive arms around me, lifts me off the floor, and spins us in a circle. "I knew you missed me."

"You're an asshole." I laugh.

His head jerks back, and he looks hurt. "What did I do now?"

"It's been a month since you've been home. We've all missed you." I squeeze him one more time before finding my footing.

He laughs and shakes his head, showing off his cute dimples. "You know where to find me, sis."

Even though he's in his junior year, I still haven't gotten used to Vinnie being gone so much. During football season, he barely made it home because of the grueling travel schedule and never-ending work-outs and practices.

"You look bigger." I take a step back and stare at him. "Soon you're going to be so big you're going to look like one of those guys with a shrunken head from *Beetlejuice*."

He's almost as tall as Angelo and Lucio, with the same thick mocha eyebrows, but his hair matches mine, filled with warm caramel browns and streaks of chocolate. His arms have grown, becoming thicker and more defined, looking more like a man than a kid these days.

"Beetle-what?"

"Never mind." I shake my head, wishing the kid would expand his horizons and taste in movies just a little bit beyond *The Fast and the Furious*.

"Shut up," he teases and shows off his way-too-big muscles, flexing them repeatedly. "I've been bulking for football."

"Uh, yeah. I can see that." I wave my hands in his direction and mock him by hunching my shoulders and raising them near my head like the Hulk. "How do I look?" I say in a deep, macho voice, stalking around my apartment like an idiot.

The perfect V in the center of his top lip flattens as he crosses his arms in front of his chest and glares at me with his striking green eyes. "Like an idiot."

"It's like lookin' in the mirror, huh?" I giggle as I continue to act a fool, and Vinnie can't help but laugh too.

"Are you going to be a pain in my ass all weekend?"

"I'm sure you're the *big* man on campus. Someone has to give you a reality check, little brother." I head toward the bedroom I made up for him. "Come on. Get settled. I've got to go to work."

He leans against the doorframe, studying me as I

finish making up the guest bed for him. "You look thinner," he says softly as he studies me.

"Is that how you compliment all the ladies? Because you're going to be single forever with lines like that." I punch the pillow and toss it near the headboard.

"No. You look good, sis. I'm just wondering why you look thinner."

I place my hands on my hips and glare at him. "I started working out. Why?"

He raises his hands in the air when I start to move toward him. "Just making an observation. As long as you're doing it the right way and not starving yourself to become a bean pole like you did after the Tommy Pasquale incident."

I blow a piece of hair away from my eyes that had fallen during my tug-of-war with the sheets that never seem to want to fit over the mattress.

"Unpack and settle in," I tell him before brushing past him in the doorway. I don't feel like rehashing the past with my little brother or explaining how my heart was a little broken after saying goodbye to Leo. "I've got to get to work."

"Okay." He stalks into the living room and stretches, barely able to hold back a yawn. "I'm going to come help out at the bar tonight."

My eyebrows shoot up because Vinnie never wants to work. "You are?"

"I figure you could use some help."

My mouth hangs open, and I blink at him, wondering if I heard him right. "Say that again."

"I figure you could use some help."

The only reason Vinnie would want to work is pussy. It's his driving force in life. Well, women and football, to be exact. "If you're planning on hooking up with some barfly, don't even think about bringing them back here. If you come there to work, that's fine, but it's not a pussy buffet."

"Come on, sis," he pleads with an innocent face. His dimples deepen, making him look sweet, when he's the furthest thing from it.

Vinnie has always caused trouble, but usually, Angelo and Lucio would get blamed because people thought Vinnie was an angel. The boy had troublemaker written all over his face, but it seemed to be visible only to us and nobody else.

"Keep that shit in your pants." I point toward his lower half. "We don't need some neighborhood skank trying to get knocked up by the great Vinnie Gallo. You got me?"

"If I pick someone up, I promise I'll put a raincoat on it."

I gag, being overdramatic, but he's still my little brother. The thought of anyone wanting to have sex with him is just plain gross. "Just cover that shit. I'd hate for you to drop out of college because of a quick fuck."

"Quick?" A smirk dances on his lips. "I'm never quick."

"Shut up." I punch his shoulder playfully.

"How's Ma?"

"Nuttier than ever. You'll see."

"I've missed her," he admits with a soft smile.

"Well, you'll get your fill this weekend."

Vinnie glances around, and I realize I haven't thrown out last week's flowers or the ones before that. They're wilted, and they look awful. "Someone likes you. Anything you want to tell me?"

I roll my eyes. "No. They're from a friend."

"I don't send roses to my friends." He smirks.

"I have to get to the bar," I tell him, changing the subject.

He yawns, walking back to his room and stretching before collapsing back onto the bed. "I'm going to close my eyes for a minute, and I'll be over."

"Sure," I mutter.

Vinnie is notorious for breaking promises—he has that much in common with my father.

"I swear to God, I'll be there. Don't give me shit. It was a long drive." He's so full of it. His college is a whopping two-hour drive from my place. That does not constitute a long drive in anyone's book.

"Bye." I close the door, leaving him to get his beauty sleep.

"DID VINNIE MAKE IT OKAY?" Angelo asks from behind the bar before I even have two feet inside Hook & Hustle.

"Depends on what your idea of okay is."

He looks up for a moment and quirks an eyebrow. "Is he alive, at least?"

"Yeah, yeah. He's alive and napping." I shove my purse under the counter, wishing like hell I was napping too.

Angelo goes back to studying a stack of papers, running his pen down the sheet before flipping to the next page. "Is that what it's like to be in college?"

"What? Laziness? I don't fucking think so."

"Must be a jock thing," Lucio says as he walks into the front of the bar, overhearing our conversation.

"I'm sure he gets an easy ride because he's the star football player," I tell them, remembering the shit he got out of doing in high school. "It's bullshit, but it's always been that way with him."

"It's just a good thing he can actually read and write with all the homework he didn't have to do," Lucio says and starts to laugh. "That little prick."

"Speaking of little pricks." Angelo smirks and turns his attention to Lucio. "How's the wife?" he asks.

I walk away as they start to talk about the honeymoon phase, something I know nothing about. At the rate I'm going, I'm not sure I'll ever experience being that blissfully happy either.

"Tino!" a few old-timers yell as my father walks through the front door, making a spectacle and a grand entrance.

He strolls through the crowd, shaking hands with his friends like he's a celebrity, before making his way to me. "Hey, doll, how's business tonight?"

He's been back a month now, but the man hasn't put in an hour's work at the bar, even though he's required to as part of his early release program.

I grab a glass, trying not to get an attitude. "Busy as always, Dad. Want to help?"

He takes a step back and clears his throat. "I can't tonight, Daphne. I'm pretty busy."

"Yeah," I mumble. "Sure looks like it."

He runs his hand through his salt-and-pepper hair and motions over his shoulder. "Well, I better go check on your mother."

I nod because it doesn't matter what I say, he's not going to pitch in. There's no use wasting my breath. "She's out back."

"Don't worry. He's still adjusting," Michelle tells me as she shoves a tip into her front pocket.

"Did your dad act like this when he got out?"

"He wasn't himself for a while, but he slowly got back into the groove," she says while she checks her makeup in the mirror behind the bar.

My dad didn't have a groove.

He had a way of life.

Even though he was released early for time served and good behavior, I have a nagging feeling he's fallen back into the lifestyle—the very one that landed him in the joint in the first place.

I settle into my usual routine, checking on the customers, chitchatting with the regulars about life, sports, and all the juicy neighborhood gossip. Hours pass and Vinnie's still MIA, but the bar is slammed and selling out of liquor at twice the rate as usual.

Michelle follows me into the back room and collapses onto a crate of vodka. "You look like shit," she tells me point-blank as I pull down a bottle of tequila from the top shelf.

"Thanks." I give her a fake smile, knowing I feel like shit too.

"Let's go out tomorrow. You need some fun in your life. You've been sulking for a month, and I can't take much more."

"I have plenty of fun in my life, and for your information, I have not been sulking."

"Sure." She cackles. "You're a party animal," she says, picking at her fingernails and twisting her lips.

"I have plenty of fun," I repeat, feeling defensive. "We have to work."

"Working doesn't mean fun. Come out with me, and I'll show you what fun really means." She challenges me because she knows I won't back down. "Vinnie can fill in."

I walked right into that one, but Vinnie will be my saving grace. "Fine. I'm game." My stomach churns even thinking about the killer hangover I'll have from this night of *fun* she's talking about.

She rubs her hands together and smiles. "I know just what we're doing too. We're going to find you a piece of ass so you forget all about Leo."

I blanch, not looking for a random hookup. "I don't need ass, and I forgot about him a long time ago."

She purses her lips. "You definitely need a guy, and you're not fooling anyone. You've been sour since the day you ended things with him."

I wave my hands in the air, showing my surrender, and walk into the hallway, leaving her behind. I'm not even five feet away when Michelle's hand lands on the fleshy part of my ass.

I yelp and glare at her over my shoulder.

"Yeah, you need some bad." She laughs.

"Vinnie!" Angelo yells across the bar when boy wonder walks in just as I walk out of the hallway from the back room.

Vinnie waves, looking so much like my father it's scary. He doesn't shake hands like Santino, but he sure has the look of importance down like he's waving to his adoring fans.

People in the bar start to murmur about the kid who went to Ignatius Prep and helped bring home a state championship in football for the neighborhood.

Now every Saturday during college football season, the only thing on at the bar is Vinnie's football game. We have a viewing party and cheer him on as he runs downfield, carrying the ball toward the end zone like the cops are chasing his ass.

My mom runs right to Vinnie. "Oh, my baby." She holds his face in her hands before she starts to pepper him with kisses much the same way I did. "You look so good." She's gushing over him.

Vinnie turns beet red, but he stays still and lets her embarrass him. "I've missed you, Ma."

"Let me look at you," she tells him and backs up a bit, leaving her hands cupping his cheeks. "You're looking good, kid."

"I've been working out." And right on cue, he flexes like the meathead he always has been and probably always will be.

She tries to wrap her hands around his biceps for a second, sticking her tongue out like she's doing something impossible. "I can tell. I can't even touch my fingertips around these guns."

"Ma, you haven't been able to do that since I was twelve."

"Finally. Ready to work?" I ask him, saving him before she does something else to embarrass him.

He glances at me out of the corner of his eye. "If I must," he says, always being whiny when it comes to anything that resembles manual labor.

"The last time I checked, you are still part owner of this place too."

"I'm the hook," he says with his chin raised and filled with cockiness. "The rest of you are the hustle."

"Whatever." I grab a towel off the counter before tossing it at him.

It smacks him in the side of the face. "Thanks," he mumbles behind the rag before peeling it away. "I'm more of a bartender, though."

"Wash the tables," I tell him and motion around the bar. "There's a lot of dirt to clean up around here."

He walks up to me and drops his voice, "Where are all the hot women?"

"Slumming it elsewhere."

"Fuck," he hisses. "I was hoping to have a little fun this weekend."

"Oh, I'm sure some trashy bimbo will walk in here at some point. Word's already spreading that you're here."

He pulls his phone from his pocket and makes flirty faces into the screen, practicing. "Maybe this will bring the girls to the yard."

My brother's ego has grown almost as big as his large Gallo head. "Don't worry, pretty boy. You look perfect. Not even a hair out of place."

He ignores me and talks into the camera. "Hey, ladies. I'm back in town and down at my bar, Hook & Hustle. Come on over and see me tonight. If you're lucky, I may even do some push-ups." He winks before pressing a few buttons.

"You're unbelievable," I mutter.

"That's what she said." He laughs.

I just shake my head and walk away.

CHAPTER TWELVE

DAPHNE

I'm barely awake, and it's already noon. I haven't even had an entire cup of coffee when Vinnie strolls through the front door with the biggest smile on his face. He strides into the kitchen, wearing the same clothes he had on last night, only with a few more wrinkles. He slides onto the stool across the counter from me and taps his hands against the granite. "How's your morning going?"

"I haven't decided yet. It's too early to think," I grumble into my coffee mug.

I've never been much of a morning person, and

that's probably why working at the bar suits me so well. I can sleep in whenever I want and never have to worry about setting an alarm. My brother is obviously a morning person, or he wouldn't be so damn chipper at this hour.

He stares down at his reflection in the polished black granite. "Mine's going amazing." He peeks up at me for a few seconds before going back to admiring himself. "Thanks for asking."

"Fucker," I whisper.

"What?"

"Nothing."

"So, Michelle and I were talking last night."

The cup is halfway to my mouth when I stop. "Please tell me you didn't sleep with her."

"She said she wants to take you out. That you need a break from working, and since I'm in town…" he continues without providing me any reassurance he didn't try to get into Michelle's pants. He stares straight into my eyes and says something I never expected. "I'm going to cover your shift so you two can have a night out."

I put my cup down and try to comprehend how any of this makes sense. Vinnie is never the first one to volunteer for anything. "Vinnie, I love you, but…" My voice trails off.

But then I think about it. The bar is partially his, and he needs to put in some time like the rest of us. He's collecting checks every month from the profits; he may as well earn a little of the money too.

"I think you're right. It's a great idea."

"Is it?" His mouth hangs open.

"It is."

I don't really care about going out with Michelle, but I think he deserves to walk a mile in our shoes.

"Well, okay then," he says quickly.

"Are you sure?" I ask, giving him one more out and expecting him to take it.

"Completely. Last night was a breeze. I'm sure tonight will be more of the same."

I don't bother telling him Saturday night is always more crowded than Friday. Last night, we were slammed after people heard he was back in town. Tonight, it will be worse. But Vinnie seemed to handle everything in stride.

All the little neighborhood women, both young and old, would be there to get a glimpse of Vinnie Gallo—the Italian football god with pristine olive skin and green eyes.

"You're smart. I'm sure you can handle it," I reassure him, even though I'm not entirely convinced.

He covers his mouth to stifle a yawn. "I'm going to lie down for a bit. Those girls exhausted me last night."

"Girls?"

"Three," he says with a smug grin.

There's no point in lecturing him about sleeping

with customers. Vinnie's going to do whatever he wants, when he wants, how he wants. We've all given him the sex talk. The rest is up to him. "Go rest. You're going to need it tonight."

"Oh, I know." His dimples appear as he rubs his hands together. "I'm hoping for round two."

My eyes widen. I shouldn't be surprised by anything or anyone my brother does anymore. "Two nights in a row with the same chicks?"

"Hell no. Variety is the spice of life."

"I'm glad to see you have your priorities in order," I say to him as he walks toward his bedroom.

He turns around, holding the side of the door with his hand. "Wear something nice tonight, and put on some makeup. Michelle has big plans for you."

Before I can reply, he shuts the door, and I can hear his laughter on the other side.

"Fuckers," I mumble. "Both of them."

Those two cooked up something without clueing me in on their little scheme. I send a text to Michelle to get the scoop, and my phone rings as soon as she reads the text message.

"Hello."

"Oh my God, Daphne. I have the best night planned for us."

"Yeah?" I try to sound excited.

"Yes!"

I stare in the mirror, running my finger along the

bags under my eyes as she chatters on about how amazing everything is going to be.

"What time are we going out?"

"I'll be there to pick you up at nine, and wear something pretty like a dress or that cute-as-fuck black miniskirt you have tucked away somewhere in the bowels of your closet."

"I have sexy clothes."

"Not since you called it quits with Leo. Anyway, a flannel and jeans do not equal sexy unless you're a lumberjack. Last time I checked, you didn't fit the bill. You've been in a rut, my friend."

I glance down and tug at the edge of my favorite red flannel. "I think I'm pretty hot. And you wore a flannel last night."

"Just look good tonight, or I'm picking out your clothes when I get there."

"Fine," I groan.

"Hey, Daphne," she says before I can hang up.

"Yeah?"

"Shave your bits too." She ends the call before I can ask why it matters. I'm not going to sleep with anyone.

MICHELLE GASPS when I open the front door.

Somehow, I managed to get my favorite pencil skirt on without falling over, and it's hugging all my curves in just the right spots. I feel a little bit like the old Daphne again. The one who didn't spend a month sulking, trying to pretend Leo Conti didn't exist.

"Dayumn!" Her eyes travel down my body, ending at my feet, which are covered in the cutest black high heels.

"I did good?" I touch my cleavage, regretting the new push-up bra I bought last week because my tits look off-the-chain huge.

"You're you again." She whistles, looking impressed. "Someone's going to get lucky."

"I'm not sleeping with anyone tonight, Michelle," I tell her again because she doesn't seem to believe me.

"Did you shave?" She grabs my arm, lifting it high in the air, but I pull it back quickly. "Phew. But did you shave everything?"

"Why do I have to shave everything if I'm not sleeping with anyone?"

"Because you need dick badly, and no man wants a bush."

I roll my eyes and already know this is going to be a very long night.

THIRTY MINUTES LATER, we're standing outside,

waiting in line for a nightclub on the North Side. "What is this place?"

"It's the hottest club right now." She reapplies her lip gloss for the tenth time since we stepped out of the car.

"This doesn't look like much of a club." I peer up at the building, and it looks like it should've been condemned ten years ago.

"Look at the line." She motions to the people behind us with the tube still in her hand. "There's the proof. Looks can be deceiving. Kind of like you in that flannel. You look frumpy, but you clean up nice."

"Watch it. I always look good. I just don't need to get all dolled up every day for Johnny and the guys at the bar."

"You never know who's walking through that door, princess. You're not getting any younger either. Stop dwelling on a guy you can't have and look for one you can ride—" she pauses and giggles "—into the sunset with."

"Michelle, baby. I've missed you," the bouncer says and totally catches me off guard. I've never been here, but Michelle's obviously been here enough to make friends with the guy.

"Hey, handsome," Michelle says flirtatiously before kissing him on the cheek. "I haven't seen you in a while."

"No man tonight?" he asks.

Man? I can't remember the last time Michelle had

a boyfriend, but it's been at least a year. This club hasn't even been open that long.

"Just my girl." She knocks her shoulder into me.

"You're holding up the line here!" someone behind us yells.

The bouncer glares down the sidewalk, and his black eyes narrow on the crowd. "The natives are getting restless. You ladies be careful in there. If you need anything, let me know."

She nods and pulls me inside the doors before people start throwing shit at the backs of our heads. "Man, they're vicious out there," she says as we step into the dark corridor with a faint light at the other end.

"How come I've never met your friend, and who's the guy you come here with?" I ask as the walls rattle around us from the thumping bass.

"Walk faster." She tugs on my arm and ignores my question. "We're missing the action."

When we reach the light, I'm momentarily blinded. I cover my eyes with my hands, and I blink a few times, trying to let my vision adjust. I spread my fingers apart slowly and take in the sight before me. "Holy fuck!"

"Come on," she mouths, her voice drowned out by the wicked beat.

As we walk, I bump into no fewer than twenty people, but no one seems to mind. People are dancing, intoxicated by the music, booze, and probably drugs too. They're too wasted to even care that I almost knock them over.

Once we're at the bar, Michelle holds up two fingers to the bartender like she's a regular.

"You like?" she yells in my ear, jutting her chin out toward the dance floor.

I shrug. I haven't decided what I think yet. I can't wrap my mind around this place. From the outside, it looks like a run-down building, though the inside is anything but.

There're massive columns with cages on top scattered throughout the large room with barely dressed women writhing inside. The DJ booth at the other end is lit up in red with a small crowd inside, jumping up and down to the beat. There have to be easily a thousand people in here.

Michelle bumps my arm and holds out a martini glass filled with something purple. I don't bother to ask what it is because I can't hear shit anyway. She pushes it toward my lips. "Drink it," she says, or at least, that's what I think she says because I still can't hear her.

Blackberry dances across my tongue as I take my first mouthful. My insides are rattling with each thump and beat as one song bleeds into another while I sip my martini.

Michelle motions toward the dance floor with her thumb and tells me to drink up. In the too-high but super-cute heels, I stagger toward the dance floor and toss back the last drop of the martini. I set the empty glass on a table before I step onto the shiny black tile with a crowd so large I can't even see the other side.

I've never claimed to be an amazing dancer, but with the intoxicating beat and the dim lighting, I feel sexy again. My body's moving, flowing with the rhythm as I dance around Michelle. She's busting moves that I haven't seen her make since high school prom.

My body's flushed and covered in sweat, but I push my embarrassment aside and keep on dancing with Michelle. She's eating it up, dropping to the floor like something straight out of a music video.

When the song ends and the group around us claps, we bow together and break out into laughter as we run off the dance floor like we're kids again. We wind our way down another hallway, different from the one we entered through, until it opens onto a giant courtyard.

"Let's get another drink and cool off out here."

The patio is lined with the tropical trees and overhead twinkling white lights against the starry sky.

I jostle from foot-to-foot, eyeing the only empty table across the patio. "I need to sit." I don't even need to look to know a blister is starting to form and the skin near my Achilles tendon is wearing away.

"Find a seat, and I'll get the drinks," she tells me before walking away.

I stand there for a moment, watching Michelle as

she heads toward the bar, before I take a step. I don't even make it more than a few feet before I collide with something solid, someone big.

I stumble backward, ready to fall until strong hands wrap around my arms. "Sorry," I say, lifting my face to see the one man I came here to forget.

Fuck.

CHAPTER THIRTEEN

LEO

"Leo," she says with wide eyes. "What are you doing here?"

"I know the owner and stopped in for a quick meeting," I lie because I don't want her to know I tracked her down.

I do actually know the owner, but my visit to the club has nothing to do with business and everything to do with Daphne.

I took a big risk. I went to Hook & Hustle, hoping no one would recognize me, and paid a waitress a hundred bucks to tell me where Daphne was. I went there with every intention of talking to her, but when I found out she took the night off, I knew this was my chance.

"Oh. Well." She glances down at her feet. "I don't want to keep you."

"How have you been?" I ask, trying to find a way to keep the conversation going and feeling her out.

"Really well." She gives me a fake smile. "And you?"

"Good." There's an awkward pause as we stare at each other.

She's so beautiful. The month apart was harder than I expected. I sent flowers every few days, making sure she didn't forget about me and always knew I was thinking about her. "Can I buy you a drink?"

Daphne glances over her shoulder, and my eyes follow hers to Michelle. "It's probably best if you don't."

I reach over and brush her hair off her shoulder, touching her skin with the backs of my fingers. Daphne doesn't pull away, and I know she's struggling as much as I am. "Just one," I beg.

Daphne turns again, looking toward her friend. "Michelle doesn't like you much."

"Well then, it's a good thing I'm not interested in Michelle. Please sit," I tell her, pulling out a chair at the table next to us. "I'll be right back."

"Don't be too long," she says as she sits down and relaxes back into the chair.

As soon as I order our drinks, Michelle walks over, tapping her fingernail against her glass. "I don't like you," she tells me, reinforcing what Daphne has already told me.

"I know."

"You're dangerous."

"I'm not." I keep my cool, knowing if I don't win over the best friend, there's no hope of ever getting Daphne. "My father may be—just like Daphne's—but I am not dangerous."

Michelle eyes me. "What are your intentions toward my best friend?" She raises an eyebrow and cocks her head.

"Intentions?"

She nods. "Are you just playing with her heart, or are you more into the whole mindfuck thing?"

"Neither." I turn toward Michelle and rest my elbow on the bar. "Have you ever met someone and wanted them so badly you can't even explain it?"

"Well, maybe," she says and fidgets with the drink in her hand as she glances down at the floor.

The only thing I can do is lay all my cards on the table. "Listen, I know there're a million reasons why we shouldn't be together, but none of them matters because of how I feel about her."

Michelle drops her chin and peers up at me. "And that would be?"

I've never been one to talk openly about my feelings, especially with a stranger. But I know Michelle's the key to my ever having a chance with Daphne, and that means I have to be open and honest.

"I love her." The words slide off my tongue with ease. Maybe because I'm not saying them to Daphne's face, but professing them to her best friend. "I know it's crazy. We barely know each other, but…"

"No," she says, cutting me off. "It's not crazy." Her words shock me. "I've known Daphne my entire life, and I've never seen her so tied up in knots over someone." She leans forward and drops her voice. "She'd kill me for saying this, but I think she loves you too. I've never seen her as miserable as I have the last month."

"Then I have to set shit straight and get my girl," I tell Michelle.

"Daphne isn't the obstacle. It's your father and hers that are the issue. I've warned Daphne about you, told her to stay away. But I can't do it anymore. I've never seen her so sad, and I can tell you care for her. I'll give my blessing and bow out tonight, giving you two time together."

"You'd do that?" I'm shocked Michelle is so willing to give us tonight.

"Of course." She smiles and glances in Daphne's direction. "Just figure out a way to make shit right, or you won't have to worry about Santino Gallo. I'll hunt you down myself."

I laugh. Michelle's small, but I can see the same

fierceness in her eyes I see in Daphne's. "I'll figure out a way."

I've made multimillion-dollar business deals before. Our fathers are no different. They're driven by the dollar and ego. I just have to tap in to how the relationship could benefit them in order for them to call a truce, making an opening for Daphne and me to be together. It sounds simple enough, but I know their egos will be the problem. If Santino is anything like my father, I'm going to have an uphill battle.

"I know what it's like when you want to be with someone so badly your chest hurts," she admits. "I'll never give up hope, and I don't think Daphne's ready to walk away from you either. Now, go," she tells me and shoos me away from the bar. "Make me believe true love is possible against all the odds."

Concern's written all over Daphne's face as I walk toward the table with our drinks in hand, ready to spill my guts. This is new territory for me. I've never wanted someone like I want Daphne, and sharing my feelings isn't something I'm used to either.

"Where's Michelle going?" she asks as I sit down and place a whiskey neat in front of her.

I glance over my shoulder, seeing Michelle head back into the nightclub. "She's giving us time alone."

"Why?" Daphne's eyes widen. "That's not like Michelle."

I don't want to go into detail, telling Daphne how I basically poured my heart out to Michelle and professed my feelings to her best friend. The first time I say the words, I want them to be special…to mean something. I don't want to say them in a trendy night-club where the seriousness of them will have less impact.

I take her hand in mine. "I can be very convincing." I smirk.

"I'm sure you can," she whispers when I swipe my thumb across the back of her hand.

The sparks are there. Flying all around us in the thick night air. I feel it. She feels it. There's no denying the connection we have. No matter what's between our fathers, it has nothing to do with us—two people with no interest in their businesses—falling for each other.

"I've missed you," I confess, and the words come out easier than I expect.

"I…"

I hang on her words, waiting to hear she feels exactly the same.

She gives me a small smile, blinking slowly across the table from me. "This is crazy, Leo."

There's no sanity in what's happening between us. "Did you miss me?" I ask her point-blank. "Nothing else matters."

"I did," she says and sighs. "I shouldn't have, damn it, but I did, which is insane."

"Then we're both crazy." I laugh and squeeze her hand. "I'll make things right."

Her fingers curl around mine. "How?"

That's the million-dollar question. There're two stubborn, old-fashioned Italian men standing in my way. I have to convince them that we're stronger together than apart. There's nothing easy about it, but I have to face the two men who're driving an invisible wedge between us.

"Don't worry about it. Let me handle things. I'd move mountains to be with you, Daphne."

"Do you understand how irrational this all is? We've known each other what…a month? I shouldn't feel the way I feel about you."

I can't hide my smile. "Sometimes the best things in life go against reason."

"Take me home," she says, and no other words need to be spoken.

The drive back to my place feels ridiculously long. Daphne hasn't stopped stroking my arm from the moment we pulled away from the valet. The second I get her alone in the elevator, I'm all over her.

Our mouths fuse together as our hands roam across each other's bodies, wanting and needing more.

"God, I want you so bad," I murmur against her lips and grip the back of her neck, holding her tightly.

"I need you," she says as her fingers slide under my dress shirt and splay across my stomach.

We tumble out of the elevator as soon as the doors open. She's in my arms, legs wrapped around my waist, kissing me with so much force my lips burn.

I carry her toward my bedroom, one hand in her hair and the other cupping her ass as she grinds her sweet spot against my impossibly hard cock. I lay her on the bed and cover her body with mine, trying to take this as slow as humanly possible.

I don't want to rush. The plane was pent-up lust, but this is something entirely different. Her hands are sliding through my hair, tugging on the ends as she deepens the kiss and locks her ankles behind my ass.

My lips glide across her jaw until I reach the soft skin on her neck and the spot I know drives her wild. "Don't you dare leave a mark," she tells me.

I smile against her neck. "Not on your neck," I promise her, but anywhere else on her body is fair game. It's childish, I know, but I want there to be no mistake that Daphne Gallo belongs to me.

CHAPTER FOURTEEN

DAPHNE

I'M ABOUT TO WALK INTO THE BAR AND HEAD UP TO my parents' for Sunday dinner when Michelle texts me.

Michelle: How did last night go?

Me: Great, but…

I stop typing and hit send. My head is no less jumbled than it was the day before. Spending the night with Leo was everything I thought it would be. The way he made love to me slow and gentle, I felt the connection between us getting stronger and more intense.

Michelle: Life's short, girl. I kind of like Leo, and I don't say that lightly.

I sigh, knowing those words aren't easy for her to say. Michelle understands the precariously sticky situation being with Leo puts us both in.

Me: I just don't want my life to be shorter because of him.

The danger is real, even if my statement is meant to be funny. I can't deny that, at any moment, we'll be found out and one of our fathers will take matters into his own hands. Leo said he'll handle everything and find a way to make peace. But it would take a miracle to bring our families together.

"Hey, stranger."

I jump when I hear Vinnie's voice. "For fuck's sake, don't do that shit."

"Who you texting?" He tries to look over my shoulder, but I put the phone against my chest.

"Michelle."

"Tell her hey. I missed her last night."

"Don't even think about sleeping with Michelle," I tell him, poking him in the shoulder as he walks by me.

"Hey, Michelle's a little too…"

"She's what?"

The thing I know about my brother is he'll sleep with just about any woman on the planet as long as she's willing. It's not that he doesn't have standards, he just loves the female body so much he seems to want to try them all out.

"She's not my type."

I grab his arm as he starts up the stairway to our parents' place with his duffel bag slung over his shoulder. "You don't have a type. What aren't you telling me?"

"Nothing." He doesn't look me in the eye when he speaks, and I know he's hiding something. "You came home late last night, or early, depending on how you look at it." He changes the subject to the one thing I don't want to talk about.

"We're almost late. You better hustle." I point up the staircase, praying he'll drop the subject because the boy is always hungry. "Ma probably already has the food on the table."

Vinnie glances up the stairs, lifting his face in the air, and inhales. "Sausage," he says with a smile. "My favorite. I'll race you."

He looks like the little kid I loved so much as he dashes up the stairs. When he was younger, everything was a competition, and I mean everything. He always wanted to be the fastest at everything he did. Usually, we let him win because he was faster than the rest of us. By the time he was sixteen, there was no competition anymore, but that didn't stop Vinnie from trying.

Vinnie flings the door open, and it crashes against the wall and almost smacks him in the face as it swings back.

"Jesus," my mother mutters as she carries the

casserole of sausage, peppers, and potatoes toward the dining room.

"Sorry, Ma. It just smells so damn good, I couldn't stop myself."

"Well, slow down, Speed Racer."

"Who?" Vinnie asks as he scratches the side of his head and follows my mom and the food into the dining room.

Angelo's already in his favorite spot in the living room, arm flung across the back of the couch, looking relaxed. "Hey." He ticks his chin at me. "Have a good night off?"

I run my fingers along the back of the couch but can't bring myself to look him in the eye. "It was relaxing. How was Vinnie last night?"

"He was Vinnie."

"Busy?"

"Packed."

"Hey. Hey," Lucio says as he carries Lulu into the living room and sits down next to Angelo.

"Where's Dee?" I ask, glancing around the living room, expecting to see her cheerful face.

Lucio pitches his head toward the bedrooms. "In Ma's office, coloring with the kids." He bounces Lulu in his lap, peppering her face and neck with kisses and making her laugh.

Delilah is such a good mom, and she's scoring brownie points in the aunt department. I'm failing miserably at spending time with my niece and nephew, especially after I promised I'd be there for them after they lost their mother.

"I have to go see them," I say before making my way down the narrow hallway. Their tiny voices fill the hall, and I watch through the small crack in the door as the three of them color.

"Do you think Daddy will ever find us another mommy?" Tate, my niece, asks Delilah.

I clutch my chest and plaster my back against the wall, fighting the tears that are threatening to fall. I can't imagine losing my mother now and I'm a full-grown woman, but Tate and Brax have experienced that kind of loss at such a young age.

"Oh, sweetie," Delilah says in a soothing tone. "No one can ever replace your mommy."

"I know." Tate's voice is almost a whisper. "But Daddy's so sad all the time, Auntie Dee."

Tate sounds wise beyond her years. In a way, she's been robbed of a happy childhood and has been forced to grow up a little faster than most kids.

"Mama," Brax says in his deep, little-man voice.

"She's not here," Tate tells him sternly. "She's never coming back."

I gasp and cover my mouth, hoping no one heard me. I'm devastated by her words.

"Come here, big man," Delilah says as I peer around the corner, watching them again.

Tate is standing at her side, holding three crayons in her hand with the other arm wrapped around

Dee's back. Brax has his face buried in Delilah's hair and his thick arms snaked around her neck, hugging her.

Delilah looks down at Tate and smiles. "Tate, your mommy's always with you. She watches over you two every day, every moment."

Tate looks around the room, no doubt trying to find her mommy. "I don't see her."

"That's because she's in your heart, sweetheart."

"My heart?" Tate whispers and glances down, pressing her hands to her chest. "She's inside me?" Her little lips part as her mouth hangs open.

"You'll always carry her with you. And maybe someday your daddy will find someone else. You'd like that, wouldn't you?"

Tate nods with her hand still over her heart.

"But when he does, your mommy will always be with you."

"Always?"

"Always."

I wipe away my tears and plaster on a smile before pushing open the door, trying to lighten the mood. "Where're my monsters?" I call out, stalking into the room like I'm going to tickle them.

"Auntie Nee. Auntie Nee," Tate calls out, running across the room and practically leaping into my arms.

I hug her tightly, running my hand down her back in soft, slow strokes. "Hey, doll. I missed you so much," I whisper in her ear. "I love you."

"Love you too, Auntie Nee."

Delilah stares at me and smiles before taking a deep breath, probably happy for the rescue. The conversation was getting heavy even for a seasoned pro like Delilah.

"Dinner," Ma calls out, saving us from having to dive deeper into the conversation.

"Who's hungry?"

Brax screeches loudly, trying to scramble out of Delilah's arms before she has a chance to stand. She lets him go, and he's out the door before Tate's feet can touch the floor.

"Thank you," Delilah says to me as we follow the kids down the hallway toward the dining room. "I was starting to lose it."

"You did well, Dee. I couldn't have handled that conversation like you did."

"Oh, please. You're a natural," she reassures me, and I know she's just being nice.

While I love my niece and nephew, I'd never call myself overly maternal. I want kids someday, but I'm not sure if I could ever be as good of a mother as mine was to us.

"Sit, sit," my father says and stands as we enter the room. I'm almost surprised he's here on time because lately he's been missing more than he's been present. "The food's getting cold."

Pop's a little more enthusiastic than he usually is, and we're all thinking the same thing as we glance at each other around the table. He's about to drop something big on us. Lately, it hasn't been anything good.

I slide into the chair, making faces at Angelo because I figure he knows what's going on.

"This smells delicious, Ma," Vinnie says as my mother scoops out a giant helping onto his plate.

"I know it's your favorite, baby." Ma hands the casserole across the table, letting the rest of us get our own food instead of babying us like she always does Vinnie.

This dish are everybody's favorite because it's the only thing she can cook that's actually edible. She's been known to mess up the easiest recipes. But this one, she's mastered, and it's perfect every time.

"Can you give me the recipe? I'd like to make it for the guys in my frat."

"It's easy. Just throw sausage, potatoes, and peppers in a pan with a full bottle of wine, red or white, along with some water. Then stick everything in the oven, covered, of course, and let it cook for a few hours until the sausage is tender."

"I don't think even I could mess it up," he says and smiles.

My father pulls out my mother's chair and waits for her to sit before he finally decides to tell us what has him flying high. "So, I know you kids think I'm up to my old ways."

There's a collective grumble from around the table because there's no thinking necessary. My dad has barely been around the last month, heading off to God knows where to do who the fuck even knows with him.

"You know your mother and I are planning our wedding," he says.

"Which is when?" Lucio asks between bites.

"In a few months." Pop smiles at my mom, who's beaming as she gives him her complete attention. "Anyway." He clears his throat. "There's a lot of reasons why your mother and I never got married before."

"We know, Pop," Angelo says, and I can hear the annoyance in his voice.

"No, you don't know, son."

"With marriage comes legalities."

That's a word my father has hated his entire life. Legalities. He's highly allergic to anything that resembles law, and that has always included marriage.

The boys are hanging on my father's every word, but I'm starving, having skipped breakfast to make it here on time after a long and very pleasurable evening with Leo.

"Our money and assets have always been in your mother's name so the government couldn't seize everything if I was arrested."

"When," I correct him, covering my mouth with my hand to hide the hunk of steaming potato that's burning my tongue.

My father sighs. "But there's always been one

thing, a big thing, that I've allowed my brother to be in charge of over the years."

I wrinkle my nose in surprise. "Huh," I mumble to myself.

"Now that you kids are old enough, and I'm finally cleaning up my act, I've asked Sal to sign those assets back over to me."

"Why now?" Angelo asks, wondering the same damn thing everyone around the table is.

"I thought of it as an insurance policy for my old age."

"What is it?" Vinnie asks before shoveling half a sausage into his mouth.

My mother covers my father's hand with hers. "Just tell them already."

"We're part owners in a winery," he says quickly.

My head jerks back. "What?"

"I thought that was Uncle Sal's," Angelo says, clearly knowing something about the entire thing.

"It's always been ours too, but I never wanted to put your inheritance in jeopardy."

"I have an inheritance?" Vinnie whispers and places his fork down on his plate.

"You do. I've asked Sal to divide up my stock equally between you kids, along with myself. In total, we own a third of the family winery in Italy, which, when divided five ways, is about six percent each."

"What?" I ask again, still in shock.

Growing up, we were never hurting for money.

My parents owned the bar, and my father had his other business dealings, always keeping us fed and clothed with a nice roof over our heads. Never in my life did I think we actually had something more. They never spoke about it, and my Uncle Sal left town when I was too young to remember anything.

"So, are we talking about a little bit of money?" Vinnie rubs his hands together, letting greed get the better of him.

"Probably a couple million dollars each," my father says, like he's talking about the weather.

I feel faint. The room starts to spin, and everything goes dark.

CHAPTER FIFTEEN

DAPHNE

"I'M FINE," I SAY FOR THE THIRD TIME AS MY FAMILY stands around the gurney I'm currently lying on in the emergency room. "This is ridiculous." I start to sit up because I'm ready to leave, but my mother pushes me back down.

"We're not leaving until we find out what's wrong," she tells me.

"I didn't eat this morning. It's no big deal."

"You've never passed out before, Daphne." Angelo stands near my feet with one hand resting against my leg. "We're not taking any chances."

"Come on," I plead, hoping someone will have some common sense. "Dad dropped a bombshell on us. My body went into shock. It's seriously no big deal."

They're staring at me like I'm a wounded animal, waiting for the moment I kick the bucket. I wonder if this is what it's like to be old or dying, and I know I'll hate every moment of it. I think of Marissa, Angelo's wife, and the way we sat vigil at her bedside for the last week of her life. I hope we brought her comfort, unlike what my family's doing to me in this very moment.

"Ms. Gallo," the doctor says as he pushes aside the cheap yellow curtain that has concealed us from the chaos of the hallways. "I have some test results back."

"What's wrong, Doctor? Is she okay?" My mother's practically in tears, gripping her chest like she's about to hear news of my impending death.

"Maybe it's best if your family leaves the room so we can discuss the results in private."

That is the worst thing the doctor could say.

"Oh. My. God. You're dying," my mother cries out and almost throws herself on top of me.

I run my fingers over her red hair, trying to soothe her. "I have no secrets from my family. Go ahead, Doc."

"First of all, you're not dying," he says right away.

Well, that's a relief. For a minute, I was wondering

if he was going to drop some giant bombshell in my lap, turning my entire life upside down. For weeks, I've been worried about how my relationship with Leo could end up with one of us dying, but I never thought some crazy-ass disease would take me before that could happen.

"Oh, thank God." My mother gasps and lifts her head from my chest. "I don't know what I'd do without you."

"Jesus. Everyone needs to calm down." I pretend like I'm not worried. But to be honest, I was petrified after the doctor came in without a smile. Asking me if I wanted my family to leave meant the news wasn't going to be something I expected.

"We're concerned, Daphne," my father tells me like I'm the one acting crazy.

The entire family is staring at the doctor, waiting to hear what the tests have revealed. "Your blood work came back, and surprise," he says and finally cracks a smile, probably thinking this will be a happy moment. "You're pregnant."

My mouth falls open. "But I just had my period. The test has to be wrong."

"How long ago?"

"I don't know. Maybe five weeks."

"So, you missed a month?" he asks.

"Not really. My periods are never on time." After a year of tracking my periods, I chucked the calendar in the trash. There was something up with my ovaries, and I was never a regular girl with a twenty-eight-day cycle.

"The blood test doesn't lie, Ms. Gallo. You are indeed pregnant. We'll order an ultrasound to make sure the baby is okay since you passed out."

"I didn't eat this morning," I tell him, still thinking he's yanking my leg.

"You'll need to be more careful about eating every few hours, and start prenatal vitamins right away. Other than that, you're completely healthy."

My world's rocked. I blink a few times with my mouth still hanging open as the doctor walks into the hallway, leaving us behind.

"You were with the baby daddy last night, weren't you?" Vinnie says as he pushes against my leg.

I glare at him.

"She was with Michelle," Angelo says, and I instantly want to punch Vinnie in the gut.

"Nuh-uh. She got in at seven this morning."

They're all staring at me like I'm about to tell them everything, but I've never been one to spill my guts.

"Daphne," my mother says, but she's so excited, she's almost shaking. "My baby's going to have a baby."

"Fuck," I hiss, dropping my head to the bed, and stare up at the ceiling.

This is the worst-case scenario. I'm knocked up. A single mother. Not just that, but I'm pregnant with

Leo's kid. It's like the big man upstairs has it out for me. Why can't I catch a break?

"Best You'll Ever Have?" Angelo says, reminding me he knows all about the mystery man. Well, at least enough to know I've been seeing someone on the side but not sharing the details.

"The father better be an honorable man," Lucio says as he clenches his hand into a tight fist. "Or we'll have a problem."

"Everyone, stop." I close my eyes and take a deep breath, wishing I could go back in time and remind myself to use a condom.

Vinnie's laughing. "You always think I'm going to knock some chick up, and look at what you've gone and done."

"Vinnie, don't start with me." I glare at him.

Just as I'm about to lose my shit, Michelle comes running into the room. "Oh my God, are you okay?" she asks as she pushes between my brothers, gasping for air. "Angelo called me and said you were in the emergency room."

"I'm fine," I tell her as my teeth grind together. "Just fucking perfect."

"She's knocked up," Vinnie says, still laughing his ass off at the irony.

Michelle's eyes widen.

"Yep." I nod.

"Oh no," she whispers and covers her mouth, looking every bit the way I feel.

Angelo turns to her, tipping his head to the side as he cracks his neck. "You know him?"

"No," Michelle lies. "I didn't know she was seeing anyone." She shakes her head, but she's a little over the top with her performance.

My heart's pounding against my chest so hard I can barely breathe. I shake my hands, feeling a panic attack about to strike. "I can't," I say, and my voice cracks on the last word. "I can't be a mother."

"I want to know who the guy is," Angelo says again, never letting shit go. "He better step up and take care of his responsibility."

"I'm no one's responsibility," I tell him, wishing they'd all just leave.

I need time to process this.

The baby.

My baby.

Leo's baby.

Our baby.

Just when I think life couldn't get any crazier, God has a way of reminding me I'm not in control.

"Can I have a minute?" I ask as my nose starts to tickle.

"Sure, baby. We'll be right outside," my ma says before she clears the room when no one moves right away.

"Michelle, can you stay?" I ask, knowing I need someone to be with me, and she's the only one who knows everything that's going on.

"Of course," she says, giving Angelo a glance as he steps out of the room.

"Close the curtain and make sure they're gone," I tell her because I don't want any chance of my family overhearing anything I'm about to say. The blowback would be catastrophic.

Michelle climbs on the gurney, tucking her leg under her bottom and grabs my hand. "Are you okay?" She laces her fingers with mine and squeezes.

"Michelle, this couldn't be any worse," I whisper.

"Why are you whispering?" she whispers back, mocking me.

I tick my chin toward the hallway, knowing full well my entire family is nosy as fuck. "You know how they are listening."

"We'll figure this out."

"How?" I ask, peering up at her with tears in my eyes.

I don't see a way this finishes with a happy ending. The one damn time I have unprotected sex, I get knocked up. *Un-fucking-believable.*

"You're going to have to tell Leo."

I squeeze my eyes shut, letting the tears spill down my cheeks. "He's going to go ballistic."

I'm not sure how I'll break the news to him. I've spent an entire month trying to pretend he never existed, and the entire time, our baby was growing inside my body. God, what if he thinks I was trying to trap him as some part of an evil plan?

"He may surprise you."

"Well, I'm about to surprise him," I say and start to laugh.

"Ms. Gallo," a woman says near the doorway as she pulls a cart behind her. "Are you ready for your ultrasound?"

Michelle goes to stand, but I pull her back down. "Stay with me."

My mother's right behind the ultrasound technician, smiling from ear to ear as she follows her into the room. "I can't believe we're having a baby," she says like she's going to be the one giving birth. "This is so exciting."

"Yeah. Thrilling," I mumble under my breath as she scans my bracelet.

The ultrasound doesn't take very long, and the technician doesn't say much while she takes pictures of my uterus. I stare at the black-and-white screen, trying to figure out what the hell I'm looking at, but I don't see much of anything.

"Did you see a baby?" I ask as she cleans off her equipment and packs up to leave.

"The doctor will be in shortly to go over the ultrasound with you."

Her words don't give me comfort. "Everything will be fine," my ma says, but she doesn't understand the absolute mess I've created.

Moments later, the doctor walks in, holding the ultrasound pictures in his hand. "Everything looks good, Ms. Gallo. You're around four weeks into your pregnancy. You'll want to follow up with your OB/GYN this week, but as of right now, both mom and baby are perfectly healthy."

"Great," I say, trying to plaster on a fake smile.

"Here's the first photos." He hands me the sheet of paper and points to a tiny speck. "There's your baby. Congratulations."

"I have to go tell everyone the baby's okay," my ma says before kissing me on the cheek and leaving Michelle and me alone.

I stare at the photo and try to think of the best way to break the news to Leo. For a minute, I think about not telling him. Breaking up with him would probably be the best solution. His life would remain uncomplicated, and our secret would stay hidden.

"Don't even think it," Michelle says as I climb off the gurney and reach for my clothes.

"What?"

"You have to tell him," she says with her arms crossed in front of her chest like she's reading my mind.

"All right. I'll tell him."

"Promise?"

"Promise."

CHAPTER SIXTEEN

LEO

"MR. CONTI, THERE'S A WOMAN ON THE LINE FOR you," my assistant, Katie, says as she stands in the doorway to my office after I hang up with some investors from Australia.

"Who is it?" I rub my eyes after staring at the computer screen for far too long.

"She wouldn't give her name." Katie shrugs. "But she said it's urgent."

"I'll take it." I reach for the phone, seeing the red blinking light for line one. "Please close the door. And,

Katie, you can go home. It's late, and I really appreciate you being here on a Sunday."

"Thank you, Mr. Conti." Katie nods and closes the door behind her, giving me privacy.

"Hello," I say, hoping it's Daphne.

I've been trying to get ahold of her for hours, and she hasn't returned a single text or phone call. I figured she was busy with her family, but with each hour that ticked by, I've become more concerned.

"Leo, we need to talk," she says, and I can tell there's something wrong by the tone of her voice. "But not over the phone."

"Where are you?"

"I'm at home."

"I'll be right there."

"I'll be waiting," she says before disconnecting the call.

I grab my keys, leaving the rest of the work I had left to do sitting on my desk for tomorrow. I rush to her place, driving like a crazy person through the streets of Chicago, not giving two fucks about a ticket or my personal safety. Once there, I slip through the front door of her building as someone walks out instead of using the fire escape.

I knock, trying not to sound too panicked. "Daphne." When she opens the door, I'm struck by the paleness of her skin. "Are you okay?" I take her hand in mine, noticing the hospital bracelet on her wrist. "What happened?" I ask before she has a chance to answer my previous question.

"I'm fine," she says and pulls me inside. "Close the door before someone sees you."

I kick the door closed, not wanting to take my eyes off her. "Why were you in the hospital? I've been trying to get in touch with you all day."

She walks toward the couch and collapses. "I need you to not freak out."

I rush to her side. "What is it?"

She pulls a pillow into her lap and hugs it tightly. "We have a big problem."

At this point, I'm thinking the worst. Either she's sick or trying to push me away again. I lift her arm and run my thumb underneath the hospital bracelet on her wrist. "Why were you in the hospital?"

"I passed out."

"Why? Did they find something wrong?" I ask, feeling like I've asked her twenty times in the last minute and she hasn't bothered to answer.

"There's no easy way to say this." She pauses and takes a deep breath as her gaze dips to the pillow.

My heart's pounding, and I can barely breathe. Daphne's never been one to beat around the bush, but right now, she can't seem to get the words out. "Just tell me, Daphne."

"I'm pregnant," she blurts out.

My head jerks back. "Say that again?" I'm pretty

sure I heard her wrong because I could swear she said she's pregnant.

She points at me. "You knocked me up."

"Holy shit. You're really pregnant?" My mind is fuzzy, and I'm rocked backward. I'm still not sure I heard her right because my heart's pounding so hard and fast I can barely hear my own thoughts. "You're sure I'm the father?"

I'm not trying to be an asshole. We've slept with each other twice, and the last time was only yesterday. That leaves the plane—where we were so caught up in the moment, we didn't use protection.

She reaches over and hits my chest with the palm of her hand. "It's yours, dammit."

"Mine?" I repeat.

I still can't process the news.

I'm going to be a father.

There will be a little Leo or maybe a tiny Daphne running around the house, squealing with delight.

"Yeah. I'm pregnant with your kid."

The news finally starts to sink in.

"We're having a baby."

"I'm having a baby," she tells me and pulls the pillow tighter against her stomach. "Unless you want to…"

"Don't say it." I hold up my hand, refusing to let her finish the sentence. "I want it." There's no way I'd even think about giving my baby away, or worse, putting an end to the pregnancy. While I'd try to support her if that's what she decided, I want this baby. Our baby.

She sighs. "How's this going to work, Leo? Our families hate each other."

"Our fathers," I correct her. "That has nothing to do with us. They'll have to figure out their own shit." I move closer and pull the pillow away from her. "You're carrying my child." Placing my hand over her stomach, I stare into her brown eyes. "Our baby."

Tears start to stream down her face, and I slide my hands under her legs and pull her into my lap. "I can't believe this is happening." She wipes her tears with the back of her hand as she rests her head against my chest.

"We'll figure it out. We'll get married and raise the baby right."

She sits straight up and blinks a few times. "Married? Are you fucking crazy?"

"Listen," I say, stroking her arms softly, trying to get her to relax. "It makes sense."

"How does anything make sense?" she snaps.

I pull her back against my chest and stroke her hair. "I can't have you and my child living somewhere else, and I most certainly don't want another man to raise my kid as his own."

"Your asshole is showing, Leo."

"Stop, Daphne. I'm being serious. Do you like me, at least?"

She peers up at me. "I've been falling in love with

you, but I'm not ready to talk about marriage. This isn't the 1950s."

I place my fingers under her chin, holding her gaze. "I'm falling for you, Daphne Gallo."

"This is all too soon. Too crazy," she says and bites her lip as she closes her eyes. "I'm not ready for this."

"I don't think anyone's ever really ready, but we will be."

"Leo," she whispers. "We can never get married. We can't even be seen in public together."

I lean forward and press my lips to her forehead. "Let me worry about that, *bella*."

She curls her fingers around my shirt and relaxes in my arms. "I don't have the energy to worry about anything else tonight," she says softly.

"Just rest. I'm not going anywhere," I promise.

Minutes later, she's fast asleep. I kick my feet up, trying to get comfortable. I know I should carry her to bed and leave, but right now, I like having her in my arms way too much to even move.

"Leo," Daphne whispers, brushing her hand softly against my cheek. "Wake up."

"What's wrong?" I grumble with my eyes closed and tighten my arms around her, too comfortable to move.

"You should go. Someone's going to see your car."

I open one eye and glance down at her beautiful

face. "I parked down the street. Don't worry. I'm not going anywhere tonight."

"I'm not comfortable."

"With me?"

She shakes her head. "On the couch. I want to sleep in my bed."

"So do I." I slide my arms under her legs and lift her into the air as I stand. I'm not going anywhere tonight unless someone drags me out of here. I'm reeling from the news, and I'm sure Daphne's still in shock too.

I gently place her on the bed and crawl in next to her, curling my body around hers. My hand rests on her stomach, protecting the very spot where our baby's growing.

I ONLY SLEEP a few hours and leave a note on my pillow, telling her I need to get some stuff done and to text me when she's awake. I know I have to find a way to make things right if Daphne and I ever have a chance of being together and keeping our baby safe.

There's only one person who can help. Someone who knows both players and has a vested interest in bringing peace.

I'm sitting outside Hook & Hustle, waiting for any signs of life and trying to figure out what I'm going to say.

The fiery redhead emerges from the front door, looking every bit like Daphne, only smaller. She looks just as I remember her from when I was a little kid, running around this neighborhood.

I slide out of the front seat and stand in between the car and the driver's door, not wanting to get too close and scare the shit out of her.

"Mrs. Gallo," I call out and wave, smiling to put her mind at ease.

Mothers are always the key. Even my hard-ass father always listened to my mother, never wanting to anger her too much.

She stops walking and looks around before her eyes find me. "Yes?"

"I'm Leo."

She eyes me curiously and takes a step closer but still keeps her distance.

"I'd like to talk to you about Daphne."

She tilts her head, and her stare intensifies. "Are you the father?" she asks.

I glance around, knowing being on the street and in front of the Gallo bar probably isn't the safest place for me at the moment. "Can we talk somewhere more private?"

"Answer the question, dear."

I nod. "I am, Mrs. Gallo."

She smiles before glancing up at the building behind her. "Come up for a coffee, and we'll talk."

I shake my head, knowing I can't step foot in the Gallo house. "I can't."

Her eyebrows draw down. "How about the little bakery down the street?"

"I'll give you a ride."

"I'll walk," she tells me, knowing better than to get in a car with a stranger.

Ten minutes later, we're sitting at a table, staring at each other over a fresh cup of coffee and a cannoli. I've spilled my guts, telling her about my relationship with her daughter.

"Leo, give her time. She'll come around," Mrs. Gallo tells me, but I still haven't dropped the biggest problem in her lap.

I move the mug around the table and know I have to come clean. "The problem isn't between Daphne and me, Mrs. Gallo."

"Oh dear." Her eyebrows shoot up. "What is it, then?"

"First, I want to say I'm falling in love with your daughter, and I want to do right by her and our baby."

"Just rip the Band-Aid off and tell me."

"My last name's Conti." I lean back, waiting for her to start yelling or maybe run out of the bakery screaming bloody murder. Worst-case scenario is the little woman is packing heat and decides to end my life right here in the middle of Mazzella's Bakery.

She blinks a few times and stares at me. "Like Mario Conti?" she asks without moving.

"He's my father."

"Oh," she mumbles and touches the base of her neck, finding the cross hanging from a gold chain. "This is bad."

"I know." I run my palms down and back up my jeans. Bad isn't really the right word for the mess we've created.

"What were you two thinking?" She shakes her head.

"We weren't," I say honestly. "I never expected to fall in love with your daughter, but here I am. In love, with a baby on the way."

Mrs. Gallo leans over the table and wraps her hands around her coffee mug. "So, I take it you're sticking around?"

I nod. "I've asked Daphne to marry me."

Mrs. Gallo glances up toward the ceiling and curses under her breath in Italian. "Did she say yes?"

"She said I was crazy."

She finally cracks a smile, but it quickly vanishes. "Are you part of your father's…"

"No, ma'am. I've never been part of my father's business."

I never would be either. Staying out of the life, his world, was my driving force through college and the reason I worked my ass off to make Excellence the premier hotel chain in the country. I never wanted to be part of his world after seeing the carnage his work caused around the city.

"Well." She pauses, turning her coffee mug in her hands. "It's not going to be easy, but here's what you need to do."

Mrs. Gallo spends the next hour laying out a plan to help keep Daphne and me both safe. I sit quietly, listening to her talk because she knows both men at the root of the problem. She is wise beyond her years. Daphne's so much like her mother—strong, funny, and beautiful.

"Can you do that?" she asks as soon as she finishes.

"I'll do anything for Daphne and to keep my baby safe," I tell her.

CHAPTER SEVENTEEN

DAPHNE

From two blocks away, I see Leo walking toward the front doors of Hook & Hustle. This can't be good. I scream his name and wave my arms like a maniac, but he doesn't hear me over the police sirens blaring on the next street. Walking faster, I make an effort to focus on my breathing, trying not to have a panic attack at all the ways this could go wrong.

Leo shouldn't be anywhere near the bar. It's too dangerous, between Johnny, my father, and any other men in my father's organization that seem to hang around like barflies. They're always on the lookout and willing to take out any threat before the enemy has a chance to strike first.

I push open the door and gasp.

My father's holding a gun straight out in front of him, and it's pointing at Leo's face. "Get out of here, Daphne," he says, only glancing at me for a moment before bringing his eyes back to Leo.

I don't move. I can't. I'm too petrified that my father will accidentally pull the trigger. "Papa, don't," I plead, clutching my chest as I try to breathe.

"He's the enemy. It's too dangerous for you to be here."

"Mr. Gallo, I'm only here to speak with you," Leo says, but he doesn't move, knowing full well my father wouldn't think twice about killing him.

Angelo walks out of the back room, and his eyes instantly widen. "Pop, what the hell are you doing?"

"Shut up, Angelo," I hiss, wishing he'd go right back into the back room.

"I have nothing to say to a Conti." My father's eyes narrow, and his top lip curls.

"I thought you were leaving the life, Papa," I remind him, still in shock over what I walked in on.

"Take this shit outside," Angelo tells my father, not realizing this isn't shit and the street isn't the place to let the world know I was knocked up by Leo Conti. "You need to leave, Daphne."

I hold my hand up, stopping Angelo as he starts to walk toward me. "Don't," I tell him.

I've never seen this side of my father. Everything he did was hidden away and out of sight. His ruthless side was only spoken about in whispers and during his highly publicized trial.

"I am, baby, but I'll go back to prison to keep you and my family safe."

I can't just stand here and let my dad shoot the father of my baby. "He's the father," I say quickly, not even thinking twice about telling my dad if it means I can save Leo's life.

My father's gaze slices to mine. "He's what?"

"Oh fuck," Angelo mutters and covers his face with his hand.

"Leo and I are in love and we're having this baby, Papa." My hand covers my stomach, instinctively wanting to protect the tiny person inside.

I thought my words would defuse the situation and make my father back down. But so far, it hasn't worked.

"You knocked up my kid?" My father's tone is venomous.

I take a step forward and hold my hand out, motioning for him to give me the gun. "Dad, be reasonable," I say, not scared of my father, but worried for Leo. "We love each other."

"He's a Conti," he repeats like Leo's last name makes one damn bit of a difference to me.

"And I'm a Gallo. Would you want Mario to hold a gun on me?"

"Never," my father answers quickly.

"Please, Mr. Gallo. Let me explain," Leo pleads. "I'm not involved in my father's business. You should know that."

I walk between the gun and Leo, stopping any chance my father will pull the trigger.

"Move," my father tells me, but I remain defiant and still.

"*Bella*," Leo says in that rich, sinful voice that started this entire mess. He grips my arms and lifts me easily off the floor. "Never put yourself in unnecessary danger. The baby." His eyes dip to my stomach as he sets me down at his side. "No one is more important than our baby."

My father's hard, icy glare lessens. "You'd give your life for my kid?"

"The mother of my child," Leo replies, raising his chin without an ounce of fear. "I'd do anything to protect them, even if that means giving my life to keep them safe."

My father finally drops the gun to his side. "How could you two be so stupid?"

This is progress.

"Papa, love isn't always rational." Leo grips my hand tightly as I speak. "We never meant for any of this to happen."

"I'm sorry, Mr. Gallo. I came here to talk to you man-to-man about what happened and ask for your blessing."

"I could've killed you." My father drags his free hand down his face and groans.

"Put the gun away, Papa." I walk toward him slowly. Leo reaches for me, trying to stop me, but I push his hand aside. "Let's talk about this."

Angelo stalks across the bar, locking the front door as my father sets the gun down on the table next to him. "I can't believe this shit," Angelo hisses.

I don't know if he's referring to my father pulling a weapon in our place of business or that I got knocked up by Leo.

"How stupid can you be to pull a gun on someone in our bar?" Angelo shakes his head and answers my question like he's inside my head.

"I wasn't thinking." Papa grimaces.

Leo walks up behind me and places his hands on my shoulders, squeezing. "You should go," he tells me, like I'm going to listen.

"I'm staying," I announce. I can't trust my father and Leo alone. And not so soon after my father was willing to put a bullet in him.

Leo's grip tightens. "We'll be fine, *bella*. Let me talk to your father, man-to-man."

I peer over my shoulder at Leo. "I don't trust either of you alone."

"I'll stay," Angelo says. "I'll make sure nothing happens."

"Angelo." Leo dips his head at my brother, his old friend from when they were little.

"Leo." Angelo almost cracks a smile.

Leo turns to me and smiles softly. "Go be with your mother and let the men figure things out."

Hello, 1950s. "You can't be serious? Are you really this much of a chauvinist?"

"No, Daphne. I'm not." He shakes his head and rests his forehead against mine. "This is about respect. Respect for your family and your father. I need to talk with him and explain. It's the only way shit will work out for us."

I tip my head up so our lips are almost touching and stare into his eyes. "Okay, but tread lightly."

Even with Angelo as a middleman, things are bound to get heated. My father has never been known for his reasonable side and has always been quick to fly off the handle. I fear that leaving Leo alone with him is a recipe for disaster.

Leo kisses me softly, not lingering too long because my family's watching.

As I back away, I grab the gun off the table. "I'm taking this with me. Just in case."

Surprisingly, my father doesn't argue as I re-engage the safety and make my way toward the staircase. I look over my shoulder, staring at the three of them, hoping they can find a way to make peace.

When I turn around, my mother's sitting halfway up the staircase with her finger over her lips. "Shh," she whispers. "Sit." She motions to the step.

"What are you doing?" I ask as I squeeze in next to her.

She takes my hand in hers, intertwining our fingers. "Listening."

"But why?"

"I'll tell you later." She shakes her head, putting her index finger back in front of her mouth.

We sit in silence with our hands locked, listening to the familiar sound of chairs scraping against the hardwood floors.

"Did you do this on purpose?" my father asks Leo.

"No, Mr. Gallo. I'm not that type of man."

"I heard you were at my son's wedding. Why were you there?"

"I own the hotel," Leo says calmly, telling my father something I still can't believe.

"You do?"

"Yes. When I saw who had booked the ballroom and heard rumors you were being released, I walked into the wedding to see if you'd show up."

"Why?"

"Because even though I'm not part of my father's business, my life, along with that of my sisters', would be in danger from your newfound freedom. I needed to know if I had to beef up security."

"We've never targeted family."

"But it's easy for us to get caught in the cross fire, sir. You should know that better than anyone."

"I do. So, how did you meet my daughter?"

"We bumped into each other at the wedding."

Leo's smart enough to leave out the good stuff like how I ended up naked in his bed or left the reception, wanting to fuck his brains out.

"And?" my father says, knowing there has to be more.

"The connection was immediate, sir. The moment I laid eyes on her, I knew I wanted her." Leo coughs, probably realizing what a stupid fucking thing that is to say to a girl's father. "I knew I wanted to get to know her better."

I grimace and look over at my mother, but she's laughing. Betty can always find the humor in the stickiest situations. I'm sure that's the only way she's been able to stay with my father as long as she has.

"Well, you certainly did that."

"I know you hate my father, but I'm asking you for your blessing. I want to be with your daughter. I want to love her. She's carrying our baby, and I want to give them the best life possible. Take care of them."

I roll my eyes, but my mother pats my hand, silently telling me to shut the fuck up.

"She doesn't need someone to take care of her, Leo. She's a strong, independent woman. She always has been and always will be. She's like her mother in that. Fiery and full of life."

I tear up a little listening to my father speak about me.

"If you think you're going to tell her what to do

and run her life, you're going to get a rude awakening."

Leo's laughter fills the bar. "I've learned that about her. It may be the thing I love most about Daphne."

They're being too nice to each other. I'm sitting on the edge of the step, waiting for shit to go south. My father is being way too sweet, especially to a Conti.

"She's already pregnant, so there's nothing I can do. I can't forbid you from seeing her. What's done is done. I'm handing my business over to Johnny Marioni. Any beef I had with your father is in the past. For the sake of my grandchild, I'm willing to make amends and forget whatever bad blood we had in the past."

"You're done?" I can hear the shock in Leo's voice.

"I've spent enough time away from my family. I'm too old to go back to prison. It's a young man's game, and I don't have a taste for it anymore."

"I wish my father thought that way."

"He needs a Betty. She'll set his ass straight. I swear, if I would've been popped one more time, Betty would've skinned me alive."

I smile at my mom. Although she's nosy and over the top sometimes, I aspire to be just like her.

"I see all Gallo women are strong," Leo replies.

"But they love hard, Leo. Remember, for all of

their bravado, there's a kind soul and a soft heart underneath that tough exterior. Don't mess this up, or you'll have me to deal with."

I guess this is progress. Although my father has threatened Leo again, it has nothing to do with his name and everything to do with how he treats me.

Someone should've set my father straight back in the day. He wouldn't have been a dumb shit for so many years. Maybe I was wrong. Maybe he has changed, and for once, no one will win the over-under.

CHAPTER EIGHTEEN

LEO

"I'll be fine," I say to Daphne over the phone before I walk into my father's home. "Don't worry."

"That's easy for you to say. You've already had a gun pointed at you today."

I laugh. "If I can survive your father, I can survive anything."

"Your dad's going to flip."

"I know, but he'll just have to deal with his shit. It has no place in my life. If he can't, I'll choose you over him and walk away forever."

"I'd hate for that to happen."

"You don't know my father. It may be a blessing." I step onto the front stoop and take a deep breath. "I've got to run. I'll call you when I leave."

"Good luck, Leo," she says sweetly.

My father's waiting for me in the dining room, reading the newspaper and drinking espresso like he does every afternoon.

As I step into the room, he pushes his thick black glasses higher on his nose and glances up from the paper. "I'm here," he says with absolutely no warmth in his voice as he folds the paper in half and sets it off to the side. "What's so important to take you away from your work?"

I pour myself a cup of espresso, letting him stew a bit. He's watching me closely like he always does. My father's an observer. He never says much, not unless it's important to him. "You're going to be a grandfather again," I say casually, not really knowing how to start the conversation about Daphne Gallo.

"Is Alicia pregnant again?"

I laugh at how quick he rushes to judging my sisters, especially Alicia. She's thirty-five and has three children by two different men, which in my father's eyes, makes her a disgrace.

"No. Alicia's not pregnant, Pop." I lean back, holding the tiny espresso cup in one hand, hoping like hell this will go easier than I expect it to. "I'm having a baby."

My father's eyebrows rise, and it's the first time he

doesn't look angry to hear he's having another grandchild. "It's about time." He pushes his cup to the side and leans forward. "I've been waiting for you to carry on the family name."

"Well, that's the thing." I pause and sip the rich, dark espresso and revel in the taste of the old country.

"Please don't tell me you knocked up some gold-digging whore." He pinches the bridge of his nose, imagining the worst thing he can think of, but he's way off base.

"No." I shake my head. "Nothing like that."

He waves his hand over the table in circles. "Out with it, son."

"The mother is Daphne Gallo."

My father's eyes widen. He doesn't say a thing as he leans back, resting his elbow on the armrest of the chair, and he places his fingers against his lips.

"Say something."

He takes his glasses off, placing them on the table in front of him. "Santino's only daughter?"

"Yes."

"Out of all the women in Chicago, you sleep with Santino's daughter?"

"It wasn't intentional."

"Your dick just happened to fall into her?" He raises an eyebrow.

"Well, no."

"Did you know who she was when you slept with her?"

"Yes."

This is how my father works. First, he loses his shit, letting his feelings and temper get in the way of rationality. Then there're a few minutes where he rants and raves before he finally settles down. Hopefully, this won't be any different.

He slams his hand down on the table, causing the espresso pot to bounce, along with everything else, including our mugs. "How could you have been so careless?"

"Love defies logic."

"You mean your prick has no boundaries."

I stay calm because anything else could be disastrous.

"Pop, Santino's out of the business, and you two used to be friends. What's done is done. Daphne's having my child, and if you can't accept them as part of our family…"

"Wait," he says and holds up his hand. "Santino's out?"

I nod. Naturally, that's the one thing my father hears and cares about.

"This changes things," he mumbles and rubs his hands together slowly.

"You're unbelievable. Even if he weren't, it wouldn't change how I feel about Daphne or my unborn child."

"Of course not." He waves his hand dismissively. "Set up a meeting. We'll handle things."

"I'll set up a meeting, Pop, but you aren't handling anything. You either make peace, or I'm done with you," I tell him before I stand. "It's your choice. You can either gain a grandchild or lose a son."

There's nothing left to say. The ball's in my father's court now. He can continue being a hard-ass, letting business get in the way of family, or he can figure out a way to coexist with the Gallos. I'm done playing games, and I sure as hell don't live to please my father.

Daphne's at the bar working, when I begged her to stay home and take it easy. The woman is defiant to the core.

"What are you doing?" I ask as I sit on a barstool across from her while she dries a glass.

She stops moving and looks up at me. "Don't start."

"Did you eat today?"

"I did." Her eyes narrow.

I know she's annoyed, but I don't give a shit. I do get to voice how I feel because she's carrying my child too. "Enough?"

She sets the glass down and leans over with her elbows pressing into the bar top. "I had plenty. Is this how you're going to be the entire pregnancy?"

I shrug and play innocent. "What way is that?"

"Overbearing."

I laugh and shake my head. "I care about your well-being and our baby's. There's a difference."

"Listen," she starts to say, but then her brother walks over, stopping her from telling me off.

"Leo. Back so soon?" Angelo asks.

"I had to check on my girl."

He runs his fingers through his dark brown hair and shakes his head. "I'm not sure how I feel about you with my sister."

Daphne smacks him on the chest with the back of her hand. "Don't be a jerk, Angelo."

"You better do right by her," he tells me with a serious look. "If you don't, you won't have to worry about my father because I'll find you first."

I stare at my old childhood friend, knowing he's a man of his word just as much as I am. "Noted."

"Takes balls to come in here," Lucio, Daphne's other brother, says as he comes to stand by their side. He's staring at me more intensely, having missed the entire conversation we had earlier.

"I can't hide."

"My father's already put the word out that you're not to be touched unless provoked," Daphne says in response to Lucio's statement.

"Provoked?" I ask as I draw my eyebrows inward.

"You plannin' on drawing a gun on someone?" Lucio asks, which explains everything I need to know.

"No. I don't even carry one."

"Don't say that too loud," Angelo says and starts to laugh, but I'm not sure I see the humor.

Lucio turns his attention toward his sister. "Daphne, it's dead in here tonight. Why don't you go home and relax? You were just in the hospital yesterday, and Leo's right, you should take it easy."

"We got this," Angelo tells her and takes the towel out of her hands. "Go."

I smile, liking her brothers more than I ever expected. For once, I feel like someone is on my side instead of fighting me at every turn.

"I could go for pizza," Daphne says as she rubs her stomach.

"Pizza, it is." I smile at my girl.

"I'll grab my things. Be right back."

I watch her as she disappears down the hallway to the stock room, and when I turn around, her brothers are eyeing me.

"You break her heart, and we'll end your life," Lucio says as he leans in so no one else can hear. "If she gets hurt because of you, we'll make sure it's painful."

"And slow," Angelo adds.

I hold up my hands. "Guys, I only want to do what's right. I love your sister. I'd never do anything to hurt her, and I'd never allow anyone to put their hands on her. I'll protect her and make her happy."

"Ready?" Daphne says as she walks toward me,

oblivious to what just transpired between her brothers and me.

"You two have a good night," I say as I stand and snake my arm around Daphne's back, gripping her hip.

"Let's grab the pizza and take it back to your place."

"Alfredo's?" she asks with a twinkle in her eye.

"From anywhere you want, *bella*."

Daphne devours twice as much pizza as I do, moaning the entire time.

"This is so good." She closes her eyes and hums her approval as she chews another bite. "Have you ever tasted anything better than this?"

"I have," I say, watching her carefully and trying not to let my lust overcome her hunger.

Her tongue pokes out and sweeps across her lips, and I lose all ability to think. "You're taunting me," I warn, feeling my resistance slipping.

"You look hungry," she says, giving no fucks what she's doing to me.

"I am, *bella*, and if you're not careful, I'm going to push the pizza on the floor and feast on you instead."

She gives me a smug grin. "Maybe that's all part of my master plan."

I grab the pizza slice from her fingers just as she's going for another bite. "You can eat later after we work up an appetite."

She tries to take the slice back, but I drop the piece to the floor and grab her wrists. “Me or pizza?”

“That’s such a hard decision.” She smirks and moves her head from side to side like she really has to think about the answer.

“If you have to think that hard”—her gaze dips to my lips as I speak—“I need to do better.”

She struggles a little in my grasp. “My answer is definitely pizza, then.” She giggles.

I pull her forward, bringing her mouth close to mine. “I’m about to change your reality in a hurry, sweetheart. Be ready to never eat pizza without thinking about me again.”

That’s the way I want it too. I want to be her be all and end all. There’s no other man in the world who’ll be good enough for Daphne Gallo, and there’s no way in hell I’ll let another man raise my child. Daphne hasn’t said yes, but she’s going to be my wife.

“Such a big talker. Let’s see if you have the moves to back up your words,” she challenges, and I’m ready to rock her world.

I pull her into my lap and stare into her eyes. “I love you, Daphne Gallo,” I whisper against her lips.

It’s the first time I’ve said the three most important and scariest words to her. We’ve danced around the topic, shared our feelings, but never actually said “I love you” to one another.

She blinks slowly and smiles. “I love you too, Leo Conti. Now you better put up or shut up.”

I wrap my arms around her back, pressing her body flush against mine. "Soft or hard?" I ask, giving her the choice in how she wants me to love her.

"Hard and slow," she says all breathless and wanton. She grinds her middle against my jeans. "I want to feel it tomorrow."

My lips crash down on hers as my arms tighten, holding her closer. She moans and rocks back and forth, riding my cock through the fabric of my jeans and driving me completely mindless with lust.

I want to own her body, claim her, as much as she owns mine. Her tongue dips between my lips, and I'm a goner. Daphne Gallo has me in knots, not knowing up from down or left from right.

I slide my hand up her back as she pulls my shirt up before touching my skin. She hums her approval as her fingers trace the dips and ridges of my abdomen, sending goose bumps across my chest.

My lips trace a path down her jaw, finding the spot on her neck where her heart's beating wildly, matching my own. Her knees tighten at my sides as I lick her soft skin and nibble her neck where it meets her shoulder blade. This is her magic spot. The one that makes her quiver in my arms.

Her fingers tangle in my hair as her head tips back, giving me full access. I stand as her arms wrap around my back, and my lips stay on her skin. She's in my arms, holding my face to her neck as I carry her toward the bedroom.

"I need you," she whispers as I place her on the bed and cover her body with my own.

"I want you," I say against her skin.

Her knees fall to the sides as I move down her body and unbutton her shirt, pushing the material to the sides. "Lower," she tells me.

I smile, unable to stop myself, because Daphne Gallo is always bossy. Even in bed.

She lets out a happy sigh, relaxing into the bed as I pull her pants down her legs, exposing her lace underwear. My mouth waters, and I want to be inside her, bury myself so deep I can't even breathe. But this is the part I savor, the moment I take slowly before I give her exactly what she wants…the hard stuff.

My fingers dip into the sides of her panties as I pull them down her legs and drop the clothes to the floor behind me. She lifts her ass toward my face, always impatient and a little greedy, just the way I like her.

Her knees touch the mattress as I bring my mouth down on her, sucking her clit gently. She lets out a loud gasp, jerking upward, offering her pussy to me. I take it, devouring her core with my tongue and lips, loving the way she tastes.

I'm calculated in my movements, following her body language and touching her the way she needs to be touched.

"Yes!" she cries out, rocking her bottom toward my face, practically grinding her pussy against me.

I want her orgasm. I want her pleasure. But not this way. I want to be buried deep inside her, leaving my imprint, owning her.

When my lips leave her body, her eyes fly open. "What are you doing?" she asks as I undo my pants and kick them to the floor.

"*Bella*, I want to make love to you. I want to feel your body squeezing me, wanting me, needing me."

"But I was…"

I bring my face close to hers and stare into her eyes. "You'll come, baby. I'll make sure of it."

Her fingernails dig into the skin of my back as I push my cock ever so slowly inside her warmth. We rock together, gasping for air and never wanting the moment to end.

I make love to Daphne. First slow and loving, and then, when she's ready and I'm finally willing, I pound into her until she can't form another word.

CHAPTER NINETEEN

DAPHNE

"ARE YOU READY FOR THIS?"

Today's the day. Our fathers have agreed to a sit-down, for a brief time, to discuss how they're going to handle our relationship and their future grandchild. They're over-the-top ridiculous and idiotic. I'll never understand why men do the crazy, silly shit they do, and age doesn't seem to help them either.

Leo leans forward and kisses the top of my head. "It'll be fine." I'm not sure if he's trying to convince me or himself.

My father wanted Mario to come to the bar for

the meeting, but we all knew that was a horrible idea. I've seen enough mafia movies to know a sit-down has to take place in a neutral location. No mob boss is willing to go into enemy territory, even if it is to call a truce.

Leo invited both men to his penthouse for a one-on-one, figuring it was the only place that made any kind of sense. He invited his father to come over early because I haven't had the pleasure, and I use that word very loosely, of meeting the Mario Conti.

"What if it's not?" I check my makeup in the mirror for at least the third time, wanting to look perfect.

I'm always a skeptic, especially when it has anything to do with my father. Leo's father is the great unknown to me, but Leo's told me he's just as much of a hard-ass as my dad. So, basically, we're screwed unless they can rise above their petty bullshit for the sake of their grandchild.

Leo squeezes my shoulders from behind me as I stare at my reflection. "Trust me. They may be pigheaded, but neither man is stupid. It's going to be all right, Daphne," he tells me when I give him a skeptical smile in the mirror.

"Why am I so nervous?"

I had trouble applying my eyeliner a few minutes ago because my hands were shaking so badly I couldn't draw a straight line to save my life. I know how much is at stake with this meeting and the myriad ways shit could go south. If my father and Mario can't work things out… Well, I don't even want to think about how that'll impact the life of my baby, *our baby*, in the future.

Before Leo can respond, the doorman calls, letting us know Mario Conti is on his way up in the elevator. I shake out my hands, trying to get rid of a little nervous energy before the show begins.

"Relax," Leo says like it's just that easy.

That's totally a man thing. My three brothers are barely ever rattled about anything. I never see them pacing with worry or popping Xanax like it's their lifeblood. That's purely a woman thing. And I'm not sexist, I'm a realist. Men let shit slide off their backs, figuring what's done is done and what will be will be, so they don't even bother spending any energy worrying about how they fucked something up. I never thought I was a worrier. But the older I get, and now with the baby on the way, my stress level is off the charts ridiculous.

The elevator chimes before the doors open, revealing an older, just as handsome version of Leo. Mr. Conti's studying something on his phone when he steps into the foyer dressed in a three-piece suit, shoes so polished I'm sure I could see my own reflection, and his hair perfectly styled like he just stepped out of the silver fox edition of *GQ* magazine.

His gaze travels up my body, but not in that creepy way, before his eyes meet mine. There's no smile on his face, no way for me to judge what the hell he's thinking.

"Pop, it's good of you to join us," Leo says, greeting his father with way more formality than I've ever greeted mine.

His father's eyes veer away from me for a moment to look at his son, and I'm thankful for a reprieve, even if it's short-lived. "Leo," he says coldly before his gaze is back on me. "You must be Daphne." He steps forward, entering the foyer which now seems way too small for the three of us.

"It's nice to meet you, Mr. Conti." I somehow smile, even though all I want to do is run and hide.

He studies me for a moment, not saying a word. I'm about to hyperventilate, wishing I could excuse myself and slink away to anywhere else but here. "I can see why my son is so enamored of you," he tells me, finally cracking what I think is a smile.

I glance nervously to Leo for a moment, looking for a rescue. "Thank you, sir." I keep my words formal, always remembering my upbringing and the respect for my elders that was practically beaten into me as a child.

"Mario, please." He dips his chin and takes another step closer.

I resist the urge to back up and flee, knowing it'll do nothing to help smooth the waters and gain favor with Leo's father. "Mario," I say softly.

Mario grabs my hand and lifts it to his mouth.

"You've grown into a beautiful woman, Daphne." He kisses the top of my hand so softly, I barely feel his lips on my skin.

Sometimes I forget the Contis lived in our neighborhood. I can't remember a time when there was peace in my life instead of the constant bullshit my father has brought on my family over the last two decades.

Leo pulls me backward as Mario releases my hand. "Would you like some coffee, Pop?" Leo asks as he moves us toward the living room like he's trying to put distance between his father and me.

"I'll take a glass of wine," Mario answers as he follows behind us to the living room.

"Thanks for coming today," I say out of nervousness as I place a hand on my stomach. "It means a lot to us."

Mario takes a seat on the couch across from me, studying my face with his steely eyes. "We're going to be family," Leo's father says a few moments later.

I nod and tug at the hem of my skirt, pulling it down over my knees. "We are." I laugh for some reason, wishing I could have a glass of wine too. Awkward moments are always easier to swallow with a drink.

Mario takes the glass of wine from Leo, looking every bit a businessman instead of a cold-hearted mobster. There's a not-so-comfortable silence as we sit on the couch, Leo and I on one side of the room, and his father on the other. In situations like this, I always talk, trying to fill the void. Silence isn't something I'm used to in my family. Three brothers and a very outspoken mom make quiet almost an impossibility.

"Leo told me you already have grandchildren," I say, trying to find middle ground for us to discuss.

"Ah, yes." He lifts his wineglass to his lips and pauses. "Alicia's always been a problem child."

Alicia is one of Leo's sisters, and from everything I've heard about her, she is, in fact, a problem. If I didn't know the backstory, I would've been taken aback by Mario's comment about his daughter. But knowing what I know, and her propensity to bed-hop, I know his father can't exactly be proud of her antics.

"Pop," Leo warns. "Be nice."

"I love my grandchildren. I couldn't cherish their little faces any more than I already do, but my daughter…" He shakes his head and sighs. "She's always taken a different path and not one I would've chosen for her."

Mario is trying to be civil. From the way Leo described him, his father is putting his best foot forward as we sit in the living room, waiting for my father. I replace Alicia's name in his sentence and know he's not exactly thrilled about the path Leo took either. I'm sure when he pictured his son having his own children, it wasn't with the daughter of his mortal enemy.

Mario leans forward and places his wineglass on

the coffee table which separates us. "Can I speak freely?" he asks as he rests his elbows on his legs near his knees, looking at us over the frame of his black glasses.

"Of course," I say, not letting Leo answer first. "I'm never one to bullshit, Mario."

"When I heard about you and my son, I wasn't exactly happy." Mario rubs his hands together in front of himself and glances down at the hardwood floor for a second. "But the way my son looks at you is much the same way I looked at his mother before she agreed to be my wife. Nothing and no one could've said anything to change my feelings for her."

I don't say anything as I peer over at Leo, who is, in fact, staring at me. I'm not sure there's anything I could actually say in response to Mario's statement, so I decide to keep my mouth shut and just listen for once.

"My approval is not needed, but I give it willingly," he says. "I only want the best for my son's first child."

There's a little misogyny in his words. I hear the sexism plain as day. There's something about the males in Italian families having their own children that always earns favor above everyone else.

"I will do my best to work things out with your father. For the sake of my unborn grandchild and the future of our families."

This is progress.

Leo's phone dings, and he glances down. "Your father is here," he tells me, covering my hand with his and squeezing.

Mario stands as Leo does, but I beat them to the elevator doors. I want my face to be the first one my father sees as he steps foot in Leo's penthouse.

"Papa," I say as soon as I see my father. He's pulled out all the stops, looking every bit as dapper as Mr. Conti in a three-piece suit and newly polished shoes.

My father's never been one for suits. He's worn them, but usually only for funerals and weddings. I can't tell which category this meeting falls into. Probably a little bit of both. One part of his life is ending, and a new chapter is about to begin.

When my father wraps his arms around me, I feel him stiffen as Mario walks behind me. "Be good today," I remind Papa. "This is for the baby, not your ego."

He kisses my cheeks as he backs away and smiles. "I know how to handle men like Mario," he tells me, and that's exactly what I'm afraid of.

I want them to bury the hatchet, but I don't even know if it's possible with all the bad blood between them. Years of turf wars, murder, and backstabbing make the possibility of a truce pretty close to impossible. These two men have to rise above their work for the sake of their children and unborn grandchild.

"Santino," Mario says as my father releases me.

My father dips his head. "Mario."

Well, this is a start. They've been in the same room for thirty seconds, and there hasn't been any bloodshed.

Baby steps. This is good.

Leo wraps his arm around my back and grips my hip roughly. "Let's go into the living room, shall we?" Leo says to both men as they stare each other down.

I take a step and immediately double over like someone just sucker-punched me in the gut.

"Daphne," Leo says, his voice filled with panic.

My hand flies to my stomach, and I gasp for air, feeling like someone's trying to rip my uterus out through my belly button.

"Something's wrong."

CHAPTER TWENTY

LEO

"I'M SURE SHE'LL BE FINE," MY FATHER SAYS AS HE stands across from me in the waiting room.

I pace, wearing a path into the off-white linoleum. "I can't believe they won't let me back there."

The nurse practically shoved me out of the emergency room, telling me they had to run tests and I should go relax in the waiting room while they evaluated Daphne and the baby.

"There was a time when they wouldn't even allow men in the delivery room for the birth of their child.

Remember?" My father asks Santino, trying to be friendlier than I've seen him in years.

"Life was easier then," Santino tells him. "Much simpler."

Besides our fathers' small talk, the only other sound in the waiting room is the tap of my dress shoes on the tile. I cross the entire room in seven quick steps, before spinning on my heels and repeating. I can't sit still. I can't chitchat and talk about the good old days.

I glance at my watch, wondering what the hell is going on. It's been an hour since they wheeled her to the back, and there's been no news or updates as I was promised.

I walk up to the reception desk and scan the surface, looking for anything with Daphne's name on it.

"Can I help you, sir?" the nurse asks as soon as she looks up from the computer screen.

"I'm here with Daphne Gallo. Are there any updates on her condition?"

She taps a few keys and shakes her head. "The system hasn't been updated yet, but I'm sure a doctor will be out soon to talk to you."

Her words don't give me any solace. I'm not used to sitting on the sidelines, waiting for updates.

"Leo," Mr. Gallo says as he walks out of the waiting room and comes to stand at my side. "You have to calm down. I know it's hard." He grabs my shoulders and stares me in the eyes. "Daphne needs you to be strong and not lose your shit. You hear me?"

I nod and clench my fists tightly at my sides. "I'll be strong, Mr. Gallo. But until I know she's all right, I can and will lose my shit."

"Daphne's a fighter," he tells me, trying to put my mind at ease.

"Mr. Conti," a woman says, standing in the doorway separating the emergency room from the rest of the hospital.

"Here." I blow out a breath and walk toward her. "Can I see her now?"

She nods. "Only one person for right now, and Ms. Gallo is asking for you."

Mr. Gallo shoos me forward. "Go. Be with her. We'll be waiting for you. Your father and I aren't going anywhere."

I follow the nurse down a long corridor of what seems like endless rooms filled with moaning patients and annoying beeping monitors. "She's resting now." The nurse motions toward the door. "The doctor will be in soon to give you an update."

My footsteps are quiet as I walk into the room, trying not to wake her. Her eyes are closed, and her hands are covering her stomach in a protective way as she lies on the gurney, covered in a thin white blanket. I slide onto the chair next to her, scared to touch her and doing my best to let her rest.

"Leo," she whispers and moves her hand to her side. "They won't tell me anything."

"Shh, *bella*." I grab her hand, squeezing it tightly. "The doctor's coming."

"What if something's wrong?" I can hear the panic in her voice.

"Everything will be fine," I lie because it's easier for me to believe that everything will work out. "I know it will be."

A doctor walks in, looking no older than a high school kid, and studies a folder of papers. "Ms. Gallo," he says before looking up at us.

"Yes." I answer for her.

He flips another page, drawing out the agony and oblivious to our terror. "First off, the baby's perfectly healthy."

I finally exhale, feeling relieved and like a weight has been lifted off my shoulders. "Were you under any stress when you started cramping?"

"A little," she says as she pulls herself upright a bit more on the gurney.

A little stress is sitting in traffic on the Kennedy when you're late for a meeting. What just happened in my penthouse rises to the level of a red alert during the Cold War.

"You're going to need to cut down on your stress as soon as possible. Also, add some fiber to your diet. You're constipated, which made the cramping worse than normal."

I laugh, covering my mouth with my free hand.

Daphne shoots me a death glare. "That's funny?" she asks and lets out a sarcastic laugh. "Ha-ha. I'm constipated."

"*Bella*." I lean forward and press my lips to her forehead. "I always knew you were full of shit, but now the doctor's confirmed it."

She swats my arm, not feeling the same sense of playful relief I am. "Thank you, Doctor."

He closes the folder in his hands and tucks it under his arm. "Maybe take it easy for a few weeks just to be safe."

"I'll make sure she rests," I tell him because I won't allow Daphne to put her life at risk as well as our baby's.

"The discharge nurse will be here soon."

"Can I get dressed?" she asks before he has a chance to walk out the door.

"Yes, but get up slowly."

Daphne blows out a breath and rolls her eyes.

I know this taking-it-easy lifestyle isn't going to sit well with her. I'm going to have to find ways to make her relax and be creative about it. If she thinks I'm handling her in any way, I'll be fucked.

She starts to sit up, and I grab her by the shoulders. "What are you doing?" Her eyes narrow as she glances down at my hands.

"Nothing," I say quickly, but I don't pull away. "I'm just helping you."

"I'm not broken."

I tighten my grip when she tries to push my hands away. "For the good of the baby."

Those are the magic words because she instantly stops fighting me. "Fine," she mutters and motions for her clothes. "Only because I don't want anything to happen to our baby."

As she gets dressed, I ask a passing nurse to bring our fathers in while we wait for her discharge. I know they acted nonchalant about everything, but they were worried too.

"Daphne," Mr. Gallo says as he rushes into the room and sees Daphne standing and fully dressed. "Is everything okay?"

My father's behind him. "Is the baby okay?"

"Everything's fine," I tell them both, but I leave out the bit about her being constipated. "She needs to avoid stress. Today was too much for her."

"I'm sorry," my father says.

I raise my eyebrows because that may very well be the first time I've ever heard him apologize. "Both of you need to work your shit out before it affects our baby, your grandchild." I punctuate the last word, reminding them a part of each of them is growing inside her.

"Yes. Yes. Of course," Mr. Gallo says and glances at my father. "We talked in the waiting room. Whatever's in the past will stay there."

"Son." My father puts his hand on my shoulder.

"Santino is telling you the truth. We've buried the hatchet."

I eye him skeptically.

"For the good of our grandchild," he adds.

"What about Johnny?" I ask, knowing he's taking over for Santino and there's bound to be some carryover.

"I've arranged a sit-down. We'll iron things out. The city's big enough for all of us."

Daphne looks at me and is just as shocked as I am that they sound like grown-ups about the entire situation. Our entire lives, we've listened to these two men trash-talk the other, ready to fight to the death.

Even though they're being overly friendly, I imagine there will come a day when the competition kicks in. Whether it be Christmas or birthdays, the other isn't going to be the cheap grandpa, giving shitty gifts. I'm fine with it. Let them spoil our baby and shower him or her with gifts.

"I'm taking Daphne away for a little while," I say.

"You are?" Daphne glares at me. "We didn't discuss anything, sweetheart." She pulls a tight smile, barely moving her lips as she speaks.

"We could both use some time away."

"I can't leave my brothers short-handed at the bar."

"I'll take care of your shifts," her father responds quickly.

Daphne's head snaps back to him. "Papa, come on."

He puts his hands up. "I'll do it. I'm retired now and have extra time on my hands. Besides, I want you to make sure my grandbaby is healthy."

"Our grandbaby," my father corrects him as the rivalry heats up, only in a new and different way.

"I don't know," she says and glances at the floor.

I place my fingers under her chin, bringing her eyes to mine. "They can handle it."

"Okay," she whispers, finally giving in.

CHAPTER TWENTY-ONE

DAPHNE

THE SUN WARMS MY FACE AS WE SIT AT A CHARMING little café in the middle of the town square. Mountains stand tall behind the buildings as if they're reaching for heaven, not realizing they are already set in paradise.

After a month in Italy, my ability to speak the language of my ancestors is still atrocious. Leo's been my saving grace, translating like he was born here.

"I could live here forever," I say, tipping my head back to soak up a little more sun.

Life is slow here. There's no rushing from one

place to the next, no traffic jams or police sirens at all hours of the night. The quaint little village of Castel di Sangro, tucked in a valley between the lush mountains and Leo's great-grandparents' hometown, is exactly how I imagined the old country to be.

"We could buy a place and raise the baby here," he says as he lifts the espresso cup to his lips.

I glance at him and shake my head. "I can't leave my family. I need my mom most of all, especially with the baby coming." I touch the tiny bump that's finally starting to grow, making the pregnancy all too real.

"We can spend summers here at the very least."

I nod, liking the idea, because I can't imagine anything better than escaping the loud, harsh city for the green countryside so filled with history and peace.

"See that church?" Leo motions across the square to a three-story white building which has seen better days. "My great-grandparents were married there, as their parents were."

I study him because Leo doesn't make small talk or drop useless information unless he's going somewhere with it. "That's so sweet." I smile, taking in the beauty of the old structure.

"I was wondering," he says as he places his cup back on the table and grasps my hand. "What do you think about getting married there?"

"Okay," I say quickly.

"Because the baby will be here soon, and I'd love

to…" He pauses, and his eyebrows draw together when my response finally registers. "Wait. What?"

"I said okay," I repeat, knowing he wasn't expecting me to say yes.

Leo's face relaxes as a smile spreads across his handsome face. "I thought I'd have to fight you on this."

I shake my head, knowing it's exactly how I want our family to start. Steeped in history and tradition, surrounded by love and joy. "It's perfect."

He stands up and takes my hand, pulling me into his arms. "You've made me the happiest man in the world, *bella*."

I peer up, staring into those sinful honey-brown eyes that captured me not that long ago. "I want us to be a family, Leo, in every sense of the word."

He leans forward and presses his lips to mine, stealing my breath like he does every time he kisses me. I wrap my arms around his middle and hold him tight, wishing we could stay like this forever.

"How about tomorrow?" he asks.

"Tomorrow, what?"

His embrace tightens. "We'll get married tomorrow."

"That's too soon. I need—" I start to say when he cuts me off.

"Your family is already on the way here. I have an appointment set for you at the dress shop in town, and the rings are already being made."

I blink a few times, totally in shock. "How?"

He's barely left my side this entire trip. How he had time to pull together a wedding, including flying my family to Italy, is beyond me. I've barely had the energy to make it to sunset every night without taking at least one catnap.

"While you sleep," he says and brushes his lips against mine.

"Oh, well," I mumble. "Tomorrow."

I try to let that sink in. Tomorrow, I'll no longer be Daphne Gallo, I'll be Daphne Conti. I wonder how Leo would feel if I decided to hyphenate my name, but that conversation can wait until another day.

"A marriage license. We need one."

"Taken care of, and this is about saying our vows before God more than the law."

Then there's no rush to discuss the legalities of which last name I'll use. I push it to the side, not wanting to ruin this perfect day.

"When does my family land?"

"Your mom is meeting you at the dress shop, and your brothers and father are already back at the hotel."

"What about your father?"

"He's at the hotel too."

I'm speechless. Somehow while we've been gone, our fathers have avoided killing each other and kept the truce in place without our having to step in the middle and remind them of their promise. It's like a modern-day miracle.

Leo places his hands on the sides of my face and stares at me. "I love you, Daphne. I want this day to be perfect. I want you to remember it always."

"I will." I rest my forehead against his lips, loving the way his hands feel on me and riding high on cloud nine.

My mother squeals as soon as we walk in the front door of the quaint little dress shop near the café. She rushes toward me with her arms open. I run to her, forgetting about Leo for a second because I've missed my mom more than anyone this month.

"Mama," I say, holding her so tight both of us can barely breathe.

"Baby, I've missed you so much." She buries her face in my hair like she used to do when I was a little girl. "You look so happy."

"I am," I whisper in her ear and squeeze her one more time before finally letting go.

"Mrs. Gallo," Leo says as he stands behind me.

My mother pushes me out of the way and tackle-hugs the man, practically knocking him over. "I'm a hugger," she tells him like he hasn't figured that one out yet.

"Well, good thing for you, I like to be hugged." He laughs and peers at me over my mother's head because she's a good foot shorter than him.

"It's so nice to see you again." She backs away

and touches his chest. "And for such a happy occasion no less."

I swear she's kneading his pecs, totally feeling him up. Leo doesn't seem to mind. He's standing still, letting her touch him. "I'm just glad Daphne said yes."

"That would've been awkward." My mother glances over her shoulder at me. "Has she been taking it easy?" she whispers.

"I can hear you."

"Oh." She starts to laugh.

I pull my mother away from Leo's chest. "I've been taking it easy. Leo's made sure of it."

"We better get started. We don't have much time, and you have a lot of dresses to try on."

"She could wear a bag, and she'd be beautiful," Leo tells my mother before he kisses my cheek. "Spare no expense, *bella*. Buy anything you want."

My mother starts to clap. "A man after my own heart," she says, staring at Leo like he's Prince Charming. "Now, go. You can't see the dress." She shoos him toward the door.

"Have fun, ladies," Leo tells us before he leaves us alone.

"Tell me he has some major flaw."

"Ma." I give her a look.

"What? I may be old, but I'm sure as hell not dead."

"Soon, we'll be picking out your dress," I remind

her, wondering what the hell happened to their wedding plans.

"Your father wants to elope to Vegas and be married by an Elvis impersonator." She rolls her eyes.

"Vegas could be fun."

"An ex-mobster in a gangster town is not a smart combo, dear."

"Yeah." I forgot about Vegas's illustrious roots, and with my father's sudden departure from his previous life, it most definitely could be a recipe for disaster.

"We'll get married at the bar and invite the neighborhood." She waves her hands toward the dresses. "I don't need all this after being together for more than three decades."

I'll have to plant the bug in my father's ear. My mother deserves something grand for putting up with his shit for all these years. I wouldn't have stuck around, waiting for him to grow up and praying every night he didn't end up in the county morgue.

"You're never too old for romance, Ma."

I GAZE at Leo as we stand on the altar of the old church, surrounded by our family in an intimate ceremony. The priest is Italian, speaking only a few words of broken English, but it doesn't matter.

"You look beautiful," Leo mouths as the priest

says a prayer over our rings, blessing them along with our union.

I picked the dress just for him, wanting to knock his socks off with something classy. The bottom of the silk gown pools at my feet and hugs my body in all the right places, even showing off the baby bump perfectly.

Leo's dressed in a black suit and silver tie, looking every bit as delicious as the night we met. That's how we ended up in this situation. Me pregnant, and him begging me to be his forever.

My mother sniffles from the first row, always the first one to cry at a wedding. I couldn't have planned a better wedding myself. I don't need the flashy reception and hundreds of guests to profess my love and devotion to my future husband and baby's father.

I've learned a lot about Leo, myself, and life during our trip away from our hectic lives in the city. Life's sweet and short, needing to be savored like a fine wine instead of chugged like a cheap beer. Italy has helped me realize that. There's no rush to be anywhere, meals are an event instead of a necessity, and everything has to do with pleasure.

In Chicago, everything is fast-paced, hectic, and anxiety-ridden. But now, after so long away, I crave the easiness of the tiny villages lined with cobblestone streets which scatter out like a spider web from the center.

Last night after dinner, I told Leo I'd be slowing

down when we returned. I know he thought I was joking, but there's no way I want to go back to the insanity of running a business when I don't have to. I'll pitch in, but my late-night shifts five days a week are a thing of the past. I want to be the mom who stays home with her baby, cuddling him or her and spoiling them rotten just like my mother did with us.

Memories are our legacy. We're not remembered for how many hours we worked or the size of our bank account. Our actions are our imprint on people's souls. How we treat others, the time we spend listening, and the way we love deeply are what will stay with a person long after we're gone. I want the memories to be sustaining, lasting well beyond my lifetime. I want to be remembered for touching their souls and leaving a lasting imprint on their hearts.

I want my friends, family, and baby to think of me for the love I showered on them and not for the time I spent chained to a neighborhood bar on the South Side of Chicago.

I want my legacy to be undeniable.

EPILOGUE

DAPHNE

Seven Months Later

"Breathe," Leo says, pushing the damp hair away from my forehead. "Remember Lamaze."

I growl and grit my teeth, wondering how I ever loved the man who put me in this situation. "I'm fucking breathing," I howl as the next contraction hits, catching me off guard.

I want to rip his face off. Scratch that, I want to rip his dick off, so this can never happen to me again.

There's no amount of classes or books that can prepare someone for labor. My body feels like it's slowly ripping in half, and there's nothing I can do to take the pain away.

Leo exhales through his mouth, sucking in a quick breath, like I'm going to do the same because there isn't a watermelon trying to come out of my cunt.

"Shut the fuck up," I hiss and push his face away, sick of listening to him.

"*Bella*, don't be that way. This is such a happy day."

"For who?" I yell, snarling at the man I showered with kisses when we woke up this morning. "You're not dying. I am."

Maybe I'm being a martyr, but every mother going through labor deserves to be whatever the hell she wants to be because the pain is immense.

I'm not talking about just a little bit. Take the worst pain you've ever experienced, magnify it by twenty, and stretch it across so many hours, you pray for death.

That's birth.

"You're being a little overdramatic."

The nurse looks over, knowing my mood went from bad to shit in under a half a millisecond.

"Leo, if I live through this, I'm going to make you pay."

"Come on. You love me," he says and tries to lean in and kiss my cheek.

I turn my head, not wanting anything to do with his lips. "So. Help. Me. God."

"How's it going?" my mother asks, bringing me a new plastic cup filled with ice chips and oblivious to the carnage that's about to take place.

"She's thinking of all the ways she can off me," Leo tells her with a small laugh like he doesn't actually think I'm serious.

"Don't laugh, kiddo. The hate is real at this stage," my mom says and shakes her head. "It's like cornering a wild bear while covered in honey. You're liable to get mauled."

Leo backs up a step, glancing down at me in shock. "Well, I…"

"She blames you for this." My mother waves her hand over my belly. "It'll take her a while before she can ever look at you the same way again."

"I'm right here," I say because they're talking about me like I'm not even in the room.

I know my mom's only trying to help. How the hell she did this four times is beyond me. I can't see myself willingly doing this again, no matter how cute the kid grows up to be.

My mother hands me the ice chips, but all I really want is a large pizza covered in pepperoni and dripping with grease.

"Thanks, Ma." I try to muster a smile.

My insides are twisting again like I'm being torn apart by the baby's fingernails one layer at a time.

"You did this shit four times," I say to my mother when I can finally breathe again. "How? Why?"

She takes my hand in hers and smiles sweetly. "When you lay eyes on your baby and fall head over heels in love, you forget the pain."

I laugh cynically. "I will never forget this pain. Never."

"Sweetheart," she says softly. "All the happy memories and years you've given me have released every second of agony you put me through when I was in labor. And I mean, it was hell on earth. Epidurals were still too new when you were born for me to get one without worry."

"I'm dying, Ma," I groan.

"Don't be a drama queen. In the olden days…"

"Don't tell me people squatted in a field, had the baby, and kept on working. I don't want to hear it."

Leo collapses in a chair next to my bed, looking more disheveled than I've ever seen him before. His hair's messy, the first three buttons on his dress shirt are undone, and his tie is loose and hanging around his neck.

"Well, if you're anything like me, sweetheart, you won't be in labor much longer."

Pain slices through me again as every muscle in my abdomen tightens. I gasp, trying to breathe to alleviate some of the pain, but nothing seems to help.

"Are we ready to see how far along you are?" the

doctor asks as he walks into the room, looking way too cheerful for me.

"Get this baby out of me," I tell him. If I could reach down and pull the baby out myself, I'd do it in a heartbeat. Anything to make the pain stop.

The doctor puts on a pair of gloves and sits down between my legs. "Have you thought any more about an epidural?"

I had always said I wanted to do natural childbirth, using the techniques of Lamaze. I thought I was a hard-ass and could take pain better than most people…which is ridiculous. I was obviously delusional.

"I want one as soon as possible. I can't take the pain much longer."

"Well, let's get in there."

By there, he means my vagina. The thing I used to love, and so did Leo. Now, it's a bringer of pain and giver of life. My poor pussy will never be the same. Permanently destroyed by the tiny human trying to rip me apart from the inside.

"Just relax," the doctor says before he practically shoves his entire arm up my cunt, feeling out my cervix. "You're dilated enough for an epidural."

"Give it to me now," I say without hesitation. I'm no longer looking to be a tough chick. There's no medal of honor for enduring the pain. The kid's not going to be the least bit impressed when they get older because I went to hell and back just so they could be born.

"Are you sure?" Leo asks, still sitting in his chair, pain-free and a lucky son of a bitch he's still breathing.

I point at him and narrow my gaze. "You shut your mouth." I would've lunged off the bed and wrapped my hands around his neck if I weren't tethered to the doctor because his hand's still up my twat.

Leo throws his hands in the air, maybe realizing the precarious position he's in. "Anything you want, *bella*."

My mother laughs and shakes her head. "Don't argue with her, Leo."

"I'd never." He shakes his head, learning not to fight me on anything because I'll just dig my heels in more. "I think an epidural is a great idea."

The doctor snaps his gloves off and stands. "The anesthesiologist will be in shortly to administer the epidural. You'll feel better once it's in place and doing its job."

"Thank fuck," I hiss.

"You're about seven centimeters dilated. We're almost there."

I don't know why everyone in the room keeps referring to my birth as a we. I'm the only one in excruciating pain. The only one about to give birth. There's no we about it. Everybody else is just an observer of my misery and not an active participant.

I groan and writhe around with each passing contraction, waiting for the epidural to arrive and wondering what the hell birth is really going to be like. The kid's still in my uterus and hasn't even started the slow and mighty tight trip down to my vagina. I think of the shoulders and cringe, knowing the real pain hasn't even begun.

A few minutes later, the anesthesiologist walks into the room with some paperwork and the biggest needle I've ever seen in my life. "Are we ready for some relief?" he asks, being chipper like everybody else who walks into my room.

"Never been so ready for something in my entire life," I say as the nurse scans my medical bracelet.

"You'll feel better quick," he says, setting everything out on a tray next to my bed. "You're going to need to sit up so I can get at your back."

Sitting up, or should I say, the act of sitting up, has become damn near impossible. My stomach's the size of a beach ball, and I don't even remember what my feet look like anymore.

Leo rushes to my side as I try to pull myself up and fail. I don't push him away or try to claw his face off because I need him to help me make this pain go away.

Leo pulls me up, and I throw my legs over the side. I have no shame left as everyone in this room has seen either my ass or my pussy. It's no longer sacred or pretty either.

"The nurse is going to help me navigate your contractions, so we can do this safely." He's doing something to my back as he speaks, but I don't bother to ask. All I want is relief, and whatever it takes to make that happen, I'll do. "You need to hold completely still while I do this procedure."

I don't even remember what it's like to be still. The pain and aftermath of each passing contraction make me move around the bed like I'm drunk dancing on the floor, too plastered to stand on my own two feet.

Leo looks me straight in the eye, holding my arms with each hand as he lowers himself so we're face-to-face. "Just look at me," he says.

I level him with my gaze. "You're the reason I'm in this much pain."

"I know. Focus on your hate," he tells me. "Plot my death in your head if you must. Just stay still."

My fingernails dig into his arms as I clutch him while he's holding on to me. The procedure's quicker than I imagined and not nearly as painful because, again, there's a human ripping out of my body.

"In a few minutes, you'll feel numb," the anesthesiologist says. "You can lie back down and relax."

"You're doing great," Leo says sweetly.

I still want to rip his face off, but the need to do so lessens every few seconds.

The nurse presses a few buttons on the fetal

monitor as I lie back down. "You should be able to get some rest now. You're going to need it for delivery."

My mother stands at the foot of my bed and smiles. "I'm going to go talk to your father and brothers. I'll be back, sweetheart. Sleep a little."

"Yeah, Ma. I'll do my best."

Moments later, everyone's gone, and it's just Leo and me left in the room.

"Better?" he asks.

"Maybe," I say, but I can already feel the epidural working its magic, reducing the agony.

Leo leans over the bed and grabs my hand. "Just rest, *bella*."

I close my eyes, thinking I can get a few hours. But I should've known better. Hospitals are not the place for any type of relaxation. People are constantly in and out of the room, staring up my birth canal like it holds some magical answers to the universe. There's a flurry of people, studying my vital signs and the baby's heartbeat. There's no rest. There will never be a moment's peace for the rest of my entire life because I'm about to be a mother.

"PUSH," the doctor says as I hold my knees, feeling more exhausted than I have ever felt in my entire life.

"You can do this," Leo cheers me on, and I'm back to wanting to end his life.

I feel like I'm attempting to take the biggest shit of my life, and no matter how hard I try to bear down and push it out, there's nothing moving.

"I can see the head," the doctor says, looking up from between my legs.

"Get the baby out of me," I plead as tears stream down my face, pushing with everything I have in me.

"Just a few more pushes," the doctor says, like that's going to make me feel any better.

I don't want to do a few more pushes. Hell, I don't even want to do one more. I want this all to be over, holding the baby in my arms, forgetting all about the last twelve hours of my life.

"You're doing so well." Leo smiles as he wipes down my face with a cool, damp cloth.

"How about you two grab her legs and help her through the last few?" the doctor tells Leo and my mother, and I know we're about to get to the grand finale.

Each one of them holds a knee, staring between my legs as I pull myself forward and push with everything I've got.

The doctor urges, "Harder, harder, more, keep going."

The hate I felt for Leo transfers to the man huddled between my legs, telling me to do something I'm doing my best at already to push the baby out.

The pain's gone, replaced by the most intense

pressure of my life. I would've straight up died without the epidural. I know that now.

Three pushes later, I gasp for air as the baby's shoulders break free.

"Oh my God," my mother says as tears form in her eyes, and she covers her mouth.

"*Bella*," Leo says, staring between my legs like he's seen the most beautiful sight.

I press my head into the pillow, feeling relieved to have survived the delivery and happy as hell to have it over.

"Congratulations," the doctor says, holding the baby in his arms before placing it on my chest. "You have a son."

Leo wipes his face, hiding the tears I have no doubt are falling fast. "A son," he whispers.

"Would you like to cut the umbilical cord?" the doctor asks Leo.

"Yes." Leo nods.

Tears stream down my face, matching my mother and Leo, but for entirely different reasons. I'm happy, for sure, but my tears of joy are that the birth is over. The baby howls as the harsh realities of life slam down on both of us.

I'm a mother.

There's no going back, only forward.

The entire family, including Leo's father, squeezed into my hospital room as soon as the nurse said it was okay to have visitors. They jockeyed for position like it was a contest, leaving Mr. Conti and Leo on one side and my mother and father on the other. Delilah, Lucio, Vinnie, Angelo, and Michelle filled in the gap, closing off a circle of people I never thought I'd see crammed into such a tiny space…well, at least not without some sort of bloodshed.

The way they're gawking at the little guy in my arms, it's like they've never seen a baby before.

"He's so beautiful," my mother says as she rests her head against my father's shoulder.

"Look at all that hair. Just like you, Leo," Mario tells Leo. He's even a little choked up but hides it well. Lord forbid he show the heart underneath his steely mob boss exterior.

"You two have been keeping his name a secret for months. What is it?" my father asks.

I smile at Leo, knowing this has bothered our families, but we still didn't give in. To be honest, we had a few names picked out and couldn't decide, leaving the decision until we actually laid eyes on our little boy.

"We're paying respect to our grandfathers," Leo announces as he squeezes my hand and looks around the room. "His name is Nino Raffaele Conti."

"It's perfect." My mother wipes the tears which

have started to fall a little harder and easier than before.

"It's a fine name," Mario says. "Strong."

My mother takes Nino from my arms, and the attention goes with him.

"How are you feeling?" Delilah asks.

"Like roadkill." I laugh.

"Yeah. That feeling doesn't go away for a while. First, it's physical and then it's mental, but," Delilah says and looks up at Leo, "at least you have someone to help you with the newborn."

I can't imagine going through any of this alone. Delilah's obviously a much stronger person than I am because I would've been a total hot mess without the support of my family and my husband.

"You're a rock star, Delilah."

"Oh, stop," she says and blushes. "I can't imagine doing it alone again."

"Again?" I tilt my head and raise an eyebrow.

She places one hand over her stomach and winks. "Don't tell," she mouths.

I had wondered why Lucio seemed happier than usual, and now it makes total sense. With the way he loves Lulu, I know he's going to be over the moon experiencing all the joys and horrors from the beginning.

"Since we're all here," my father says and clears his throat. "Your mother and I have an announcement."

The room goes silent.

"We set a date," my mother explains.

I roll my eyes. It's been almost a year since my father announced they were getting married, and in typical Santino fashion…there was absolutely no hurry.

My father pulls my mother close. "We're getting married on December 23rd."

"Way to go, Pop," Vinnie says as he punches my father in the shoulder, almost knocking him over.

"It's about fucking time," Angelo adds.

"Are you sure about this?" Lucio asks my mother and somehow keeps a straight face.

"He's finally going to make an honest woman out of me." My mother laughs. "It only took four kids and four grandkids, but it's finally happening."

The normal life I craved not too long ago has finally become my new reality. Happy family, sexy husband, beautiful baby, and for once, everyone is getting along…even with Mario, which is a miracle in itself.

I shift in my bed, finding it damn near impossible to get comfortable because my poor body has just been through battle. Anyone who says otherwise is being a goddamn martyr.

"Maybe we should go," Angelo tells my family when he glances down at the bed, and we lock eyes as I grimace.

"No, no. I'm fine," I say, trying to play it off because I never like to look weak.

"You're right, Ang. I'm sure Leo and Daphne would like some time alone," Lucio says.

Vinnie walks up to the side of the bed and kisses my cheek. "I love you, sis. You should've named him Vinnie, but I totally understand. He would've had some big shoes to fill."

"Shut up," I say, trying not to laugh because everything in my body hurts. "Get out of here."

My father's phone rings, and he turns his back to us as he answers. "Yeah?" There's a short pause before my father's shoulders slump forward. "When? Where?" All eyes are on my dad as he turns around. "I have to go," he says and walks toward me. "I'm sorry."

"What's wrong?" I ask because he's tense and all traces of happiness he had moments ago are gone.

"Don't worry about it, sweetheart." My father kisses my cheek and brushes my hair away from the side of my face. "Enjoy my new grandson. I'll be back to check on you later."

"Pop." Angelo takes a step toward our father before he has a chance to leave. "What happened?"

My father's pale. The only other time I saw him like this was when he was about to be arrested. "Are you being arrested?" I ask, jumping to the only conclusion that makes sense.

Vinnie places his hand on my father's shoulder and squeezes. "Just tell us, Pop."

My father faces Mario, staring him straight in the eyes. "Johnny's been shot."

And the serenity and normalcy I thought I finally had disappears.

The Men of Inked: Southside series continues in Hook, book three!

Visit *menofinked.com/news-bm* to sign up for my VIP newsletter, featuring exclusive eBooks, special deals, and giveaways!

or

text **BLISS** to **24587**

to sign up for VIP text news

There's other ways to follow me…

BookBub | Twitter | Facebook | Instagram

I'd love to hear from you.

www.menofinked.com

Join my PRIVATE Facebook Reader Group

MEN OF INKED: SOUTHSIDE SERIES

Join the Chicago Gallo Family with their strong alphas, sassy women, and tons of fun.

- Book 1 - Maneuver (Lucio)
- Book 2 - Flow (Daphne)
- Book 3 - Hook (Angelo)
- Book 4 - Hustle (Vinnie)
- Book 5 - Love (Angelo)

MEN OF INKED SERIES

"One of the sexiest series of all-time"

-Bookbub Reviewers

Download book 1 for FREE!

- Book 1 - Throttle Me (Joe aka City)
- Book 2 - Hook Me (Mike)
- Book 3 - Resist Me (Izzy)
- Book 4 - Uncover Me (Thomas)
- Book 5 - Without Me (Anthony)
- Book 6 - Honor Me (City)
- Book 7 - Worship Me (Izzy)

ALFA INVESTIGATIONS SERIES

Wickedly hot alphas with tons of heart pounding suspense!

- Book 1 - Sinful Intent (Morgan)
- Book 2 - Unlawful Desire (Frisco)
- Book 3 - Wicked Impulse (Bear)
- Book 4 - Guilty Sin (Ret)

SINGLE READS

- Mend
- Enshrine
- Misadventures of a City Girl
- Misadventures with a Speed Demon
- Rebound (Flash aka Sam)
- Top Bottom Switch (Ret)

NAILED DOWN SERIES

- Book 1 - Nailed Down
- Book 2 - Tied Down
- Book 3 - Kneel Down

TAKEOVER DUET

What happens when you sleep with your biggest enemy?

- Book 1 - Acquisition
- Book 2 - Merger

FILTHY SERIES

- Dirty Work
- Dirty Secret
- Dirty Defiance

LOVE AT LAST SERIES

- Book 1 - Untangle Me
- Book 2 - Kayden

BOX SETS & COLLECTIONS

- Men of Inked Volume 1
- Men of Inked Volume 2
- Love at Last Series
- ALFA Investigations Series
- Filthy Series
- Takeover Duet

View Chelle's entire collection of books at menofinked.com/books

To learn more about Chelle's books visit *menofinked.com* or *chellebliss.com*

ABOUT THE AUTHOR

Chelle Bliss is the *Wall Street Journal* and *USA Today* bestselling author of Men of Inked: Southside Series, Misadventures of a City Girl, the Men of Inked, and ALFA Investigations series.

She hails from the Midwest, but currently lives near the beach even though she hates sand. She's a full-time writer, time-waster extraordinaire, social media addict, coffee fiend, and ex history teacher.

She loves spending time with her two cats, alpha boyfriend, and chatting with readers. To learn more about Chelle, please visit menofinked.com or chellebliss.com.

JOIN MY NEWSLETTER

Text Notifications (US only)
➔ Text **BLISS** to **24587**

WHERE TO FOLLOW CHELLE:

WEBSITE | TWITTER | FACEBOOK | INSTAGRAM
JOIN MY PRIVATE FACEBOOK GROUP

Want to drop me a line?
authorchellebliss@gmail.com

www.chellebliss.com

facebook.com/authorchellebliss1

bookbub.com/authors/chelle-bliss

instagram.com/authorchellebliss

twitter.com/ChelleBliss1

ACKNOWLEDGMENTS

I should really start writing the acknowledgements as soon as I have the first words in any story. I always wait until the book is ready to publish and then remember every person who has played a role. Sounds like a solid plan, right? Wrong. It's an epic failure. By this point, my mind is practically useless and I'm rushing toward the finish line to press the publish button. But here I am. Again. Trying to remember every person who played a role to helping me create this book and I'm staring into the darkness, wishing I could even remember what I did yesterday.

So, lets try see how many people I can forget… again.

Lisa Hollett, Julie Deaton, and Rosa Sharon — ladies, you're a killer teach of editors and proofreaders. You're quick, kind, and always willing to dive right into my words. I know sometimes I sling a hot mess in your lap, but you never complain. I can't thank you enough for your hard work and support.

Lori Jackson — Thanks for an amazing original cover. I wish I could've used it and it'll show back up again. I swear. It's too beautiful not to be for sale. Your graphics are always spot on and totally beautiful.

Wendy Shatwell of Bare Naked Words — You're amazeballs. You totally put up with my crazy shit and never cuss me out. I don't know how you do it, but you have the patience of a saint.

Readers — What can I say? I'm a lucky son of a bitch for having an crazy fabulous group of readers who love my Gallo's. I don't know what I did to get so fucking lucky, but thank you for joining me on this crazy ride.

Betas and ARC readers — Ladies, you are hands down the best.

Brian — I know there are days I totally disappear as I chase a deadline. Thank you for always being understanding. I promise I'll get ahead someday. I swear. No really. It's all part of my plan.

Bliss Romance Hangout — You ladies (gentleman too) are always great at keeping my moral up and the words flowing. Any time I'm feeling down, just a quick stop into my fabulous reader group, and I'm right back on track. Thanks for loving my words.

I don't know who else I forgot. It's 5am and the

sun's not even out yet. I'm on my second cup of coffee, but my brain isn't functioning at maximum capacity just yet.

All I can say is thank you. Thank you to everyone. Without you I don't know where I'd be…

ACKNOWLEDGMENTS

I don't even know where to start with the acknowledgements for this book. Life has been crazy ridiculous and there has been an army of people behind me, making sure I got this sucker written.

You (yeah, you) — Thanks for wanting to read my words. You help motivate my ass. Without you, this would just be a hobby. I can't thank you enough for your Gallo love. Remember, your words mean the world to me.

Brian M. — thanks for giving up time with me so I could slave away at the keyboard to bring this book to life. I know I'm not an easy human, but you love me anyway. Thanks again for going another month without smothering me when I snore.

Lisa Hollett— Girl, I don't even know what to say. You worked your ass of editing this book. Thanks for not crawling through the computer screen and strangling me when I said I needed it back within forty-eight hours and gave you no warning. I know you consumed A LOT of wine because of me. Please tell your liver I'm sorry.

Julie Deaton — You killed it on the proofread. Thanks for always taking me and not making me beg. I'd totally beg though because you're the bees knees (is that right?). Anyway, I'm thankful I found you and happy you're in my life.

Rosa Sharon — You never cease to amaze me with your ability to find the small details. Thanks for not telling me to kick rocks when I asked you to proof the book at the last minute. You're the bestest kind of human.

Seeing a pattern yet? I was stupid late.

Corinne Michaels — Your words inspire me. You probably have no idea, but when I get stuck, I grab one of your books and read for an hour and voila, I can write again. Your words are magical and your men are fucking hot. Then there's the fact you're a HH too, which is pretty fucking fantastic. Don't ever go soft on me… or I'll hunt your ass down.

To my beta girls — I love you. Thanks for putting up with my crazy ass. I know I'm a little off kilter.

Mom — Thanks for giving up some time with me this summer so I could write. You're my best friend and someday you'll master that damn fancy new phone you have.

Lori Jackson — Thanks for the amazing graphics.

You save me soooooooo much time. You're fabulous and someday we'll have coffee together. I can't wait for everyone to see the rest of the sexy covers in this series.

Anthony Colletti — Thanks for talking me off the ledge. I went from a full fledged panic attack to relatively calm after our phone call. Thanks for always being a good listener and only sighing sometimes.

Xanax — Thanks for the peaceful nights and a quiet mind.

Bliss Hangout Members — I fucking love each and every one of you. Thank you for driving me forward and keeping me motivated during times when I could barely concentrate.

I'm sure I'm forgetting a million people. Hell, I almost forget my name sometimes.

Just THANK YOU! THANK YOU! THANK YOU!

www.ingramcontent.com/pod-product-compliance
Lightning Source LLC
Chambersburg PA
CBHW030332310726
48979CB00001B/1

* 9 7 8 1 9 5 0 0 2 3 6 9 1 *